The second novel in an
original new paperback series
—Wagons West—
about the first
great wagon train westward.

NEBRASKA!

By the author of INDEPENDENCE!

WAGONS WEST

NEBRASKA!

STALWART MEN AND SPIRITED WOMEN BLAZING A TRAIL OF PASSION AND GLORY ACROSS THE PROUD AMERICAN NATION . . .

CATHY VAN AYL
Though a young widow, she is sexually
innocent, and both drawn to and frightened
by the manly ways of Whip Holt.

MICHAEL "WHIP" HOLT,
the lean, taciturn mountain man who is
master of the frontier, yet a rank amateur
when it comes to understanding women.

TONIE MELL
Hard-riding, fast-shooting, and
beautiful, she may pay with her life
for her Russian ancestry—and with the
lives of the entire wagon train.

DR. ROBERT MARTIN,
the physician whose skills win
even the respect of hostile Indians.

★★★★★★★★★★★★★★★★★★★★★★★★

CINDY,
a former prostitute in search of a
new life in the West. She once hated men—
now one man could change her mind.

TED WOODS,
who would kill to protect the woman he loves.

MAJOR LAURENCE WOODLING,
a South Carolina aristocrat who lost his
plantation but not his faith in the future.

CLAIBORNE WOODLING,
the Major's son. A demon rider,
an expert swordsman, and a dangerous man.

EULALIA WOODLING,
the Major's daughter. A flirt,
and a selfish beauty, until she suffers
the ultimate degradation.

HOSEA,
an escaped slave who risks
his life to save the wagon train.

STALKING HORSE,
Cherokee warrior, Whip's closest
friend and blood brother.

PIERRE LE ROUGE
Tricked into an act of treachery, he
redeems himself by a deed of daring heroism.

PRESIDENT VAN BUREN,
leader of the nation, who, in a desperate
race against time, must save the
wagon train from sabotage by foreign powers.

★★★★★★★★★★★★★★★★★★★★★★★★

Bantam Books by Dana Fuller Ross
Ask your bookseller for the books you have missed

WAGONS WEST * VOLUME 2
NEBRASKA!
DANA FULLER ROSS

TM

Created by the producers of
White Indian, Children of the Lion,
Saga of the Southwest, and
The Kent Family Chronicles Series.
Executive Producer: Lyle Kenyon Engel

BANTAM BOOKS
TORONTO · NEW YORK · LONDON · SYDNEY

NEBRASKA!

A Bantam Book / July 1979

2nd printing . . . . . . July 1979	9th printing . February 1980
3rd printing . . . . . . July 1979	10th printing . . . March 1980
4th printing . . . . August 1979	11th printing . . . . April 1980
5th printing . September 1979	12th printing . September 1980
6th printing . . . October 1979	13th printing . November 1980
7th printing . December 1979	14th printing . . . March 1981
8th printing . . February 1980	15th printing . . October 1981

Produced by Book Creations, Inc.
Executive Producer: Lyle Kenyon Engel

ISBN 0-553-20417-3

Published simultaneously in the United States and Canada

PRINTED IN THE UNITED STATES OF AMERICA

24 23 22 21 20 19 18 17

NEBRASKA!

THE DARING TRAIL
OF THE MEN AND WOMEN
OF WAGONS WEST AS
THEY CROSS THE GREAT
PLAINS TOWARD A NEW
ERA IN AMERICA

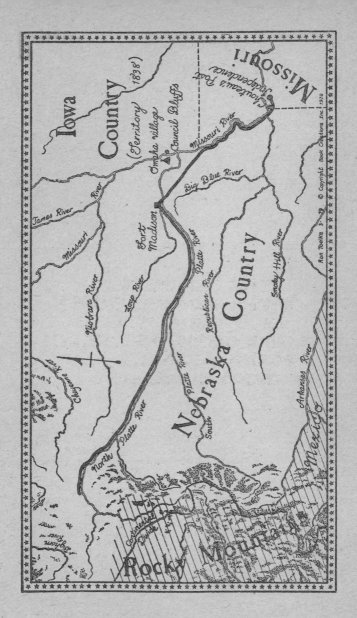

I

Heavy clouds, thick, black, and ominous, blew east-ward from the Rocky Mountains across the Great Plains wilderness, obscuring the moon and stars. The ground was still warm from the early autumn sun that had shone down on Missouri the previous day, but the night air was cool. A white mist, as impenetrable as a bale of cotton, rose from the broad waters of the great Missouri River, bathing the area in a blanket of swirling mists.

High on the bluffs of the eastern bank of the river, a short distance from the frontier village of Independence, Missouri, stood the symbols of the future—covered wagons arranged in a circle. Within the scores of wagons, hundreds of men, women, and children were asleep. Some had begun their journey in the East and had been joined by others along the way in a daring and unique venture. They were the first pioneers who were blazing a path across the country to Oregon and to the Pacific Ocean.

Inside the circle, the horses and oxen were asleep, too, as were the dogs. There seemed to be nothing to fear. Independence was a sturdy little community of ranch owners and farmers—people who took the law into their own hands when necessary because no other law existed at this remote outpost. Bloodshed was not unknown, but violence occurred infrequently.

No one in the wagon train heard the two boats being rowed across the Missouri from the west bank; no one saw the little craft hauled ashore, beached and made secure; and certainly no one in the train knew that six armed men, frontier drifters who preyed on fur trappers or isolated farm owners, had found a tempting target.

The six men crept up the hill, pistols and knives in their hands. A shepherd dog stretched outside one of the wagons awakened and raised his pointed ears. Quietly the bandits crept closer, struggling as they made their way up the bluff.

Suddenly one member of the wagon train, a tall, lean man dressed in buckskins, awoke. Instantly alert, he threw off his blanket; he reached for his long rifle automatically and quickly rose to his feet from the grassy spot where he had been sleeping.

The mist was too thick for him to see through it, so he listened intently, his head cocked to one side. Then a faint, grim smile appeared on his face. Moving silently, with the experience of one who had spent years as a hunter, trapper, and guide in the Rockies, he went quickly to several key wagons.

In almost no time he was joined by three men, all of whom carried rifles. One was a burly blacksmith who had spent a decade in prison for murder. Another was a high-ranking Austrian nobleman who had joined the wagon train because he loved adventure. The third was a mild-mannered physician, a widower who sought a new life, far from the sorrows he had known.

The trio followed the man in buckskins to the lip of the bluff. No one could see more than a few feet ahead, nor could they hear a sound—they were reacting instinctively. Within a few seconds they were joined by an Indian brave, also clad in buckskins, a warrior who almost casually notched an arrow on the string of his bow. Like the man in buckskins, he had no need to see the approaching menace.

A broad smile appeared on the face of the man in buckskins. There was no doubt that he thoroughly enjoyed the challenge of danger. He didn't need to speak; his companions had traveled far with him and knew what was expected of them. They all waited.

By now the robbers were no more than five yards from the lip of the bluff, almost within reach of their goal. The man in buckskins nodded, almost casually, and four rifles spoke simultaneously, the weapons deliberately fired over the heads of the approaching men.

The startled bandits paused, then turned and fled down the steep slope, sliding and stumbling, falling and scrambling as they raced to the safety of their waiting boat.

Now it was the Indian's turn. He sent arrow after arrow toward the retreating men. The bandits saw the arrows dropping around them and increased their wild pace as they dragged their boat into the water and rowed off to safety.

The man in buckskins listened, heard the fading sound of oars, and nodded. His companions turned and strolled back to their wagons for another hour of sleep. He and the Indian wrapped themselves in their respective blankets. Within a few minutes they had drifted back to sleep.

The men, women, and children of the train were still asleep. Even those who had awakened briefly had mistaken the firearms volley for a crack of thunder.

The wagon train was secure.

As always, Cathy van Ayl looked lovely as she emerged from her wagon. Totally unaware of her beauty, she paused on the back step to tuck some stray strands of her long, blonde hair under her sunbonnet, then tightened the sash of her dimity dress. She looked like a young girl in her teens rather than a widow of twenty-three. That air of innocence wasn't accidental. She had never been intimate with her elderly husband, Otto, a miserly farmer from Long Island, who had died in a raid on the wagon train.

Cathy stepped down to the ground just as Whip Holt, the hired guide and wagonmaster of the Oregon-bound caravan, came into view. Tall and sinewy in his buckskins, he was armed, as usual, with a brace of pistols and a long bullwhip, wrapped around his middle, that gave him his name. His skin was leathery after years of exposure to the outdoors, and his eyes were hard. But when he saw Cathy he grinned at her, and suddenly he looked younger than twenty-nine.

She smiled at him in return, her heart skipping a beat. When Otto was alive, it had been necessary to conceal her interest in Whip, but all that had changed since the young mountain man rejoined the train, several weeks ago, as it moved westward across Missouri. Now she had no reason beyond her own sense of discretion to hide the way she felt.

Certainly Whip made no secret of his own feelings. "Morning, ma'am," he called, sauntering toward her.

"You're wearing a new buckskin shirt and trousers, I see," she said politely.

He was surprised that she had noticed what he was wearing. "Well, you know how it is. I get restless just sitting around Independence while we put in supplies and wait for the new folks joining us to show up. So one day I went hunting. He cleared his throat awkwardly. "You look mighty nice, all dressed up for a day in the city."

Cathy couldn't help laughing. Certainly no one else in 1837 would dream of referring to the frontier town of Independence, Missouri as a "city." One of the last outposts of civilization east of the Great Plains, it was visited by trappers, hunters, and traders bringing their furs from the Rocky Mountains to the East. Now, with other wagon trains scheduled to follow Whip's caravan across the wilderness to the fertile Oregon country, Independence promised to develop into a major supply center.

"I told my sister I'd buy some things in town for her and bring them along tonight."

Only a few days earlier, Cathy's older sister, Claudia, had been married to Sam Brentwood, the former leader of the wagon train. The couple would remain in Independence to establish a supply depot, sponsored by Sam's mentors, former President of the United States

4

Andrew Jackson and John Jacob Astor, a fur baron and the leader of a group of wealthy businessmen who were encouraging the settling of the Oregon country.

"Claudia and Sam asked me to supper tonight, too," Whip said, and shifted in embarrassment. "I—I wasn't so sure I wanted to go, seeing as how I don't sit down at a table indoors very often. But if you're going, ma'am, I'll be happy to escort you."

"I'd like that," Cathy said. She smiled again before turning away, then added, "I'm not really dressed up, you know. All I own are a few dresses like this, except for the old woolen things I wear on the trail."

"Could you use a doeskin dress, ma'am?"

"I'd love it, Whip." Cathy hesitated. "But I wouldn't want you to think I was hinting."

"No matter. Stalking Horse," he said, referring to his close friend, a Cherokee scout, "has been pestering me to go hunting again, so I reckon I'll have some skins for you by the time we push off."

Cathy thanked him, embarrassed by his generosity, then left the circle of wagons. Needing time to think, she stood, looking beyond the bend in the Missouri River, imagining the limitless wilderness and mountains that the wagon train would have to cross before reaching Oregon.

Otto van Ayl had been determined to go to Oregon and had given his wife no choice. But the widowed Cathy was free to make up her own mind. Claudia and Sam had offered her a home with them in Independence. And she wouldn't be dependent on their charity, either. Her wagon was as solid as any made in New England, where they had come from, and the four horses that pulled it were strong, surefooted and healthy. She could get a substantial sum for the wagon and team if she decided to stay behind when the train moved out. In addition, Otto had left her the fortune he had saved in a lifetime of miserly living, two thousand dollars in gold.

When they had started on the journey, Otto had concealed the money beneath a false floor in the wagon, but after his death, at Claudia and Sam's insistence, she had moved it for safekeeping to the enormous special wagon where the caravan's medicines, extra weapons, and emergency rations were stored.

So Cathy was wealthy, at least by the standards of the pioneers who were heading to Oregon. Certainly she could pay for her keep if she decided to stay with her sister and brother-in-law. Fortunately, she wouldn't have to make up her mind for a few days; she felt pulled in both directions.

Because of Whip and because of what she had heard about Oregon, she wanted to go on. But she was a grown woman, not a romantic adolescent, and she couldn't allow her interest in him to become too great a factor. On the other hand, she had begun the long trek, and she did believe in finishing what she started. Also, if any of the stories she had heard about Oregon were true, she knew it would be heaven on earth. ·

Tugging her in the opposite direction was the knowledge that powerful forces were at work trying to prevent the American settlers from reaching their destination. The ownership of the Oregon country was in dispute, with both the United States and Great Britain claiming it. A British agent, Henry St. Clair, who had joined the wagon train posing as a settler, had already made several violent attempts to halt the train. After he had been discovered and left the train, he had inspired a vicious attack on the caravan by army deserters.

The British attempt to sabotage the train wasn't the only one. Imperial Russia wanted to stop it from reaching Oregon, too. Russians had been the first to settle in Oregon. Although international pressures had forced the czar seemingly to abandon his claim, the government in St. Petersburg actually was doing no such thing. Cathy was one of the few members of the caravan who knew that attempts had been made by the czar's secret police to blackmail a lovely frontier girl named Tonie Mell into working for them. Tonie's parents, whom she hadn't seen since early childhood, were still in Russia. She had been forced to join the pioneers early in their journey and had been told that her parents would not be allowed to come to America unless she committed acts of sabotage against the train. But, thanks to her own courage and the help of Sam and Whip, she had outsmarted them. Now she was continuing on to Oregon, this time in the company of her uncle, Arnold Mell, who had decided to sell his farm to Sam and Claudia and join his niece on her journey. But it was fair to assume that the Russians would try again.

In addition, there were terrifying rumors among the settlers about hostile Indian tribes in the wilderness ahead. Some pessimists predicted that every last man, woman, and child in the train would be murdered. But Cathy refused to believe these stories. No matter how great the menace of Indians might become, she had unbounded faith in Whip Holt's abilities. She had seen him in action, and she was confident he would lead the band of settlers, already four hundred strong and growing every day, safely to their Oregon destination. She was convinced that no Indians could prevent Whip from reaching his goal—for that matter, neither could the British and Russians.

Tonight, perhaps, she would discuss her situation with her sister—it might clarify her thinking.

Remembering her promise to buy some things for Claudia, Cathy headed toward the town of Independence. She passed log cabins and houses of whitewashed clapboard. Until the past year, Independence had been little more than a village. But now it boasted two general stores, a stable, and, on its main street, two brothels and at least a dozen taverns and saloons.

When Sam and Claudia finished making changes in the ranch, their property would become the principal supply depot for later wagon trains. The depot would sell both horses and oxen, as well as spare wheels, axles, and yokes. Claudia planned to put in a full supply of such provisions as bacon, flour, beans, and sugar—the staples that every family needed on the trek across the continent. Thanks to the generosity of Astor and his associates, as well as the official encouragement of the new President, Martin Van Buren, Sam would have enough funds to put in a stock of firearms, gunpowder, and ammunition, too.

As Cathy walked down the main street, the morning sun was warm, almost hot. The breeze was gentle and it seemed to her more like summer than the beginning of autumn. It was small wonder, she thought, that Whip was eager to start the march across the plains as soon as possible. Cathy knew from her own experience in the past six months that the caravan could travel ten to twelve miles per day in good weather, but that progress was slowed to a crawl when it rained. And when the rains were very heavy, it sometimes became necessary to call a complete halt.

Pondering her dilemma, paying scant attention to her immediate surroundings, Cathy was suddenly aroused from her reverie by the sound of a man's harsh, deep voice.

"That there one is the prettiest I've seen since we got to this town. I claim her!"

"Like hell you do," another man replied. "Maybe we'll draw lots for her, all of us, or maybe we'll leave the choice up to her. We got to be fair about this."

Startled, Cathy saw eight or nine men who had just emerged from a tavern directly ahead. In spite of the early hour, they had been drinking heavily. Some of them were dressed in shabby linsey-woolsey and others in worn, greasy buckskins. They had not shaved for days, and their hair was dirty and unkempt. All were armed with skinning knives, as well as either pistols or rifles.

These were the men Whip and Sam contemptuously referred to as "frontier scum," opportunists who earned a precarious living. Sometimes they bought furs from trappers down on their luck and sold them to traders. Sometimes they did odd jobs for local homesteaders. They were as unsavory as they were unreliable, and Cathy blamed herself for failing to see them in time to avoid them.

But she had little time for regrets. The group had spread across the road, blocking her path, and noting their leers, she was afraid that they would maul her if she tried to crowd past them. But she might be in even worse trouble if she turned and tried to flee; certainly that would encourage them in their game. There were no other pedestrians or riders in sight, so it would be useless to call for help.

The best way to handle the situation, she decided, would be to keep moving forward, remaining calm and ignoring the brutes. So, despite a strong urge to run, she continued to walk at the same even pace, her head high.

One of her tormentors muttered something, and the group quickly surrounded the girl. The man with the rasping voice, appointing himself the spokesman, grinned at her.

"You look like you need some lovin'," he said, "so take your pick."

"Let me pass, please." Cathy knew no escape was possible, but made an effort to speak calmly.

"Don't put on no airs with us, girlie," another declared. "You women up the road charge enough, so it's high time you give us somethin' free."

The stunned Cathy suddenly realized they had mistaken her for a girl from one of the brothels. Certainly they were in no mood—perhaps in no condition—to heed her denials. She was in real danger, and she didn't know how to escape.

Arnold Mell, leading two pack horses laden with the last of his belongings from the ranch, felt a sense of relief he wouldn't have admitted to anyone. The house was no longer what it had been prior to the recent death of his wife. It was crowded with too many memories, so he was glad to be rid of it, pleased that he was joining the wagon train.

Tonie had argued against the sale, thinking he was doing it just for her sake. She was partly right. He realized that in the time she had spent with the caravan before it reached Independence, she had fallen in love with the wagon train's personable and competent physician, a widower named Robert Martin. He wanted to give the romance every opportunity to develop. In fact, he was delighted. Never before had the tomboyish girl shown an interest in any man, and she deserved happiness. He and his wife had tried to substitute for his brother and sister-in-law, the parents she had left behind in St. Petersburg, but he had often felt she had missed her real mother and father. And she had been under a great strain ever since she had been black-mailed by the czar's secret police. Her courage in defying the might of a huge and powerful nation had been splendid, and she had earned the future she so badly wanted for herself.

But Arnold had his own reasons for joining the train, too. He had settled in Independence when it had been a wilderness, but life here was too tame now. At the age of sixty, he was in better physical condition than men half his age, and he looked forward to meeting the challenges of the Great Plains and the Rocky Mountains. What was more, his talents as a rider and marksman and his intimate knowledge of the Plains Indians would be a great help to Whip Holt, who would need all the assistance he could get in shepherding so large a company of men, women, and children all the way to Oregon.

Glancing at Tonie, who was riding demurely beside him, Arnold smiled to himself. A superb horsewoman and expert rifle shot who had spent most of her life in buckskins, she had chosen a different role for herself today. Her fiery red hair, which usually flew free, was piled high on her head, and she had used cosmetics subtly, to emphasize the depth of her green eyes and the fullness of her mouth. Instead of buckskins, she was wearing a snug-fitting dress of green linen with a low, scooped neckline—a gown that showed off her lithe, trim figure to its best advantage. And, thanks to the dress, she was actually riding sidesaddle.

Shaking his head, he started to laugh. The girl glanced at him archly, raising a slender eyebrow.

"I'll have to call you Antoinette instead of Tonie," he said.

She knew precisely what he meant, and she blushed. "I'll be wearing trousers most of the time crossing the Great Plains, Uncle Arnold," she said. "Whip Holt has already asked me to keep the job of monitor. So I'll be riding up and down the lines of march all day, making sure there are no problems or wagon breakdowns. The only chance I'll have to wear dresses and really look like a woman will be on Sundays when we rest."

"I'm not blaming you, Tonie, just teasing you a little," he said. "Your aunt would have been proud to see you looking like such a grand lady."

"Do you really think I do, Uncle Arnold?"

He nodded, chuckling again. "You bet, and I won't be the only one."

"Bob Martin doesn't know I'm alive," Tonie said flatly.

"Don't be so sure of that. And if he hasn't noticed you before now, he'll come to life in a hurry when he sees you today. I wondered what took you so long this morning. Now I know—and I must say the results are worth the time you spent."

"They'll be worth it," Tonie said as they reached the road that would take them into the heart of Independence on their way to the wagon train encampment, "if Dr. Martin really pays some attention to me and stops taking me for granted. What's that up ahead, Uncle Arnold?"

He looked, then shrugged. "Just some frontier men, seems like."

"They're up to something."

"That wouldn't surprise me."

As Tonie peered ahead, she became increasingly concerned. She caught a glimpse of a sunbonnet, blonde hair, and a flounced skirt in the middle of a circle of men. The men were taking turns tormenting the woman, trying to caress her breasts and reach up under her skirt. "I don't like this, Uncle Arnold!"

"Nobody thinks very much of men like that, and one of these days they'll have to be driven out of town. But they're not bothering us, Tonie, so I suggest we leave well enough alone." Arnold spoke mildly; a lifetime of fighting for the sake of principle had left him weary.

Suddenly Tonie saw the face of the trapped girl and was horrified. "It's Cathy!"

Before her uncle could stop her, Tonie spurred forward, her anger replacing her common sense. She was able to look after herself when she was armed, but she carried no weapons today and consequently was helpless. Arnold Mell followed close behind her, calling in vain for her to stop.

Tonie sent her mare charging into the circle, breaking the formation. "Clear the road and leave that lady alone!" she cried.

"Here's another!" one of the men shouted, then easily hauled Tonie from her horse.

She fought him, trying to kick him and rake his face with her nails, but her long-skirted, tight-fitting gown hindered her. "Take your hands off me, you filthy pig!" she screamed.

He subdued her easily, laughing as he pinned her arms to her sides. "I got to teach you to show a little respect."

"Ain't this nice?" the leader asked of no one in particular. "Now we got two."

"Let's see which is livelier, the blonde or the redhead," one of the men suggested.

Arnold Mell, still mounted, raised his rifle. "Take your hands off these ladies and go about your business," he said in a cold, quiet voice, "or somebody is going to get hurt pretty badly."

One of the men quickly stood behind Cathy and, using her as a shield, he twisted her arm behind her back. At the same moment, he held his skinning knife to her throat. "Grandpa," he said, "the first one to get hurt will be this woman. Pull that trigger just once, and I'll cut her from ear to ear, I swear it." Arnold knew he wasn't bluffing.

Cathy stood very still, scarcely daring to breathe. The long, slightly curved blade was only an inch or two from her throat. Tonie, too, stopped struggling in the grasp of her captor. Deadlocked, Arnold stared at the men and they returned his gaze.

Although those who were participating in the frozen tableau didn't yet realize it, the scene was being witnessed by three pedestrians who were approaching the site. They had been walking single file along the narrow part of the road when Dr. Robert Martin, who was in the lead, halted abruptly. "My God! Tonie and Cathy!"

Seeing the group, Stalking Horse, clad only in a loincloth, a bearskin cape, and moccasins, reached for his bow and an arrow from the quiver he always carried over one shoulder. "Me fix," he said.

Instantly Whip Holt assessed the situation. In sheer numbers the odds favored the gang, but he knew that he and Arnold Mell, even without Stalking Horse and Bob Martin, could overwhelm the gang. If a real fight developed, however, Cathy and Tonie might be hurt, or even killed. Their safety was his first concern.

"No, Stalking Horse," he said, taking charge. "Put down your bow. Bob, your belt is the right place for your pistol. Let it stay there." He sauntered forward casually, discreetly tugging at the handle of his whip to uncoil it.

"Mr. Mell, it would be a big help all around if you'd put down your rifle for a minute or two."

Arnold was surprised but instantly realized that Whip had a plan in mind. "You're the boss, Mr. Holt," he said, lowering his rifle.

Tonie displayed astonishing poise by grinning appreciatively at her uncle. She knew what the others did not— that he could fire with pinpoint accuracy even while holding the rifle in his lap. The muzzle, she noted, continued to point at the leader of the gang.

Whip strolled still closer to the men and their captives, his tone amiable. "I reckon we ought to have a little chat about this situation," he said. "Hanging may be too good for you boys, but we might let you go if you release these ladies. Right now—with no arguments."

"Don't come one step closer, I'm warning you!" the man who held his skinning knife at Cathy's throat shouted.

"Whatever you say," Whip replied, halting.

At the same instant his whip sang effortlessly through the air, and its leaded tip cut a deep furrow in the man's hand.

13

The man screamed in agony as the knife fell to the ground from his nerveless fingers.

The leader drew his pistol. "You were warned," he called.

Again the lash leaped toward its target, this time wrapping itself around the wrist of the gang's leader. Whip tugged gently, and the man's hand was forced up over his head. His pistol discharged harmlessly into the air. Whip tugged again, and the pistol dropped to the ground.

Not yet satisfied, Whip disengaged the lash, then let fly a third time, and the rawhide coiled around the leader's neck. A less than gentle tug brought him to his knees, and an instant later he pitched forward onto the ground, clawing in vain at the taut leather line.

"Mr. Mell," Whip said pleasantly, "I'd be obliged if you'd cover these bastards now. You, too, Stalking Horse. Shoot to kill if any one of them makes a single move." He continued to pull in the whip, dragging the leader toward him.

The Cherokee had already notched an arrow on his bowstring, and Arnold happily raised his rifle again.

Whip continued to pull in the rawhide line. Rather than be choked, the man was forced to wriggle forward on his stomach, unable to rise and unable to resist the steady pressure.

"Cathy," Whip said. "Come over here, please. Take your time and walk slowly."

Cathy felt like running but did as she had been directed.

"That's it," Whip said, still pulling on the lash and keeping a sharp watch on the rest of the gang. "Get behind Stalking Horse and the doctor."

As she did so, Whip said, "All right, Tonie, it's your turn."

"I'll be with you in a minute." Tonie turned to the man who had hauled her from her horse. Smiling slightly, she reached up and raked his face with her fingernails. Blood spurted from the scratches, and he groaned. But, keenly aware of the rifle and bow pointed at him, he did not dare even to raise a hand to protect himself, much less strike the girl.

Tonie spat in his face, then laughed. Turning away from him, she strolled toward her deliverers, the picture of elegance.

"Are you all right, Tonie?" Dr. Martin asked, his voice deep with concern.

"Never better, Bob," she replied lightly.

Arnold chuckled. His niece could look after herself, no question about that. And although she couldn't, and wouldn't, have planned the unsavory incident, she had certainly succeeded in calling herself to Robert Martin's attention. It was unlikely that he would ever forget the impression she had made.

"What about you, Cathy?"

"I—I'm all right now, Doctor. Thank you." Cathy was still shaken.

By now the leader of the gang was within arm's reach of Whip, who let the lash fall free. Then he coiled it around his waist with practiced ease.

As the burly man stumbled to his feet, Whip told him, "We don't like it when our ladies are molested." Quickly, before the man could move, Whip smashed his fist into the man's face.

The man tried to protect himself, but to no avail. Whip landed two hard rights to his face, followed by a solid blow to the pit of the stomach. The man doubled over. A hard, driving right straightened him for a moment, and then he toppled backward, sprawling on the dusty road.

"I'm giving you boys fifteen minutes to clear out of town," Whip said, nudging the body of the fallen man with his foot. "Take this one with you and don't come back, any of you. My Indian friend here hasn't taken any scalps lately, and he can have all of yours."

Several members of the gang came forward hesitantly to carry their fallen companion. Then the entire group, suddenly sober and badly frightened, left the scene as rapidly as they could, scattering as they ran.

Cathy was calmer now, and her eyes were grave as

15

she turned to Whip. "I'm very much obliged to you. More than I can ever say."

Although he was always self-confident in moments of crisis, he flushed beneath his heavy tan. "I just did what had to be done," he replied.

Gratefully he turned to Arnold Mell. "I'm glad you held off and didn't start blasting. The girls might have been hurt."

Arnold grinned. "Years ago when I was one of the first to settle in these parts," he said, speaking with no more than a trace of a Russian accent, "I learned two things. Always keep your gun loaded, but keep your finger off the trigger whenever shooting might cause more problems than it solves."

Whip nodded soberly, pleased with Arnold's answer. The old man was going to be a valuable member of the company. Anyone who understood the wilderness as he did was a valuable asset to the wagon train.

Dr. Martin's manner seemed professional as he looked at Tonie Mell. If his concern was personal, he succeeded in concealing it. "You look none the worse for wear after a nasty experience."

Tonie, outraged at his cool, professional tone and at his failure to compliment her on her appearance, said coldly, "Thanks to Whip and Stalking Horse, I've managed to survive rather nicely, thank you."

Then she turned to Cathy. "Cathy, were you heading into town?"

Cathy nodded.

"Good," Tonie said. "I have some errands to do, myself. Uncle Arnold, if you'll take my horse with you, I'll meet you at the wagon train later."

Bob Martin watched with consternation as the two girls walked off arm in arm, down the road. As a physician and as a widower, he thought he should have had a better understanding of women. But he could not figure out why Tonie had suddenly seemed so angry. What had he done to insult her?

A large, newly painted sign which had just been hung over the front door identified the ranch house and its outbuildings as Brentwood's Depot. It wouldn't be long, perhaps two or three months, before supplies and provisions would begin to arrive from the East and the depot would be busy. Today the air was festive as Sam and Claudia Brentwood gave their farewell party to the people he had escorted this far on their long, arduous journey to Oregon.

The lean and grizzled Sam, limping due to an arthritic hip, had butchered a steer and was roasting two sides of beef over a fire built in a trench behind the house. He had also slaughtered a hog for the occasion. Piled up in mounds were potatoes and fresh sweet corn, still in shucks, to be cooked in the coals.

Two enthusiastic young helpers were turning the spits for him. Danny was a former bound boy in his mid-teens, who, indentured to a cruel and violent man, had escaped and joined the wagon train. He had endeared himself to the whole company by his willingness to work hard. He worked in perfect harmony with Chet Harris, the eldest surviving son of the widowed Emily Harris, who was intent on making a new life for her family. The two boys were about the same age and had become such close friends that when one appeared the other was always close at hand.

The most intriguing member of the wagon train had insisted on taking charge of preparing the drinks. Baron Ernst von Thalman was a wealthy, middle-aged Austrian nobleman, formerly a cavalry officer in the Imperial Austrian Army. Lean and athletic, a deadly shot, he lived in a custom-built wagon that resembled an elegant home on wheels. He had jugs of hard cider for the men who wanted it, a less potent cider for the women, and a non-alcoholic cider for the children.

Cathy van Ayl and Tonie Mell helped Claudia Brentwood in the kitchen, as did Cindy, a former prostitute from Louisville who had reformed and was making a new life for herself. Working together, as they had learned to do on the road, the young women prepared salad greens and baked loaves of white bread, corn bread, and a variety of fruit pies.

Stoking the wood fire for them, carrying the baked

breads and pies to tables in the yard was Ted Woods, a blacksmith by trade. He was a swarthy, powerful giant, and it was no accident that he was always found in the vicinity of the slender, bubbling Cindy. It was obvious to her, as well as to her companions, that Ted had developed a deep interest in her, although he had said nothing about his feelings to anyone. Some thought he was shy, but Cathy knew better. Ted had spent ten years in an Indiana prison after killing his wife and his brother when he had discovered them in bed together. That experience had scarred him deeply, and Cathy, at least, wondered if he would ever dare to tell Cindy of his interest in her.

As they worked, Cathy and Tonie told the story of what had happened to them earlier in the day in Independence. Claudia Brentwood was concerned.

"Now I can understand why Sam taught me to shoot and makes sure that I keep a rifle close at hand whenever he's away from the house. This town isn't much better than the wilderness."

"Don't worry," Tonie told her. "Once word gets around the neighborhood that you know how to handle firearms, you won't be molested. In all the years I lived here, I never had any trouble until today. And it serves me right for getting dressed up. Bob Martin didn't even know I was alive."

Pushing a lock of hair out of her eyes, Cathy laughed. "You're fooling yourself, Tonie. I saw the doctor's expression when those troublemakers had us trapped. He may not even know it himself—yet. But he's sweet on you."

"Of course he is," Cindy declared. "I know men, and it's just a question of time before he proposes to you."

"By that time," Tonie said defiantly, "I may want to turn him down."

At that moment Ted Woods came into the kitchen carrying another huge load of firewood, so the girls quickly changed the subject.

"Was there no way you could protect yourselves this morning?" Claudia asked.

Tonie's smile was rueful. "It was the first time in longer

18

than I can remember that I wasn't carrying a rifle. If I'd been armed, I would have put a bullet between the eyes of the man who was encouraging the others, and that would have been the end of the matter."

"I think that learning to handle a rifle is the best thing that ever happened to me," Claudia said. "I can't tell you how grateful I am to Sam for teaching me."

"I've been wondering if I ought to learn to shoot," Cathy said.

"The same idea has been going through my mind," Cindy said as she put apples into a pie shell.

Ted, who was throwing short logs into the oven, made no comment, but his back stiffened.

"You don't approve, Ted?" Claudia asked.

He dusted his hands as he stood and turned. "No, ma'am. Tonie here grew up knowing how to shoot. You learned because it was something you really wanted to do. But Cindy here—and Cathy, too—they'd do themselves more harm than good. People shouldn't fool with guns."

Cindy couldn't resist the urge to tease him. "But we've got to be able to look after ourselves in country where there are Indians and renegades and goodness only knows what other dangers."

Ted stared at her for a moment. "The reason there's menfolks in this train is to look after ladies who can't take care of themselves." Then he turned and stamped out of the kitchen, heading in the direction of the wood shed.

The girls were silent for a time after he had left. Cathy was the first to speak. "Ted is sweet."

Tonie dared to ask what all of them were wondering. "What do *you* think of him, Cindy?"

Her strawberry blonde curls danced as Cindy shook her head. "As you know," she said, "I have my reasons for not thinking very highly of men. Oh, there are a few gentlemen in the world. Sam Brentwood is one, and Baron von Thalman is another. I don't yet know Whip Holt well enough to judge him, but Dr. Martin is a real love."

Tonie acted as though she had been physically struck.

Looking up from the dough she was mixing, she glared at the other girl.

Cindy, unaware of her reaction, continued to chatter. "I haven't made up my mind about Ted Woods," she said. "My first reaction to him was that he was a nuisance. But he's been so kind and helpful to me that I can't help feeling grateful to him. Beyond that—well, I don't yet know."

The kitchen door opened again, and Sam came in, followed by Arnold Mell and Whip Holt. "There are two hundred or more of the guests out there already," Sam told his bride, "and more are arriving every minute. A couple of the men are keeping an eye on the meat while we have a little private chat." He led the men into the parlor.

"Whip," Sam said as they settled into plain wooden armchairs, "I wanted a word with you, and I asked Arnold to join us because he's spent more time than either of us in this part of the world. You're aiming to push off pretty soon, I believe."

"We'll be ready in another couple of days," the new wagonmaster replied. "Nine more wagons joined us today —with about thirty-five people in them—and I want to give them time to pick up emergency provisions before we start."

"You'll be leading about four hundred and fifty people, then," Sam said.

"Closer to five hundred."

"That makes my worries all the more real. That's one hell of a lot of mouths to feed."

Arnold Mell absently rubbed the arm of his chair. "That shouldn't be a problem. There are enough herds of buffalo out yonder to keep us in meat."

"Until winter comes," Sam said. "Don't let this summer weather fool you. It's still the end of September. Arnold, how long do you estimate it will be before heavy snows start to hit the plains?"

The old frontiersman looked out of the windows at the sea of green grass that stretched toward the horizon. "Eight weeks, maybe, if the cold hits early. Ten or eleven weeks if the nasty weather holds off."

"That's pretty much the way I had it figured," Sam said. "Whip, I'm not interfering, and I'm sure as shooting not trying to tell you what to do. But I've been wondering about your plans for winter."

Whip Holt always found it difficult to think while he was sitting. He rose and began to pace up and down the length of the roughly furnished parlor. "The way I see it," he replied, "I've got two choices. Either I can play it safe and stay right here in Independence until spring, or I can get a good head start across the plains. Staying here has its advantages, but there are arguments on the other side. President Van Buren has made it plain he wants us to reach the Oregon country as soon as we can—before the British start establishing settlements on the Pacific coast south of Fort Vancouver or the Russians take heart and come back. Also, some of our people aren't the bravest in the world. They're making this trip because the U.S. Government will guarantee every householder a plot of six hundred acres —almost four times as much free land as they can get anywhere else. I'm afraid that many of them will lose what little courage they have and change their minds about going out to the Oregon country if they have to stay here in Independence until spring."

Sam nodded. "That makes sense."

"So I plan to push out across the plains and go as far as we can before the cold weather comes," Whip continued. "With luck we can travel as far as five hundred miles before we have to hunker down— provided the British and Russian agents leave us alone. Even if they stir up trouble, we should go quite a distance."

"Fair enough," Sam said. "I'm sure you realize as well as I do that the wagons are too flimsy for winter living and that buffalo will be harder to find once the snows come. So that brings up the question of finding a campsite near forests, where there will be enough wood for cabins and fires, and close enough to salt licks that buffalo use."

"You're right, Sam," Arnold said. "In all the trips I've made out into the plains, I've found very few patches of woods. I'm sure that Whip and I, between us, can pick a site in an area that buffalo frequent, even when the snow is thick. But finding forests is something else."

Whip continued to pace. "I'm going to trust my instinct. President Van Buren has been pestering us, and so has Sam's friend, Andrew Jackson. I want to put as many miles as I can between the wagon train and Independence. We'll keep our eyes and ears wide open. We know there are a few forests out in that Godforsaken wilderness, and somehow we'll find one of them before the snows come."

II

Members of the wagon train were frantically busy as they made their final preparations. The women emptied the few stores in Independence of their supplies of bacon, flour, beans, and other essential foodstuffs. Those who had traveled from the East Coast replaced the worn canvas covers of their wagons. Ted Woods worked from daybreak until night fitting new steel rims on wheels. The men bought lead, bullet presses, and gunpowder.

Everyone reacted to the approaching trek into the unknown in his own way. There was a good deal of tension between Lena and Terence Malcolm, one of the wagon train's most popular young couples. Lena had joined the caravan on her seventeenth birthday with her father and her illegitimate baby daughter, Lenore, in the hope of creating a new life. Terence Malcolm, nineteen, who had believed when he first joined the train that he was dying of consumption, had married her in order to give her baby a name. But the rugged life in the open air had cured him, and subsequently he and Lena had fallen in love.

The others believed that Lena and Terence had found happiness together, but no one seeing them as they sat on the rear stoop of their wagon would have thought so.

Terence stared off into the night, running a hand through his hair, while Lena glanced at him furtively. At moments like this he made her think of her father, now dead, who had become violent under the influence of alcohol.

"Terry," she said, speaking softly so they wouldn't awaken the baby who was asleep inside the wagon, "you pulled into a shell right after we got to Independence. Please—what's wrong?"

Her young husband continued to look at the few stars shining in a cloud-filled sky. She put a hand on his arm, and Terence felt her trembling. He could remain silent no longer. "I'm scared," he said.

Lena was shocked. "Of what?"

"Not for myself. For you and Lenore. You came on this expedition because your pa made you do it, not because you wanted to go to Oregon. I've been talking to some of the older men, and they say we face terrible risks. I have no right to subject you and Lenore to them. You might be killed by Indians or die of starvation. All kinds of awful things could happen to you."

"What are you trying to tell me, Terry?"

"I have to go to Oregon. I have you and the baby to support. At six dollars an acre, I can't afford to buy a farm anywhere in the East, or even in Illinois or Indiana. No matter how rough the travel may be, I'm obliged to go on to Oregon and stake my six-hundred-acre claim."

"You'd leave Lenore and me?" Lena was on the verge of tears.

"The way I see it, we have enough cash to pay for your room and board right here in Independence, where you'll be safe. Once I get to Oregon and build us a home, I'll send for you."

She was silent.

"All right?" he asked, sounding apprehensive.

Lena exploded. "If I didn't believe it's wrong for people to hit each other, I'd box your ears good, Terence Malcolm. Nobody made you marry me. You did it of your own free will, and I'm your wife!"

"Sure you are," he said, trying to soothe her. "That's the reason I suggested—"

"I don't want to hear one more word!" Lena cried. "I'd rather starve with you or have all three of us killed by Indians—together—than to be separated from you for even one single day. If you want us to drop out of the wagon trail, we'll do it, and maybe we can find jobs as a hired couple somewhere."

"That isn't practical. I want the best of everything for you and Lenore."

"Then we're coming with you, and that's the end of the discussion," she said. "Goodness mercy, I was afraid you didn't love me any more."

"There's no chance of that," he replied softly, his voice shaky.

Lena looked at him, her eyes shining. "We took a vow when we got married. We promised to stay with each other for better or worse. So far everything has been pretty wonderful, and that's the way it will always be."

The sound of her voice awakened the baby. "Mama! Papa!" she called.

"We're right here," Terence called. "Go back to sleep, Lenore." He looked at his wife, his expression sheepish. "You just don't know how worried I've been."

Lena pulled his head toward her, and they kissed. Terence's worries vanished, and he knew he was the most fortunate of men.

Whip Holt had no wagon, preferring to sleep in the open. Now, returning to the train late in the evening after a busy day that had started at daybreak, he intended to get his blanket and spread it on the ground just inside the circle of wagons. But he was delayed by the approach of a portly man in an expensively tailored suit, who was accompanied by two exceptionally handsome young people.

Whip had met them only two days earlier but knew them by sight immediately. They were not a family one could easily forget.

Major Laurence Woodling was a South Carolina aristocrat whose military title had been earned in his state's militia during the War of 1812. He had lost his plantation in the financial crisis that now gripped the United States, just as so many smaller farmers had gone bankrupt, and he was traveling to Oregon in the hope of starting life anew.

With him were his twenty-one-year-old son, Claiborne, whose arrogant strut indicated he knew he was good-looking, and his daughter of nineteen, Eulalia. As spoiled as her brother, Eulalia was a beauty, with a full, ripe mouth and seductive eyes. She wore a skin-tight dress with a daringly low-cut neckline that left little to the imagination.

Whip instantly sensed trouble.

"Mr. Holt," Major Woodling said in a deep, soft drawl, "we've been waiting for you all evening."

"What can I do for you, Major?" Whip was cordial but not effusive.

"We have two requests. We find one wagon very crowded for the three of us, and I wonder if we might be able to buy another."

Whip shook his head. "You'll have to travel a thousand miles or more toward the Atlantic to find a wagon and a team of horses or oxen that you could buy, Major."

"You see, Papa?" Eulalia was so annoyed she barely avoided stamping her foot. "I've been telling and telling you!"

Her father ignored the outburst. "What do you suggest we do, Mr. Holt?"

"You have two choices, Major. Either you make do with what you have, or you make other arrangements." He turned to the son. "You look as though you can ride and shoot."

"I was practically born in the saddle," Claiborne Woodling declared. "And if you'd care to make a wager on a shooting contest, you may pick your own type of firearms and the target."

"I don't shoot for pleasure," Whip was abrupt. "As it happens, I've been putting together a team of scouts, line monitors and the like. If you can shoot and ride as well as you seem to think, we'd gladly have you join us. Certainly I'm willing to give you a tryout.

We'll be sleeping in the open most of the time, so your wagon wouldn't be as crowded."

As he spoke, he realized that Eulalia Woodling was flirting with him. She was so open in her approach that she wasn't offensive. Unaccustomed to women flirting, he warned himself to be careful. But her violet eyes exerted such a magnetic power that he couldn't ignore her gaze, nor could he ignore the slight smile that parted her lips.

"I'm not that partial to the outdoors," Claiborne said. "What do you do when it rains?"

Whip grinned wryly. "We get wet."

"I see." The young man fingered his silk cravat. "I could use some spare money for entertainment on our journey," he said. "How much do these positions pay?"

"Pay?" Whip stared at him incredulously. "Boy, we're heading into country where the odds against survival are two or three to one. If you're a gambler, just think about that for a spell. Everybody in the train has chores to do. You'll be given your assignment tomorrow, Major, as will you, miss. You, too, boy, unless you try out for a monitor's job and are good enough to hold it. Folks in this company volunteer their services for the good of everybody, and they're happy to do it. We work together or we die!"

"You give me little choice, sir." Claiborne bowed stiffly. "I accept your offer. Just tell me what I'm to do."

"You'll work for Tonie Mell, who will give you your instructions in the morning." Whip turned to the Major. "I believe you said there were two matters you wanted to take up with me, Major."

"There are, Mr. Holt. I still have some funds, fortunately, and I'm willing to pay a reasonable sum for a slave who can attend to the chores of wagon-train living."

Whip didn't know whether to be annoyed or to laugh. "Major," he said, "you'll be driving your own wagon, hitching and unhitching your team, and looking after your horses all the way out to Oregon. Miss, you'll be washing clothes, keeping the inside of your wagon tidy, helping fix meals, and drawing water. From here to the

Pacific. The Oregon country is free soil. There are no slaves there. What's more, most members of this company come from the North and wouldn't tolerate slavery in the caravan."

Major Woodling's eyes burned, but he remained courteous. "I thank you for your information and interest, sir," he said, then turned and started off toward his own wagon. Claiborne clicked his heels, bowed, and walked off with his father.

Eulalia lingered for a moment. "Don't mind Papa and my brother, Mr. Holt," she said. "They've only known one way of life, and they haven't yet learned how to get along in the world." She turned away and, aware that he was watching her, allowed her hips to sway as she walked to her wagon.

She, too, had a great deal to learn, Whip reflected. If she flirted this brazenly with others on the journey, she would create an uproar. As he took his blanket from his saddlebag, he wished she were less attractive, and he warned himself to be wary of her.

Whip Holt had announced they would make an early start, so most members of the company had retired early. By ten in the evening, the campsite was quiet, and everyone seemed to be asleep.

Shortly before midnight, however, fifteen-year-old Chet Harris sneaked out of the wagon he occupied with his mother and two brothers and walked to Ted Woods's small, ramshackle wagon. Standing there, he coughed gently. Instantly Danny, who shared the wagon with Ted, crept silently into the open. The two boys hurried down to the bank of the broad Missouri River, following it to an area where the grass was waist high.

There they halted, and Danny called softly, "Hosea!"

Most members of the company would have thought they were dreaming if they had seen the man who emerged like a wraith from the thick, deep grass. Totally bald, with skin of shining ebony, he was attired only in a loincloth.

Much shorter than Danny and Chet, he was no more than five feet tall, but he was fully developed physically,

28

with powerful shoulders, strong arms, well-muscled legs, and a thick torso. Around his middle, on a thong, he wore rows of what appeared to be decorations resembling small tenpins. Actually they were small weapons—wooden throwing clubs weighted with metal. Unknown in America, they were used in Africa by the Ashanti tribe to kill small game and, when necessary in battle, to stun an enemy whom the Ashanti wanted to capture rather than kill.

Over one bare shoulder, the black man also carried a leather container no more than six inches long. It appeared harmless, but he had already shown the two boys the contents—a blowgun and darts that he had dipped in the venom of snakes he had killed.

He grinned at the boys, waved, and then joined them, making no sound as he moved forward through the tall grass.

"Did you find the supper we left for you?" Chet asked. "We didn't dare call you because there were too many people around."

"Hosea find," the man said. "Good supper. Plenty much to eat." He patted his flat abdomen.

"We march in the morning," Danny said. "We'll take you to the special wagon and show it to you. Make sure you hide there before dawn and stay there until it's dark. We'll bring you food whenever we can."

"Hosea like food!"

"If you stay hidden until we put Independence far behind us, they won't send you back."

Danny felt a great sympathy for this African who had been captured by Arab traders and sent to the United States as a slave. Only recently had he removed his identification anklet, with a file the boys had brought him.

Danny had been a fugitive, too, and knew how difficult it was to live on the run. He was awed by Hosea's remarkable journey, all the way from the plantation in Georgia where he had been given his Biblical name, to Independence, Missouri. Anyone who could travel all that distance on foot, wearing only a loincloth, had to be an extraordinary person. No matter what Ted Woods might think, no matter how Whip Holt might react when he learned what the boys were doing, Danny intended to help the man he and Chet had befriended.

"The special wagon," he said, "is filled with all kinds of things. Barrels and sacks of emergency food supplies, medicines, spare wagon parts, and harnesses. Firearms and ammunition, too."

Hosea smiled slightly as he touched his blowgun container, then let his fingers slide over one of the tiny clubs hanging from his middle. He remained silent, but his reaction was plain: others could use firearms if they wished; he would place his faith in the ancient weapons of his people.

"There are lots of odd corners in the wagon, so it shouldn't be too hard for somebody of your size to hide there," Danny said.

"Easy," Hosea replied, then laughed.

"Just be careful, that's all," Chet said. "Somebody will be inspecting the wagon every day to make sure everything is in place. They won't go through it carefully, but they'll take a long look inside from the back flap. So stay up near the front, where nobody ever goes."

"Not worry," the escaped slave assured them. "Hosea be very safe in special wagon."

"Let's go, then." Danny was nervous, afraid that one of the adults, Whip in particular, might wake up and see them.

The boys walked together, assuming an air of nonchalance they were far from feeling, and Hosea followed them at a distance of a dozen paces. He managed to blend in with his surroundings in some mysterious way. The boys glanced repeatedly over their shoulders to make certain he was still behind them.

When they reached the special wagon, they halted behind it. Danny pointed to a burlap sack outside the circle of vehicles, which he and Chet had filled with a loaf of bread and dried buffalo meat.

Hosea's sense of smell, as highly developed as his other senses, immediately told him the contents of the sack. He scooped it up and slung it over his shoulder in a single, swift gesture. Opening the rear flap, he climbed inside the special wagon and closed the flap behind him.

It was astonishing to the boys that he could be so quiet; those who were asleep in the wagons to the front and rear were totally unaware that anything unusual had taken place. Danny and Chet stood outside for a moment, exchanged uncertain smiles, then went off to their own wagons.

Ted Woods opened one eye when Danny stealthily crept into their wagon. By Danny's movements, Ted knew that he had been up to something. Turning over on his pallet, Ted smiled as he went back to sleep. No secrets could be kept for long on the wagon train, and soon whatever it was would come out into the open.

St. Joseph, Missouri rivaled Independence as the principal frontier outpost in the United States, although it was gradually losing ground. The atmosphere was similar: fur buyers purchased the wares of trappers, traders, and hunters, and the saloons and brothels in the town quickly separated the mountain men from their hard-earned money.

There were very few respectable boarding houses in town, and Henry St. Clair lodged in one of them. A man in his thirties, dashing and trim, he wore expensive clothes and was sometimes mistaken for a sharp-witted representative of a fur company. Henry did nothing to discourage such ideas.

He had arrived in St. Joseph more dead than alive after being viciously beaten by the leader of a gang of army deserters who, at his instigation, had attacked the wagon train and, after suffering a catastrophic defeat, had taken out their anger on him. The one physician in town had been taking care of him. He was mending very well and considered himself fortunate—none of his bones had been broken and, although he was still somewhat battered, he could get around without too much difficulty.

Fortunately, the army deserters had not known about the money belt he carried around his waist. On the frontier, men would kill for much less. It was filled with gold and United States coins, more money by far than he would require to complete his mission. That task was a simple one, or so he had believed when his superiors in the British secret service had given him the assignment. He was under orders to slow the progress of the first major wagon train to cross the continent and, if possible, to prevent it from reaching Oregon. Obviously it would be far easier for Great Britain to claim all of the Oregon country, which it now held jointly with the United States, if Queen Victoria's subjects rather than American citizens were the first to settle there in large numbers.

The job was proving to be more difficult than Henry had imagined. When he had passed himself off as a settler, his sabotage attempts had been ineffective. He had suffered an even worse defeat after he had been discovered, fled, and enlisted the aid of the deserters.

Not that he himself cared whether the caravan reached the Pacific—he had no personal interest in the matter. But he was a professional agent, with a long history of achievements in Europe, Africa, and Asia. His reputation did not allow him to tolerate failure.

St. Clair also had high hopes for his future. He had been promised that he would be permitted to retire from the field once he ruined the plans of the United States. He would be given an office in London and a title, and he would remain in that city, spending the rest of his professional life as a supervisor.

London! Just the thought of returning there dazzled Henry St. Clair. It was his favorite place on earth, filled with inns that served the kind of food he most enjoyed and studded with taverns that employed amenable barmaids. After a long career devoted to hard work in unpleasant and uncomfortable surroundings, Henry was ready to retire to a desk and the joys of London.

Walking slowly up the dirt road that constituted St. Joseph's main street, he went to the office of the physician and, because he always paid his bills immediately, he was admitted without delay.

The doctor gave him no more than a cursory

examination. "You're healing," he said. "You were lucky you didn't do much worse to yourself falling down that cliff."

"How soon may I leave?" St. Clair demanded. He had to get on with his assignment.

The doctor tugged at his chin. "Well, if you could rest for another couple of weeks, it sure wouldn't do you any harm."

"But would it hurt me if I took off as soon as I get my gear together? I have urgent business elsewhere, sir."

The physician hesitated. "You seem to be in fairly good shape, I'll admit. I won't take responsibility if you suffer a relapse, but if you want to take that chance yourself, I'm not in a position to stop you."

That was all Henry wanted to know. He paid his bill and left the office. Wasting no time, he headed straight for the market district that faced the Missouri River. He approached a barn where a sign hung over the entrance: *For Sale or Rent—Horses and Carts.*

The proprietor smelled of the stables, and Henry wrinkled his nose in distaste. Americans were still a barbaric people. "I want to buy the largest wagon in your shop and a suitable team to pull it," the Englishman said.

The man gaped at him. "You ain't thinkin' o' gettin' a prairie schooner, Mister?"

"Whatever." Names meant nothing to Henry, and he shrugged, wanting only to complete the transaction as quickly as he could.

"Prairie schooners are as scarce as white buffalo, Mister. You got t' pick them up in New York or Hartford or Boston. Where are you aimin' t' travel?"

Perhaps the man thought he was being helpful, but in England no tradesman would dream of asking such a personal question. "I intend to do rather extensive traveling on behalf of my employers," Henry replied curtly.

The proprietor shook his head. "The best I got is a freight wagon I bought last month when the owner got himself killed in a bordello fight down the street. It'll carry merchandise, with room left over for people t' live in."

"I'd like to see it."

The man took him outside to the rear of the barn where several vehicles, most of them in bad condition, stood. "There you be," he said, pointing.

Henry stared at the largest wagon he had ever seen. It had twelve wheels and a yoke for six horses. This wagon was not only huge but cumbersome; on the other hand, it could easily accommodate all the goods he planned to purchase. And there would be more than enough room for him to sleep under the arched canvas roof.

The proprietor saw that he was impressed and began to push. "Do you want horses or oxen? We got both."

"If you have a strong team of horses, I'm interested. I know nothing about oxen."

The man frowned; never had he encountered anyone unfamiliar with oxen. But a major sale was pending, so he did not dwell on the matter. Instead he took the prospective client to a string of stables that stood at right angles to his other buildings.

There Henry found a team of six workhorses in prime condition, sturdy animals that appeared to be in robust health. His luck was better than he had dared to hope, and he exulted inwardly. "How much for the freighter and the team?" he demanded.

Judging by the stranger's clothes, the expensive dueling pistols he carried in his belt, and his superb, English-made rifle with a polished walnut butt, the proprietor knew Henry was a man of means. "Five hundred dollars," he said.

Henry grinned at him. "I'll give you two hundred."

The stranger wasn't a fool, after all, the proprietor thought, then sighed aloud. "Make it two hundred and fifty, and you've got a deal."

"That includes harnesses, of course," Henry said, driving a hard bargain.

The man hesitated. Then, unwilling to jeopardize a sale, he capitulated. "You got a deal, Mister," he said.

Giving him no opportunity to change his mind, Henry counted out the sum in American paper money. "Have the team hitched and ready to go by early this afternoon," he said, and gave the man an extra dollar.

Next he went to St. Joseph's largest general store and, in less than an hour of whirlwind buying, he had purchased everything he needed for his own use. He found two sets of buckskin shirts and pants that fitted him reasonably well, along with a buffalo-skin cloak to wear when the weather got colder. He could have planned to shoot his own on the Great Plains and cure the skins, but this would save him the trouble. He laid in a generous store of rations, including salted fish and smoked venison, as well as barrels of such staples as pickled beef, sacks of flour, beans, sugar, and salt, and sides of bacon and ham.

Even more important, he bought a mattress and several blankets, two pairs of oiled boots, and several rolls of canvas to replace the covering on his wagon. He found extra wheels, two axles, and a spare yoke for his team and, as a final precaution, he bought a hammer, a keg of nails, and two knives. Now he was almost ready.

Arranging to pick up most of his purchases later, he took one set of his new clothes with him and went to the better of St. Joseph's bordellos. It might be a long time before he would have another opportunity to bed a woman. He acquired the services of a blonde who satisfied him, even though she wasn't up to his London standards. Then he dressed in his new buckskins and boots.

Returning to his lodging house, he picked up his few belongings, paid his bill, then went to the stables for his waiting team and freight wagon. His next stop was the general store, where his morning's purchases were loaded into his wagon.

Finally, he went to a warehouse with a somewhat questionable reputation where he had engaged in intensive bargaining the previous day. A dozen unmarked, innocent-looking crates containing rifles were loaded onto the wagon, along with containers that were filled with gunpowder and heavy boxes loaded with lead bars from which bullets could be fashioned. Finally a large number of barrels of cheap whiskey were rolled onto the wagon. Ever since colonial days, it had been against the law in the New World to sell or give liquor to Indians, but Henry had paid more than the asking price for the whiskey, so the owner of the warehouse had conveniently forgotten to fill out the form required by the federal government when alcoholic beverages were sold in quantity.

Ready at last, Henry St. Clair drove his team to the bank of the Missouri River. There he paid the operator of a ferry fifty cents—double the usual price—to take him and his heavy load to the west bank.

"Where are you headed?" the operator asked.

Henry gave him the first answer that came to mind. "I'm starting a new kind of business. I'm taking supplies out to the Rockies to sell to mountain men."

The explanation made no real sense, but it satisfied the ferry operator.

Sitting on the front of the wagon and keeping his team under tight rein while the ferry traveled across the broad river, Henry St. Clair smiled to himself. He was truly pleased. Ahead lay the Great Plains, and he felt reasonably certain he would be moving into the area before the wagon train reached the region. He could travel far more rapidly than could a caravan of fifty or sixty wagons.

The unknown did not frighten him, the wilderness held no terrors for him. The liquor and weapons were virtual guarantees that he would be able to make a mutually satisfactory arrangement with one or more of the Indian tribes. The odds against him had been overwhelming, but he told himself he had every right to be proud of his accomplishments so far. The wagon train was doomed.

Sam and Claudia Brentwood intended to bid a last farewell to their friends on the wagon train, so they awakened two hours before dawn, dressed hastily, and hurried to the kitchen. There they found that Cathy, who had decided to spend the night with them, was not only fully dressed but had already made coffee.

Once on the road into Independence, Claudia exchanged a glance with Sam, and he raised the question that both had been reluctant to ask. "Cathy, you still haven't told us your plans, and you can't really hold off any longer. Are you staying with us and turning your wagon and team over to somebody, or are you going on to Oregon with the train?"

Cathy smiled faintly and sounded very sure of herself as she said, "I'm going to Oregon."

Claudia was surprised. "I thought that nasty experience you had in town a couple of days ago might have robbed you of any spirit of adventure you had left."

"I'm not interested in adventure," Cathy said. "What I enjoy is the freedom to live my own life in my own way. I went straight from papa's supervision to Otto's, and now, for the first time ever, I can do what I please."

Sam reflected that he would never understand any woman. "I know you and Otto worked a farm on Long Island," he said, "but I thought that life didn't appeal to you very much."

"It's the only life I know," Cathy replied.

"Then," he persisted, "you'll take six hundred acres from the government, build yourself a home, and start to farm the property?"

Claudia couldn't help smiling at the note of astonishment in his voice, and she couldn't blame him. A girl as pretty and petite as Cathy didn't look capable of cutting down huge trees, uprooting the stumps, and plowing the earth for planting, much less putting up her own house in the wilderness.

Cathy's smile indicated that she was fully aware of the difficulties that lay ahead of her. "I still have Otto's money, and if I can't work this out in some other way, I can always pay somebody to do the hard physical labor for me."

Sam wondered what she meant by "working this out in some other way," but Claudia knew instantly.

"I know you've entertained a rather high opinion of Whip Holt ever since you first met him," Claudia said directly, "and I suspect your opinion of him is even higher since he saved you from those roughnecks."

37

"Claudia!" Cathy grew scarlet, mortified because her sister had raised the matter openly in Sam's presence.

Claudia knew what was going through her sister's mind and was firm. "Sam is family now, so we'll keep no secrets from him. You can trust him to be discreet."

"Of course," the bewildered Sam said.

Cathy was badly flustered and peered off into the night. The stars had disappeared, and she could see only a short distance down the road. "It—it so happens I have a very high regard for Michael Holt."

At last Sam understood. He had never heard anyone else refer to Whip by anything other than his nickname.

"But I have no intention of throwing myself at him," Cathy went on. "I'm not a hussy. And I have no intention of marrying anyone so soon after Otto's death. What's more, I have no idea whether Michael Holt will ever want to settle down with any woman. I may be young, Claudia, but I'm not giddy, and I do try to be realistic."

"Are you sure there's nothing more to all this," Claudia asked, "than gratitude to Whip for rescuing you the other day?"

"I'm not sure of anything, but I plan to find out!" Cathy retorted.

Sam decided to intervene. "Cathy," he said, "watch your step. I've known Whip for a long time, and I've been as close to him as anybody can get, which isn't all that close. He's a good man, but he holds everybody at arm's length. And he values his freedom more than life itself. I don't think any girl, not even one as pretty as you, could ever lasso him and put a brand on him."

Cathy absorbed her brother-in-law's words in silence. Then suddenly the clouds parted, and the moon appeared, illuminating the wagons that stood in a circle high on a hill overlooking the Missouri River. Dark figures scurried around a roaring breakfast fire. She felt a lump in her throat, and for a few moments her heart raced faster. "No matter what," she said, "I'm going on to Oregon!"

The man who called himself André Sebastian arose early, as he always did. He ate a substantial breakfast in the dining room of the one respectable inn in St. Louis, then lingered at the table over coffee. He lit one of the expensive Latin American *segaros* that were his only weakness.

Perhaps he would leave today on the next stage of his journey, but he felt no need to rush. It wouldn't matter if he waited an extra day or an extra week. He could cover fifty miles in a day without exerting himself, while the most the American wagon train could manage was ten miles. There was no way the train could move fast enough to leave him far behind. And his own timing was of primary importance: he had no desire to make his approach in Independence. It would be far easier to strike after the wagons moved out into the lonely, unending reaches of the Great Plains.

That was something the *chargé d'affaires* of the Imperial Russian Legation in Washington failed to understand. But the *chargé*, like so many desk officers in the employ of the secret police, was an imbecile. In order to serve in a supervisory capacity, one had to have family connections in St. Petersburg, but common sense would indicate that men with field experience should be promoted to the higher posts.

Not that André Sebastian sought or would accept a desk job. He was too restless to shuffle papers, and his distinguished career, almost all of it served in the New World, proved that he was superbly efficient in the field.

It was difficult for anyone to tell whether he was twenty-five years old or forty, and that was one of his advantages. His hair was dark, his features were ordinary and his suit of broadcloth, although made for him by a tailor, was a dirty gray color. André Sebastian was not a man whom people remembered, which was precisely the appearance he had long cultivated.

Now that he was closing in on his quarry, he thought the time was appropriate for a review of this case. His one regret was that he hadn't been given the assignment to begin with. He had been on another job at the time, and Tonie Mell, who had been chosen for this one, had obviously failed to act.

This assignment required great finesse and stamina,

Sebastian reflected. Only a man who had crossed all of Siberia on horseback could be asked to follow the Yankee wagon train into the untamed vastness of the Great Plains.

At an appropriate moment, he would approach Antoinette Melichev, the girl who called herself Tonie Mell. St. Petersburg's terms had become harsher. He would notify her that if she failed to cooperate—perform acts of sabotage that would bring the wagon train to a halt—her mother and father not only would be required to remain in Russia, but might be imprisoned, sent in exile to Siberia or even executed.

André Sebastian hoped the threat would mean enough to the stubborn girl to convince her to act on behalf of the Russians. If not, he was authorized to take any steps necessary to force her compliance. Only if she continued to refuse did he have orders to intervene directly, to perform acts of sabotage that would disrupt and disorganize the train.

The reasons for this had been stressed to him repeatedly by the *chargé,* who had treated him like an idiot, but the purpose of the order was plain. Russia was posing as the one great power that was friendly to the United States; Martin Van Buren and his State Department were taken in by the ruse, just as Andrew Jackson, the previous President, had been. Great Britain, France, and even failing Spain might connive against the young, growing nation that was expanding so rapidly across the face of North America, but the government in St. Petersburg stated that it had no conflict with Washington.

The facts were far different. Imperial explorers and settlers had been the first to find and make their homes in the fertile lands of Alaska. The Oregon region then stretched from Alaska to California. Based on their explorations along the northern Pacific coast, Russia had laid claim to parts of the Oregon country.

The Americans and British, the United States and Canada, lying relatively close to the Oregon territory, also had laid claim to the area. Russia had faced a cruel choice: either withdraw or go to war. Granted that Oregon was a paradise, rich with timber and salmon, marvelously fertile soil, and precious minerals in her mountains. But she was not worth a war with Great Britain, at present the strongest nation on earth, or even with the Yankees, who had demonstrated in their War of Independence and War of 1812 that they continued to fight until they achieved victory. So Russia signed treaties with Great Britain and the United States, giving up its interests. Now Russia wanted the lands back and was taking a subtle approach to accomplish its goal.

André Sebastian knew he was the right person for the task that lay ahead. He was a crack shot, a deadly knife thrower, and capable of sustaining himself in the wilderness for long periods. Studying the glowing tip of his *segaro,* he calmly sipped his coffee. He felt confident that, one way or another, he would persuade or compel Antoinette Melichev to perform the deeds that the government of the czar demanded of her. And no one would ever learn of the Russian secret police's involvement.

Members of the wagon train ate a hearty breakfast of pancakes and bacon and, while the women washed the dishes and tidied the campsite, the men hitched their teams of horses and oxen. There were four barges used for river crossings in Independence, and Whip Holt hired all of them. The transfer of the animals and wagons took the better part of the morning, but at last the task was completed, and the company assembled on the west bank of the Missouri in a land occupied by the Kansa Indians and a few white men.

The route selected by Whip was simple. The company was so large—four hundred and seventy-six persons— that the need for water was constant. So he intended to travel almost due north along the Missouri until they came to one of its principal tributaries, the Platte, in the land of the Omaha nation. There they would turn west and would follow the Platte—and subsequently the North Platte—all the way to the Rockies.

The grass was high, but there were only a few, small, scattered trees dotting the landscape. The land that stretched out toward the horizon was flat. There were no hills here, no rises; it was evident that the Great Plains had been aptly named.

The absence of natural obstacles made it possible for Whip to arrange his caravan in three parallel columns of about fifty wagons each. The place of honor of the first wagon of the right column was held by Baron Ernst von Thalman. He had been elected president of the train by a unanimous vote—a rare sign of confidence in a foreigner. As the head of the community, he would act as judge in disputes between members of the company and would also act as spokesman for the travelers in dealings with the wagonmaster.

To lead the center column, to the surprise of many, Whip placed a couple who had been the butt of numerous jokes when they had joined the caravan months earlier. Nat Drummond, in his mid-forties, was short, slender, and balding, a quiet man who minded his own business and rarely raised his voice. His wife, Grace, towered above him by a head, outweighed him by fifty pounds, and subjected him to a constant barrage of criticism, which he ignored. Others had learned—and perhaps Grace was discovering, too—that little Nat was a solid man, a valuable member of the expedition. He never became flustered and never lost his head in a crisis.

The position of the first wagon of the left column was awarded to Cathy van Ayl. Some thought she had been given the place because of Whip's personal interest in her, but they were mistaken. She, her late husband and her sister had been the first members of the wagon train, so she held the coveted post by right of seniority.

Three scouts fanned out ahead of the wagons. After today they would depart every morning after an early breakfast and not rejoin the group until evening. Later, when the company traveled further and further from civilization, they might absent themselves for two or three days at a time, reporting back only when necessary. All three were the best men available. In the center was Stalking Horse, who had left his Cherokee Village in Tennessee as a boy and had spent much of his life in the West—which he knew intimately—and who had no ties to any of the Indian nations of the Plains. On the left was Arnold Mell, tireless in spite of his age, as experienced as Stalking Horse at smelling danger and reading signs that indicated bands of hostile Indians or other dangers.

On the right was a hunter whom Whip had known in the Rockies. Mack Dougall was almost fifty years old, stocky and with a potbelly. When he had joined the expedition at Independence, he had immediately made arrangements for Ted Woods to carry his supplies—which consisted mainly of two barrels of cheap whiskey. His thirst was insatiable, and his complaints about the aches in his bones were endless, but Whip knew from experience that Mack allowed nothing to interfere with his duty. When necessary, he could stay in the saddle day and night.

Danny was driving Tonie Mell's wagon. She had happily accepted when Whip promoted her to the post of chief monitor, and she and her assistants rode up and down the lines of wagons, making certain there were no breakdowns and that no animals became lame. If a serious emergency occurred, a halt would be called.

The buckskin-clad Tonie was introduced to one of her assistants, young Claiborne Woodling, at breakfast, and there was an immediate clash when he announced, "Taking orders from a woman will be something new for me. A man should be in charge of the monitors."

Tonie eyed him coldly. "I've been monitoring the line for months and I know what I'm doing. That's why Whip put me in charge. So you'll be working for me." Trying to be conciliatory, she added, "But I see no problems. The work is routine. As a matter of fact, sometimes it gets dull. You've got to resist the temptation to gallop as you go up and down the line."

"What's wrong with a gallop?"

"You tire your own horse unnecessarily," she replied, "and sometimes the workhorses and oxen get too excited. Just maintain a nice, steady pace and make sure you keep checking—wagon by wagon—as you ride. That's all there is to it."

Claiborne made no reply, but he had his own ideas.

When he felt like galloping, that was precisely what he intended to do.

Claiborne wasn't the only member of his family causing trouble. Eulalia was seething as she sat with her father on the board of their wagon.

"I just can't believe it," she said, shaking her head so her long black hair swayed. "That woman is impossible."

"What woman?" Major Woodling asked.

"That Van Ayl person. She actually had the nerve to ask me whether I wanted to join the dishwashing detail or the water-fetching group. When I told her that neither appealed to me, she said that was my choice. I refused, and she plain assigned me to washing dishes."

Her father sighed. "This is a new way of life for us, Eulalia. We've got to accept chores when they're given to us."

"Well, I went straight to Baron von Thalman during breakfast, and that's what he said to me, too. But I won't!"

"You will, Eulalia," the Major said firmly. "If we had any choice, we'd be back home, not riding in this convoy all the way across the continent. But we've got no alternative, so we have to accept their rules."

"I'll do it—for now," she replied grudgingly, "but I'll get even with that bossy Van Ayl woman. Just you wait and see."

A short distance from them, in the next line, Danny maneuvered the Mell team into place directly behind the special wagon. Waiting nervously for the march to begin, he hoped Hosea wouldn't get curious and peer out of the wagon. It would be all too easy for Whip and Baron von Thalman to send the escaped slave back across the river to Independence. And that would be the end of him. Many people there would be happy to pocket the reward given for any slave returned to his master.

At last all of the wagons reached their assigned places. The scouts had long since vanished, and Whip Holt took his place at the head of the column. "I reckon we'll be on our way," he said quietly to Tonie Mell. His horse started forward toward the northwest only a short distance from the banks of the Missouri.

Tonie, who had taken the center line for herself, started to ride toward the rear, giving the signal that the caravan was beginning to move. The moment was very special to her, but it was spoiled when she saw that Claiborne Woodling, on her right, was deliberately disobeying orders by galloping.

Soon the entire caravan was in motion. Between each wagon there was a comfortable gap so no one would breathe too much dust. The sun shone almost directly overhead in a hazy sky, and the gentle breeze from the west carried the faint but distinct scent of sweet prairie grass.

Now, after the long halt at Independence, the veterans in the caravan heard the familiar music made only by a wagon train. The newcomers, aware of it for the first time, soon would become accustomed to the harmonies. The hoofbeats of the horses set a steady, sharp rhythm on the hard ground, and the surprisingly softer, more delicate drumming of the hoofs of the oxen provided a counterpoint. The leather of harnesses creaked in time to the pounding, pulsing throb, and the squeaking wheels of the wagons provided the major theme. These pioneers to Oregon had no way of knowing that, until the coming of the railroads a half-century and more later, the music of their wagons and of all the wagons to come would echo and reecho across the continent.

The days of organizing, planning, and arranging were over. The long trek was under way.

III

By the third day of the journey into the wilderness, even the most inexperienced of the new arrivals had become accustomed to the routines. Each morning, the men of the fire-making detail were the first to arise, leaving their wagons as soon as the glow of the false dawn appeared in the sky. Since wood was scarce throughout many portions of the Great Plains, the men learned from Whip to make their fires of what were called "chips," dried buffalo dung, available in large quantities and sanitized by long exposure to the elements. A score of women volunteers led by Cathy van Ayl prepared breakfast each morning, and by dawn the entire company was assembled. All major chores, including the gathering of water and washing of dishes, were organized communally, but individual householders harnessed their own animals and moved into their assigned places in the three lines. The breakfast fires were extinguished, and the sun was rising by the time the caravan began to roll.

At midday the train always halted for an hour or more to rest the horses and oxen. This period was known as "nooning," and those who were hungry usually ate cold leftovers. Some people took naps, but the security-conscious Whip Holt assigned the men and older boys to sentry duty on a rotating schedule, and a watch was kept for bands of hostile Indians or stray, wild animals. Whip made it very plain that, in the event a buffalo herd was sighted, all male members of the company who could handle firearms should be summoned without delay.

The journey was rescued after the nooning, and the company rode on until about four in the afternoon. Whip knew where to call a halt for the night, the scouts having told him in detail what lay ahead. The first task was that of forming the wagons in a protective circle. The oxen and horses were set free inside the circle, to safely graze. Meanwhile water was carried from the Missouri, the older boys gathered buffalo chips and firewood when it was available, and the women went to work to prepare supper, the main meal of the day.

While the women cooked, foraging parties went out into the prairies to search for game. Deer were plentiful, as were rabbits, and there were wild geese and ducks to be found in ponds partially concealed by tall grass. Few fish were found in the Missouri River, but the smaller streams that fed into it were filled with them. The company tried to be self-sufficient. The provisions carried by every family were to be kept for emergency use only.

It was during this pre-supper time that Dr. Martin treated those who needed it; fortunately, most of the ailments were minor. On days when Ernie von Thalman didn't go hunting, he listened to complaints and tried to settle quarrels and disputes.

Supper was the highlight of the day. Newcomers tended to go off by themselves, but they swiftly learned that everyone mixed freely during the social hour. Many lasting friendships were formed. People who had been total strangers planned to become neighbors when they reached the Oregon country.

The scouts ordinarily arrived before the meal was served, and reported in detail to Whip concerning what lay ahead. It was during this hour, too, that the wagon-master's other lieutenants reported to him.

Tonie Mell waited for several days before going to Whip, but on the fourth night of the journey, she announced bluntly, "I may need a new monitor in place of Claiborne Woodling."

Whip pulled a blade of grass out of the ground, then nibbled on the white portion at the base. "What's wrong with him?"

"He'd be fine if he did what he's told. But he wears out his horse galloping up and down the line all day, and he's so busy showing off to the women that he doesn't really check to make sure there are no problems with any of the wagons."

Whip nodded, rose, and sauntered off toward the Woodling wagon, where Claiborne was chatting with his father and sister.

The wagonmaster stopped and beckoned to Claiborne. "You're a good rider," he said when the young man joined him.

Claiborne grinned, pleased that he was winning recognition.

"Your trouble," Whip continued, "is that you don't follow orders."

The younger man's smile faded. "I don't like working for women."

"That's what I figured. But nobody in this company is more competent than Tonie, and nobody has contributed more to our safety. You can go back to helping your father drive his wagon, and I'll find another monitor."

"Hold on." Claiborne enjoyed his assignment because he felt it set him apart from the other settlers. "It isn't fair to—"

"I'll give you one more chance," Whip said, interrupting. "In this train, folks work together and do what they're told. If Tonie comes to me again, you're finished."

Just then, Cathy van Ayl, standing near the fire, banged a cooking spoon on the bottom of a frying pan, the signal that supper was ready.

Whip did not look at the young man again. He turned and went off to eat with his scouts. Their good news caused him to forget Claiborne. Arnold had bagged a buck on the way back to the campsite, and Mack Dougall had shot a doe in the same vicinity.

"There wasn't time to cook 'em tonight," Mack said, reeking of whiskey as usual, but sober. "But Nat Drummond says he'll butcher 'em before he turns in, so we'll have plenty o' venison for tomorrow's supper—well, not quite enough for this many folks."

Stalking Horse was annoyed because, unlike the other scouts, he had not found any deer. "Where you catch?" he demanded.

"About five miles up the Missouri and three miles to the west," Arnold said. "There's a salt lick hidden behind some high brush near a little stream that flows into the river."

Stalking Horse said nothing, but his eyes indicated he had no intention of being outdone by his older, white colleagues. As soon as the meal was over, he slid a pair of knives into his belt, picked up his bow and his quiver of arrows, then went to fetch his gelding, a farewell gift from Sam Brentwood.

He led his mount beyond the circle of wagons and was about to vault onto the horse's back when he sensed that someone else was near. He stared, then reached for one of his knives just as a wraith-like, curious figure emerged from the special wagon and came toward him.

The man was blacker than the night, as short as a child, and almost totally bald. Hosea halted, then raised a hand in the Ashanti greeting.

The gesture was remarkably similar to the Indian sign of peace, and Stalking Horse loosened his grip on the hilt of the knife. He had never seen this little man before, and it was odd that he should have come out of the special wagon. But the Cherokee, unlike his white friends, had a live-and-let-live philosophy, and he felt a twinge of sympathy for this strange creature who was clad only in a loincloth.

Stalking Horse raised his own hand in reply to Hosea's gesture, then leaped onto the back of his horse and started off toward the north, quickly increasing the gelding's pace to a canter.

Hosea ran beside him, moving effortlessly. The Cherokee was startled—he had never encountered a man

50

who could keep up with a cantering horse. But he admired the man's speed and stamina, so he allowed him to come along. Besides, he appeared harmless, carrying nothing other than a small container slung over one shoulder and some strange little objects tied to his middle.

Stalking Horse wondered how long the man could maintain the pace. Mile after mile the horse continued to canter, and mile after mile Hosea ran beside the horse, untiring, his breathing easy and unlabored, his gait steady.

Then, when they came to a place within a mile of the salt lick Arnold had described, Stalking Horse slowed to a halt, dismounted, and walked beside the horse. Hosea followed him. He must have overheard the conversation with Whip, Stalking Horse thought, and somehow figured out that he was going hunting.

They came to a small tree, and Stalking Horse tethered his gelding. Making no sound, he moved forward again. Hosea was equally silent.

The wind was blowing from the south into their faces, which was good since any deer in the vicinity of the lick wouldn't be able to get the scent of humans. The grass grew higher, and the pair snaked through it side by side, Stalking Horse telling himself that whoever this stranger might be, he was an accomplished hunter.

They circled the pond that Arnold had mentioned and saw the lick ahead. Peering through the thick grass, they saw a buck and a doe feeding.

Stalking Horse reached into his quiver and notched an arrow on his bowstring. As he did, his small companion removed one of the unusual objects hanging from his waist.

They struck simultaneously, Hosea hurling his miniature, weighted club at the same instant that Stalking Horse fired the arrow.

The Indian fully expected to kill his quarry and was in no way surprised when he put the arrow into the doe's heart. What amazed him was that the black man's club, aimed with unerring accuracy, had caught the buck on the head, and he toppled to the ground, too.

"Wait here," the impressed Stalking Horse commanded, then hurried off to fetch his horse.

Returning with the mount, he and Hosea loaded the deer onto the gelding's back. Because the horse was so weighted down, the walk back to the campsite took several hours.

Some members of the expedition had already retired, but the cooking fire was still burning. A number of people were sitting and standing around it, drinking coffee. Stalking Horse halted and removed the deer.

Hosea stopped outside the circle of the wagons.

"Use knife," Hosea said. "Need shirt and pants."

At last Stalking Horse understood. He handed him a knife, took his gelding and, entering the circle, immediately found Whip. He began to explain what had happened, deliberately speaking in his own language so that others wouldn't know what he was saying.

Whip immediately accompanied the Cherokee, who was still explaining when they approached the place where he had left Hosea. Working with great speed and dexterity, Hosea had already skinned the buck and was butchering the carcass. He looked up, the knife still in his hand, but he appeared resigned now to whatever fate might await him. He neither ran away nor tried to defend himself.

Whip had his hand on the butt of a pistol, but refrained from drawing it. "Who are you?"

The little man drew himself up proudly. "Hosea."

"Somebody had to hide you in the special wagon and bring you food. Who helped you?"

The black man hesitated, but knew that lies would only complicate his situation. "Boys."

"What boys?"

"Name of one Danny. Name of other Chet."

"Fetch them," Whip said, and Stalking Horse hurried back to the fire.

"Is it true," the wagonmaster demanded, his curiosity overcoming him, "that you actually killed that buck with one of those clubs?"

Hosea grinned and handed him one of the little clubs.

Whip held it in his hand, noted that it had a perfect

balance, and handed it back to him. At that moment Stalking Horse reappeared with the sheepish boys.

Danny was eager to explain before he received a tongue-lashing. "Hosea here is a wonderful fellow," he said. "He escaped from a plantation in Georgia and crossed the whole United States all the way to Independence without being caught."

"That's why we had to help him," Chet added. "Please, Whip, we don't care how you punish us, but don't send him back."

"Let him stay with us!" Danny begged.

Whip raised a hand for silence, then turned to the black man. "Anybody who can keep up with a cantering horse for miles and can kill a buck with a crazy weapon like this doesn't need to hide. Besides, all men have a right to be free." He grinned, then extended his hand. "Welcome to the wagon train."

Hosea shook his hand with great dignity.

The boys whooped with delight.

"Help him finish skinning and butchering these deer," Whip told them. "Hosea, tomorrow night you'll eat roast venison, and you'll eat with all the rest of us."

The little man bowed to express his appreciation, then suddenly waved the boys away from the deer. "No!" he told them. "Hosea take off skins. Best skinner in world. Then boys cut meat. Need skins for clothes."

Whip had skinned more wild animals than he could recall, and watching Hosea skin the doe, he had to concede that his boast was justified. He was remarkably nimble, his speed was dazzling, and at no time did he injure the skin. Had he chosen a career as a mountain man, he would have succeeded, and Whip could think of no higher praise.

"Sleep beside the fire, Hosea, until you can make yourself some buckskins. The nights are chilly." He turned and went back into the circle.

Stalking Horse continued to watch until Hosea was finished, and then, as the boys butchered the carcasses, Hosea allowed Stalking Horse to help prepare the skins. He and Hosea cut away the hair, scraped the insides clean of flesh, then rubbed the skins vigorously, using a mixture of salt, fat, and the brains of the deer, along with bunches of grass. It was late before they were done. Danny, returning after a final trip to the fire with the venison, which would be cooked lightly before being roasted the following night, brought word that Ernie von Thalman would allow the skins to be cured in the sunlight on the roof of his wagon. Finally, Hosea retired to the side of the fire.

In the morning, he created a sensation, and by the time the entire company assembled for breakfast, he was the center of attention. In spite of his scanty attire, he continued to conduct himself with grave dignity, bowing courteously to everyone who approached him and shaking hands with those who held out their hands to him. He answered all questions the members of the company asked, although some of his replies were vague.

Most of the travelers seemed to accept him, although some appeared uneasy when, in response to requests, he showed them his blowgun and miniature, weighted clubs. A few southern farmers and their families avoided him, but only the Woodlings were openly hostile. Eulalia solved the problem by pretending he didn't exist, but her father glared at the black man, and Claiborne went out of his way to be rude. "He should be sent back to Georgia in chains and whipped every day for a month," he announced to no one in particular.

Others more than compensated for this hostility, however. Ernie von Thalman and Dr. Martin offered him places in their wagons during the march, and Tonie said she would be pleased if he rode in her wagon with Danny. Cathy van Ayl and Cindy made certain he had enough food for breakfast.

Still courteous but offering no explanations, he refused all offers of places in various wagons. Then, when the workhorses and oxen were harnessed and the wagons broke up their night formation to start moving into line, he walked quietly to Whip, who was just mounting his stallion.

"Hosea go with chief," he announced.

Whip was puzzled. "That's fine with me, but I'm afraid I don't have a spare horse for you."

"No need horse. No want horse," Hosea replied. When the caravan began to move, he trotted amiably beside Whip's mount, never showing any sign of fatigue, never complaining.

During the next ten days, the weather gradually became cooler, and on two nights rain fell. On the second occasion, lightning filled the sky, thunder rumbled across the plains, and several wagon owners insisted that Hosea sleep under cover. He refused with the same gentle dignity he always displayed, but he did accept a blanket from Dr. Martin and consented to sleep under Ernie von Thalman's wagon.

Hosea was clever with his hands, but when the skins were finally cured, Cathy noticed that he appeared puzzled and sat for a long time after supper studying the shirts of several of the men. Realizing that he didn't know how to sew, she insisted on making his new wardrobe for him. She cut the skins for him, and for the next three days he drove her team while she sat on the board beside him and sewed his new shirt, pants, moccasins, and the short outer cloak he would wear when the weather turned still colder.

Her kindness won his loyalty. Thereafter, when she was preparing meals, he invariably appeared beside her and quietly performed tasks that required physical strength.

One evening, refusing food until Cathy was done with her work, Hosea finally accepted a dripping chunk of meat, which he placed on a slab of bread. The conversation near the fire was too noisy for him, so he retreated to the shadows near the special wagon. Sitting cross-legged on the ground, he began to eat. Suddenly he raised his head, listening intently.

Danny was coming toward him, but Hosea gestured for silence, then rose quietly and hurried to the far side of the fire, where he beckoned urgently to Stalking Horse, Arnold Mell, and Whip. They followed him without question.

Hosea halted near the spot where he had been eating his supper and stood still. Stalking Horse, too, heard the sound that had alarmed him. Then Whip and Arnold picked it up at the same instant and, exchanging glances, cocked their rifles. Although none of the others who were gathered around the campfire realized it, intruders had broken into the wagon directly behind the special wagon.

Whip took charge, indicating with gestures that he and Arnold would go into the open through the narrow space between the vehicles while Stalking Horse and Hosea crawled out under the special wagon.

Danny, curious and excited, wanted to accompany the men, but he was halted by a sharp, curt wave from Whip, who didn't want the burden of the boy's safety on his mind. Danny reluctantly stopped.

Rifles were less effective at short range than smaller firearms, so Whip and Arnold both carried their rifles in their left hands and drew pistols from their belts with their right.

As soon as they moved out into the open, they flattened themselves against the outside of the special wagon. They took in the situation at a glance. Six horses were tethered a short distance away, and a half-dozen Kansa warriors were systematically looting a settler's wagon.

The braves, their nationality identifiable by the bright red and deep purple stripes of paint on their cheeks and foreheads, had slashed the canvas at one side of the wagon. Making silent trips between the wagon and the spot where their horses were tethered, they were apparently stealing everything—sacks and barrels of emergency food supplies, bundles of clothing, and an old clock. They had piled more on the ground than they could comfortably carry, and were so intent on their thievery that they didn't realize they were being observed from the shadows a few yards away. Two of them, after jointly carrying a barrel of pickled beef, started back to the wagon.

Stalking Horse was the first to strike. Leaping to his feet and bounding forward, a knife held above his head, he gave his intended victim no opportunity to defend himself or even to shout a warning to his companions. Before the Kansa realized what was happening, the

56

Cherokee had slashed his throat, and he crumpled to the grass.

While Whip and Arnold watched, Hosea proceeded to dispose of the second Indian. Waiting only long enough to make certain that Stalking Horse was not in his line of fire, he sent a tiny dart from his blowgun at the warrior, who was reaching for the knife in his own belt. The needle-sharp point of the dart penetrated the Indian's face, and he grimaced, as though stung by a bee or wasp. He raised his free hand to his cheek to brush away the insect, but by that time the poison was taking effect. For a moment he stood erect, a bewildered expression on his face. Then the knife dropped from his nerveless fingers, and he collapsed in a heap, dying as he sprawled on the ground.

Whip and Arnold exchanged a quick glance. The same thought had occurred to both of them. The silent tactics instinctively employed by their companions were proving remarkably effective. The other Kansa who were rummaging inside the wagon didn't even know they were under attack. So Whip silently indicated to Stalking Horse and Hosea that they were to continue. Not only did Whip not want to warn the Indians, but he was afraid that any gunfire might attract members of the wagon train to the scene. The presence of hostile Indians could easily start a panic among the less experienced members of the wagon train, and it was possible that some of them might be injured.

Stalking Horse placed himself in the open space between the wagons, where it would be more difficult for him to be seen, and Hosea seemed to melt into the night as he dropped to one knee in the shadow of the special wagon. Soon two more of the Kansa emerged from the wagon, carrying a sack of grain. Stalking Horse literally flew as he hurtled toward the warrior closest to him and plunged his knife all the way to the hilt into the man's back. The brave had no chance to fight back, and, sprawling face forward onto the ground, he died without realizing what had happened to him.

Then there was a faint, popping sound as Hosea directed a strong puff of breath into the mouthpiece of his blowgun. The tiny dart was invisible as it flew toward its target. Again his aim was accurate—the dart penetrated the back of the other Kansa's neck.

He dropped the sack of grain, and began to reach up to swat what he thought was an insect. Then he staggered in a circle, agony reflected in his eyes. Dropping to his hands and knees, he crawled a few feet in the direction of the tethered horses and then silently collapsed.

Before Stalking Horse could remove his knife from the back of the warrior he had just killed, a fifth Kansa emerged from the wagon. The man carried a pile of clothes in his arms, but he immediately took in the situation. Quicker and more agile than his colleagues, he flung the stolen clothes aside, drew his own bone-handled knife, and leaped at Stalking Horse.

The Cherokee was still unarmed, and he rolled to one side to avert the full force of the impact, deflecting the Kansa's vicious attempt to knife him.

The Kansa landed on top of Stalking Horse. A deadly tug of war began for possession of the blade, with the Cherokee hanging on to his foe's wrist while the Kansa struggled ferociously to free himself. They rolled over and over in the grass, both men kicking, both hitting and punching with their free hands. Neither spoke, and only their deep grunts indicated the intensity of their combat.

Whip and Arnold were helpless. The two men writhing on the ground were twisting and turning so rapidly and convulsively that it was impossible to shoot at the Kansa without running the risk of killing Stalking Horse.

Hosea dropped his blowgun into its container and took one of his tiny clubs from the loop around his middle. Again and again he raised the club, but could not throw it for fear of striking his friend.

Whip had counted the intruders' horses and had realized that if each of them had ridden a separate animal and had brought no spare mounts, then one Kansa remained inside the wagon. So, even as he watched Stalking Horse, awaiting an opportunity to fire, he knew that at any second the last Kansa might appear and join in the fight.

Stalking Horse's opponent was taller and more power-ful than he was, so the Cherokee had to rely on cunning as well as strength. Still unable to gain possession of the knife that meant life or death, he relaxed his grip for an instant. Then, as the Kansa gathered himself for the final blow, Stalking Horse drove a knee into his groin. The other Indian gasped and involuntarily doubled over.

The opportunity was momentary, but Stalking Horse took full advantage of it and punched his opponent in the solar plexus. The blow was sharp and deft, and the Kansa gagged.

Now the Cherokee had gained the upper hand. He seized the knife the Kansa had dropped, then stabbed the man repeatedly. Spurred by the violent intensity of the fight, he struck again and again, thrusting and stab-bing, slashing and cutting in a frenzy until long after his foe was dead.

Arnold started forward, intending to stop him, but just then the last of the raiders emerged from the wagon.

Hosea immediately reached for his blowgun, and Arnold raised his pistol.

"No!" Whip ordered, his tone urgent.

Both stopped, without question.

The Kansa took in the scene of carnage, realized his companions were dead, and wanted only to save his own life. Dropping the hammer and saw he had been about to steal, he sprinted madly toward the little grove where the horses were tethered. Leaping onto the back of one of the mounts, he galloped off, not once looking back as he crouched low over his horse's neck.

Arnold knew why Whip had prevented the killing of the last Kansa, as did Stalking Horse. But Hosea was still confused. "Why Whip let Indian go?" he asked.

"Because I wanted him to go back to his own people and tell them what happened here. I want every warrior of the Kansa nation to know that any of them who try to steal from us will pay with his life."

Whip turned away, slipped through the opening be-tween the wagons and called to everyone to join him outside. By the time the settlers assembled, Stalking Horse had scalped all five of the dead Kansa. Trying to be generous, he offered three of the scalps to Hosea, but they had no value to the black man, so he refused them. Stalking Horse promptly hung all five from his belt.

Some of the women became sick, and a number of the children wept when they saw the grotesque corpses illuminated by torchlight. Many of the men didn't seem too happy, either, but an angry Whip insisted that everyone look at the bodies.

Standing between two of the warriors' bodies in the dark field, he spoke. "Folks," he said, "if it wasn't for our friend Hosea being alert, we might not have learned we were being robbed. Thanks to him and Stalking Horse, all but one of the thieves were killed. I'm hoping the Kansa will take heed and keep their distance from us from now on. I know you don't enjoy looking at dead, mutilated bodies, but I wanted all of you to look —and look hard—at these warriors. I hope that this will help you remember we're a long way from civilization, and we're going a heap further. Those of you who carry firearms, keep them with you at all times. Don't wander away from camp without permission, or you may end up looking like these dead Indians. Keep your eyes and ears wide open, and don't take chances."

Somberly the families filed back into the circle. There was little conversation. A number of volunteers remained behind, some of the men removing and burying the braves' bodies while others gathered the scattered property of the family whose wagon had been ransacked. Several of the women, directed by Grace Drummond, got out needles and heavy thread and began to repair the slash in the side of the canvas. The woman to whom the wagon belonged sobbed silently with relief. Her husband put his arm around her and thanked God that their small children had not been in the wagon at the time. He tried not to think what the savages would have done to two pretty blonde girls.

These tasks were soon finished, and as the campfire burned lower, the company retired. But the circle of wagons no longer seemed as secure and safe as it had been, and many of the travelers lay awake listening to the strange and no longer friendly sounds of the night. The plains, which had seemed so similar to the prairies of civilized, settled Illinois, were desolate and wild. The Indians in these parts weren't dependable friends like Stalking Horse; they were savage creatures eager to rob and murder those who trespassed on their territory.

Somewhere in the distance a wild animal, probably a coyote, howled dismally.

Many of the travelers—burrowing beneath their blankets because the winds blowing across the Plains felt increasingly colder—wished they had never come on this lonely journey.

Mack Dougall was filled with a sense of excitement when he returned to the campsite from his scouting duties one evening. He indicated he wanted a conference with the company's leaders. Whip, Arnold Mell, and Ernie von Thalman sat down with him in the Baron's comfortable wagon, but Mack wasn't yet ready to talk.

Removing a bottle of whiskey from his hip pocket, he pulled out the cork with his teeth, wiped off the mouth with a grimy hand, and took a long swallow. "My joints are achin' somethin' fierce," he said, "and this here is the only medicine there is that saves me from bein' a complete cripple." Looking as though he felt sorry for himself, he offered the bottle to the other men, but they all declined.

Mack belched, drew the back of his hand across his mouth, and settled back in the Baron's only padded chair. "About twenty miles from here," he said, "I seen the biggest herd of buffalo I ever set eyes on. There had to be a thousand of them."

Whip whistled under his breath.

Arnold explained for Ernie's benefit. "Most herds run to two or three hundred buffalo. A really big herd may number as many as five hundred. I've only seen that many once or twice."

"I don't believe I ever have," Whip added.

"The way I figure it," Mack said, "two or three herds got together because they liked the taste o' the grass. They was nibblin' and munchin' away like crazy."

Whip nodded.

"It seems to me," Mack said, "that if we send out a big enough huntin' party—and can get anywheres near the combined herd—we can have enough meat to see us into the cold weather and enough hides to make winter cloaks for as many as wants 'em."

Arnold nodded but said nothing, lost in thought. Whip was silent, too, thinking.

Ernie became impatient. "Why do we wait? With the extra horses we got from the Kansa raiders, we must have enough mounts for at least twenty men. We can take the twenty best riflemen and go with Mack at once to find the herd."

Whip shook his head. "You don't understand, Ernie," he said. "It isn't that simple."

"Buffalo," Arnold added, "are strange, skittish critters. They're bound to hear twenty horsemen coming toward them, and they'll get so jittery they'll take off. And once they start to move, there's no telling which direction they'll go."

The Baron frowned. "Suppose we make a circle around to their rear—a few of us, that is—and drive the herd toward our main body of hunters, who will be waiting for them."

The others laughed. "Before we reached Independence, Ernie, you saw one small herd of buffalo stampede, and even that was a scary sight."

"I shall never forget it," Ernie replied.

"Just thinkin' about a stampede of a thousand buffalo freezes my innards," Mack said, reaching into his hip pocket for his whiskey.

"Mack is right," Arnold said. "Not only is it impossible to point them in the direction we want them to go, but there's no way to control even fifty buffalo. A thousand of them could tear a forest apart or destroy a town."

"There's something else to be considered. We can't make a detour to their grazing grounds with the whole wagon train." Whip was emphatic. "We'd need at least two days to get there, and then we'd have to spend two more days hauling ourselves back to the right trail."

"Why would we have to do that?" Again Ernie was confused.

"Consider this," Whip told him. "Suppose we take twenty hunters and kill as many as seventy-five buffalo."

"A reasonable assumption. Perhaps we could bring down even more," the Baron said enthusiastically.

Whip's smile was wry. "A bull may weigh a ton or more. A cow runs at least a thousand pounds. After we butcher the carcasses, we'll have to smoke the meat, which means building some mighty extensive trenches and fires. But that's just the beginning. Unless the entire wagon train is nearby, how can we transport thousands and thousands of pounds of smoked meat to the wagons? We'd need at least fifteen freighters—which we don't have."

At last Ernie von Thalman grasped the enormity of the problem. In the long silence that followed, Mack Dougall took another swig from his bottle.

"I see no way to solve this," Whip said at last. "I'd love to bring down enough buffalo to feed us for many weeks. But I see no practical way of doing it."

"Neither do I," Arnold agreed. "What's more, even if we go after them, they may have disappeared by the time we reach the grazing grounds. The worst thing about buffalo, Ernie, is that they're completely unpredictable. Nobody knows what sparks a stampede. Oh, it can be something obvious, like a rifle shot, or it can be nothing at all that any human being can figure out."

Mack chuckled. "I've seen it many times. One second the damn buffalo are just standin' around like cattle, chewin' away on grass as peaceful as you please. But the very next second, for no rhyme or reason, they're high-tailin' across the plains as though Beelzebub himself is chasin' 'em."

"They do have a marvelous instinct for avoiding large objects," Whip said. "Even when they stampede, they'll never run down a horse and rider, for instance, or a wagon. But they get so crazed that they probably wouldn't even notice a man just standing in the prairie."

"I believe they'd trample him to death," Arnold said. "Me, I don't intend to try the experiment. But that's not the point. There doesn't seem to be a way we can handle this oversized herd."

"There isn't," Whip said regretfully. "None of us has ever faced a situation that's involved so many people. It's too big a headache for us."

The next morning, however, there was an unexpected development. The scouts were served their breakfast early, and Whip was eating with them, as was his custom. Suddenly, Stalking Horse dropped to his hands and knees, placing an ear close to the ground.

Whip immediately followed his example. After a moment or two, he heard a faint, rumbling noise. Shaking his head in astonishment, he scrambled to his feet. "Until now I never believed in miracles, but that herd of buffalo seems to be heading this way. There's no telling whether they'll veer off, but we want to be ready. Mack, get Ernie for me, quick. Arnold, start rounding up the best riflemen in the train."

The group worked with frantic speed to prepare for the possibility that the giant herd might come close to the campsite.

While Ernie von Thalman sifted through the many volunteer hunters, selecting only those whom he knew were marksmen, Whip issued succinct orders to the entire company. All workhorses and oxen were to be kept penned inside the circle of wagons. Even if they became nervous and tried to bolt, they were not to be allowed out into the open, where they might be trampled by the stampeding herd. No women or children were allowed to go outside the circle, and every mother was to be held accountable for the whereabouts of her own family.

Tonie Mell protested. "Whip," she said, "you know I'm a better shot than most of the men. Why can't I join the hunt?"

"Because you're needed right here," he told her. "You've had more experience than anyone else in controlling the animals. You'll know how to calm them if they get panicky."

The girl sighed, but knew he was too busy for an argument.

"If I needed your rifle," Whip assured her, "I'd call on you, believe me."

Claiborne Woodling started to make a scene when he wasn't included in Ernie's band. "None of you has ever seen me shoot, so you don't know whether I'm good or bad. I have my own horse, and I demand—"

"All right," Whip told him, interrupting curtly. "Join us, then, provided you do what you're told—without argument."

Every few minutes Stalking Horse placed his ear to the ground and reported on the location of the herd. "Still coming this way," he said repeatedly. "Coming fast!"

Twenty-two horsemen followed Ernie into the open beyond the circle of wagons. Breakfast was forgotten by all but a few inside the compound.

Whip remained behind for the moment, giving final instructions. Realizing that Tonie couldn't handle such a large number of horses and oxen alone, he appointed Nat Drummond to help her. "Call on as many men as you need to keep the animals quiet," he said. "Panic is contagious, and we don't want them smashing into wagons and hurting people by trying to break loose."

Hosea was loitering nearby, looking anxious. Whip could read his mind. "You want to join us out yonder, I know, but you don't have a horse."

"Never need horse," Hosea replied.

"This is one time you'd need one." Whip was firm. "Stay here, and if any of our animals get too upset, put them to sleep for a while with those little clubs of yours. Gently."

Pleased because he had been given a major responsibility, Hosea bowed, then glided away.

As Whip headed toward his stallion, he found his path blocked by Danny, who held a gelding's rein in one hand and Tonie's rifle in the other. "Please, Whip," he said. "Let me join the fun."

Not only could Whip remember how he himself had felt when he had been in his teens, but he knew Danny deserved a reward. Hard-working and eager to help everyone, the boy with no family of his own had a harder lot than most. And Whip knew that a boy could grow to manhood only when he was given a man's duties to perform. "Come along," he said.

An ecstatic Danny followed him through the opening between two wagons into the high grass.

Ernie had arranged the riders in a single line, as though they were cavalrymen ready to charge an enemy. Whip held back the laughter that rose within him, not wanting to hurt his friend's feelings. He would have to reorganize the column, but first he needed more information.

Stalking Horse had already anticipated Whip's desire and was squatting, his ear close to the ground. "Buffalo come very fast," he said. "This way." He pointed off to the left, then mounted his own horse and started in that direction. Willing to let him take the lead, Whip rode behind him, beckoning to the others to follow.

No one spoke as they made their way in single file across the prairie, halting after they had ridden about three-quarters of a mile. The rumble of the approaching buffalo could now be heard by everyone, and the roar was quickly growing louder and louder.

Whip lost no time reorganizing the party into two columns. They formed in a V, and he placed himself at the critical point in the center, facing the direction the buffalo would approach. The next most important places were those on the flanks, at the outermost open ends of the V. Because of their experience, as well as their marksmanship, Arnold Mell and Mack Dougall were given those positions.

In the distance they could see a cloud of dust that grew thicker and rose higher as it came closer. The thunder of four thousand hoofs was so loud that Whip had to shout to make himself heard. "Hold your fire until I shoot," he told the party, "and make certain you hold your horses steady. That's as important as anything else you'll do. A horse gets skittish when he sees an army of buffalo charging toward him. All right?"

Everyone seemed to understand.

"Most important of all, there will be one bull in the lead. Leave him be."

"What would happen if we shot the lead bull?" Claiborne Woodling interrupted.

Whip curbed his irritation. "None of us would live long enough to find out. If he is brought down, the whole herd will lose its sense of direction. They would panic, and roll over us like a tidal wave."

The roar was so loud now that conversation was no longer possible, but Whip made a final adjustment. Pantomiming what he wanted, he moved Danny directly behind him to the left. The boy, excited and pleased, grinned at him, then kept checking his borrowed rifle.

The buffalo loomed on the horizon. They ran shoulder to shoulder in a solid mass nearly half a mile wide. Whip was awed. Mack was right; never had he seen a herd that spread out so far.

Glancing back over first one shoulder then the other, he saw that the hunters were holding their positions. None were openly panicked, and what was more important, all of them were in control of their horses. Rifles had been checked, and the hunters were ready for action. Whip looked at Danny and winked at him.

It was possible now to make out individual animals. The buffalo's eyesight was less acute than his other senses, and the leader, attracted by the blurred mass of the hunting party, galloped toward the men, unaware of the danger. The ground trembling beneath his churning hoofs, he ran recklessly, his head lowered.

The waiting men could see the buffalo clearly. The leader was a massive, mature beast, shaggy and unkempt, who weighed at least a ton and a half. Whip couldn't help admiring him, secretly glad that such a magnificent beast would be spared.

The organization of the herd was remarkable. Behind the lead bull were scores of other adult males, all of them in the prime of life, their horns fully grown. Others were stretched out on both flanks in single files, to keep strays in line. In the center, pounding forward, came the younger bulls, adolescents who had not yet reached maturity but had great strength and stamina. Behind them came the old bulls, whom seasoned hunters preferred to ignore because their meat was so tough. Their horns were gnarled, their fur was matted, and many of them found it difficult to maintain the pace. But still they ran, for their lives depended on their ability to keep up. Frequently an old bull's strength finally drained away, and he crumpled to the ground. The others then ran around him, never trampling him, and it was not uncommon to find the rotting carcasses of old bulls on the plains.

Next, although invisible in the surging mass of beasts, came the cows and their calves, the mothers nudging their young and driving close on their heels to force them to keep running. And at the very end of the formation were several more rows of strong, mature bulls who would not permit stragglers to drop out.

At the moment there was no way of determining the depth of the charging, seething mass of animal flesh. The herd charging toward the men reminded Whip of towering waves he had seen rolling toward the shore of the Pacific Coast wilderness.

Whip's stallion, ordinarily calm and responsive to his master, became skittish, pawing the ground and tossing his mane. His instincts urged him to throw his rider and flee, but Whip patted him, stroked him, and, hoping the animal could hear him above the roar, spoke to him soothingly. The stallion grew quiet.

The buffalo now stretched as far across the plains as the eye could see. Arnold and Mack, the only members of the party other than Whip who were experienced in dealing with buffalo, were even more awed by the size of the herd than the newcomers. The ground shook as though from an earthquake, and the thickening cloud of dust threatened to choke the riders and their horses.

But the hunters maintained their tight, V-shaped formation. The size of the group presented a large enough obstacle for the buffalo to notice it in the midst of their mindless charge, and so the men would be relatively safe—if the herd followed the usual patterns. But anyone who left the formation surely would be trampled.

The lead buffalo, in spite of his size, was remarkably swift and sure-footed. He actually seemed to pick up speed as he thundered across the prairie. The bulls in the rows directly behind him were being challenged and had to exert themselves to keep up the mad pace. As the females and older bulls tired and fell back, the size of the herd spread menacingly.

It seemed certain that the lead bull intended to smash through the barrier of men and horses. His momentum was so great that not even a hail of bullets would have prevented him from rocketing into the riders and their mounts. Whip's only protection was his knowledge of the buffalo's habits. If this leader and his followers were unpredictable, however, Whip would be the first to die, and it was doubtful if any of the others would be able to save themselves.

Whip could now see the red eyes of the lead buffalo. They were glazed, and there was no way of knowing what the maddened beast might do. He was almost close enough to touch when, suddenly, he veered to the right and swept past the point of the V-shaped formation.

The danger was far from over. Most of the bulls in the rows directly behind him followed his example, but others appeared leaderless; they could smash at any moment into the men and their mounts.

But the instinct for survival was as strong in the buffalo as it was in humans. A powerful, mature bull took it upon himself to become a sub-leader, and rather than crash through the barrier, he swerved to the left.

The hunters were like an immobile obstacle in a swift-flowing river, as the buffalo charged past them by the hundreds on both sides. Men and horses choked on the dust, their eyes stinging and watering: the stench of the herd was so unbearable that many of the new hunters retched.

Whip had won his gamble. He raised his rifle. It would have been difficult to avoid hitting a buffalo in that roaring, thundering mass, but he chose his target with care. He squeezed the trigger, and a bull in the prime of life staggered, lost momentum, and pitched forward onto the ground. Others in the herd instantly made detours around his body without slackening their pace.

The men had been waiting for Whip's signal. Arnold and Mack immediately opened fire, too. Stalking Horse let fly with an arrow, and Claiborne Woodling demonstrated that he was as good a marksman as he claimed, bringing down another bull with a single shot.

Rarely had hunters enjoyed such an opportunity, but suddenly a new crisis developed. Danny's gelding, already unnerved by the charging herd, was further upset by the sound of rifle fire. The boy could no longer handle him, and the horse reared, then plunged forward, throwing Danny to the ground.

Whip was powerless to save the horse. The frightened animal moved into the path of the onrushing buffalo, who knew only that he was not one of their number. The gelding was knocked off balance by the bulls and then disappeared from sight as he was trampled by the buffalo. For a moment or two, the horse's screams rose above the thunder, then faded away as he died.

Whip's only concern was Danny. The boy was dazed and stood indecisively, wavering on his feet. If he lost consciousness, he would fall directly into the path of the buffalo.

Whip quickly freed the rawhide lash from around his middle and took aim. The whip coiled around the boy's body. Meanwhile buffalo were charging so close to him that they missed him by inches. Little by little, Whip hauled him closer, finally bringing him to relative safety behind his own stallion.

Stalking Horse, who was next in line on that side, needed no instructions to close the gap; he moved his horse closer to Whip, and the two horses provided a wall for the boy, who now stood safely inside the point of the V.

The rawhide whip fell away, and Danny recovered his equilibrium. Gradually, as his fear and confusion subsided, he was filled with a sense of shame. He felt responsible for losing a horse, and he was afraid the men would regard him as a child who was unfit to become a member of their company.

He felt the urgent desire to redeem himself, and there

was only one way. Shielded by Whip and Stalking Horse, he could prove he was a man by bringing down buffalo, and that knowledge made him calmer. When he had been thrown, he had retained enough presence of mind to hold on to the borrowed rifle, and he still held it in his hands. He raised it and fired, and was pleased when a young bull stumbled and dropped.

Seeing this, Whip was relieved. He knew that Danny would do nothing foolish now.

As the cows and their calves were running past the V-shaped formation, Whip saw a young calf that was pure white. He was stunned—a white calf was very rare and extremely valuable.

Stalking Horse saw the calf, too, and caught his breath. Less superstitious than the Indians of the Plains nations after having spent long periods with civilized men, he nevertheless shared the deeply ingrained belief of the plains tribes that the rare white calf was a reincarnation of the moon god. The skin of such a calf brought its owner great good fortune and could not be sold or bartered. When presented by its owner as a gift, however, the fortunate recipient then became blessed by good health and prosperity.

Whip, knowing the value of the white calf, didn't want to mar the hide. Steadying himself, he took particularly careful aim and put a bullet between the eyes of the young buffalo.

Soon the bulls at the rear of the herd appeared. The hunters continued to shoot, firing and reloading as rapidly as they could, until the last of the column roared off across the prairie. Ernie took out his pocket watch and announced that almost forty minutes had passed since the buffalo had first started to move past the formation.

The ground was littered with the carcasses of bulls, cows, and calves, and Whip immediately sent a rider to fetch the wagon train. The detour would take the caravan out of its way, but that couldn't be helped. The entire company had to be put to work.

Whip himself first skinned the precious white calf, taking great care not to inflict any unnecessary cuts on

71

the hide. That one skin could mean as much to the members of the caravan as the entire supply of carcasses.

As soon as he was done, he went to Danny and clapped the boy on the shoulder. "I'm proud of you," he said.

Danny looked up from the young bull he was skinning and flushed. "I feel terrible, Whip. I let everybody down."

"What happened to you could have happened to anybody. What I liked was the way you got hold of yourself and started shooting. You're doing fine."

Danny grinned, his self-confidence restored.

Without delay, the hunters went to work skinning the carcasses of the buffalo they had killed. Only Claiborne Woodling balked. "I'm a hunter, not a butcher," he declared.

Whip had no patience with him. "Winter is coming," he said, "so we'll need meat and hides. Anybody who won't work for the good of all can get out—and try surviving by himself."

A sullen Claiborne picked up his knife.

The caravan caught up with the hunters early in the afternoon, and everyone in the company was given a specific assignment. Mounted groups using wagons for hauling went off to the nearest woods and returned with piles of dead brush and logs. After the buffalo were skinned, some of the women began the tedious process of curing the hides. Meanwhile, the carcasses were butchered, long trenches were dug, and fires were lighted in them. The meat had to be smoked for seventy-two hours, and in all the journey was delayed by a week.

But no one minded. There were few who actually enjoyed the taste of smoked buffalo meat, but at least the travelers knew they wouldn't starve. And the cured hides would be used for coats, cloaks, and blankets.

Whip allowed no one to touch the skin of the white calf. After preparing it himself, he stretched it on the roof of Ernie von Thalman's wagon to dry.

At last the task of preserving the meat was done, and every family was given an appropriate share. Skins were spread on the canvas roofs of wagons by day, then removed at night when the air was damp. Cathy van

Ayl, who had already made herself a doeskin shirt and skirt, as well as Hosea's clothes, was besieged with requests for advice on the making of leather garments.

The younger children had a new game, buffalo hunt, and every evening they raced up and down inside the circle of wagons, screaming and shouting as they alternated playing the roles of hunter and buffalo.

The hunters in the company remained active, bringing venison and small game to the campsite at night. The smoked buffalo meat was intended strictly for winter use, when other meat would be unavailable.

Whip Holt breathed more easily after the encounter with the giant herd. He knew there were many dangers threatening the future of the wagon train, but the possibility that people would starve before spring was now remote.

IV

Hosea acquired the skin of a large bull buffalo, and after the westward journey was resumed, he spent most of his time in the evenings working on a special project of his own.

Danny and Chet, still fascinated by him, noted that one night he had cut several boughs of strong oak. Working with meticulous precision, he fashioned the wood into a double, diamond-shaped frame, binding the sections together with lengths of rawhide. Over the frame he stretched buffalo hide until it was taut. When he was satisfied that it was snug, he added a second layer of rawhide.

Not until Hosea placed a crossbar over the middle of his contraption, on the inner side, did the boys realize he had made a shield.

"Like Ashanti make in jungle," he said proudly.

Danny examined it and was dubious. "If anybody shoots at you with a rifle, Hosea, it won't stop bullets. It isn't that strong."

"No good for guns," the black man agreed. "But stop arrows, stop tomahawks, stop knives."

Two days later Hosea and Stalking Horse set off hunting. The Indian was mounted, as always, and carried his bow, arrows, and a spear. Hosea, trotting beside him, carried no weapons other than his clubs and deadly blowgun. There were those who claimed he was inadequately armed, but Whip did not agree.

"Hosea," he said, "will do as well as somebody carrying a whole arsenal."

There were many prairie dogs in the high grass of the plains—animals resembling woodchucks but smaller. Prairie chicken were everywhere, too. These were a variety of plump grouse that mountain men and others who traveled through the plains regarded as delicacies. The animals and birds were very shy, sensitive to the approach of humans, so they were difficult to catch.

The pair, far more silent than most white hunters, soon devised a system of their own. Hosea moved ahead, planted the base of his shield in the ground, then crouched behind it. There he stayed, making no sound and no movement, while Stalking Horse remained at a distance, ready to take part at an instant's notice.

Eventually a pack of prairie dogs or a flock of prairie chicken appeared, and curious about the immobile rawhide shield, they moved toward it. Once they came within range, Hosea threw his little clubs, always striking at least one or two. The others fled, and Stalking Horse was able to kill some of those with his arrows.

Hosea was a perfectionist, so he devised something new that aided him and his partner. Picking tufts of the long grass, he arranged them in his shirt and hair, making himself virtually invisible as he concealed himself behind his strange shield.

At noon the pair paused beside a small brook to drink, water Stalking Horse's mount, and eat some smoked buffalo meat. Hosea left his shield a short distance away in a field of tall grass.

Stalking Horse had begun to teach the escaped slave the language of the Kiowa nation, which virtually all the tribes of the plains used, and as the two men sat near the brook, relaxing, Stalking Horse took the opportunity to teach Hosea a few new words. But even when they were relaxing, the two men did not forget they were in the wilderness, and they remained alert.

At the same moment, both heard a faint but alien sound. Stalking Horse leaped to his feet, instinctively reaching for his bow and an arrow from his quiver.

Hosea dropped to his hands and knees and, virtually invisible thanks to his camouflage, snaked through the high grass until he reached his shield. Leaving it standing in the ground like a miniature fortress, he crouched behind it and peered out cautiously.

Five Indians, who had been hiding in the grass, approached on the far side of the brook. They were armed with bows and arrows, spears, and knives. Their scalp locks were stiffened with heavy grease, and their faces and torsos were smeared with streaks of white and yellow paint, identifying them as warriors of the small but warlike Topeka tribe. Silently one of them hurled a spear at Stalking Horse.

They had seen Hosea, too, although they didn't know what had become of him, but they weren't concerned with him, at least for the moment. They were concentrating on Stalking Horse.

The Indians moved closer. Perhaps they could capture their victim alive and take him back to their village as a slave.

But they had not reckoned on Hosea. While Stalking Horse held the Topeka at bay momentarily with his bow and arrow, Hosea fitted a dart into his blowgun. There was a scarcely audible popping sound, and one of the braves clapped a hand to his cheek. The man's scream of agony broke the silence, and he collapsed.

One of his companions threw a stone-tipped spear with all his might at Hosea, but it struck the rawhide shield, bounced off it, and fell harmlessly to the ground.

The Topeka were astonished, and a hail of arrows followed the spear. All but one fell into the grass after striking the shield, while one became embedded in the rawhide and remained there.

Hosea blew another dart from his blowgun. Again he found his target, the dart cutting into the lower lip of a warrior who stood for a moment, stunned, before he, too, dropped to the ground as the poison took effect.

Stalking Horse fired an arrow at the foe, but he was

77

too angry to concentrate, and for the first time in years, he missed his target.

A third Topeka boldly approached the shield. Neither he nor the other survivors had actually seen the tiny darts that had felled two of their number, and he was determined to destroy this strange and lethal contraption.

Hosea removed one of the little clubs he carried around his middle and hurled it. It struck the warrior in the temple, and he fell unconscious.

Only two of the braves were still in the fight, and Hosea, still protected by his shield, coolly killed one with another dart from his blowgun. He could have dispatched the last one, too. But, himself a warrior, he was conscious of the pride that Stalking Horse took in his own prowess. So he left the last of the warriors for his companion to kill.

This time Stalking Horse did not miss. His aim was true, and his arrow penetrated the brave's chest.

As he fell backward onto the ground. the Topeka struggled briefly and tried in vain to remove the arrow.

Now only the warrior who had been knocked unconscious by the club was still alive, and again Hosea left the honors to his friend. Stalking Horse went over to the man, stared at him coldly for a moment, then drew his knife, and cut the man's throat.

Emerging from the safety of his little fort, Hosea began to collect his spent darts and club.

While he was retrieving his weapons, Stalking Horse scalped all five of the Topeka and collected their weapons. In an attempt to be fair, he offered them to his companion, who had played the larger role in their victory.

Hosea regarded the spears as cumbersome, heavy weapons, so he had no use for them. He had never tried a bow and arrow, so he had no need for these weapons, but he finally selected a bone-handled knife that had belonged to one of the Topeka and slid it into his belt. Spoils meant nothing to him. He also declined an offer of the Topekas' scalps—wanting only what he might find useful.

Leaving the bodies where they had fallen, the pair resumed hunting.

"Not much time left," Stalking Horse said as he shaded his eyes and looked up at the sun. "Maybe we catch more chicken." The battle having ended, he saw no need to dwell on the matter.

But Hosea had something on his mind more important than prairie chicken. "Need more poison for darts," he said.

Stalking Horse recognized the urgency of the request, so they forgot the grouse and prairie dogs and searched instead for large rocks, which they cautiously overturned. They found no snakes, however, and they were about to give up their quest when Hosea stopped and pointed. Directly ahead the prairie grass was much thinner, and the area, stretching out for a distance of about two hundred yards, was strewn with a jumble of rocks. With unspoken accord they divided the field, taking care to leave Stalking Horse's mount safely behind. They hunted silently, swiftly—two wilderness men who knew precisely what they wanted.

At last Hosea's patience was rewarded. As he pulled apart a nest of rocks, a rattlesnake more than four feet long slithered into the open. Hosea's quiet grunt of satisfaction told his companion that he had found what he had been seeking.

The snake halted, saw the man, and instantly coiled itself, head swaying and fangs showing. Hosea remained calm. He had dealt with many kinds of snakes in his native Africa and with copperheads in the United States. If rattlers were new to him, that fact was irrelevant. He knew what he needed to do, and although he entertained a healthy respect for his deadly enemy, he felt no fear. Grasping his shield in one hand and the knife he had just acquired in the other, he took two steps backward, then waited.

Stalking Horse wanted to put an arrow into the snake. But the confidence of the little black man was so obvious that he decided it was wiser not to interfere and to let him handle the delicate situation as he saw fit.

Hosea could see that the snake, angry that its rest had been disturbed, was positioning itself to strike. He tightened his grasp on the handle of his shield, balancing his weight on the balls of his feet. He was reminded of an old Ashanti saying, that a battle with a serpent was a dance in which the loser died and the victor was rewarded with life.

The reptile stopped swaying, and the rattle in its tail sounded a warning that it was about to strike. A split second before the snake's head shot forward, aiming at its enemy's calves, Hosea lowered his shield to the ground. The snake struck viciously, its fangs making two tiny holes in the rawhide cover.

At that same instant Hosea retaliated, his own timing perfect. Leaning around the edge of the shield, he brought the knife down hard in a swift, slashing movement. His aim was as accurate as the rattler's, and before the snake could recover sufficiently to strike again, Hosea had severed its head from its body.

The head dropped to the ground, and Hosea picked it up. Placing it on a flat rock, he cut it open, his hand as steady as a surgeon's. At the back he found what he was seeking—the snake's twin sacs of venom. Taking all his darts, he inserted their needle-sharp points into the sacs. Poison oozed out onto the flat stone, and he took care not to touch it. Slowly, cautiously, he removed the darts from the venom sacs one by one, holding them by the blunt end, and placed them on another rock to dry.

Stalking Horse had joined him and stood a short distance away, watching.

Next Hosea picked up the body of the rattlesnake and deftly skinned it. Leaving the body for ants to devour, he placed the skin in his rope belt.

"Make new belt," he said, breaking the silence. Then he picked up the darts and dropped them into the container hanging from his shoulder.

It was dusk when the pair reached the campsite, and they went straight to Whip. For Hosea's sake Stalking

Horse spoke in English as he emptied the saddlebag of grouse. "Hunting not too bad today," he said.

Whip took note of the five scalps, not yet dry, which were hanging from the Cherokee's belt and saw the rattlesnake skin, yet to be cured, which dangled from Hosea's waist. These two could take care of themselves anywhere, any time, but apparently they did not consider their day's exploits worthy of mention. So Whip felt compelled to treat the matter lightly, too. "It seems to me," he replied, his voice dry, "that this was a pretty fair day for hunting."

The wilderness of the plains seemed desolate, devoid of all human life, but it was an illusion. Every evening, when the scouts returned to the campsite, they reported to Whip that they had seen Indians, some riding their ponies in pairs, some traveling alone and, occasionally groups of them. Arnold saw Kansa, Mack was certain he had spotted several Wichita, and Stalking Horse twice made out Topeka warriors in the distance.

The warnings to members of the wagon train were repeated. Men who owned firearms were once more reminded to carry them at all times. And under no circumstances were any members of the company to leave the circle of wagons after dark.

Cindy, who was now working on the cooking detail with Cathy van Ayl, found that order irksome. One night, their work done and their own supper eaten, they retired to the back stoop of Cathy's wagon for a chat.

They were a pretty pair. Cindy had given up the heavy makeup she had once worn, and both of them had given up trying to avoid the sun and were attractively tan. They wore shirts and skirts of doeskin.

Cathy was feeling depressed and, for reasons she couldn't quite understand, wanted to enjoy a few confidences with a friend. As nearly as she could figure, it was the vast emptiness stretching out endlessly in every direction that gave her a feeling of being lost, rudderless.

Recently she had found herself thinking more and

more of her earlier life, and she was able to see where she had gone wrong. It had started in New Haven, after Mama had died and her older sister, Claudia, had moved into the old house with her first husband. Richard had been so unsure of himself, so insecure that he had turned to the bottle in a vain attempt to bolster himself, and his drinking had not only made Claudia miserable, it had influenced her little sister, too.

Only now was Cathy beginning to perceive that her contempt for weak men had come from that period of her childhood. Then, the very night she had attended her first grown-up party, wearing a lovely pink silk dress that she and Claudia had made together, she had met Otto van Ayl, Papa's friend and a man old enough to be her father, who had been visiting the family. Shortly after that, he had asked Papa for her hand.

How eager she had been! She had mistaken Otto's rigid ways, his autocratic manner, and his insistence that he was right in all things, for strength of character. How stupid she had been. An innocent sixteen-year-old, an adolescent who had nurtured romantic dreams, she had been unprepared for the realities of life and marriage.

No, it wasn't the mistake of marrying Otto that was bothering her. She had slept with him only on their wedding night, and after that disastrous experience, he had treated her like a daughter rather than a wife. For all practical purposes, although she could not admit it to anyone except Cindy, she was still almost a virgin, even though she had been married to Otto for six years.

And now, whatever her married life had been, she was alone, left to fend for herself on this journey across the trackless plains.

"You know, Cindy," she said, "I think it's the emptiness out here that bothers me. Life wasn't easy on our farm—on Long Island. But the scenery was so varied—something different no matter which way you looked. We had a little brook out in back of the house that flowed into the Atlantic. And sand dunes! Sometimes I'd climb to the top of a dune and sit for hours, just watching the waves rolling in."

Cindy nodded. "From the window in my room at the —" she paused, "—house I could see the Ohio River. And watching the river is what saved my sanity in Louisville more times than I can remember. It was so dependable."

"We're very much alike."

"There's one way we aren't," Cindy said. "Now don't be offended, Cathy, but you're much more of a romantic soul than I—especially about Oregon."

"I'm looking forward to settling in the Oregon country," Cathy replied, "but I don't expect it to be the land of milk and honey that some people on this wagon train are so certain it will be. No land could be that perfect. But there will be mountains and forests and the sea. At least I hope we'll settle somewhere near the ocean. What I miss most is the sight of waves. Even that won't be enough, though." She became pensive.

"It sounds like you want a man." Cindy smiled.

"Not that I necessarily *want* one. I—I just have the feeling that I *need* one."

"Sex is overrated. Believe me, I know what I'm talking about, honey."

Color rose in Cathy's face. "I wasn't even thinking about that part of it!" she exclaimed. "I've come to know myself better in the months since this train left our farm. And I've pretty much come to the conclusion that I'm the sort of woman who needs a man to lean on."

"Don't you believe it, not for a minute!" Cindy was emphatic. "You're pretty, and I—well, I've got an air that makes me attractive to men, even though I couldn't compete with you in looks. So neither of us will ever have a lack of suitors, I can promise you. But we certainly don't need any of them."

Cathy became uncertain. "After being around people all day, dealing with all those women when we're fixing meals, talking to a couple of dozen men every time we stop, I'll admit I need privacy—"

"Of course you do. That's why we eat so quickly and leave the fire. I'd give anything if I could just

83

wander out into the prairie by myself for an hour, but I know Ted Woods would follow me."

Cathy giggled. "He's terribly shy, but it's plain enough that he's sweet on you."

"I'm not ready for a romance with him—or with anybody else. I'm too busy getting men out of my system. The very idea of marrying anybody and settling down makes me a little bit ill."

"I can imagine how you feel," Cathy said, sobering, "but it isn't that way with me."

Cindy grinned at her. "From what you've told me about your life with Otto, you'll really be marrying for the first time when you do get married again."

"It scares me half to death, but it's what I want."

"Anybody special in mind?" Cindy raised an eyebrow.

Cathy shook her head. "Well, yes and no."

"You mean Whip, of course. Sometimes, when he looks at you, he just melts."

"And other times he doesn't seem to know I even exist. I tell myself it's because he has so many responsibilities for the whole train and has so much on his mind."

"You're the only one who can decide, but don't be in too big a rush."

"Oh, I won't."

Cindy's eyes became bright. "The way I look at it, a man is convenient to have around. On occasion. He can do all kinds of physical work that a woman doesn't have the strength to do. But I'll never let any man become my lord and master."

"I wouldn't want that, either."

"In the marriage service," Cindy said, "you're obliged to promise you'll obey your husband. That's not for me. There isn't a man in this world I could ever respect so much that I'd agree to take second place to him for the rest of my days."

"When you put it that way," Cathy said, sighing, "I can't possibly argue with you. It's just that I feel helpless when I don't have a man of my own to look after me and protect me."

"It strikes me you're taking care of yourself these days without a man."

Cathy paused, then laughed. "Why, so I am," she said. "I never thought of it that way."

"You see? You can do whatever you please, and you're not accountable to anyone but yourself."

"That's fine for now," Cathy said. "But I don't really think I'd like it this way forever."

Cindy sighed. Her friend's traditional background made it difficult for her to realize that marriage was not necessarily the right goal for every woman. Sometimes it was the beginning of a new way of life in which her freedom would be restricted. On the other hand, she wanted to be fair. "I'm not claiming that all marriages are bad. All I'm saying is that I don't know anybody I could love so much that I'd be willing to marry and make all the sacrifices and compromises that marriage demands from a woman."

"You'll agree, won't you, that frontier life isn't easy for either of us?"

"Easy?" Cindy looked out beyond the wagons at the endless prairie, as vast and uninhabited as the oceans that seemed to mean so much to her friend. "If I had known how hard it would be, I'm not sure I would have joined the train."

"A man," Cathy said, "could help make it more bearable. That's why I'd like a—well, a partnership."

Cindy's smile was cynical. "If there is such a thing as a partnership. Just remember this. A marriage to the wrong man is far worse than a marriage to no man!"

Suddenly Cathy sensed that they were not alone. She turned slightly, and a chill crept up her spine when she saw two tall, husky Indian warriors standing only a short distance from the opening between her wagon and the wagon behind it in the circle. They were so close they could almost reach out and touch her. Their scalp locks were greased stiff, and each sported a feather. They carried bows, with quivers of arrows slung over their shoulders, and the bone hilts of knives protruded above their belts.

They continued to stare, making no hostile moves, but Cathy found it difficult to catch her breath. Cindy was saying something she didn't hear, and Cathy managed to touch her on the arm and incline her head silently in the direction of the two braves.

Cindy saw their glittering eyes and the heavy streaks of dark brown and pale green paint on their faces. She screamed involuntarily at the top of her lungs.

In a moment Ted Woods appeared. Whip wasn't far behind him, and a score of others started toward the girls. The warriors held their ground, continuing to stare.

Immediately Whip took charge. "Folks," he called, "I'll handle this. Go back to the fire, drink your coffee, and tend to your own business." Reluctantly they obeyed.

Cathy noted, however, that Arnold Mell, Mack Dougall and Stalking Horse remained, and Ted Woods retreated only as far as the next wagon. Hosea came up beside him, a hand resting on one of his miniature clubs. Then Tonie Mell appeared, looking like a boy in her buckskin shirt and pants. She was also holding a rifle.

The support of so many armed friends was comforting, and Cathy felt somewhat relieved. But she was afraid a fight with the two Indians would erupt at any moment. Her experience with Indians was limited. She had no idea what the savages would do next.

Whip raised an arm, his hand held palm upward in a greeting that indicated friendship. The warriors returned the salute. Whip addressed them in Kiowan, his tone courteous, and they replied in the same tongue. Then they entered the circle, leading two Indian ponies.

As Whip conversed with the Indians, Cathy realized that social amenities were being observed. It bothered her, however, that the two braves continued to stare at her and at Cindy while they talked. She couldn't help fidgeting uncomfortably.

Then one of the warriors launched into a long, impassioned speech, occasionally flinging his arms wide. To Cathy's astonishment, Tonie Mell exploded in silent laughter. Afraid she would laugh aloud, which would have been discourteous, she hurried away and went back to the fire.

Arnold was grinning openly, as was Mack. But Stalking Horse remained wooden-faced, and Whip looked grave. After the warrior finished speaking, Whip replied at length. Ordinarily brusque in his speech, he now seemed to be indulging in flowery rhetoric. The two braves listened intently, but their eyes remained fixed on the two frightened girls huddling together on the stoop.

At last Whip offered a partial explanation in English. "Our visitors," he said, directing his gaze toward Cathy and Cindy, "are senior warriors of the mighty Omaha nation. They welcome us to the Great Plains and offer us peace. We haven't yet come to their land. They are on a scouting trip because their people are at war with the Kansa. They saw our fires, so they investigated, and they wish us no harm."

The two girls remained tense.

Whip sounded more casual. "Ted," he said to the blacksmith, "go to the special wagon. Bring me a little iron frying pan and a blanket. Don't appear to be in any hurry—I don't want our visitors to be alarmed."

Ted Woods was reluctant to leave while Cindy appeared to be in any danger, but he had received a direct order, and he obeyed it, sauntering off toward the special wagon. Again Whip and the two Omaha engaged in a spirited conversation.

Cathy became restless. "I'm cold," she said. "Let's go to the fire, Cindy."

Whip interrupted himself in the midst of a long statement to the Indians. "Stay right where you are," he said, his voice suddenly urgent. "Don't move!"

Cathy, who had started to rise, sank back onto the stoop and sighed. It was absurd that she and Cindy had to remain while Whip held his endless discussion with the Indians. She didn't want to argue in front of the others, however, so she obeyed his request, but she made her feelings clear by glaring at him.

After a short time, Ted returned with a small frying

pan and blanket. Whip took them from him and made another interminably long speech to the two warriors. At the end of his address, he handed the skillet to one and the blanket to the other.

The braves examined their gifts at length, then replied to Whip's address with even longer speeches. Then the warriors raised their arms in the peace gesture. Whip did the same, and the Omaha departed, leading their horses out of the circle.

Before they rode off, however, they turned for one long, final, lustful look at the two girls. Then they mounted their horses, and in the silence that followed, the retreating hoofbeats of their mounts sounded clearly.

Standing, Cathy asked with elaborate courtesy, "May we know what that was all about?"

The other men decided that discretion was advisable and retreated. Only Ted Woods remained.

Whip tried to keep a straight face. "The Omaha," he explained, "are one of the biggest and strongest of the Great Plains tribes, and these men were two of their senior warriors, which means they sit in the council of elders that decides questions of war and peace. The friendship of the Omaha will be very important to us when we move through their territory. They don't attack friends, so we'll be saved running battles and many casualties. That's why I treated the warriors so carefully and presented them with gifts."

Cathy nodded impatiently. "That's fair enough, I'm sure, but why did we have to stay?"

He hesitated for an instant, then said, "Because you two were the subject of our negotiations. They wanted to buy you and take you home to live with them as their squaws. In fact, their interest in you was so great they offered me their horses for you."

Cathy was outraged. "I don't take that as a compliment. You could have told them that in our world freeborn women aren't for sale!"

"But we're in their world now," Whip said quietly.

"All the same, you could have sent them on their way!" she retorted angrily.

"Not without offending them. I had to go through the

motions of considering their offer. I let them believe you were my squaws, and I finally told them I needed you more than I needed two new horses. But I gave them the gifts to show them I didn't resent their offer."

"*I* resent it very much," the furious Cathy said.

Cindy giggled. "No wonder Tonie was laughing so hard."

Cathy realized the situation had certain amusing aspects, but her sense of humor had deserted her. It didn't bother her that a barbaric Indian brave had wanted to trade her for a horse—the man simply didn't know any better. But it upset her that Whip had even pretended to negotiate, instead of putting the savage in his place. Suddenly, to her mortification, she burst into tears. Unable to stop crying, she raced into her wagon and pulled the flap down behind her.

Cindy could have explained her reaction to Whip, but she had no chance. Turning, he stalked off, angry that his efforts had not been appreciated.

Ted Woods vanished, as he always did when there was a chance to be alone with Cindy, so she walked back to her own wagon. She knew that Cathy would want to be alone.

Cindy envied Cathy who was a near virgin. She would marry again, be it to Whip or someone else. But no man, she thought, not even the lonely Ted Woods, would seek more than a temporary attachment to a woman who had been a whore. At moments such as this, Cindy wondered if she had been wise to stake her whole future on the Oregon-bound wagon train. Perhaps she should have saved more money, then gone to an Eastern city like New York or Philadelphia, where she could have kept her past secret.

As she drew near her own wagon, she saw a man standing in the shadows. Even before she could make out his face, she knew his identity by the cut of his expensive clothes and the sheen of his boots.

Claiborne Woodling came to her, smiling broadly. The expression in his eyes, which she had seen so often, told her what he wanted.

"I hear you had quite an experience tonight," he said. "Everybody is talking about it."

"Let them talk." Cindy tried to brush past him.

Claiborne grabbed her arm. "Don't be in such a hurry. I'm just trying to be friendly."

"Take your hands off me," Cindy told him, "and don't ever touch me again. I know your kind of friendship, and I want no part of it."

He tried to protest.

Suddenly she pulled out a knife, which she had bought in Independence, from the pocket of her dress. Ordinarily she would have tried to be civil to this arrogant young man. It didn't pay to make personal enemies on the long journey. But his appearance at that particular moment was unbearable, and her patience was exhausted.

"I'm not going to warn you again," Cindy said, brandishing the knife.

Claiborne was tempted to take the knife from her, but too many people were still awake, and he didn't want a scene. "You're a shrew," he told her in a low, menacing voice, "but one of these days I'm going to tame you." Then he turned and stalked off into the darkness.

Cold autumn rains fell steadily every day for a week, turning the vast prairie into a quagmire and forcing the wagon train to halt. Rivers overflowed, soaking the ground even more, and when the journey was resumed, it was difficult for Whip to pick a path wide and dry enough for the train to travel in three columns. The alternative was to place the wagons in single file, but he refused to consider the idea.

"If we move in one line," he told Von Thalman, "the train will stretch out for nearly three miles, and that's a risk we can't afford to take. We'd be too tempting a target for roving bands of Indians. Warriors could attack the rear of the train, kill the monitor, and those of us up front wouldn't even know what happened until hours later."

So the three-column formation was maintained, even though less ground was covered. The horses and oxen grew tired because the footing was uncertain, and several times a day the entire company had to halt because a wagon's wheels had become mired in deep mud. The train did well to cover eight miles in a single day.

By mid-November the sun rarely appeared, the sky overhead remained a dull, dark gray all day, and the winds that swept across the Great Plains grew steadily colder.

A number of people became ill, all suffering from sore throats, high fevers, and aches in their bodies that lasted for days. Dr. Martin made the rounds every morning, at the nooning hour, and again after the train halted each day. There was little he could do for his patients other than give them doses of an elixir of coal tar, along with oil of sassafras to rub on their chests. It was essential, he told them repeatedly, that they remain in bed. He would not allow anyone who was ill to drive a wagon, so the healthy pioneers from other wagons were pressed into service.

Available throughout the night to those who needed his services, Bob Martin refused to spare himself and began to look haggard. Tonie Mell worried that he would fall ill, insisted on helping him each day after she completed her own duties.

Then Mack Dougall became ill even though he tried to ward off the disease by fortifying himself with larger quantities of whiskey than usual. In spite of Mack's protests, Dr. Martin put him to bed in one of the wagons, thus leaving the wagon train with one scout less. No other member of the company was familiar with the Great Plains or the ways of the Indians. Tonie volunteered, but Whip rejected her offer.

"That would be tempting Providence," he told her. "If a band of warriors discovered that one of our scouts, operating alone, was a woman, they would haul you off to one of their villages and keep you there as a slave for the rest of your days."

"You forget that I'm a first-rate shot," she said.

"I'm well aware of it," he replied, "but don't you forget that you're a woman."

It was necessary to appoint a scout to act in Mack's place, and with great misgivings, Whip gave the position to the only other volunteer, Hosea, who refused the offer of a horse. Early each morning he went off at a run, carrying his rawhide shield, and every night he returned, still energetic. He learned his duties quickly and, somewhat to Whip's surprise, soon became expert in the difficult art of spotting the presence of Indians. Stalking Horse patiently coached him until he could easily distinguish one tribe from another. In an area where different tribes held different attitudes about white men, this identification was crucial.

One afternoon in late November, there were snow flurries in the air. That night Whip held a private conference with Ernie von Thalman.

"Once the snow really starts to fall, we'll have to call a halt," he said. "So from now on, we've got to search for a likely place to make a winter camp, and that won't be easy."

Ernie was well aware of the problems. "We'll need wood to build cabins because people can't spend the winter in their wagons. Buffalo chips are all right for cooking, but they don't give off much warmth, so we'll need wood for fires. And we've got to have shelter for the horses and oxen, too. Where can we find all that wood in a country where there's little but grass?"

"If many more people get sick, we'll have to stop out here in the middle of nowhere," Whip said, "and that means trouble. We're coming into the Nebraska country now, so we have two choices. There's a fine forest just south of the junction of the Platte and Missouri rivers, but I don't like it much."

"Why not?"

"Just a little ways to the north, on the Missouri, is one of the biggest towns of the Omaha, almost directly across the river from a trading post in the Iowa territory called Council Bluffs. By and large, the Omaha are a peaceful tribe, but they're strong, and there's no telling what they might do if a wagon train filled with horses and oxen, blankets and kettles and guns—not to mention good-looking womenfolk—made winter camp less than a day's ride away."

"I don't believe in putting my head into a noose and

handing someone the other end of the rope," Ernie said, frowning.

"Our alternative," Whip told him, "is to head west as well as north. About forty or fifty miles west of the Omaha town, right on the Platte River, there's another, even bigger forest. There's everything there—oak, maple, elm, pine, hickory, and juniper. It's a huge forest that spreads northward for many, many miles, so you can bet that plenty of deer and other game will be foraging there throughout the winter."

"That sounds better to me."

"I agree," Whip said, "although there's a possible problem. I'm told the U.S. Army has built an outpost at the edge of the forest, right on the river, called Fort Madison. The soldiers might not want us as near neighbors for the winter."

"But the government is sponsoring this expedition, and we have the personal approval of President Van Buren," Ernie said. "I don't see how the army could object to our making winter camp nearby."

"Not officially." Whip's smile was wry. "But, hellfire and damnation, Ernie, you were a colonel in the Imperial Austrian Army. Put yourself in the place of the commander of Fort Madison, which was just built and was put into operation only this spring. He's a king in his own realm, and he leads a pleasant life except when the Indians kick up a ruckus. All of a sudden he has to share his forest with a company of almost five hundred civilians. People will die; civilians will need help and protection; and his soldiers will start messing around with our young women. Van Buren or no Van Buren, he may tell us to take ourselves to the far end of the forest and not bother him."

"It's possible," Ernie said, "but there's only one way to find out."

Whip grinned broadly. "Ah, that's what I wanted to hear. As long as I have your support, we'll do it. And if the garrison commander doesn't like us, that's just too bad. He doesn't own either the forest or the Platte River."

The next morning Whip spoke briefly to the scouts, and that day the wagon train changed direction, moving more toward the west than the north.

Progress was still painfully slow. The caravan could travel no more than eight miles each day. The weather continued to grow colder, and frost killed much of the prairie grass. Mack Dougall, who had recovered and had resumed his scouting duties, was heard to remark that he couldn't remember a year when winter had threatened to come to the Great Plains this early. His dire comment spread through the camp, and some of the newcomers panicked.

But the veterans reassured them. "Trust Whip Holt," they said. "He knows what he's doing."

A week after changing direction, the wagon train approached the Platte River, one of the principal tributaries of the Missouri. The scouts returned during the nooning hour to report the news. In mid-afternoon the caravan came within sight of the river, which was swift flowing and more than a half-mile wide. On the far bank stood a large, solidly constructed log fort, with the flag of the United States flying from its highest ramparts, and behind the fort stretched what appeared to be an endless forest.

Many of the Oregon-bound settlers cheered when they saw the flag. However, there was one member of the company who was thinking seriously of returning to civilization. Arthur Elwood, who was approaching forty, had joined the expedition in the hope that he could buy some of the colonists' land-grant claims of six hundred acres per householder, and resell them, at a profit, to land speculators. He had offered cash for such tracts. But so far no one had responded to his offer, and he was tired of the inconveniences of wagon train living.

The wagons were moved into their customary circle for the night. Even before the task was completed, two officers in blue army uniforms trimmed in gold started across the river. To the surprise of many in the caravan, they rode rapidly across the Platte, which appeared to be very shallow.

94

Whip and Ernie walked to the river bank to meet them.

"Captain Haskell and Lieutenant Thompson," the senior officer said after they dismounted.

Whip introduced himself and the Baron.

"So you're Holt," the Captain said, smiling broadly. "The Colonel has been wondering whether we'd be seeing you."

"Then you've heard of our expedition." Whip said.

Both officers laughed heartily, and the Captain said, "We've heard of little else in the past two months. Two entire battalions of our regiment haven't shown up here yet, and it doesn't look as though we'll see them before spring. But the War Department has sent Colonel Jonathan at least three letters of inquiry about your wagon train, and even President Van Buren has written to him. The Colonel has been so nervous he's been on the verge of sending out patrols to search for you."

Whip and Ernie smiled at each other. The company would be welcomed at Fort Madison.

"We're relieved you decided not to make a crossing today, Mr. Holt," Lieutenant Thompson said. "There are only a couple of hours of daylight left, and you're going to need a full day for your crossing."

Ernie von Thalman was surprised. The water appeared shallow.

"The problem," Whip said succinctly, "is quicksand."

The two officers nodded.

Ernie was dismayed. "Obviously we'll have to move either upstream or downstream to an area where there is no quicksand."

Captain Haskell shook his head. "I'm afraid that isn't feasible, Baron. In those places the river is much narrower, and the water is deep, with the current so swift that no wagon could make the crossing."

"If the bed of the river here is similar to what I've seen elsewhere on the Platte," Whip said, "the quicksand acts fairly slowly. I watched you as you came across, and I saw you didn't give your horses much chance to tarry, so I figured there was quicksand here."

Whip turned to the Baron. "Ernie, we'll have no

trouble as long as each wagon stays in motion. The minute a team of horses or oxen stop, though, they'll be mired, and the only way to save them will be to cut them loose, drag them ashore on the far bank, and sacrifice the wagon—and its contents."

"A fair analysis, Mr. Holt," Captain Haskell said. "This Platte River quicksand is like glue. It may be slow acting, but once it catches hold, it sucks up anything and everything that gets stuck in it. Any team that tries to haul a trapped wagon will be mired, too, and the only thing left to do is shoot the poor beasts before they get sucked under."

"Our people," Whip said, "have been driving their wagons day after day for a long time. Those who came from the Eastern Seaboard have been traveling for more than a year. They're good at it. They know what they're doing, they don't get rattled, and they don't scare easy. I'm sure we'll make out just fine, provided we take a few precautions."

Ernie was dubious. "What sort of precautions?"

"Perhaps I can be of help to you, Mr. Holt," Captain Haskell said. "I have the honor of commanding what I believe to be the finest cavalry troop in the army— eighty men, all of them veterans. I suggest you send two wagons across at a time, about one hundred yards apart. I'll assign a full platoon to each passage, with Thompson here in command of one and my other lieutenants in charge of the second. I'll keep myself free to supervise the enterprise, and I'd be very pleased if you'd join me, Mr. Holt. Between us, I believe we can keep those wagons rolling."

They shook hands after agreeing to start early the next morning.

Whip and Ernie strolled together toward the wagon circle, where campfires had already been lighted. "As I see it," Whip said, "the problem is strictly one of confidence, especially for those who have to wait for hours on this side of the river for their turn to cross."

Ernie nodded thoughtfully. "I suggest that anybody who might get nervous be sent across fairly early. It won't bother the more experienced people to wait."

"Fair enough," Whip said, "and we'll start with women we know won't panic. Like Cathy van Ayl." Without realizing it, he was paying Cathy a compliment.

"I like that," Ernie said. "Any men who have doubts about their own abilities will feel much better after they've seen a couple of ladies negotiate the crossing. Do I gather you'll have no use for our own riders?"

"None," Whip replied flatly. "Our scouts do good work in their own operations, but they wouldn't know how to deal with quicksand, and neither would the monitors. Besides, young Woodling is so arrogant and unpleasant that somebody might get ornery just to spite him and stop dead in the middle of the river."

When they reached the fire, Whip summoned the entire company and told them in detail about the next day's operation. He didn't overemphasize the dangers of the quicksand, but at the same time he concealed nothing. "You'll have no trouble." he said, "as long as you keep moving. I've crossed the Platte dozens of times myself, and I know what I'm talking about."

The brief meeting came to an end, and Whip immediately sought out Cathy. "You'll go first in the column on the right," he told her, "so you'll have to be awake and ready extra early. You can turn over the cooking detail to somebody else for breakfast."

"Why me?" Cathy asked in surprise.

Why, he asked himself, did he always become tongue-tied in her presence? Unable to repeat what he had told Ernie, he replied curtly, "It makes sense, that's why." Then he walked away, leaving her staring angrily after him.

The fire-making detail started to work an hour before dawn the next morning, and Cathy organized the breakfast cooks before preparing for her departure. Whip joined her for a quick mug of coffee, but she was cool to him, and little conversation passed between them.

The stars vanished, and the sky was growing lighter as Whip rode his stallion into the chilly waters of the Platte, the scouts and male monitors strung out behind him, with each man carefully leaving a gap of about ten yards between him and the rider in front of him. Whip's stallion could feel the soft sand giving beneath his hoofs, and he responded instinctively. Lifting his legs high, almost as though he were prancing, he made the crossing without difficulty.

The others encountered no problems, either. But Claiborne Woodling, who brought up the rear, couldn't resist showing off. He walked his horse at a crawl most of the way across the Platte, then raced the final hundred feet, his horse splashing water madly.

The cavalry troop was already drawn up on the north bank, ready for action. Captain Haskell was standing near the water, holding the reins of his horse, and beside him was a handsome, white-haired officer with a small beard whose silver epaulets identified him as a full colonel.

"I'm Bert Jonathan," he said, extending his hand as Whip dismounted. "Welcome to Fort Madison. You can't imagine how pleased I am to see you, Mr. Holt. Now, perhaps, Washington City will stop pestering me."

"My people and I are grateful to you, Colonel," Whip replied. "We haven't enjoyed many luxuries on our trek."

Daylight had come, although the sky remained sullen and the river, ruffled by a cold, damp wind from the west, was leaden. Captain Haskell led his troop across the Platte, Whip riding with him at the head of the line, and the veterans proudly moved in formation.

Whip had decided that Tonie would lead the left-hand column, and the cavalrymen brightened when they saw her and Cathy van Ayl seated on the boards of the first wagons. Pretty girls were unknown at this remote wilderness outpost, and the men stared at them, grinned and saluted, then began to call greetings to them.

Whip felt an unexpected twinge of jealousy when he saw the attention Cathy was drawing. But there was no time now for personal reflection.

"Let's go!" Whip called sharply, and Cathy and Tonie drove their teams into the water, a soldier riding beside each wagon.

Whip and Haskell gave them a head start, then caught up with them, passed them, and led them to the far bank. The girls had become expert drivers. Their wagons moved at a slow but steady pace, and they came ashore safely.

The foot soldiers who would act as guides to the campsite were as delighted by the appearance of attractive young women as the cavalrymen had been, and even Colonel Jonathan and the three middle-aged officers who comprised his staff looked pleased. Again Whip felt a twinge of jealousy.

The second wagons in each column were arriving now, and the third wagons were beginning to cross. The operation was proceeding smoothly.

Extreme precautions were taken to get the special wagon with its irreplaceable supplies across. Twenty horsemen accompanied it, holding ropes that were tied to its wheels and axles. Trusting no one else to the delicate task, Whip drove.

The wagonmaster uncoiled his whip, and the twenty cavalrymen picked up their ropes. "All set, Mr. Holt?" Haskell called.

"Ready, Captain!"

The whip cracked over the heads of the eight oxen, who slowly moved into the chilly water. Two cavalrymen on each side accompanied them, and as the wagon inched forward, the other horsemen followed.

In spite of the cold, Whip discovered he was sweating. The regular driver who sat beside him shuddered slightly.

The oxen didn't like the feel of the soft sand under their small hoofs, and two of them hesitated. Before they could stop altogether, however, the wagonmaster's whip lightly touched one on the back, then the other. The blows were not hard enough to break the animals' skins, but stung them just enough to keep them in motion.

The cavalrymen strained at the ropes, forcing their mounts, unaccustomed to such degrading labor, to keep in motion. The wagon's progress was maddingly slow.

Having once established a rhythm for the oxen, Whip knew it had to be maintained. "Ee-yup-ho!" he shouted, standing on the platform so he could keep a sharp watch on the entire team. "Ee-yup-ho!"

The oxen responded to the cadenced call and continued to trudge forward through the chilly water, their pace unvarying.

Captain Haskell moved back and forth constantly behind the wagon, veering first to the left, then to the right. "Flint, hold your rope tighter!" he called. "Budman, don't slow your pace! Not too fast, Harrigan. Hold your place or you'll upset the balance."

"Ee-yup-ho!" The wagon had passed the center of the Platte and was crawling closer to the north bank, where soldiers and members of the train who had already made the crossing stood and watched anxiously.

The wind increased, and a wave struck one of the lead oxen, splashing the animal's face. Bewildered by the unexpected cold slap, the beast halted.

The whip sang out immediately, touching him lightly, then struck again with somewhat greater force. As everyone held their breaths, the animal began to move again, and the rhythm of the other oxen continued unbroken.

The special wagon inched nearer to the north shore. The worst was over now. If necessary, members of the cavalry troop waiting on the bank could ride into the water and assist their comrades with the ropes. But Whip kept up his cadenced call, and Captain Haskell called a steady stream of orders to his men.

At the bank, Arnold Mell plunged into the water, caught hold of the front end of the yoke, and guided the oxen ashore. The heavy wagon followed, its wheels cutting deep furrows in the bank, then rolling more smoothly on the hard ground.

Whip halted the team, turned the wagon over to the regular driver, and jumped to the ground.

Captain Haskell joined him, and they shook hands. "That was great!" the officer cried. "I owe you a drink!"

"I'll take it, tonight," Whip said, "when our day's work is done."

Meanwhile the crossings of the other wagons had been resumed, and in midstream Whip passed the wagon driven by Major Woodling, who was concentrating his full attention on his horses.

Eulalia, sitting on the boards beside him, looked as though she had just left her father's plantation for an afternoon's ride in the country. Her eyes were rimmed with kohl, her lips and cheeks were rouged, and she wore a fur-collared coat with a matching, frivolously feathered hat. Smiling broadly at Whip, she removed a hand from a fur muff to wave at him, and then, unable to resist the temptation, she smiled provocatively at Captain Haskell.

The officer made no comment, but Whip could see that the girl had sparked his interest, and Whip couldn't blame him. Eulalia might be somewhat irresponsible, but she was far friendlier than some members of the expedition —particularly Cathy van Ayl.

No serious accidents marred the crossing of the rest of the wagon train. Occasionally a horse balked or a frightened team of oxen faltered, but the drivers and the cavalry escorts kept the animals in motion.

The cavalrymen and their commander were tired after the long ordeal. Only Whip still had a spring in his step.

Members of the train had followed their usual practice of arranging the wagons in a circle, this time in the clearing behind the fort. The wood-gathering detail had done its work, and the women in charge of meal preparations were gathering. No soldiers intruded because, Whip was told, the area had been declared out of bounds.

He was just completing his own inspection of his charges when an officer approached him. "Mr. Holt," he said, "the Colonel would like to see you and the president of your train in his office as soon as you find it convenient."

V

Colonel Bert Jonathan leaned back in his leather-padded chair. Folding his hands on the plain pine table that served as his desk, he smiled at Whip and Ernie.

"I've had many weeks to think about the offer I'm going to make to you, gentlemen. I can get no information from Washington about why my men—two battalions—haven't arrived. That's typical of the War Department. In any event, I'm dead certain the rest of my regiment won't be here before spring. Now then, I assume you've been intending to build cabins for your winter quarters?"

"That's right, Colonel," Whip replied. "I've hunted in the forest behind your fort many times, so I know it well."

"There's no need for you to build anything," the Colonel replied. "You have about five hundred people in your train, so there's ample room for you here. The quarters my new battalions will occupy are empty. There are barracks, as well as private quarters for officers and noncommissioned personnel. The fort is solid, you'll have access to two large kitchens, and there are a number of fireplaces scattered throughout the quarters. You'll have to supply your own food and firewood, I'm afraid."

Whip was overwhelmed by the offer. "I don't know how to thank you, Colonel. Food will be no problem. There's plenty of game in the forest, and there are more fish in the Platte, winter or summer, than your troops and our people can eat."

The Colonel smiled. "I neglected to mention that we also have extensive stables to house your horses and oxen. You may need to send foragers out to find food for them before the heavy snows come, but they'll certainly be dry and warm."

"Your kindness is so great I can scarcely believe it," Ernie said, bowing slightly.

Bert Jonathan chuckled. "Not at all. I'm not charitably inclined, but I'll be obeying President Van Buren's request to extend every hospitality to you. And I have something else in mind, too. Some of the Indian tribes in my area are beginning to kick up their heels."

Whip nodded. "I've heard that the Kansa and Omaha may be going to war against each other."

"You're well informed," the Colonel said. "So I'm sure you can appreciate my dilemma. I don't have enough troops to police the region, and if trouble does break out, I have too few men to halt it."

"Perhaps," Ernie said politely, "we might be able to assist you."

"That's what I had in mind," Colonel Jonathan replied candidly. "How many effectives could you put into the field?"

Whip and Ernie pondered the question. "I'd guess about eighty," Whip said. "What do you think, Ernie?"

"As part of a larger force, not acting independently, I would place the total closer to ninety."

"I bow to greater knowledge." Whip turned to the American officer. "Baron von Thalman is too modest to tell you this himself, but he gave up command of a cavalry regiment in the Imperial Austrian Army when he came here and joined us on the march to Oregon."

"Splendid," Colonel Jonathan said. "I'm delighted to have a colleague on hand."

Ernie smiled. "You may be less happy if you call on us. Our scouts are the best anywhere, and if Whip

Holt goes scouting for you, there's no man in his class. But don't expect too much from the bulk of our people. They are American civilians, which means they are strong individualists who resist discipline. They work together best in a crisis. But some are able horsemen and expert shots, so I think we can give you solid support if you call on us."

"That's comforting to know," Colonel Jonathan said. "I just hope I won't need your help. Now, before you start moving your people indoors, there's only one more question to be resolved. I shall speak frankly. At a frontier outpost like Fort Madison, the men see no women for months at a time. There are a number of attractive—very attractive—young ladies in your train. I trust that my officers are gentlemen, and I'll place your quarters permanently off limits to the enlisted cadre. I trust you can exert some controls, too, in order to hold untoward incidents to a minimum."

Whip sighed, and Ernie said, "We cannot act as nurse-maids, but I've observed that most of our younger women are sensible, and I'm certain they'll avoid problems. Our older women are a stabilizing influence, of course, so I think—at least I hope—you'll find that everyone will settle into routines here after the novelty wears off."

"Until then," Whip said, "It might create more problems to try to keep people apart. Colonel, we'll be pleased if you and your officers will join our company for supper tonight."

Colonel Jonathan accepted graciously, then sat back in his chair and smiled. "You may be having problems on your train, but your people are having smooth sailing compared to what they'd face back home."

"How so?" Whip demanded.

"I had some dispatches from Washington City and a couple of letters from New York when the mail pouch was delivered the other day. And frankly, gentlemen, between us, the United States is going through the worst period in her history." The Colonel became more serious. "The panic has been growing worse, and President Van Buren and his Treasury Department don't seem to be able to cope with it. There are thousands upon thousands of men out of work in New York, Boston, Philadelphia—and every smaller city and town. There were bread riots in New York, and troops had to be called out to restore order."

Ernie whistled under his breath.

"The banks," the Colonel said, "have had to crack down on people who can't pay their debts. Not only are factories going out of business, but farmers and city folks alike are losing their homes and property. And more than one hundred banks have failed. Think of it—more than a hundred!"

"That means Oregon will start looking better and better to the dispossessed," Whip said thoughtfully. "So will all the free land between Independence and the Pacific."

"That's why this fort has become so important," the commander explained. "We've got to keep order and stop Indian wars here for the sake of the settlers who are going to pour out here. Free land is the only salvation for people who would otherwise starve to death."

"We're lucky to be the first," Ernie said. "We'll have our choice of a place to settle when we reach the Oregon country. I hadn't realized that conditions in the East were so bad."

"They're bad," Colonel Jonathan said. "Henry Clay's giving Van Buren no peace. A friend of mine in the War Department says that Clay is making an average of three or four speeches a week, attacking the administration. All the newspapers that don't care much for Van Buren—and that includes most of them—reprint every last word that Clay and the other Whigs say. Van Buren was a first-rate diplomat, but I'm afraid that the present situation is more than he can handle."

"What we need," Whip said, "is Andy Jackson back in the White House."

The Colonel grinned. "I served with Jackson a great many years ago, in his Florida campaign. There's never been another like him, I can tell you. He had an instinct for knowing the precise moment to attack, but he also knew when to lie low. He's no financial genius, any more than Little Van is, though, and I'm afraid that even if he were still president, he'd have to lie low, too."

"What I don't understand," Ernie said, "is how a growing country like the United States could be in such great trouble."

"You've just explained it, Baron," the Colonel said. "We're suffering growing pains. We've been primarily an agricultural nation since our founding, but the industries of the East are growing as rapidly as the frontier is moving to the West. The whole nature of our society is changing."

Whip looked glum. "I reckon you're right, Colonel," he said. "I can see the changes coming out this way—and beyond."

Ernie was surprised. "Really?"

Whip nodded. "Before we took off from Independence, Sam Brentwood and I ran into a couple of mountain men we knew. They had just come from trapping on the Green River in the Wyoming country, and they said it was pretty damn sad. The old haunts are trapped out—you can't make a living at it these days. I guess the country isn't fit for anything but settlers. It won't be long before the whole region is civilized—people and more people every place you look."

"Yes, it's coming," the Colonel said. "The Indians sense it, too, you know. That's why so many of the tribes that have been living in peace for centuries are suddenly so touchy, ready to go to war with anyone who comes near their territory. They realize that things are changing."

"Forgive me," Ernie said, "but I come from the Old World, and I am not accustomed to seeing this huge amount of space. Both of you talk so blithely of settlers moving in. But how will they be supplied? How will they build their cities? How will they trade with other parts of the United States and the world?"

"I reckon they'll use wagon trains that carry only freight," Whip said.

"Not for long," Colonel Jonathan said. "Moving freight by wagon train is slow and cumbersome. I'm looking ahead twenty years now, but I believe—and a number of my War Department colleagues agree with me—that the day isn't too far distant when a network of railroads will extend to the Pacific in the West and as far as Texas in the South."

"Texas?" Whip was startled.

"In case you haven't heard," Colonel Jonathan said, "the Americans who have been settling down there won their war of independence with Mexico and have set up their own republic. It's only a matter of time before Texas is admitted to the Union. Sam Houston was the general who won the war, and now he's President of Texas."

Whip chuckled and shook his head. "I would have guessed if I'd known Houston was involved."

"Sam Houston was one of Andrew Jackson's protégés," the Colonel explained to Ernie, who looked puzzled. "He became Governor of Tennessee, and one day he quit. Nobody has ever found out why. He went to live with the Cherokee for three years—he had lived with them when he was in his teens—and he was known as the Big Drunk. Now he's the head of a new republic and certainly will be the first governor when Texas becomes a state. What's more, I'm told he doesn't touch liquor any more."

Ernie shook his head. "The more I find out about the United States, the more convinced I am that there's no other country on earth like it."

"That's the truth!" Whip said. "I remember an old bear out in the Rockies, mean and tough and ornery. He was wounded by an Indian arrow one autumn, and he went off to his lair. Everybody expected he'd die there. But he showed up the next spring, meaner and tougher and more ornery than ever. That's the United States. We may have unemployment, and banks may be failing, but don't think this country will shrivel up and die."

Afterwards the Colonel took them to inspect the quarters that members of the wagon train would occupy. When Whip and Ernie returned to the campsite, they called a meeting. When the settlers heard that they would be spending the winter indoors, they were elated.

Emily Harris suggested that sheets could be hung in the barracks to create separate areas where families would be able to enjoy a measure of privacy. The idea was enthusiastically received.

Ernie, who was acting as chairman of the meeting, announced that there were thirty private rooms, each large enough to hold two people. "So that everyone has a fair chance," he said, "I suggest we draw lots for these quarters."

Everyone agreed, but Emily Harris had a further idea. Still attractive and vigorous after losing not only her husband but also, in the earlier stages of the journey to Oregon, one of her four sons, she spoke in a loud, clear voice. "Mr. Holt and Baron von Thalman carry more responsibilities than the rest of us," she said. "So I propose that they be exempt from the lottery and that we simply give them one of the private rooms."

Whip intervened quickly. "I appreciate the thought," he said, "but I can't accept."

"Neither can I," Ernie added, "but I thank you, Emily. We'll take our chances with everybody else."

Straws were prepared, with sixty of them shorter than the others. They were placed in two bundles, and all who were eligible, including single people and the heads of households consisting of two persons, filed past the youngest of the Harris boys and a little girl who held the straws.

The first winners were Cathy van Ayl and Cindy, who promptly agreed to room together. Terence and Lena Malcolm, who were considered a family of two because their baby was so small, were elated when they drew a short straw. Arnold Mell was a winner, followed by Mack Dougall, and people roared with laughter when Arnold announced with mock ferocity that he didn't think he could survive a winter spent in close quarters with Mack.

A small barracks was assigned to the single women and another to the single men, with the four remaining rooms, all of them larger, turned over to families. Some people began to move bedding and other belongings indoors immediately. All property had to be taken into the barracks because the canvas covers would be removed from the wagons to prevent the canvas from rotting during the winter.

Eulalia Woodling was furious when she failed to win a place in one of the private rooms and complained to anyone willing to listen to her that the drawing had been unfair. But she quickly recovered her good humor when the officers arrived en masse for supper. Soon she was flirting outrageously and impartially with them; five of them were particularly attentive to her throughout the meal.

The other single women were far more reserved, and Cindy whispered to Cathy and Tonie, "Eulalia is really asking for trouble. God help her before we get out of here in the spring. She'll need all the help she can get."

The members of the expedition, some of whom had lived in their wagons for more than a year, could scarcely believe their good fortune. To them, Fort Madison seemed palatial. The outer walls were made of thick oak logs, filled in with clay, and the floors were fashioned of rough-hewn wood. Thick oilpaper covered the windows in the sleeping quarters. There were brick fireplaces in the infirmary, the dining halls, assembly rooms, and the larger barracks. The wood-burning ranges in the two kitchens provided their own heat.

Work schedules were reassigned. The best marksmen were made permanent members of the hunting party. Others were given the duty of fishing in the Platte River and in a lake about a half-mile to the northwest, and still others became foragers who would collect grass and hay for the animals and find edible roots in the forest.

Cathy remained in charge of one kitchen, and Emily Harris took firm command of the other. When Eulalia Woodling tried to win release from the kitchen detail, Emily firmly put her in her place.

"I don't know who you think you are, young lady," the robust woman boomed in a voice that everyone could hear, "but if you want to eat, you'll work, just like the rest of us."

Hosea, who was given no immediate responsibilities, found what Colonel Jonathan later described as the "junk shack," located behind the main fort. In it were two defective three-inch cannon, the smallest size used by the army, each complete with its own carriage and firing platform; sheets of tin, the remains of the roofing used in the Colonel's office and the officers' mess hall; and a number of broken tools, bent nails, and used, discarded horseshoes.

Hosea went at once to Whip, who agreed to go with him to Colonel Jonathan, and the amused commander of the fort gave him permission to take whatever he wanted.

Ted Woods volunteered to provide new horseshoes for the cavalry mounts whenever it was necessary. He had already moved into the fully equipped blacksmith's shop adjoining the stables. These quarters were so large that he was happy to allow Hosea to use one corner of the shop.

Hosea promptly went to work on projects of his own, but offered no explanations to anyone.

A scant seventy-two hours after the wagon train had reached Fort Madison, Whip announced that he smelled snow in the air. All of the men and older boys, with the exception of a small hunting party, quickly went off into the forest to chop down dead trees and bring firewood back to the fort.

The men labored for two and a half days, cutting and chopping so much wood that they had to harness workhorses to three of the bare wagons in order to haul the wood back to the fort. They returned with enough wood for a month, but Nat Drummond, who had shown a remarkable aptitude for the task in spite of his small stature, argued that more should be cut as soon as possible, before the winter weather became too bad.

The next morning the snow began to fall, drifting down lightly at first, then becoming thicker. "This will be a heavy one," Whip predicted, and Stalking Horse agreed.

The snow fell for two days and nights. During that time, only the military sentries ventured outdoors.

When the snow finally let up, hunting, fishing, foraging and wood-gathering activities were renewed. The temperature continued to drop, and a thick layer of ice formed on the nearby lake. Stalking Horse showed the fishermen, including a fascinated Danny and Chet, how to cut a hole in the ice, drop a baited line into the water, and haul up fish, which responded to the lures more rapidly than they did in warmer weather.

The company's quarters were snug, and the settlers were grateful for their good fortune. Tonie, however, always restless unless she spent time in the open, persuaded Whip to allow her to accompany the hunters. She proved her worth by bagging more game than many of the men. Cathy and Cindy made a point of going out for a brisk walk each day, but took care to obey Colonel Jonathan's firm order that no individual—and no woman, in particular—wander more than a mile from the fort. Only armed groups of men were granted that right.

Some people rarely left the warmth of the fort, and one of them was Eulalia. Other than performing her kitchen duties, which she did with ill grace, she had little to occupy her time. She made it her business to learn the off-duty hours of the officers who were showing interest in her, and at those times she could invariably be found in one of the assembly halls, which members of the expedition were using as social gathering places.

Hosea continued to work long hours in private. Only Ted Woods knew what he was doing, and he kept it secret. It was two weeks before the Ashanti was ready to reveal the results of his activities, and then he invited Whip, Ernie, and Arnold to accompany him to the blacksmith's shop.

The astonished visitors could only stare at what he had accomplished. A grinning Ted Woods stood nearby, watching them.

Hosea had built a tiny forge, a replica of the ones he had used in Africa. It was only two feet long and eighteen inches wide and was made from scrap metal.

Near it stood a pot he also used, and Ted explained how it had been created. "Damnedest thing I ever saw," he said. "He made a little pot out of clay, and he fired it in a tiny mound filled with charcoal. You'll notice there's a hole in the pot. Well, damned if he didn't make himself more charcoal, smash it into hunks no bigger than my fingernail, and then he fired the pot still more. Show them the special tool you made for the pot and that you use on your forge, Hosea."

The Ashanti held up for inspection a miniature bellows, fashioned of wood, metal and discarded chunks of leather.

That was just the beginning. With little persuasion Hosea showed the men some of the objects he had been making with his tools. Among them were arrowheads of steel and strong, tiny fishhooks for Stalking Horse. He presented Whip and Arnold with tiny knives, their blades razor-sharp. And he gave the surprised Ernie a pipe reamer only two-and-a-half inches long.

Ted picked up some nails. "The army uses a finer grade of nail for horseshoes than I use," he said, "and there plain aren't any here right now. So Hosea made me these nails. They're an exact, perfect fit for the cavalry shoes."

Whip shook his head. "I reckon you can make just about anything," he said.

"Make anything," Hosea replied, then showed them several pairs of delicate earrings, no two pairs alike, which he had made for Cathy and some of the other ladies.

At supper that night Hosea's handiwork created a sensation. He basked in the admiration of the people who had become his friends.

Then Eulalia approached him. "There's a necklace I've been wanting for a long time," she said, "ever since I saw a friend of mine wearing the original. I'll describe it for you, and you can make it for me."

Hosea shook his head.

"But I want it!" the girl declared.

He met her gaze, but said nothing.

"If I must," Eulalia said, becoming angry, "I'll even pay you for it."

"No make," Hosea said, then turned away from her.

Angrily she stalked off, her heels clattering on the rough wooden floor.

Hosea would do anything in his power for those people he considered friends, but he would have nothing to do with anyone who looked down on him or treated him with contempt.

Two days later a sudden, critical need developed for Hosea's special skills. A breathless Danny brought the word to the blacksmith's shop. "Dr. Martin wants to see you, Hosea, in the infirmary. Right away."

The Ashanti sprinted to the fort so rapidly that he far outdistanced the boy.

He found Terence and Lena Malcolm standing in the examining room. They were obviously worried. Hosea heard Dr. Martin's voice on the far side of the operating chamber door and went inside without bothering to knock.

Tonie was holding the Malcolm baby in her arms, taking care to keep her upright, while Dr. Martin searched frantically through his instrument case.

"Lenore swallowed a thimble," Tonie said.

"I believe the thimble has lodged in her wind pipe," the doctor said, indicating that portion of the anatomy on his own body. "If she starts to cry or makes any sudden, jerking movement, she could dislodge the object —and choke to death. And because she's so small, I have no instrument I can use to fish up the thimble. If I draw you a picture of what I want, can you make an instrument for me?"

"Hosea can do," the little man replied without hesitation.

Bob Martin took a sheet of paper, dipped a quill pen into a bottle of ink that stood on a small corner table, and began to draw. "I'm no artist," he said, "but I'm making this picture as precise as I can. Here's the instrument and here's the handle. It must be as thin as a hair, as thin as you can make it. It will have to bend and conform to the shape of the baby's wind pipe as it goes down, but if it breaks, it will surely kill her."

114

Hosea watched carefully as the doctor drew.

"How long will it take you?" the physician asked. "I know you can't do the impossible, but every minute counts."

"Already working with forge today, so charcoal plenty hot. Will make in one hour. Maybe not so long." No one had ever heard Hosea deliver such a long speech. Snatching the sheet of paper, he bolted from the room.

When Hosea returned to the blacksmith's shop, Ted, who had just learned of the crisis, was at work, building up his own bed of coals, bringing them to a deep, intense red with a large bellows. "Anything I can do to help?"

"Make fire very hot," Hosea replied, and began a swift, systematic search through the objects he had taken from the junk room.

Soon he found what he wanted, the thin crossbar of a cavalryman's broken spur. He handed it to Ted, who immediately placed it directly over his roaring fire and used his great strength to coax still more heat from the coals with his bellows.

In a short time the steel strip was glowing, and Hosea went to work on his own forge. With two sets of pliers he made the bar thinner, then began to shape it with a little hammer and a curious, all-purpose tool that had a knife blade, a hook, and a sharp point.

Occasionally he glanced at Dr. Martin's drawing of the instrument, but he had the shape sufficiently clear in his mind to use the sketch only as a general guide. His fingers seemed to fly, and Ted marveled at his delicate, sure touch and complete concentration.

Hosea sighed gently. "Is done," he said, and holding the instrument with a pair of tongs, he plunged it into a bucket of cold water until it cooled. Then, still grasping it by the tongs, he raced back to the infirmary.

Lena Malcolm was cradling the baby in her arms, taking care to hold her upright while she and Terence tried to keep Lenore amused.

Bob Martin eagerly inspected the instrument. "Perfect," he said, and handed it to Tonie, who carefully dropped it into a bowl of brandywine to clean it.

115

"Lena," the physician said crisply, "give the baby to Tonie. You and Terence wait outside and please close the door behind you."

The young mother obeyed reluctantly.

After the door was closed, Dr. Martin said, "Tonie, place the baby's feet on the table. Stand behind her, hold her arms and body steady, and no matter what happens, don't let her move."

Tonie did as she was told, but Lenore, still too startled to cry, began to kick her feet.

Hosea stepped forward and standing beside Tonie, he gently but firmly grasped the baby's feet and held them still.

The physician worked swiftly, his touch sure and delicate. Taking the dripping instrument from the bowl with one hand and opening the baby's mouth with the other, he inserted the remarkably thin strand of steel down Lenore's throat.

Tonie spoke to the baby in a steady, calm voice, trying to soothe her.

Bob Martin seemed to know precisely what he was doing. He jiggled the handle slightly, for what felt like an eternity to Tonie but actually was only a few seconds. Then he grunted with satisfaction and slowly removed the instrument. Attached to the end was the thimble.

But there was still work to be done. As the angry, frightened baby opened her mouth to wail, the doctor snatched a glass containing a milky liquid and poured some of it down her throat.

Lenore almost gagged, swallowed a quantity of the liquid in spite of herself and then let loose with a scream of protest.

The smiling Bob Martin opened the door and beckoned. "She'll be fine now," he said as Tonie handed the shrieking baby to Lena.

Suddenly, abruptly, Lenore stopped wailing and dropped off to sleep.

"Here's your thimble," the physician said, handing it to Terence. "You may want to keep it as a souvenir."

The young couple stammered their thanks, but were

somewhat bewildered. "I'm worried," Lena said. "Why did she drop off to sleep the way she did?"

"Oh, that. I gave her a diluted dose of laudanum. It's an opiate, rather unpleasant to the taste, but very effective. She'll sleep for several hours, and when she wakes up she'll suffer no ill effects except a slight sore throat."

Lena managed to smile as she cradled the baby in her arms.

Bob Martin picked up the instrument, then silenced the couple as they tried to express their gratitude to him. "Don't thank me," he said. "Any experienced doctor could have done what I did. It was Hosea who performed the miracle, making this instrument to my exact specifications in less than half an hour. I'll never understand how he did it."

"Hosea." Terence said fervently, shaking his hand, "our whole family is in your debt as long as we live."

Hosea was embarrassed. He shuffled his feet, stared down at the floor, and suddenly bolted. His air of self-confidence had deserted him, and all he could murmur as he fled was, "Much work to do."

Snow continued to fall intermittently, and the weather turned bitterly cold. Whip said the winter promised to be the worst he had ever known in the ten years he had spent in the West. But the hunters and fishermen continued to enjoy good fortune. The foragers and wood-cutters remained active, too, and the women busied themselves indoors making clothes of buffalo hides and preserving winter berries.

Fears of friction between the civilians and soldiers, spending the winter together in a place remote from civilization, gradually subsided. The troops discovered that the ladies were much like the mothers and sisters they had left at home. Occasionally there were disputes between individual soldiers and male members of the wagon train that developed into fist fights, but Colonel Jonathan and Ernie von Thalman wisely ignored these eruptions.

To be sure, the future settlers did not find living conditions at the fort easy. The men who went hunting or fishing, woodcutting or foraging, always in groups, considered themselves fortunate to get away; the others were forbidden to go beyond the palisades and soon became restless.

Although accustomed to communal living, here they were forced to remain in close quarters. The scene was unchanging, and they had to find ways to keep busy.

"I'm beginning to hate this place," Tonie said to Cathy one day. "Whip and Ernie make such a fuss about my going out with the hunters that I hang around here most of the time. I'm not used to being confined and having so little to do. Even if I do work at the dispensary, sometimes I have to keep myself from screaming from boredom."

"So do I," Cathy said. "Would you believe that I actually miss the farm? I hated living there mainly because of Otto, but it's the *place* I miss. My own snug bedroom. My own kitchen, where I could keep my pots and pans and knives exactly as I wanted them. And my own parlor, even though I didn't sit in it all that often."

"I know what you mean," Tonie replied. "When the wagon train was moving, we had a feeling of accomplishment. Now we're just twiddling our thumbs, so we think of home."

"Because we have no homes other than the wagons parked out yonder," Cathy said sadly.

"It must be harder for you than for me," Tonie said, "because you're basically such a homebody."

"I suppose I am. I never had much of a spirit of adventure, you know, and it was Otto who decided that we were going to Oregon. I had no say in the matter, and if he had given me my choice, we'd have stayed home. Home. How I like that word."

"For someone who didn't want to go west and who wanted to stay put," Tonie said dryly, "it seems to me you've performed miracles. You've adjusted better than most to wagon train life."

"That's sweet of you to say, but you'd change your

mind if you worked on one of my kitchen shifts. I scream and shout and carry on something awful when some of those women don't work as hard as they should. Really, Tonie, I'm becoming an awful shrew."

"You couldn't say an unkind word to anybody," her friend assured her.

"What really bothers me," Cathy went on, "is what we're going to do about celebrating Thanksgiving and Christmas. Not that I mind for myself. I honestly don't care. But some of the children were asking me the other day, and I didn't know what to tell them. There's no point in going to Ernie because he's not familiar with American customs. But I'm wondering if I ought to speak to Whip. And Colonel Jonathan. What do you think?"

Tonie laughed. "Don't speak to anyone," she said.

"But—"

"Uncle Arnold let something slip a couple of days ago, so don't dare repeat it—it's a big surprise. The hunters have found wild turkeys in the forest and have been shooting them, then freezing them in snow so they'll keep until Thanksgiving. Believe me, you'll have more birds to clean and stuff and roast than you'll ever want to see again."

Cathy was delighted. "How wonderful! Who thought of the surprise?"

"Whip, I believe. He's much more sensitive than some people realize, and he knows that with everyone just sitting around doing nothing for day after day, morale is low."

"He really *can* be sensitive," Cathy said. "I suppose that's why I become so furious with him when he behaves like—like such a lump of callous old mountain man."

What she was really saying, Tonie thought, was that she became angry when Whip, who found it difficult to overcome his shyness, could not express himself clearly in her presence. The way he looked at Cathy, however, particularly when she wasn't aware of his gaze, indicated his interest in her. But obviously Cathy hadn't made up her mind about Whip. His way of life was so alien to

119

all she had ever known that she would need more time before she decided, as Tonie felt sure she ultimately would, that she wanted him.

"I have an idea," Cathy said, clapping her hands together in childlike enthusiasm. "Why don't we get some of the women together and make dolls and other toys we can give to the children at Christmas? Presents from all of us that they can open under the tree. We'll need a tree, of course."

Tonie laughed. "There are enough pines out beyond the palisades that the tree will be the least of our problems. As for the gifts, let's do it. That should help raise everybody's spirits."

They began work on the project that same day.

The first visitor to Fort Madison after the arrival of the wagon train was André Sebastian. He rode a handsome stallion and traveled with two heavily laden pack horses. Claiming to be a surveyor, he said he was on his way to the Rocky Mountains, and that he had been hired by a new fur company to determine approximately how many years beaver, lynx, and other animals whose pelts were in great demand would continue to abound in the Rockies.

Colonel Jonathan welcomed him, as did the people of the Oregon-bound caravan, and he accepted the invitation to stay for a few days. At mealtimes he always managed to find a place beside Tonie Mell at one of the long tables. A few people noticed and speculated that he was attracted to her.

Whip happened to be sitting on the far side of the table on the second night of André Sebastian's stay at the fort and engaged him in conversation. "It's none of my business, Sebastian," he said, "and I don't want to shove my nose into places where it doesn't belong, but I think you have more courage than good sense."

"How so?" Sebastian was smiling faintly.

"The worst of the winter is still ahead. Crossing the Great Plains at other seasons is no joke. And if you've spent any time in the Rockies, you know that mountain men hole up at this time of year. So do the Indians."

"True enough, and I certainly can't get much of my work done before the thaws come," Sebastian said, "but I want to be there when the weather turns nicer."

Whip made no further comment, but his shrug spoke for itself.

André Sebastian felt the need to offer some further explanation. "I have friends who have cabins in the mountains. I plan to stay with one of them."

Whip's interest was sparked. "Really? I've been spending about half of each year in the Rockies for a long time, so I know a good many of the hunters and trappers. Maybe I've run across your friends."

Sebastian's bland smile indicated that he had no intention of identifying his future hosts.

Whip immediately let the subject drop, but afterwards, he took Tonie aside. "There's something odd about that fellow," he said.

Tonie agreed.

"I can't figure him, Tonie, but it may not matter. He'll probably be leaving the fort soon, and it could be we'll never see him again. On the other hand, I had warnings from the government in Washington City and from Sam Brentwood—as you know better than most— that there are people who would do nearly anything to break up the wagon train. This André Sebastian seems kind of sweet on you, so maybe you could keep your ears open for as long as he's here, and you might just find out something."

She had tried hard to forget that she had ever been requested to commit acts of sabotage against the train, and she was happy that she was treated like other members of the company. But what Whip said made sense, and she agreed to do what she could.

The thought depressed her, however, making her restless, so at an early breakfast the next morning, she asked for permission to join her uncle, Whip, and Mack, who were going hunting in the forest.

Arnold Mell frowned. "There's snow in the air."

"If I get wet, I'll dry off when we come back here," Tonie replied. "I promise you I won't get lost in the forest."

The men had to laugh, and Arnold Mell raised both hands in a gesture of surrender. "You win," he said. "You always do."

They went off to their separate quarters for rifles, ammunition, and powder horns, and Tonie donned her new, hooded buffalo cloak.

When the little group reassembled at the back gate of the fort, they were surprised to see that André Sebastian was waiting for them. He, too, carried a rifle.

"I don't want to intrude," he said, "but I'm hoping you'll allow me to come with you. I'm leaving soon for the mountains, and I need to get in shape again after several days of soft living."

It would have been rude to reject his request, so the hunters nodded, and he fell in beside Tonie as they entered the forest and made their way through underbrush mixed with patches of snow.

"What game have you been bagging here?" Sebastian asked the girl.

Tonie didn't want to encourage conversation with him, but she remembered what Whip had said the previous evening. "The usual," she replied. "Plenty of deer and all kinds of small game. An occasional wild boar, although I haven't been lucky enough to spot one myself. And one day we came across a small herd of buffalo grazing on young evergreens. That was to the west of here, at the edge of the forest."

André Sebastian listened as though he cared. "Any bears?"

She shook her head. "Whip Holt has seen them here during the summer, but none of us has even caught a glimpse of bear tracks. Whip has a hunch they go up farther north to the Minnesota country to hibernate."

"Quite a fellow, this Whip Holt."

"That he is," Tonie said. "The best hunter and guide in the West, and a good, loyal friend. But I'd hate to cross him."

"I'll remember that," Sebastian said.

Tonie glanced at him obliquely, but his expression seemed innocent enough.

They trudged for the better part of an hour, covering

two to three miles, and then they scattered, agreeing to meet at noon at a place Arnold called "the red rock."

Sebastian looked blank.

"I assume you're planning to tag along with Tonie," Arnold said.

"Yes, if she doesn't mind," Sebastian declared. She felt compelled to agree to the man's company, and nodded.

The girl took the lead, heading eastward, with André Sebastian following several paces behind her, and she set a lively pace—too lively, she thought, for successful hunting. Wildlife would be sure to scatter when they heard the thumping of her boots on the frozen ground.

Sebastian must have known she was behaving like an amateur, but he made no protest and remained silent until she halted beside a patch of winter berries to search for deer tracks. "I've been waiting," he said quietly, "for an opportunity to have a truly private chat with you."

She looked at him, saying nothing, and waited.

"You are Antoinette Melichev," he said.

Tonie's heart pounded. Only the staff of the Imperial Russian Legation in Washington and agents in the employ of the czar's secret police knew her by the formal name under which she had come to the United States as a small child. "Who are you?" she demanded.

"My identity is unimportant."

"You're on the payroll of the Russian secret police."

"That is also unimportant. Miss Melichev, I bring you a message." His eyes seemed to bore into her.

"Don't bother repeating it," Tonie said wearily. "I'm sure I know the message."

"I think not." André Sebastian's voice became gentle, almost caressing. "Many months ago, in Washington, when you applied for a visa for your parents to come to America, you were asked to help your native country in a time of need. And in return, you were told the visa would be granted."

In spite of her attempt to remain calm, she could feel herself growing angry. "That isn't quite accurate. I was told that unless I cooperated, no visa would be granted. Well, I understand why the Russians don't want

123

to sabotage the wagon train themselves. They don't want to become involved. It's so much better to have someone else do it. But I've made it clear I don't intend to be that person. I'm an American, not a Russian, and I'll do nothing to harm *this* country—even if it means that the mother and father I haven't seen since I was very little stay in St. Petersburg for the rest of their lives."

"The nature of the bargain has changed." His voice was barely audible now. "So I beg you to be sensible. The conditions here at Fort Madison are perfect for what has been asked of you. All you need to do is collect a number of pine branches. Surely you know how fiercely they burn. Place them on the flooring of the empty wagons that stand behind the fort, then take a tinderbox and flint to them. The winter wind will do the rest, and the wagons will burn to the ground. Your friends will be forced to return to their homes—traveling some distance on foot, to be sure—and it will take years for the Americans to organize another venture to the Oregon country."

"I think you're contemptible," Tonie said quietly. Suddenly she raised her rifle to her hip. "Come just one step nearer, and I'll kill you. I assure you I can fire from this position."

"I don't doubt your word," Sebastian said, seemingly calm, "but such heroics are unnecessary. I am merely a messenger."

She watched him narrowly.

"I mentioned a moment ago that the essence of the bargain that was offered to you has been altered. I have been asked to inform you that if you fail to accomplish what has been asked of you, Ivan and Olga Melichev will not spend their declining years in St. Petersburg. A formal charge of treason will be lodged against them. They will be found guilty and sent to a work camp in Siberia. They will remain there for the rest of their days—and the elderly do not survive long there."

"But they've committed no treason, and you know it. They've done no harm to anyone," Tonie protested, aghast.

"I form no personal opinion in these matters. They

are not my concern. I was sent into this wilderness to carry a message to you, and this I have done." He bowed mockingly and turned away, disappearing into the forest with surprising speed.

A blind rage enveloped Tonie; she wanted to follow him and shoot him down. But in spite of her fury, she could not do it. Besides, as he had said, he was only an agent, and his death would not remove the threat to her parents.

She could hear him running and knew she could not match his speed. Also, it would be dangerous for her to follow him alone. His one desire now had to be that of escaping before he could be captured, turned over to Colonel Jonathan, and taken to Washington City as a foreign agent. To avoid being captured, he would become the hunter rather than the hunted, and she was sure he would not hesitate to shoot her down.

Tonie cupped her hands at the sides of her mouth and gave the piercing cry of the owl—the prearranged emergency summons that indicated she was in distress. She waited a few minutes, then repeated the cry, again and again, to guide her companions to her. The wait was agonizing.

Mack Dougall was the first to arrive.

He knew nothing about Tonie's troubles with the Russians, and there was little he alone could do for her. Rather than give him a detailed explanation, she said, "There's a nasty problem. Wait until the others get here."

Mack shrugged, then helped himself to a generous swallow of whiskey from his flask.

Tonie repeated the owl cry, and this time it came back to her from a distance. But another quarter of an hour passed before Arnold and Whip arrived. By now over half an hour had elapsed since André Sebastian had left.

In spite of Tonie's attempt to speak dispassionately, her voice shook as she gave them a verbatim report of her conversation with the agent.

Arnold Mell cursed volubly in Russian.

"I made my decision months ago," Tonie said. "No matter what happens or becomes of anyone, I refuse to commit treason against the United States."

"You owe nothing to Ivan and Olga," Arnold said angrily. He paused before speaking the next words. "They were happy to get rid of you, Tonie, when Sophie and I offered to bring you to America. My brother's position as court jeweler to the czar gave him an inflated sense of self-importance, and they were having so much fun that they didn't want to be burdened with a daughter."

"Thank you for telling me, Uncle Arnold," she said softly. "This makes my decision easier to bear."

Until now Whip had said nothing. A white line had formed around his mouth, and when he spoke, there was a snap of authority in his voice. "I knew there was something strange about that bastard. You say he has at least a half-hour head start on us, Tonie?"

"By now it must be closer to an hour." It was difficult to tell the time, for the sun was hidden behind dark clouds.

"We've got to catch him if we can," Whip was grim.

"I want the pleasure of dealing with him," Arnold said.

They all started off, walking as quickly as they could, through the forest in the direction of Fort Madison.

Walking rapidly, Whip called over his shoulder, "We've got to turn him over to the government. Depending on what President Van Buren and the State Department want to do, this could mean breaking relations with St. Petersburg."

"First," Arnold replied, his voice harsh, "we must catch the man."

At last they saw the log palisades of the fort looming up through the snow that was now swirling about them. As they moved through the gate, Whip slowed his pace. Not knowing how André Sebastian might react, he didn't want to give the man warning.

Ernie von Thalman was just emerging from the blacksmith's shop, and when the group saw him, they came to an abrupt halt.

Tonie was sobbing for breath, on the verge of collapse, and her uncle placed an arm around her for support.

Ernie knew something was amiss, but before he could say anything, Whip asked him curtly, "Have you seen André Sebastian?"

"Yes," Ernie said. "As a matter of fact, he behaved very strangely. He came dashing in from the forest and went straight to the stables, where his horse was already saddled and his pack horses were ready to travel. He saw me—I was just going to have some words with Ted Woods—but Sebastian didn't even stop to say hello or goodbye. He just went riding out of the fort as though he were being chased by the devil!"

"How long ago was that, Ernie?"

The Baron removed a thick, gold watch from a waist-coat pocket and looked at it. "At least an hour."

Arnold cursed again in Russian.

Whip looked down at the ground. The snow was falling so rapidly and heavily that the footprints he and his companions had made only moments earlier were already obliterated. "There's nothing we can do," he said wearily. "We can ride much faster than a man on the move with two pack horses, but we don't know whether he's gone east, west, or south across the Platte."

"It doesn't really matter," Arnold said harshly as he squeezed his niece's shoulders reassuringly. "Our path and that of Mr. André Sebastian will cross again, and when that happens, we have a score to settle with him."

Tonie Mell sat alone before a roaring fire in what had been one of the small officers' parlors in the fort. Brooding and withdrawn, she stared into the flames, not noticing that Ernie had entered the room.

Ernie, aware of what Tonie was feeling and wanting to help her, had searched for her until he had found her. He knew that she had undergone a shattering experience and needed comfort and support. More objective than her uncle could be, he felt that his worldly background and his understanding of human nature on many levels would make it possible for this proud young woman to lean on him; yet he hoped he could help her without her quite knowing what he was doing.

He cleared his throat gently.

Startled, Tonie looked away from the fire, blinking at him.

"You needn't tell me," Ernie said. "You're still upset over your experience with André Sebastian."

"I'm angry," Tonie replied brusquely. "Furious, if you must know. If he came into this room right now, I could murder him with my bare hands."

The Austrian nobleman nodded calmly. "You wouldn't be human if you reacted in any other way."

"How dare he threaten me? And what makes the Russians think I'd harm my friends and be disloyal to my country? I'm an American, not a subject of the czar. Just because the parents I haven't seen since I was a baby happen to be living in Russia is no reason for me to become a hostage!"

"It makes no sense," he agreed. "But governments frequently are neither logical nor ethical. They do whatever they think is in their own best national interests, and they give no thought to individuals who may be made to suffer the consequences of their policies."

"It isn't fair!"

"Of course it isn't. But what you fail to take into account, my dear Tonie, is that life itself isn't fair. Animals kill in order to survive and so do humans. That's the basic law of nature, like it or not."

The girl stood, moved closer to the fire and, averting her face, looked into the flames again. "If you must know, I'm frightened. And until this experience, I was never in all my life afraid of anything."

Ernie smiled. "You sound as though you're ashamed of your fear."

"I am. I hate being weak!"

"Fear very often is a sign of strength, Tonie, not weakness. The hunter who knows no fear when he faces an angry mountain lion intent on destroying him is more than a dolt. He's an idiot. Fear sharpens one's reactions and enables us to be among the survivors."

"You really think so?"

"I know it," he replied quietly. "Before I came to

America, I took part in three major campaigns and fought in eight battles. Before and during those battles, I was badly frightened."

"But the Emperor of Austria personally decorated you several times."

"Only because I had the good sense to be afraid. Brother officers who knew no fear are in their graves today, but I'm here. There's a difference between recklessness and bravery, you know. The wise person knows when to lie low, when to protect himself or herself, when to fight back. There are moments when one should be bold, when one should press an attack. But there are times when one simply covers one's flanks."

Tonie slowly turned toward him. "Why are you telling me all this?"

"Because you're one of the few people I know who does this. There are women in this wagon train who would become hysterical if they had gone through your experience with André Sebastian. There are women who would give up the struggle, who would succumb to the pressure he was putting on you."

"I have no intention of doing that," she said, clenching her fists.

Ernie looked at her as she faced him defiantly, her eyes blazing, and he chuckled. "You prove what I've been saying about you. Of all the women I've ever known, you're better able than any to face whatever may lie ahead. Because you're self-reliant, my dear. You have faith in yourself."

"Well," she admitted, "I won't let the Russians or their agents stomp on me. I don't start fights, Ernie. But I fight back!"

"Every word you say proves my point," Ernie said. "As the Russians are learning to their sorrow, they chose the wrong person to intimidate."

For the first time since he had entered the room, she laughed. "You're giving me a swollen head, you know."

"Not at all. I'm merely being honest. And I'm enjoying this experience myself. It isn't often that I've seen a powerful nation being humbled. The inner strength you provide and the help that your loyal friends give you make a formidable combination, Tonie." He crossed the room and kissed her gently on the forehead. "This is one battle that Imperial Russia simply cannot win."

The girl was silent for a few moments, then nodded. "No, they won't win," she said softly. "I will, because I'm doing what I know is right."

VI

Roaring fires burned in the hearths of the adjoining dining halls providing warmth for members of the wagon train, who, grateful to be spending the bitterly cold winter indoors, sat at the long tables and ate their supper quietly. The lack of privacy was creating friction, but so far common sense had prevailed, and no serious quarrels had disturbed the peace of the community. Eulalia and Claiborne Woodling were being ignored by many people who regarded the brother and sister as obnoxious, but their far less abrasive father had won general acceptance.

In the midst of the meal, an aide to Colonel Jonathan came into the dining halls looking for Whip and Ernie, and when they went off with him, leaving their meal unfinished, people exchanged apprehensive glances. Obviously something was wrong.

The commander of Fort Madison was waiting for the men in his office, and when they entered, he wasted no time on preliminaries. "I need your help, and I need it fast. Holt, what do you know about the Ponca nation, whose territory is north of the Omaha's land?"

"I can't tell you much about them, Colonel, because I've always avoided them," Whip said. "You know where you stand with most tribes, but not with the Ponca. They're shifty, always trying to gain an advantage over

131

everybody else. They break alliances as fast as they make them. A friend of mine—a chief of the Cheyenne—told me years ago to stay away from them, and I've always followed his advice."

"Is it true that they're good fighters?"

"From what I've heard, they're tricky," Whip said, "They wait for their enemies to make a mistake, and then they pounce. What's happening, Colonel?"

"Just a few minutes ago," Bert Jonathan replied, "one of my scouts arrived with word that the Ponca are on a rampage."

Whip whistled under his breath. "How many are there?"

"About fifteen hundred, all mounted," the Colonel said. "They're looking for loot—as well as women and children to take prisoner. I'm not worried about an attack on Fort Madison. They're too clever for that, and I'm almost certain they'll stay away from us. But they're bound to raid Omaha and Kansa villages and maybe attack other tribes."

"They'll stay out of Blackfoot country," Whip said. "No Plains nation would dare to raid a Blackfoot town."

"Attacks on the Omaha and Kansa would be bad enough, with those nations already sparring with each other. Before you know it, all of the minor tribes of the area will be joining in a free-for-all. And when Indians go to war with each other, the fighting can last for years. I've got to put a stop to it before it starts. My directive from the War Department is to keep the peace in this region."

"With your limited personnel," Ernie said bluntly, "I don't see how you can do it."

"I'm leading an expedition against the Ponca tomorrow morning, leaving here at daybreak," Colonel Jonathan declared. "I need your help, and I can supply you with as many as fifty horses if you don't have enough good mounts. How many men can you give me? I want only good riders—first-rate shots—men who are willing to obey orders."

Whip thought for a moment. "In warmer weather I might be able to scrape up ninety, but some of our people can't function too well in the snow and ice. Ernie and I will ask for volunteers, and then we'll screen those who respond. My offhand guess is that we can supply you with about seventy effectives."

The Colonel was pleased. "They'll be augmenting two of my cavalry troops, so that should be enough, and I'll leave fifty men behind to guard the fort."

Ernie was startled. "One moment, Colonel. You said the Ponca have fifteen hundred warriors in the field. Each of your cavalry troops numbers eighty men. So the addition of our seventy will give you fewer than two hundred and fifty. Surely you don't intend to send a force that small into battle against fifteen hundred mounted braves!"

Whip and Colonel Jonathan exchanged smiles. Frontier warfare in the New World in no way resembled the battles to which Europeans were accustomed.

"An attack on their whole body would be suicidal," the Colonel said. "Even if we won such a battle, we'd suffer a defeat. The Ponca would feel humiliated, and they'd come back at us again and again. They'd give us no peace for years."

"Ernie," Whip said, "our aim is to discourage them just enough so they'll come to their senses and go back to their own towns."

"I think I can explain," Colonel Jonathan interrupted. "A few years ago I was an instructor at the Military Academy at West Point. I taught our cadets the techniques used in the Imperial Austrian Army by your Hungarian cavalry regiments."

"Ah!" Ernie brightened. "Salami tactics!"

"Precisely," the officer replied. "We find ways to split the main body of the Ponca into segments, then inflict enough punishment on each portion to persuade them they ought to give up the whole idea of waging war. We don't follow the Hungarian salami tactics to their logical conclusion, however. At no time do we try to annihilate any segment. That would just be borrowing trouble for the future."

"We'll report back to you as soon as we have our

133

people set," Whip said. He and Ernie shook hands with Colonel Jonathan, then left his office and returned hurriedly to the dining halls.

There, they announced the Colonel's request for aid, and Whip made their own position clear. "When Colonel Jonathan took us in for the winter, we promised to help him in situations like this. But we want only men who can tolerate the hardships of a winter campaign. Anyone who might have to give up and return to the fort will be a burden."

He was not surprised when virtually every one of the men volunteered, and even the older boys begged for the right to go. A notable exception was Arthur Elwood, who had confided to various members of the company that he was thinking of leaving the wagon train.

Grace Drummond made a scene when her husband rose to volunteer. "I forbid you to go!" she cried in a loud voice. Nat ignored her protests.

Whip found it difficult but necessary to reject the services of Major Woodling. "Let your son represent your family," he said. "Your daughter needs protection. What would happen to her if both you and Claiborne were killed?"

The Major knew it was unlikely that both he and his son would suffer mortal wounds. "Mr. Holt," he said with a wan smile, "you've found a diplomatic way to tell me I'm too old for a venture like this."

Whip nodded.

"Thank you, sir, for being diplomatic." Woodling returned slowly to his place at the supper table. The others felt sorry for him.

Hosea was refused the right to accompany the party, too, and was distressed. "Hosea plenty good fighting man," he said with an injured air.

"There's none better," Whip agreed. "But no matter how long you can run without getting tired, the Colonel wouldn't approve of having one man on foot while almost two hundred and fifty others are mounted. Don't worry. You'll have plenty of other chances to show your skills as a warrior before we reach Oregon."

The following morning Cathy van Ayl and her helpers

went to the kitchens far earlier than usual to prepare breakfast for the departing men. Most members of the wagon train were on hand to see the group leave.

The cavalry troops were assembling on the snow-laden parade ground. Each volunteer was given a saddlebag containing enough dried beef and parched corn for a four-day journey, a blanket, and those whose supplies of ammunition were limited were given additional powder and bullets.

Colonel Jonathan had a brief talk with Whip. "I assume your scouts will join mine. Will you take charge of all scouting yourself, Mr. Holt, and coordinate your three men with my eight? Mine will be directly under your command."

"Sure. Glad to oblige."

The Colonel unfolded a map. "Here's where we'll camp tonight, on the western tip of this lake."

Whip borrowed the map, brought all the scouts together, and showed it to them, instructing them to rejoin the regiment whenever they could after sundown. All of them were veterans long familiar with the terrain. Whip then assigned each man a separate sector, reserving for himself the area in which he believed it most likely that the Ponca warriors could be found.

"It isn't enough just to locate the braves," he said. "Try to get a fairly accurate estimate of their numbers."

Whip said goodbye to Ernie, who was commanding the wagon train contingent and whom he would rejoin later, then bade farewell to the Colonel. After saluting Cathy, who had followed him out of the kitchen, he returned to the waiting scouts. "There's no need for us to wait for the main body," he said. "We'll be on our way."

Dawn had not yet broken as Whip led his scouts out of the rear gate of Fort Madison. They immediately scattered, each moving off in the direction of his assigned sector. The hoofs of the horses made a squeaking sound on the snow, and the cold was so intense that Whip gave his stallion his head.

The horse quickly began to canter to keep warm, as his master had known he would. When he tried to increase his pace to a full gallop, however, Whip had to give the reins a gentle tug. "No, boy, we'll do no galloping on this ground until we have to. Both of us will be in trouble if you take a tumble on the ice and break a leg."

The stallion settled back into a canter. Dawn came, and then the sky grew brighter, but the clouds overhead formed a thick, gray mass, and the sun did not appear. Whip was warmer now, but he kept his buffalo-skin cloak closed and his fox hat pulled low on his forehead. A man who grew careless in such weather could suffer frostbite long before he realized it.

Riding toward the northwest, with the edge of the forest off to his right, Whip saw the endless prairie stretching out ahead and to his left. This was his world, silent, forbidding, and alien to the outsider, but comforting to those who truly knew and loved the wilderness. The prairie looked deserted, but that was an illusion. There were herds of buffalo here if one knew where to find them. There were antelope and deer as well as small game, and somewhere in the vast space ahead there were fifteen hundred Ponca warriors intent on making war.

Whip was enjoying himself thoroughly. Although he liked leading the wagon train because the job was a challenge, this was infinitely better. On the other hand, he realized he couldn't spend the rest of his life as a scout and mountain man. Mack Dougall had lived such a life and was now forced to find his companionship in a bottle.

Some day, Whip reflected, he would settle down, establish a homestead claim, marry, and raise children. Until this moment the idea of staying in one place and putting down roots had not crossed his mind. He had taken it for granted that he would deliver the company to its destination and then return to his own way of life in the Rocky Mountains.

What, he wondered, had caused this sudden change? He suspected it was Cathy van Ayl. He couldn't put her out of his mind. Ridiculous—no woman was going to tie him down. The worst of it was that he could imagine himself married to her, living in a house he built himself near the great blue-green forests of the Oregon country. He tried to get rid of that mental picture, but it refused to disappear.

Whip sighed and reassured himself he wasn't being forced to make any drastic decision in the immediate future. Another year at least would pass before he guided his charges to Oregon, and many things could happen to change the situation. Cathy might fall in love with and marry someone else. She had the money she had inherited from Otto, in addition to her natural talents and beauty, so any bachelor in the wagon train who didn't court her was being shortsighted. Not that he himself gave a damn about her money, but it made her independent, and less likely to be interested in a mountain man like himself.

Cathy aside, Whip told himself, he had to think in terms of his future. But he found searching his own mind a painful process. He was a mountain man, no more and no less, and for years he had been content with his lot. He loved the thrill of pitting himself against the unknown, of using the forces of nature as his allies. He gloried in his ability to react instantly in an emergency, to act quickly and instinctively when danger threatened. But those abilities wouldn't be enough in the future. The world he had known and loved for so long was changing rapidly.

The five hundred men, women, and children in the wagon train represented the future. These pioneers soon would be followed by countless others, until the whole continent would become populated. The wilderness was vanishing, and the day was not far distant when the mountain man would become a figure of the past. In his place there would be the patient, steady farmer, the persevering rancher, the solid townsman who sought rather than shunned the company of others.

Where would he fit into this America of tomorrow? He doubted that he could ever be happy in a small town, much less a city. The regimen of a farmer, who performed the same chores again and again, did not appeal to him. He understood horses, though, and could handle cattle, so perhaps he could be happy as a rancher.

It shocked him when the thought occurred to him that he might be wise to claim a parcel of land for himself in the Oregon territory and settle there. He could, of course, lead other parties across the country to the

Pacific, and perhaps he could cling to his present way of life for as long as another decade. But in ten years he would be nearly forty, perhaps lacking the qualities needed to buckle down and start a new career. He knew mountain men who had turned into hopeless drunks when they had grown too old for the rugged out-of-doors life they had chosen, and he had no intention of becoming a member of that pathetic band.

Not that he had to make a decision today. The wagon train was still far from Oregon. Whip turned to the task immediately at hand.

At noon he paused beside a small lake, cutting a hole in the ice so he and his stallion could drink. He ate some smoked beef, along with a handful of parched corn, and was satisfied.

About an hour later he made out a smudge on the horizon that he first guessed might be buffalo. But the smear was spread out across the landscape, moving toward him, and he well knew that buffalo herds formed in depth as well as laterally.

It must be the Ponca. He needed to confirm the supposition, however. After making certain his rifle and pistols were ready he headed off in the direction of the blur on the horizon.

The next quarter of an hour passed slowly, Whip's suspense mounting. By the time he was sure that he was indeed approaching braves on horseback, the Ponca were well aware of his presence, and a group of twenty warriors separated from the main body and raced in his direction.

Thanks to his civilian attire, which they could distinguish at this distance, they had no idea that he was performing a task on behalf of the United States Army, so that much was to the good. It would not be difficult for them to tell immediately that he was a white man, however, as Indians of the Plains tribes rode far smaller horses. So those who had come in pursuit of him probably wanted to kill and scalp him, then take his stallion and his firearms.

He knew he could hold his own against a fairly large force, particularly when he was carrying a rifle and two pistols, and his foes were armed only with bows, arrows, and spears. But the odds of twenty to one were too great on the prairie, where there was no place to hide.

Whip's courage was unlimited, but he was practical, and he realized the time had come for him to retreat. The Ponca were reckless horsemen, indifferent to their own safety or that of their mounts, so he had no time to lose. He wheeled, then headed back in the direction from which he had come.

Glancing over his shoulder he saw that the braves were gaining on him. He would have to risk his stallion's neck and his own. He gave the horse his head, in spite of the ice and snow underfoot, and the stallion accepted the challenge, breaking into a full gallop. If he skidded or stumbled, he would fall, and that would be the end of him—and perhaps the end of his rider.

Again Whip looked over his shoulder and was relieved to see that the distance between him and his foes was increasing. Compelled to keep up his dangerous pace, however, he had to trust the stallion's instincts. In places the snow was at least a foot deep, and a hoof striking a hidden rock would mean sudden disaster, but he had no alternative.

He was outdistancing his pursuers, and a few minutes later the braves gave up the chase. The Indians were realists, too, and the prospect of the limited quantity of loot they could take from a lone traveler wasn't worth the effort they were making.

Whip immediately slowed his stallion to a safe canter. Only then did he realize that, in spite of the cold, he was covered with sweat. He shivered as he turned in the direction of the rendezvous point.

He rode for two more hours. The day was dying, and the regiment obviously had just arrived because only now were sentry outposts being established.

"Where's the Colonel?" Whip shouted, scarcely slowing his pace.

The sergeant of the guard pointed. Tents that would provide a minimal shelter were being removed from the backs of pack horses, and Bert Jonathan, who had himself dismounted, was watching the operation.

Whip jumped to the ground, noting that Ernie von Thalman, the commanders of the two cavalry troops, and members of the regimental staff, having seen his rapid approach, were hurrying to the Colonel's side.

"I've located the Ponca," he said, wasting no words, and gave a succinct but full account of what had happened to him.

Colonel Jonathan did not interrupt him, but waited until he had finished before questioning him. "How many were there?"

"I had no chance to make even a rough head count," Whip replied, "but there were so many that I know I saw their main body. On the other hand, I couldn't even guess whether there were five hundred or two thousand."

"At least we have an idea where to find them tomorrow," Captain Haskell said.

Ernie nodded in agreement.

"I hate to contradict you, gentlemen, but you're dead wrong," Whip said. "I know where they were a couple of hours ago, riding at a moderate pace, and I know the direction in which they were heading. But it doesn't necessarily follow that we can figure out where they'll be by morning. By then they could be blame near anywhere. Finding them again could be as hard as locating a kernel of corn you dropped in a field of tall grass."

Frowning, the Colonel asked, "Are you suggesting that we ought to make direct contact with the Ponca tonight?"

"That's right, Colonel. By this time they'll be stopping and making camp for the night. But they travel lighter than we do, and they don't have tents to pack. They'll be on their way again at dawn, and by the time we get organized and on the move, they can be far away. We might not locate them again for at least a week."

The Colonel glanced up at the darkening sky. The heavy, solid clouds would be certain to hide the moon and stars. "A night attack can be tricky. What do the unit commanders think? Captain Haskell?"

"My men are up to it, sir."

"Captain Smith?"

"So are mine, sir."

"Baron von Thalman?"

"I have no idea, Colonel Jonathan. Our people did defend their wagons admirably once when they were attacked by a band of army deserters, but they've never operated together as a formal cavalry troop, so I can't make predictions."

Whip felt compelled to interrupt. "Colonel," he said, "I suggest you hold the civilian troop in reserve. Once they see the way the army troops act, they'll have an example to follow, and I believe they can do it. But they're not up to initiating a complex maneuver."

"If our objective was to destroy the Ponca," Colonel Jonathan said, "I wouldn't even consider a night attack. Under those circumstances I'd prefer waiting until tomorrow, even if we lost them for days. However, since our aim is that of giving them a good case of cold feet that will send them back to their own towns for the rest of the winter, I'm willing to try. Gentlemen, reassemble your units and call in your outposts. We'll march again in ten minutes."

The officers hurried away.

"One more suggestion," Whip said. "The scouts are going to start trickling in soon and will be arriving here for the next hour or so. They won't know quite what to do if no one is here, so I suggest you leave a few men behind to direct them. I'm sure they'll catch up in time to join in the fight. And my own scouts can double as Baron von Thalman's lieutenants once we're all reunited."

"You think of everything, Mr. Holt." There was admiration in the Colonel's voice.

Less than a quarter of an hour later, the regiment was on the move again, with Captain Haskell's troop in the lead, Captain Smith's following, and the men of the wagon train bringing up the rear. Whip rode alone. There would be no opportunity to pause for supper later, so he ate some smoked beef and munched on parched corn in the saddle.

Within an hour he was joined by Arnold Mell and Mack Dougall, and ultimately Stalking Horse appeared. One by one the cavalry scouts also joined him.

"I'm worried about Stalking Horse," he confided to

141

Arnold. "The soldiers don't know him, and in the dark—with those feathers stuck in his scalp lock—he looks like any other Indian to them. So they might not be able to distinguish between him and the Ponca once the fighting starts."

They rode on for another hour, with Whip selecting the route by estimating how far the Ponca might have come if they had maintained their same pace and had not changed direction. He was guessing, he knew, but at last his gamble paid off—he and Arnold spotted several glowing clumps in the distance. Then the army scouts saw them, too, and tensed.

"Ponca campfires," Whip said, and called a halt. Summoning the commander of the vanguard, he said, "Send someone to the rear and ask the Colonel if he'll join us."

The request proved unnecessary. As soon as the column halted, Colonel Jonathan rode forward, followed by members of his staff.

The scouts counted eleven fires.

"There aren't as many Ponca in the main body as you were originally informed, Colonel," Whip said.

"That's right," Arnold declared. "Not that the difference is all that significant, but we've counted eleven fires, and I happen to know the Ponca traditionally assign one hundred to a fire. So we'll be facing about eleven hundred instead of fifteen hundred."

"It's still far too many for a full-scale attack," the Colonel said.

"I believe we can ride about a mile closer without being detected by their sentries," Whip told him.

"What would be the advantage, Mr. Holt?"

"I don't know—yet. But the closer we are the better we can make out their defense perimeter."

"Fair enough," Colonel Jonathan said.

"Just one thing, Colonel. We don't want to let the Indians know we're breathing down their necks. So I suggest you impose silence on the whole regiment. Don't allow anyone to light a pipe or *segaro*."

Whip waved the column forward again, and, with Arnold still beside him and the army scouts spread out in a line behind them, they rode on for another quarter of an hour. The eleven fires became more distinct, although it was too dark to make out anything else.

One fire, the fourth from the left, was bigger than the others, and attracted Whip's attention. Arnold reached out to tap him on the shoulder, and he nodded in agreement. They had advanced far enough. At this distance they could still consult, and the Colonel could issue orders without fear of being heard. Whip halted the regiment again and engaged in a low-pitched, earnest conversation with the army scouts and Arnold.

Again the Colonel moved forward to join them.

"We have noticed something we all find interesting. Look at the fourth fire from the left."

"Now that you mention it," the Colonel replied, "it looks twice the size of any other fire. What does it mean?"

"We think the sachem—the leader—of the Ponca is using that fire," Whip said.

Colonel Jonathan nodded. "I gather by your tone that you have a specific plan of action in mind."

"We've just been discussing it. I'll try it out on you. Just suppose," Whip said, "that you spread the regiment out in a semicircle—a thin line that starts parallel to the fire on the left and extends all the way to the fire on the right. At a given signal, the entire regiment—after first moving as close to the Ponca sentry outposts as we can—will open fire. Have the men reload and keep firing as rapidly as they can."

"But they can't possibly hit any target at that distance," the Colonel protested, "especially on a night as dark as this."

"I hope not," Whip replied. "The idea of the fireworks display is to confuse and frighten the Ponca and make them think they're being attacked by a force far superior to their own. Two hundred and thirty rifles can make a hell of a lot of noise."

"Aside from the fact that your wagon train civilians won't be making a direct attack, I don't see the advantage."

"While you're putting on your show, your scouts, Arnold and I will ride to the big fire. By now the Ponca are either sleeping or on their way to sleep. Tell him the rest, Arnold."

"It's this way, Colonel," Arnold Mell said. "A few years ago I visited a Ponca town and slept in the local chief's hut. The chief had a special blanket—beaded, with a lot of feathers stuck in it, so that even when he was asleep, people would know he was the chief."

"The principal sachem must be using a fancy blanket like that," Whip said. "He's our goal. We'll scoop him up and ride back to our lines with him. We'll arrange some signal with you so you'll know we're coming, and when we give the signal, the whole regiment pulls back, falls into formation, and rides back this way, fast. The sachem will be expecting us to kill him, and in the dark he'll have no idea how many of us are taking part in the overall attack. But you'll spare his life and send him back to his people unharmed—provided he gives you his word that he'll take his warriors home and stay there. When an Indian's honor is at stake, he'll keep his pledge."

"Astonishing," Colonel Jonathan said.

"We'll be holding casualties down to an absolute minimum," Whip explained. "We may have to put bullets in some of the senior warriors who are sharing the sachem's fire, but only if they get in our way. We may get out of this without any of my men or your troopers being killed or even hurt."

The Colonel shook his head, then stamped his booted feet to keep warm. "What about those of you who are taking part in this raid?" he demanded. "It strikes me you'd be taking a frightful risk."

"Not that bad." Whip shook his head. "Obviously the whole regiment will avoid shooting in the direction of the sachem's fire so we aren't hit by our own bullets."

"I'm thinking in terms of the Ponca capturing and murdering you!"

"If we do this right, we'll be in and out before they realize what's happening. And once we've captured the sachem, they won't dare to fire at us. They'll be afraid of hitting him."

The Colonel appreciated Whip's daring, but continued to disapprove. "I still think you're taking too great a risk. I hardly need remind you that your first obligation is to the people of your wagon train. If you should be killed, injured, or captured, they'd be forced to return to Independence and wait there until another wagonmaster competent to lead them could be found. The expedition to the Oregon country could be delayed for many months, and you know as well as I that the President is eager to settle that territory as soon as possible."

"I won't fail the wagon train company," Whip replied. "I've been in far more ticklish spots and have come through without a scratch. Believe me, Colonel, I've weighed the odds."

The expressions on the faces of the army scouts indicated they agreed with him. One of them, a grizzled trooper with leathery skin, spat into the snow. "I'm due to retire on a pension next year. I'm buying me a little farm near my brother's in Kentucky, and I aim to spend the rest of my days there, all peaceful and quiet. I'll be damned if any good-for-nothing, lazy Ponca warrior is going to deprive me of something I've been waiting for ever since I first volunteered for this army after the British burned Washington City more than twenty-three years ago."

"There can't be more than a hundred or so warriors at that fire," another scout, leaner and younger, said contemptuously. "In hand-to-hand combat or when they're making a raid of their own, they're dangerous. But with ten of us, all carrying rifles and pistols, I don't see how they can stop us."

"They can't," a third scout said flatly.

"We're not treating the Ponca lightly, Colonel," Whip said. "But conditions are perfect for an action that could solve all our problems. Sure, we'll be taking a measure of risk. But I didn't join you on this outing to sit back, twiddle my thumbs, and enjoy the winter air."

"I'm afraid I'll have to go along with you, Mr. Holt," Colonel Jonathan said, "but I'm doing it against my better judgment."

The Colonel summoned his unit commanders and gave the specific instructions. The two army troops moved to the flanks, leaving the weaker and less disciplined wagon train civilians to hold the center. Then all three units moved further apart until they formed a rough semicircle around the Indian encampment. There was a distance of ten to fifteen feet between each man, sufficient space to give the Ponca the impression that the attacking force was far larger than it actually was; yet the distance was not so great that the units would find it difficult to close ranks quickly in case a sudden, unexpected emergency developed.

When Whip told Stalking Horse that he did not want him to accompany him into the Ponca camp, he faced a personal problem. It was evident that Stalking Horse was hurt. "Whip no longer trusts his brother," he said in his own tongue.

"That is untrue," was the instant reply. "Whip has trust and faith in his brother as he has in no other man. It is because of his love for his brother that Stalking Horse must stay behind."

The Cherokee bristled. "Does some man question my courage?"

"I question the mind that was given to you by the great god of your nation," Whip said tartly. "You have a scalp lock with feathers in it. The Ponca have scalp locks with feathers in them. The animal skins you wear are like the animal skins they wear. You carry a bow and arrows, and so do the Ponca. It is very dark, and there will be great confusion when we ride into the camp of the enemy. I want no army scout to fire at you because he mistakenly thinks you are a Ponca warrior. I won't take that chance."

A reluctant Stalking Horse returned to his place in the wagon train line.

The scouts started forward again, moving cautiously as they advanced two hundred yards beyond the three units following them. They remained close enough to each other to see signals given by hand, and eventually a message was passed to Whip from the far left side of the formation: a Ponca sentry outpost was only a short distance ahead.

Whip permitted the main body to move forward another one hundred yards, and then they stopped. So far the conduct of the civilians was as professional as that of the cavalrymen.

With Arnold beside him, Whip motioned the scouts into a single line. Then Whip raised a hand, and when he let it drop, the scouts rushed forward, permitting their mounts to gallop. Not until they had raced far beyond the sentry line did the Ponca on guard duty realize their security had been breached. They raised a shrill, penetrating cry—a perfect imitation of a crow's call—to alert their companions.

By that time the scouting unit was rapidly approaching the large fire. One of the scouts recognized the ornate blanket in which the sleeping sachem of the tribe had wrapped himself. He rode straight toward the prone figure, the scouts on either side of him veering inward sharply.

Leaping to the ground, the scout struck the Indian leader sharply across the back of the head with a pistol butt, knocking him unconscious. He threw the leader across his horse. Then, mounting his horse again and holding the prone body of the Ponca in front of him, the scout began a wild dash back toward the regiment's lines, a scout on either side of him.

Whip, Arnold, and the five other scouts stayed behind for a few moments in order to give the others time to effect their escape. Ponca warriors were awakening now, leaping to their feet and reaching for their weapons. One, more agile than the others, managed to fit an arrow into his bow. Seeing him, Whip coolly shot him with a pistol, the bullet striking the unfortunate brave between the eyes.

The sound of the shot not only alerted the entire Ponca force, but was the ultimate signal that the regiment awaited. A volley of rifle fire erupted, the flashes briefly illuminating a vast semicircle.

Dazed, the Ponca believed that they had been surrounded by a superior force of white men with firesticks, and in their momentary confusion Whip and his companions began their own hasty retreat.

Crouching low in their saddles, they urged their horses

forward, and in a short time they overtook the other members of their party.

Meanwhile, the regiment directed a steady stream of rifle fire at all of the Ponca fires except the large one, leaving Whip, Arnold, and the scouts a narrow channel through which they could escape.

By now the Indians were sending shower after shower of arrows after the men who had abducted their sachem. But the warriors were afraid to pursue the fleeing scouts. The rifle fire held them at bay.

A whistle that Colonel Jonathan had given Whip dangled from his neck on a rawhide thong. He blew one high-pitched blast after another, indicating the successful return of the scouts with the still-unconscious chief of the Ponca nation.

Only now did it occur to Whip that he had neglected to make allowances for one vitally important detail. Instead of heading toward one of the cavalry troops, he and his companions were riding directly toward the men of his own wagon train, who might easily become rattled, think the riders bearing down on them were Ponca, and direct their fire on them. But Stalking Horse and Mack Dougall steadied them, and Whip was pleased to see a grinning Nat Drummond excitedly waving him closer.

Only one of the future Oregon settlers failed to obey orders. Claiborne Woodling suddenly moved forward out of the stationary line. Intoxicated by the success that had been enjoyed so far, he appeared determined to ride into the Ponca camp, which would have been a suicidal gesture. Mack raced after him, caught hold of his reins, and, blistering him with a string of oaths, forced him to return.

By now the scouts had reached relative safety behind their own lines, and a succession of whistle blasts conveyed this information to the regimental commander.

Colonel Jonathan promptly ordered his units to begin a withdrawal. His own troops obeyed quickly, still firing as they withdrew, but the maneuver was far more difficult for the civilians to accomplish. They managed to achieve it with some hesitation, however, and then the lines were contracted so all three units formed a solid phalanx.

Once the regiment halted, it was discovered that two of the scouts had suffered minor injuries. Dr. Martin, who had come to the center of the line with Colonel Jonathan and his staff, quickly took charge, cutting the arrows out of the flesh, pouring brandywine on the wounds, and then bandaging them.

The still-unconscious Ponca was removed from the scout's horse and laid on the ground. Two knives were removed from his belt. Then Dr. Martin revived him by placing a container of sharp, dried herbs under his nostrils.

The dazed Ponca sat up and saw that he was surrounded by white men, many on horses. Colonel Jonathan and Whip dismounted and were joined by Stalking Horse. All three of them faced the dazed sachem, who was just beginning to realize the seriousness of his predicament.

Colonel Jonathan, long accustomed to dealing with Indians, knew, as did Whip, that the chieftain had to be treated with the dignity his high office demanded if the ultimate goal of the maneuver was to be achieved. "Tell him, please, that we mean him no harm, Mr. Holt. Tell him we want no war with him and his people and that we seek only peace."

Whip translated his words, adding a few flourishes of his own.

The sachem drew himself to his full height, even though his head still ached, and gathered his beaded, feathered blanket around him. No matter where he looked, he could see white men with firesticks, many of them in uniform. The presence of Stalking Horse indicated there were Indians in this war party, too. "Why has White Eagle, the sachem of the Ponca, been taken from his sons? They will not rest until this insult has been avenged!"

Whip translated, then added, "Let me answer him, Colonel. I think I can handle this myself."

"The father of our warriors," Whip said to the Ponca as he inclined his head in the direction of the white-haired colonel, "means no disrespect to White Eagle. It is his wish that he and his sons become the friends of White Eagle and his people. White Eagle was brought to this place because there was no other way the father of our warriors could hold a powwow with him. He and his

149

sons want to live in peace with the Ponca. They wish also to live in peace with the Omaha, the Kansa, and all of the other great nations of this land. Only those tribes that break the peace are our enemies."

Suddenly Stalking Horse intervened with a gesture that startled the Ponca chieftain. Holding White Eagle's knives on the palms of his hands, he gave them to him.

Only an Indian or someone who knew the tribes intimately could have understood this gesture. The sachem was being treated as a free man and an equal rather than as a hostage. Reacting slowly because undo haste would have appeared unseemly, he took the knives and slid them into his belt. His face remained stiff, expressionless, but his eyes betrayed his feelings and indicated that some measure of his pride had been restored.

Colonel Jonathan took advantage of this situation by making a gesture of his own. Slowly, elaborately, he withdrew his own army knife from its sheath and presented it to the sachem.

The blade was made of tempered steel, the handle was fashioned of metal and covered with leather. The weapon was far superior to the crude knives of the Ponca, and White Eagle was overwhelmed. It appeared that these men who used firesticks meant what they said and were not trying to trick him.

Aware of the impression that had been made, Whip made up his mind to bring the talk to its climax. The night was already well advanced, and if the negotiations continued until daybreak, the Ponca warriors would see how heavily they outnumbered their foes and might be tempted to launch a full-scale attack in the hope they could rescue their sachem.

"White Eagle," he said, "return with your warriors to the villages and towns of the Ponca. You will go with honor. You will take with you the friendship of our chief and his sons. Only if you make war against the other nations that occupy this land will you and your people be harmed."

Whip spoke quietly to one of the scouts. The man nodded, then left, and returned a few minutes later with a pack horse relieved of its burdens. Whip presented it to White Eagle. The sachem knew he was free to leave. The gifts he had been given had been presented to him unconditionally. If he violated the spirit in which they had had been given, he would be denying the ancient traditions of hospitality that the Ponca, like all other Plains tribes, regarded as sacred.

Whip glanced at Bert Jonathan, indicating that now was the time to strike a bargain.

The colonel extended a hand. "I pledge you peace," he said.

Whip translated, his voice sonorous.

White Eagle hesitated for an instant, and in that moment the question of war or peace hung in the balance. Then he held out his own arm, and he and the Colonel gripped each other's wrists. "White Eagle pledges peace," he declared.

The formalities were complete. Solemn promises had been exchanged, and the sachem would be dishonored if he violated them. He mounted the pack horse, which was far larger than any mounts the Ponca knew, and started toward his own lines.

Colonel Jonathan immediately gave the order for the regiment to withdraw an additional quarter of a mile. The crisis was not over yet—it wouldn't be completely resolved until the warriors accepted their chieftain's agreement.

Dawn broke as the dignified White Eagle rode slowly back to his own camp. He vanished from sight. His followers were undoubtedly astonished to see he was alive and well. There was a long wait, presumably while he conferred with his lieutenants. Then the Ponca campfires were extinguished, and the warriors began a quiet, orderly retreat toward the north.

Colonel Jonathan gave the order to return without delay to Fort Madison. Peace had been restored in the eastern Nebraska country at a cost of one dead Ponca warrior and two wounded scouts. What pleased Whip more than anything else was the knowledge that the men of the wagon train company had gained valuable military experience. They would need it when they resumed their own journey through hostile Indian territory.

The two mountain men who arrived at Fort Madison unexpectedly, on the way from the Rockies to Independence, were named Welden and Burke. One was tall and heavyset, the other shorter but equally brawny. Both were bearded, in their early thirties, raucously profane, and they were dressed alike in greasy buckskins.

"They're scum," Mack Dougall said in disgust. "The minute I saw them, I hid my cask of whiskey. They're the kind I'd send on their way if I saw them in the mountains."

"I know their type, too," Arnold Mell agreed. "When fellows like that showed up at my ranch in Independence, I'd meet them at the front door with my rifle in my hands and swear I'd shoot them if they didn't leave my property fast. I would have done it, too, but they always took me at my word. Colonel Jonathan should have sent them on their way."

"He couldn't," Whip explained. "They're U.S. citizens, and with a new blizzard threatening, he had to give them shelter. I know how you feel, but we've got to put up with them for as long as they hang around here. I reckon, though, that we ought to pass the word for folks to be on their guard."

There were no locks on the doors, so members of the wagon train company were warned to conceal their valuables and to keep watch over their other possessions. Most people tried to be courteous, however, and treated the mountain men politely. The pair were given bunks in the bachelors' sleeping quarters.

Tonie Mell was the first to have an unpleasant encounter with the two men. Since the storm made hunting expeditions impossible, she had spent the day working in the infirmary with Dr. Martin, and at sundown, as she left to return to her own quarters before supper, she was somewhat miffed. That day she had put on a dress, hoping to attract the doctor's attention. Bob Martin had appreciated her efforts on his behalf, as he always did, but he had made no comment on her appearance. If she didn't know better she would have sworn he was blind. Wiping her hands on the apron she still wore, she angrily made her way down the long hallways of the fort, her heels clicking on the rough-hewn floor.

Suddenly her path was blocked by two bulky figures. As they lurched toward her, she could smell the nauseating odor of cheap whiskey.

"Ain't she somethin'?" Welden demanded, leaning against the wall. "Sweetheart, you got no idea how long it's been since I've had a romp with somebody like you."

"Me first," Burke said. "I'm the one who saw her first!"

"We'll toss a coin for her," Welden declared, reaching for her.

Tonie, like her uncle, had dealt with men of their sort at home in Independence, and she reacted without hesitation. Reaching into her apron pocket, she withdrew the long, pointed pair of scissors she had been using in the infirmary to cut cloth for bandages. Holding the scissors like a dagger, she pointed them at the larger man.

"Touch me again, just once," she said, "and I'll carve out your gut."

Welden could only stare at her, speechless.

Burke laughed. "You goin' to let a woman talk t' you that way?"

"The same goes for you," Tonie told him. "But your stomach is smaller, so you'll get it in the groin."

The pair continued to gape at her, then looked at each other.

Tonie knew she was no match for them, but she was not intimidated. If they persisted, she would inflict as much serious damage on them as she could and would make enough noise to bring the entire wagon train company and a troop of cavalry to her assistance.

Welden was still sober enough to realize he had made the mistake of approaching a wildcat. He took a single step backward. His experience with respectable women was limited, but he could tell by her expression that she would not hesitate to use the scissors. He wanted a girl, but he did not want to be stabbed.

"Get out of my way," Tonie said, her green eyes

blazing. "I'm not going to tell you again." Her arm poised and her body tense, she was prepared to strike.

Welden wilted and stepped aside.

"You, too," she told the shorter man.

Burke flattened himself against the log wall.

Tonie swept past them, disdainfully, without a second glance.

"Holy Lord," Burke muttered. Taking a flask from his hip pocket, he drank so quickly that some of the whiskey dribbled down his unshaven chin.

Weldon took the flask from him and helped himself. "To hell with her," he said, wiping his mouth on his greasy sleeve. "She ain't the only doe in the forest."

Tonie didn't mention the incident to anyone. She knew what her uncle and Whip thought of the pair, and having defended herself successfully, she put the matter out of her mind.

An hour and a half passed before the members of the wagon train company were belatedly called to supper. As the men, women and children filed into the adjoining dining halls, a scowling Ted Woods, who stood near the entrance, tapped Whip on the shoulder and drew him aside.

"The reason supper is late," he said, obviously concerned, "is because Cindy and Cathy didn't show up to take charge."

"It could be they're resting," Whip replied. "They may have fallen asleep and not wakened."

"That isn't like either of them," Ted said stubbornly. "I don't like this one bit, and I aim to find out what's going on." He started off down the long corridor.

Sighing quietly, Whip decided to accompany him. He knew about Ted's volatile temper. If Cathy and Cindy were sleeping through the supper hour, a luxury they deserved, he didn't want Ted making an unwarranted scene.

They walked together in silence. Then, as they drew near the officers' room the two girls were sharing, they heard sounds of a scuffle and increased their pace. The door was closed, but they could hear a man's harsh laugh. "Hold still, sweetheart, you're goin' to like this!"

Whip quickly opened the door. Cathy and Cindy were lying on their beds, sprawled on their backs, their hands tied behind them and gags in their mouths. Looming over them were Burke and Welden, but the girls had not been completely subdued and were kicking violently, their skirts flying high, as they tried to ward off their attackers. Furniture had been upset, and clothing was scattered around the room. Cathy and Cindy had fought hard.

Just as the door opened, Cindy managed to free herself from her bonds and, reaching up, she clawed Welden's face.

He cursed her and cuffed her hard across the face.

Seeing this, Ted Woods gave a low, animal-like growl and hurled himself at Cindy's attacker.

Burke had been in the process of lowering himself onto Cathy's body when he heard Ted, and he looked across the room in surprise. At that moment Whip grasped him by the collar, hauled him to his feet, and drove a fist into his face.

Burke was drunk, but he had enough sense to realize he had to protect himself. He drew a knife.

Whip gave him no chance to use it. He put all of his weight behind a short punch to Burke's stomach and, as Burke doubled over, Whip took the knife from his hand and threw it under Cathy's bed.

"Fight like a man," Whip said, moving forward again.

Burke tried to protect himself from the hammer-like fists that battered his face and body, but even if he had been sober, he would have been no match for the thoroughly aroused Whip.

It was one of Whip's maxims that the man who wanted to win a battle had to keep his head. Now, even though he was angry, he was able to follow his own advice. His mind continued to function clearly as he gave Burke one strong blow after another.

One of Burke's eyes was closed, blood trickled from a corner of his mouth, and he retreated to a corner where he cowered, trying to escape the beating by covering his face with his arms. But his feeble attempts were useless.

Whip broke through his guard with a right to the face that straightened him. Then a well-placed left caught

Burke in the stomach, again doubling him over, and another right caught him full in the face again, slamming him against the wall. He crumpled to the floor and stayed there.

Cindy had removed her own gag and Cathy's, then untied the other girl's wrists. They huddled together, still dazed by the rape that had so narrowly been averted.

Whip had temporarily forgotten Ted and the other intruder. He turned to see the blacksmith sitting astride Welden's chest. Ted's powerful hands were clutching the man's neck, choking the life out of him, while at the same time he was raising the man's head and smashing it repeatedly on the floor.

"Enough, Ted! You've finished him, so leave him be!" Whip shouted.

Ted didn't hear him; he was conscious only of the man who had assaulted Cindy. There was a wild, maniacal expression in the blacksmith's eyes, and it was plain he was determined to kill the man. Welden tried in vain to remove the hands that were choking him. No man could long survive the punishment he was getting. Whip came up behind the blacksmith and tried to pull him away, but Ted's strength was too great.

All at once the room was filled with soldiers. Two of them joined Whip, and all three, straining together, finally managed to pry Ted away from Welden, who sucked in air painfully.

Colonel Jonathan was standing in the entrance to the room, and Whip quickly told him what had happened.

By the time he had finished, Ted Woods had regained his senses. He stood quietly, flexing his fingers and gazing at Cindy. "I—I hope you're all right, ma'am," he said diffidently.

Cindy could only nod. Not only was she shaken by her own experience, but Ted's violence had frightened her, too. She knew that if Whip and the officers had not intervened, Welden would be dead by now. She couldn't yet think straight, but it was frightening to know that a man with Ted's temper and bull-like strength had appointed himself as her protector.

"Haul those two into the corridor so the ladies can compose themselves," the Colonel directed.

Soldiers propelled the guilty pair into the hallway. Burke was still bleeding, trying to focus with one eye, and Welden, not yet breathing normally, grasped the back of his head, his gaze flicking apprehensively in the direction of Ted, who was following behind, along with Whip and Colonel Jonathan.

"What do you have to say for yourselves?" Colonel Jonathan asked, after closing the door to the girls' room.

There was a long silence before Burke mumbled, "We was just havin' an innocent little jamboree. Nobody got hurt until these two bulls came into the room."

"Are you suggesting that the ladies were accepting your advances willingly?" The Colonel spoke quietly.

Welden nodded as best he could.

"You lie!" Ted roared, and would have started forward again had Whip not laid a restraining hand on his arm.

"If that's the case," Whip said, "perhaps you'll be good enough to tell me why the ladies' hands were tied and gags were placed in their mouths."

The accused pair had no reply and remained silent.

Hearing what Whip had said, Colonel Jonathan said, "You're guilty." His voice was icy. "You were granted the privilege of a sanctuary here, and you abused our hospitality—mine, the army's, that of our civilian guests, and above all, that of the people of the United States, who own this property. Gather your belongings and leave. At once!"

The two men were shocked by the severity of the sentence. "We told you when we got here how we lost our horses," Burke said, speaking with difficulty. "Lord Almighty, Colonel! It's more'n forty miles from here to the tradin' post at Council Bluffs!"

Desperation made Welden eloquent. "Even in good weather, we'd have the devil's own time tryin' t' reach Council Bluffs, what with all them towns o' the Omaha b'tween here and there. But there ain't nobody can make it there in the kind o' weather there is out yonder right now."

157

Colonel Jonathan was unyielding. "Where you go or how you proceed there is none of my concern."

"But we'll die out there!" Burke was alarmed.

Colonel Jonathan ignored him. "Lieutenant Myers," he said to his aide-de-camp, "see to it that these men are escorted to the back gate. Make sure all of their belongings are delivered to them there, and have them escorted off government property. Notify the sentries that if they return or are caught loitering in the barns or elsewhere, they're to be shot on sight."

"Yes, sir," the aide said, and saluted.

"I deeply regret this incident, Mr. Holt," the Colonel said. "I'll be grateful if you'll tell the ladies I'll apologize to them in person tomorrow, when they'll be better able to receive me." He turned and went off to his own quarters.

Welden and Burke knew they could not disobey the order, so they allowed themselves to be led away.

Whip and Ted found themselves alone in the corridor.

The door opened, and the two girls emerged. They had changed into clean dresses and combed their hair.

"We heard Colonel Jonathan's verdict, but I can't say I feel sorry for those two," Cindy said.

Cathy went straight to Whip. "Thank you," she said simply. "It would have been ghastly for me if you hadn't arrived when you did—and taken care of that beast."

Whip was embarrassed and shrugged aside Cathy's thanks. "Are you all right?"

"Oh, yes. My wrists are raw, but they'll heal fast enough."

Still uneasy because of Cathy's obvious gratitude, Whip turned to the other girl. "What about you, Cindy?"

"Oh, one side of my face may be black and blue tomorrow, but I'll cover it with rice powder and nobody will know." She laughed, and there was an element of bravado in the sound. "I knew worse in the place where I worked in Louisville."

It was the first time Whip had heard her refer to her previous life as a prostitute, and he hastily changed the subject, pointing to Ted. "It was Ted who got me to come here with him to investigate. He's the one who figured there was something the matter when you didn't show up to fix supper."

Shuffling his feet, Ted stared down at the floor. This shy, tongue-tied giant bore scant resemblance to the wild-eyed demon who so easily would have killed a man only a short time earlier. For the moment his murderous impulses had been quieted. But his problem, as he knew better than anyone else, might flare up again without warning, and the consequences could be disastrous.

VII

Henry John Temple, Third Viscount Palmerston, was irascible, imperious, and endowed with unlimited energy, qualities that caused him to be feared by his subordinates, shunned by his peers, and disliked by his superiors, of whom he recognized only one, the young Queen Victoria. Palmerston held an Irish peerage, which made it possible under the rules of Parliament for him to hold a seat in the House of Commons. Passionately devoted to the protection and expansion of the world's greatest empire, he was, in his mid-fifties, universally recognized as perhaps the best Foreign Secretary in his nation's illustrious history.

One of the few men in England who was not afraid of him was the equally aristocratic Sir Edwin Knowlton, who had been his classmate at Harrow four decades earlier. Their goals were identical, but Knowlton elected to serve the Crown in the shadows. Not only had he created an espionage and counterespionage service of extraordinary efficiency—an organization that operated with precision around the globe—but his own desire for anonymity gave him a leverage in his dealings with the mighty, even the powerful Palmerston. Although such people knew him to be extraordinarily competent, they also knew he would never be a threat to their power or position.

Knowlton sat quietly in the enormous office overlooking Pall Mall, a faint smile on his face, making no comment as he listened to the Foreign Secretary speak.

"The Oregon country," Palmerston said in his booming voice as he paced the length of the Persian rug that covered the magnificent hardwood floor, "is ours. By right of discovery, by right of occupation, and by right of international law. The Americans go too far when they claim it, and I refuse to tolerate their impudence!"

"Do sit down, Temple," Sir Edwin said mildly. "Or you'll lose your voice before you make your policy speech in the Commons this afternoon."

"Quite so." Palmerston retreated to his desk, sat, and drummed his restless fingers on the polished surface. "Obviously the Americans want an outlet to the Pacific, and I say to them, take California from the Spaniards. Everything north of it belongs to us!"

"Temple, you're wasting your time and mine by telling me a policy we've been following for years."

"Edwin, you're being impertinent."

"Who has a better right? Get to the point."

"Very well,'" Palmerston said crisply. "American newspapers and magazines are filled with articles about the excitement being created by the first wagon train to cross North America. Congressmen make patriotic addresses on the subject, and a dozen new wagon trains are being organized. We must act—quickly—to prevent that first wagon train from reaching Oregon, or we'll be forced to compromise our own claims. Last year I made it clear to you that the train now in motion must be halted."

"So it shall." Knowlton spoke with confidence. "One of my very best agents is in the field attending to the matter."

"Who is he?"

"A chap named St. Clair. He has a distinguished record, and he's completely reliable."

"What is he doing?"

Knowlton was deflated. "To tell you the truth, Temple, he hasn't been in touch with my office in recent months. He's functioning somewhere in that Godforsaken American wilderness, and until he can get in touch with our garrison at Fort Vancouver, his means of communication with us are limited."

Palmerston's temper rose. "Then send out another agent, Edwin. Send a dozen! You know the stakes are high!"

As Sir Edwin Knowlton's subordinates knew, he, too, had a short temper. "Obviously you haven't considered the consequences. A mission of this sort is extremely delicate. If the American government should get wind of what we're doing, there will be hell to pay. The former President, Andrew Jackson, will demand that America go to war with us again, and he'll be supported by public opinion, even though President Van Buren is a civilized man who wants peace."

"I don't want war with the United States," Palmerston said slowly. "I'm not certain our own people would tolerate it. But the Oregon territory is a rich prize, Edwin, and we can't let it slip out of our hands. The American claim is as valid as our own, and if they settle there first, we'll have the devil's own time trying to squeeze them out."

"It will be the better part of a year before that train reaches Oregon. Long before then, I expect a report from St. Clair telling me he's succeeded. On the off-chance that something untoward should happen to him, of course, I have several competent agents I can send from Fort Vancouver to help him."

Again Palmerston drummed on his desk. "The situation does seem to require patience."

"I have faith in St. Clair," Knowlton said.

The Foreign Secretary stared at him. "For your sake, Edwin, for his and for the Empire's, I hope your confidence in him isn't misplaced."

Henry St. Clair was annoyed with himself. Driving his wagon across the Great Plains with his riding horse tethered to it, he bundled himself in his heavy cloak, pulled his hat lower onto his head, and reflected that he was stupid. A senior British agent, engaged in carrying out a delicate, vital mission had to think in terms of the present, and he had been remiss. He should have known he was leaving St. Joseph far sooner than necessary, since he could cover three or four times as much territory in a single day as the accursed wagon train could manage. St. Joseph wasn't London, not by a long way, but at least he had slept in a comfortable bed there, consumed edible meals, and had found a whore to his liking. Now he found himself in the middle of nowhere. Regardless of where the wagon train might have halted during the cold weather, he had to find adequate shelter for himself and his horses during the rough winter months that still stretched ahead.

Certainly he could take no action against the wagon train until spring, no matter what his superiors ordered. Men who spent their entire careers behind London desks had no real understanding of what went on in the field, so he usually ignored their specific directives. When he became an executive, he wouldn't demand miracles from his subordinates.

His problem, as he well knew, was that he had performed seemingly miraculous feats in India, North Africa and Siberia, so London was expecting him to produce again. Very well, he would, but he had no intention of moving alone against the wagon train. He had tried that approach and had almost been captured for his pains. His last venture had been ill-starred from the outset, but now he was confident he had a workable plan, both for surviving the winter and for sabotaging the wagon train.

Since leaving St. Joseph, he had encountered bands of Indians from several tribes, and thanks to his ability to speak Kiowan, which all of the Plains nations understood, he had avoided trouble. Now he was driving into territory controlled by the ferocious Cheyenne, who were alleged to be the equals of the dreaded Blackfoot. He hoped the Cheyenne would stop him, for they were part of his plans.

That morning he had been sighted from a distance by a lone warrior, riding bareback, who had watched him across the snow-laden prairie for a time and then had cantered away. The brave had been a Cheyenne, easily identified by his multi-feathered headdress, and Henry expected a return visit at any time. No tribe, the Cheyenne in particular, would be able to resist the temptation of killing a lone white traveler who owned several horses.

The day dragged on. Henry was chilled and wanted to halt to build a fire, but it was wiser not to change his plans at this point. At last his patience was rewarded. He saw four riders in the far distance, all of them moving rapidly toward him.

He halted his wagon team, mounted his riding horse, and waited confidently. Tactics he had used in dealing with other savages would be effective again.

The riders were coming toward him at a breakneck pace, obviously intending to overwhelm him. Holding his rifle across his knees, Henry St. Clair drew a pistol and fired it into the air, then took care to reload it with all possible speed.

As he had anticipated, the riders immediately slowed to a trot and became more cautious. Their headgear told him they were Cheyenne, so he was pleased.

The braves were carrying bows and arrows. They realized, however, that he was carrying a rifle, which had a far greater range, so they conferred on how to subdue this stranger without being hurt themselves.

Henry cut short their talk, astonishing them by raising his right hand in the universal Indian sign of friendship and greeting. "The son of the great sachem," he called at the top of his voice in Kiowan, "bids his brothers of the Cheyenne nation welcome."

His words and his fearless attitude bewildered the warriors, and they inched closer.

Henry had aroused their curiosity, which was precisely what he wanted. Now he had to dispel their suspicions. "The son of the great sachem brings gifts for all," he told them. Reaching into his saddlebag, he withdrew four old pistols, which dated back to the American Revolution. He held them over his head so the warriors could see them.

The Cheyenne, fascinated continued to draw nearer. The black and white streaks of paint smeared on their faces gave them a gruesome appearance.

They were close enough now for Henry to throw each of them a pistol, which he did. Then he repeated his initial gesture of firing one of his own pistols harmlessly into the air. While the warriors continued to observe him closely, he reloaded it. Now came the critical moment: he took a handful of bullets from a pouch and showed them to the Cheyenne.

His pantomime needed no explanation. The braves knew this white man was offering them the magic arrows he used in his firestick. They also knew that, although it would be easy enough to cut down this lone traveler with their spears, they didn't know how to use these powerful, alien weapons.

They had risen to the bait, and Henry became even more confident. "The son of the great sachem across the sea," he told them, "has many firesticks for other Cheyenne. And he will teach them how to shoot."

Greatly impressed, the Cheyenne communicated with each other with gestures.

Then Henry provided the final, clinching argument. He reached into his saddlebag again, and, drawing out a small flask of the cheap whiskey he had procured in St. Joseph, he tossed it to a brave whose intricately fashioned headdress indicated that he was the leader of the group.

The warrior examined the container, frowning in puzzlement as he turned it over in his hands. Then he saw the cork, pulled it out cautiously, and sniffed. Suddenly his stern expression vanished and, grinning broadly, he raised the flask to his mouth and drank. He shuddered in pleasure and passed the flask to the nearest of his companions.

Henry waited patiently until each of the Cheyenne had consumed a portion of the whiskey. There was no doubt in his mind that he would achieve his objective. "The son of the great sachem has drink for all of the braves of the Cheyenne."

The last resistance evaporated. The senior warrior raised his arm and gave the peace sign, and the others followed his example.

The rifle remained in place across Henry's knees as he calmly repeated the sign. He had dealt with too many savages in too many parts of the world to take unnecessary risks.

"Will the son of the great sachem ride to the town of the Cheyenne?" the senior warrior asked.

"It will be a great honor," Henry St. Clair replied gravely. He bent down and picked up the reins of the horses that pulled his wagon, then indicated he was ready to depart.

The Cheyenne formed a protective escort, two riding on the left and the other two on the right as Henry moved ahead, leading the wagon team. Even if they should encounter a war party of another tribe, none would dare attack a man who was enjoying Cheyenne hospitality.

The British agent rejoiced silently. He had found the perfect shelter for himself and his animals and would be safe through the rest of the winter, regardless of whether his hosts lived in huts or tents of skins. And, although the Cheyenne didn't yet know it, they would become his allies and would become the best of all instruments that would destroy the Oregon-bound wagon train.

The latest blizzard was the worst yet, and it raged for seventy-two hours. When the skies cleared, the reflection of the sun was dazzling, and the civilians and soldiers at Fort Madison saw that the snow covering the prairie was at least three feet high, while some drifts were mountainous. Whip predicted there would be a thaw soon, ultimately to be followed by another freeze, and that during the temporary warm spell the snow would melt appreciably. Arnold, Mack, and the army scouts agreed with him.

Until the temperature rose, however, it was impossible for anyone to leave the fort—even to hunt, fish, or gather wood. Now everyone understood why Whip had insisted that large stores of meat and fish be smoked and preserved and why he had demanded that high stacks of wood be cut and stored.

Many people had little to occupy their time. Small children became cranky, crying for no apparent reason, while older boys and girls were mischievous, playing tricks on their elders and trying to blame each other. Men became edgy, and women started to snipe at one another.

Ernie von Thalman, in his capacity as president of the train, was required to act as judge of countless petty disputes. He performed ably, doing what was required of him, but privately told Whip he was weary of senseless, infantile arguments.

No one was more bored than Eulalia Woodling. The young officers of the garrison had discovered, one by one, that she had no real interest in any of them and was flirting with them only for entertainment, so they now tended to avoid her. Members of the wagon train company, who resented her patronizing airs, were polite when necessary but paid her little attention.

The worst of her predicament, in her own eyes, was working as a kitchen assistant. On her father's plantation, all cooking had been done by slaves, and she hadn't even been responsible for planning meals or approving menus. Now, wearing an apron covering dresses that would have been more appropriate at a lawn party than in a frontier fort, she made pancakes by the hundreds, rolled dough for bread, butchered meat, and cleaned winter berries and root vegetables. Eulalia deeply resented the authority exercised by Cathy van Ayl. She was convinced that the other women working in the kitchens were united against her and forced her to perform the most menial tasks.

Her weary father was not sympathetic to what Eulalia regarded as her plight. "We aren't the first people to lose a fortune during hard times," Major Woodling said, "and we won't be the last. You and Claiborne should be glad for the opportunity to make new lives for yourselves. It's for your sakes that I joined this expedition to the Oregon country, and your lack of gratitude and understanding pains me. I know of no reason you should be spared when all the other women are doing their fair share. Besides, you spend only a few hours in the kitchen every day, and the rest of your time is your own, so I can't feel sorry for you."

Unwilling to accept advice that conflicted with her own desires, Eulalia devised a scheme that, she hoped, would win her release from the kitchen detail that she loathed. Perhaps, she thought, if she demonstrated her incompetence, she would be discharged.

She put her plan into operation that same afternoon. Sitting alone in a corner of the kitchen, she paid no attention to the chatter of the others as she peeled potatoes.

There an apron-clad Cathy van Ayl, holding a wooden spoon she used for tasting, came upon her. Stopping and watching her for a few moments, Cathy became irritated. "Really, Eulalia."

"Is something wrong?" Eulalia's wide eyes were innocent.

"Food is our most precious commodity, and we're lucky to have the luxury of enough potatoes for a meal. But look what you're doing to them!" She reached down and picked up a length of peel, to which almost a half-inch of potato still adhered. "This is wasteful. You're throwing away almost as much as you're using."

Eulalia became sullen. "If you don't like what I'm doing, give the work to someone else. You won't hurt my feelings."

Cathy kept a firm grip on her temper. "You've been assigned to the kitchen staff, so we're stuck with each other. I don't enjoy giving orders any more than you like taking them—"

"Oh yes, you do! You just love lording it over me!"

The other women stopped talking and listened to the confrontation.

"What I think or feel isn't important," Cathy said, still speaking quietly. "It's my duty to see that no food is wasted and that our meals are well prepared. I didn't ask for the job. I was given it, and I try to discharge my duties to the best of my ability. I suggest you do the same. Not for my sake but for your own and for the sake of everyone else in the company."

Several of the women nodded in sympathetic agreement.

Their opposition infuriated Eulalia. Not one of them had enjoyed the advantages she had known throughout her childhood. Not one of them had ever lived in a great mansion and had an army of servants to wait on her. Not one had ever owned a huge wardrobe of silk gowns or had been known throughout several counties as a belle. They were jealous of her, and the worst was this blonde who put on airs without cause.

"If I don't peel potatoes to your liking, Miss High and Mighty," she said, "get someone else to do it." She started to rise.

Cathy surprised herself by putting a hand on the girl's shoulder and pushing her back into the chair, then brandishing the wooden spoon only inches from Eulalia's face. "Anyone in this wagon train who wants to eat must do a fair share of the work, and that's final," she said. "If you don't know how to peel potatoes, I'll show you. Watch!" She dropped the spoon onto a counter, snatched the knife from Eulalia, and expertly, swiftly, peeled a potato. "There," she said, "Even a child can do it, and I'm sure you're not all that clumsy."

Reluctantly Eulalia returned to work. That was the end of the unpleasant incident, but the basic problem remained.

The next day Eulalia complained to Whip about her situation, but he firmly rebuffed her. Next she flirted with Dr. Martin, much to Tonie Mell's irritation, but stopped when she realized he was not in a position to help her.

Gradually it dawned on Eulalia that Ernie possessed considerable power and influence because of his position as president, and because he was an Austrian baron, she regarded him as a social equal who should understand her situation. So she went to him. He succeeded in curbing his annoyance at her requests, but nevertheless made it plain that no one was exempt from duties. Girls of thirteen and fourteen were required to perform chores, he told her, and suggested that if she disliked the kitchen so much, she might be able to trade responsibilities with one of the girls who curried and watered the horses. Suspecting that Ernie was laughing at her, Eulalia dropped the subject.

So she continued to work in the kitchen, and the rest

of the time she was restless and bored. She had no interest in sewing or preserving berries, and she shrank from such activities as smoking meat and fish or curing buffalo or deer hides.

Whip was unfailingly courteous to Eulalia because he was polite to all women. However, she was so eager to win approval from men that she misread his attitude and assumed he was interested in her. So she made up her mind to make another attempt to win his support, and this time she planned her campaign with care.

She made it her business to spend at least a few minutes each day chatting with him. Aware of his basic shyness with women, she adopted a subtle approach rather than flirting with him openly. She spoke to him only on matters that she knew were of concern to him, such as his hunting trips, and she made no mention of her own situation. She went out of her way to make certain he was served his favorite cuts of meat at meals.

Cathy knew that Eulalia was making a play for Whip, but she refused to compete. If Whip wanted to develop a closer relationship with her, Cathy told Tonie and Cindy, he would have to do it on his own initiative. Consequently she withdrew even further than she intended or realized: the result was unfortunate. It gave Eulalia an even better chance to strengthen her ties with Whip.

In the days that followed the big blizzard, Whip spent all of his time at the fort, so Eulalia was able to talk with him more frequently. Observing his routines, she discovered that he visited the kitchens late each afternoon, before the cooking staff reported for duty to prepare supper. So she made certain to be the first of the cooks to appear.

Eulalia learned that Whip checked the contents of the cold bins, shelters partly exposed to the winter air, where frozen and smoked meats and fish were stored. It was no accident that he usually arrived just in time to find her braving the elements in the open passageway outside the twin kitchens, taking meat or fish from one of the shelves.

These tactics failed to bring him any closer to her, however. Although he was still pleasant and polite to her, he remained somewhat remote. Eulalia made up her mind to step up the pace of her campaign.

One afternoon, after dressing in one of her prettier frocks and applying cosmetics, she made certain she arrived at the kitchens before he did. She listened for his approaching footsteps, which she recognized, then quickly went out into the freezing passageway and began to tug at a heavy, frozen section of buffalo meat.

The cold chilled her, the frozen meat stung her hands, and she dropped the heavy piece of meat onto the snow underfoot. As a child, she had learned to weep at will when she had wanted something that she could attain in no other way, so when Whip came out into the passageway, he found her shivering in the cold, her cheeks wet. "What's this?"

"I dropped this meat," she sobbed, pointing at it. "I can't leave it on the ground, but it's too heavy for me to carry."

"I see no problem, ma'am," he said, hoisting the section onto his shoulder and carrying it into the kitchen for her.

Eulalia's lashes were still attractively damp, but her smile was radiant as she followed him. "I'm so grateful to you, Mr. Holt," she said fervently.

"I didn't do much of anything," he protested.

"Oh, but you did. You don't understand. I don't know much about cooking, and the women are always teasing me. You've saved me from an unpleasant night. They would have spent our whole time here this evening finding ways to tell me how clumsy I am."

He was embarrassed by her frankness.

Seeing this, Eulalia instantly changed her approach. "If you have a moment to spare, Mr. Holt, perhaps you could help me."

"I'll be glad to try, ma'am."

"Until we came to Fort Madison and the weather turned so cold, I'd never even heard of frozen meat. In fact, I was afraid to eat any of it for days."

"No need to be," he said. "Throw a frozen buffalo steak or a leg of venison on a campfire, and it tastes as fresh as if it had been shot just an hour earlier. What most folks don't know is that frozen meat won't keep long after thaws come. Then, if the weather becomes very cold again, you have to throw it away. Meat that's been frozen twice makes people sick. I learned that from the Cheyenne tribe when I spent a winter with them."

"That's very good to know. I'll remember it." She actually didn't care in the least what they were discussing. "My problem is that I have a dreadful time cutting it. This section is too big to put on a kitchen fire, and it takes forever to thaw. So it has to be butchered now."

"Show me how you do it," Whip said.

Eulalia selected a long knife from a rack and began to saw the hard buffalo meat.

"No wonder it takes you so long. Here, I'll show you." Whip picked up a large cleaver and, wielding it deftly, cut about halfway through the entire section. "That's the first step. Now, try your knife again."

The girl made another attempt to saw. "You see? Nothing happens."

"Your knife is plenty sharp, and the point is just right, but you're using it the wrong way. I'll show you what I mean." Whip placed his hand over Eulalia's. "Push the point into the frozen meat this way, following the seams. As deep as you can. Then slowly push down on the handle so the metal blade digs into the rest of what you're trying to slice."

Eulalia paid scant attention to the instructions. At last she was making progress with this incredibly bashful man. They were standing so close together that their shoulders and hips touched. What's more, whether he knew it or not, he was actually holding her hand!

At that moment Cathy came into the kitchen, saw the couple in what looked like an intimate pose, and stopped short.

"Point and press, point and press," Whip said, unaware of Cathy's presence. "That's all there is to it."

Cathy inadvertently caught her breath. Eulalia turned

for an instant, saw the other girl, and couldn't resist smiling in triumph. Cathy picked up her skirts and swept out of the kitchen, her head high.

"Now you try it by yourself," Whip said, not aware that Cathy had entered and left the kitchen.

Trying to concentrate for his sake, Eulalia made an attempt to cut the meat alone.

"That's better. Keep practicing, and you'll soon get the hang of it."

"Thank you, Mr. Holt," she said. "You'll never know how much these few minutes have meant to me."

He thought her expression of appreciation was overdone, but decided that was just her way of talking. "Glad to oblige, ma'am," he said.

Going back out to the passageway, Whip checked the contents of the bins, then went back inside by way of the other, adjoining kitchen.

He went through to the corridor beyond it and there came face to face with Cathy. Why, he wondered, was her only greeting an icy glare?

The thaws came, as those experienced with plains winters had predicted, and vast quantities of snow melted. The weather gradually became colder again, but it was now possible for men to penetrate the forest, either on horseback or on foot. Early one morning several parties of hunters left the fort. Meat supplies were shrinking, Whip said, and needed to be replenished. Even Ted Woods was pressed into service because his great strength would speed the process of hoisting the carcasses of game onto the backs of pack horses. So Hosea was alone in the blacksmith's shop, where he busied himself at his miniature forge.

In late morning a visitor arrived, riding a gelding and leading two pack horses. His name, he told the officer of the guard, was Emmett Watson, and he had business with the wagon train company. He was admitted to the fort and taken to the section occupied by the future Oregon settlers.

Dr. Martin was busy in the infirmary, and both Whip and Ernie had gone hunting, so he was received by the two oldest men on hand, Nat Drummond and Major Woodling. Watson, who was husky, bearded and fair-haired, was disappointed when he learned that neither the wagonmaster nor the president of the company was on hand. He preferred, he said, not to discuss his business with anyone else.

The noon meal was about to be served, and since so many of the men were hunting, everyone who had stayed behind could be accommodated in one dining room. Watson was invited as a matter of course to stay for the meal, and he quickly accepted, going into the dining room with Major Woodling while Nat moved off to join his wife.

"You're a Southerner, judging by your accent," the Major said.

"I make my home in Georgia, sir. But I travel all over the United States. This trip, I must admit, is the longest I've made." Watson kept an eye on the door and stiffened when Hosea came into the dining room, but he made no comment.

The main course consisted of a thick soup, made of beans and buffalo meat flavored with wild onions, one of the company's favorites. Major Woodling, enjoying the dish, noticed that the visitor continued to watch Hosea, who sat on the far side of the dining hall.

"This isn't bad," Watson said. "But I'd give my soul for a bowl of real gumbo. Well, it won't be long before I'm eating it again."

The Major made a shrewd guess. Although they were sitting by themselves at one end of a long table, he lowered his voice. "You're a bounty hunter," he said.

The man made no attempt to deny it. "Does it show all that much?"

"Only to me, I imagine," the Major replied, smiling. "I lived my whole life in South Carolina before I came on this expedition. Whenever one of my slaves ran away, I hired somebody like you to find him and bring him back."

"I've spent a half-year on the trail of that one," Watson said, his voice quietly menacing as he nodded in the direction of Hosea. "He's led me one merry chase."

"Six months." The Major was musing. "He must be valuable."

"His master is paying me twenty-five hundred dollars, plus all my expenses, to return him alive."

"That's a small fortune."

"So it is, but this one is no ordinary slave. They claim he's very clever."

"Indeed he is," Woodling agreed.

"What's more, his master owns a very large plantation, and he's afraid he'll lose many more slaves unless this one is returned. So the bounty is cheap in the long run."

"You're not going to earn it," Major Woodling said.

Watson eyed him.

"Hosea is enormously popular with everybody on the expedition. He has more than made himself useful. He's made some valuable contributions to the company's welfare, and he's regarded as a free man."

"Is that the way you regard him, sir?"

Major Woodling was uncomfortable. "The way I feel doesn't matter. There are hundreds of people in this group, and if a vote were taken, I'm sure it would be unanimous in Hosea's favor."

"Nobody has asked for a vote," Watson said, and ate the rest of his meal in glum silence.

People began to file out of the dining hall, Hosea among them, but Major Woodling continued to sit with the visitor. "There's no chance that Whip Holt, who's the wagonmaster, or Baron von Thalman, our president, will agree to let you take that black man away with you."

"I don't plan to ask them," Watson said. "Where do you suppose he's going now?"

The Major hesitated, and there was a long silence.

"You claim you're a Southerner and that you owned a plantation," Emmett Watson said. "I don't want your active help. I wouldn't even think of asking for it. I know you've got to live with these people, that they're going to be your neighbors in Oregon. All I want from you is a simple answer to a simple question."

Woodling stared down at the table, looking ashamed. "He spends most of his time in the blacksmith's shop."

"Where's that?"

"In back of the main buildings, near the stables."

Watson stood and held out his hand. "I'm glad to have made your acquaintance, sir," he said. "If you ever come back and have a need for my services, my partners and I have our office in Savannah. Anybody there will tell you where to find me." He strolled away, looking unconcerned.

Major Woodling sat at the table for a long time, his face buried in his hands.

Eulalia saw him and came to him. "What's wrong, Papa?" she wanted to know.

"I have a touch of indigestion, that's all," he told her harshly. "I'm going to lie down for a spell."

She watched him as he left the dining hall, his face averted.

At least an hour later, Danny and Chet returned from the lake, where they had been fishing. Their catch filled a large basket, which was so heavy that both boys had to carry it to the kitchens.

"We lost a lot of our hooks today," Chet said.

"If Hosea isn't too busy, maybe he'll make some more for us. Come on." Danny led the way to the black-smith's shop. There they found a small fire burning, but Hosea was nowhere to be seen.

"I'll wait here for him," Danny said. "Why don't you see if you can find him somewhere in the fort?"

Chet agreed and dashed away.

Danny wandered around the shop, looking at a set of horseshoes Ted had just made, and pausing to admire some metal arrowheads that Hosea had fashioned for Stalking Horse. Then something on the Ashanti's work-table caught his eye, and he picked it up.

It was a partly eaten chunk of a sugar confection known as a praline, and without thinking, he raised it to his mouth, then stopped himself. Holding it there, he reminded himself that the praline was Hosea's, not his. All at once he realized it had a disagreeable odor, and still holding it, he stared at it. It certainly didn't smell like sugar.

He was still holding it when Chet returned.

"I can't find him anywhere, Danny. There was a visitor

177

here earlier in the day, and the last anybody knows, he was on his way out here to see Hosea. My mother and one of my brothers saw the man."

"Smell this," Danny said, and handed him the praline. "I found it on Hosea's worktable."

Chet held it beneath his nose, inhaled deeply, and then sniffed more cautiously. "This is strange. It smells like the medicine we had to give Pa when he was so sick. He took it every single day before he died; it's a smell I'll never forget."

"What did the medicine do for him?"

"It was supposed to make him hurt less. I'm not sure it did him much good, but it sure did make him sleep." All at once Chet realized what he had said and stared at his friend.

"It's a drug!" Danny exclaimed.

"Do you reckon this stranger used it to put Hosea to sleep? Why would he do that?"

"He's gone, isn't he? We'd better see the officer of the watch!"

The boys sprinted to the front gate of the fort, paying no attention to the slush through which they had to wade. There the officer of the watch confirmed that the visitor who had arrived earlier in the day had already departed, his pack horses heavily laden.

"Which way did he go?" Chet demanded.

The young lieutenant shrugged, indicating that he hadn't noticed and didn't care.

Chet thrust the piece of praline into his shirt pocket and spoke frantically. "Danny, we got to find Whip— fast!"

They raced to the rear of the fort, ran into the open, toward the forest. Melting snow impeded their progress, and they stumbled and slipped frequently, sometimes falling. But they refused to slow their pace. Although they were breathless, once they were in the forest, they shouted Whip's name again and again. The forest remained silent.

The boys moved deeper and deeper into the woods, not knowing how much time was passing, and after an eternity, they heard an answering shout. Soon an angry

Stalking Horse came into view, leading his pony. "Why boys make noise?" he demanded. "Deer run away!"

In their excitement, they spoke simultaneously.

The Cherokee raised a hand to silence them, then pointed an accusing finger at Danny. The boy explained until his breath failed, and then Chet took up the narrative, concluding by taking the partly consumed praline from his pocket.

Stalking Horse's eyes narrowed, but his expression did not change. "Man put Hosea to sleep? Steal Hosea and go away?" he asked incredulously.

"That has to be what happened," Chet replied.

"Right," Danny added. "Hosea isn't in the fort. And the last anybody knows, the visitor was going out to the blacksmith's shop."

"My ma and brother saw them," Chet said. "We talked to the officer of the watch, and he told us the visitor is gone. He only stayed a few hours, and that's mighty peculiar all by itself."

"He was riding one horse, and he had two pack horses, piled up with bundles. You know how little Hosea is. He could have been inside one of the bundles." Danny was still in a frenzy.

The Cherokee's eyes glittered, and he took charge. "Boys go back to fort. Wait for Whip, then tell. Stalking Horse go now. Find Hosea. Bring back." He leaped onto the bare back of his small mount, and the animal started off through the melting snow and slush.

The Indian had no intention of returning to Fort Madison; he wanted to waste no time. Going around the fort rather than through it, he halted outside the main gate, facing the Platte River, and studied the ground, searching for prints in the rapidly melting snow.

Stalking Horse proceeded methodically. There was virtually no chance that the man who had abducted Hosea had crossed the river, which was overflowing its banks. The Platte was filled with rapidly moving ice floes, and no one trying to handle three horses would be able to cross it safely. No man in his right mind would try.

Logic dictated that the kidnapper was more likely to have taken his victim in the direction of the white man's civilization rather than out across the endless plains. So Stalking Horse first searched the ground that extended eastward. Crouching and moving slowly, he carefully studied the snow, ice, and slush. Nothing escaped his notice. He covered one hundred feet, then another hundred, but did not pause.

Something off to his right, a few yards from the waters of the swollen river caught his eye. He went to the spot at once, squatted, and looked more closely. There, in the melting ice, was a partly obliterated hoof print, a portion of the mark made by a metal horseshoe still visible. It was the only sign he needed.

Now he understood the kidnapper's tactics. The man was riding close to the water's edge deliberately, in the hope that the overflowing waters of the Platte would wash away his trail. Clever, but not quite clever enough.

Mounting his pony again, Stalking Horse rode eastward at a canter, staying close to the bank of the river. Unless the abductor knew the area intimately, he would use the river as his guide, at least for a time.

Dusk came, and Stalking Horse slowed his mount to a walk, waiting for night. The sky overhead was clear, he noted. That was all to the good. A three-quarter moon would be a great help.

Now that the sun had vanished, the weather was growing colder again, and the Cherokee grunted in quiet satisfaction. The slush and melting snow were starting to freeze. Within an hour it would be impossible to hide hoofprints. And the ice floes continued to move swiftly toward the junction of the Platte with the Missouri some fifty miles away, so there was virtually no possibility that the man would try to cross to the south bank.

Stalking Horse grunted again when the moon rose. The ice was becoming slippery, so he moved farther from the river bank, certain that his quarry would be obliged to do the same.

The moon rose higher, and suddenly the Cherokee dismounted. There was no need for him to bend low now as he studied the ground. He could make out the hoofprints of three horses, two of them the huge beasts that white men used to pull their wagons and freight carts.

He knew beyond all doubt now that he was on the trail of the right person.

He checked his bow, which he replaced over his shoulder, then touched the point of his knife with his fingertip. He was in no hurry now. A tracker traveling alone and unencumbered could move far more rapidly than a man burdened with a prisoner and two pack horses. The moonlight was sufficiently clear for Stalking Horse to easily follow the trail in the snow. He was relaxed but alert, conscious of the possibility that he could overtake the bounty hunter and his victim at any time.

Another hour passed, however, before the sound of a man's voice somewhere ahead told him that he had reached the end of the trail. Apparently the man had made camp for the night. The voice rolled on, but the Cherokee couldn't yet make out what was being said.

Now Stalking Horse saw three horses, tied to trees, and he made a wide detour around them, then dismounted, telling his superbly trained pony with a double pat on the neck not to wander away.

Now the man's voice was clearer. "Damn you," he said. "You've got to eat, or you won't live long enough to get back to Georgia. I tell you plain, I'm going to collect that bounty, so you'll eat if I have to cram the food into you."

The man was crouching with his back to the Indian, speaking to Hosea. The Ashanti was propped in a sitting position against a saddlebag, his hands and feet tightly bound.

The moonlight enabled Stalking Horse to see that his friend's expression was indifferent. Apparently he was still under the influence of the drug.

Nevertheless, Hosea was conscious. He heard the Indian, a sound his captor failed to discern, and for an instant, he raised his eyes. No recognition showed in them, but he lowered his gaze again so swiftly that Stalking Horse knew Hosea realized that help was at hand.

The distance between the Indian and his quarry was so short that it was impractical to fire an arrow. Stalking Horse silently laid his bow and quiver on a snowbank, then reached for his knife.

181

Watson was holding a chunk of dried beef in front of his prisoner's face, waving it angrily as he tried to force the captive to eat.

Hosea was sufficiently recovered from the effects of the sleeping potion to cooperate actively with Stalking Horse. He had been on the verge of giving in to the demands that he eat, but now he stubbornly closed his mouth and clenched his teeth.

The bounty hunter cursed him, then pressed the fingers of one hand against the sides of his captive's cheeks in an attempt to force his mouth open. At that instant Stalking Horse leaped across the intervening space, his upraised knife ready to strike.

Watson had not achieved success in his unpleasant trade by being unaware. Instinct told him he was being attacked from the rear, and he rolled to one side. Stalking Horse brushed against him, but the full impact of the collision was lost, and it was impossible for the Cherokee to wield his knife.

All he succeeded in doing was toppling the helpless Hosea onto his side. Because of his bonds, the Ashanti found it extremely difficult to struggle back to a sitting position.

Watson started to reach for the pistol he carried in his belt, but Stalking Horse knew, once his initial rush had failed, precisely how his foe would react. Unable to use his knife for the moment because he had thrown himself out of position, Stalking Horse reached out with his free hand, caught hold of the bounty hunter's nose and simultaneously tried to jam his fingers into the man's eyes.

Unaccustomed to this primitive but effective form of attack, Watson emitted a scream of pain and rage as he groped in vain for his pistol. Then the Cherokee's knee landed with full force in his groin. The bounty hunter doubled over.

He was immobilized for no more than a second or two, however, and Stalking Horse realized his first move must be to disarm the man. He took hold of the pistol and managed to yank it out of the man's broad belt. Having used firearms only infrequently, he threw it aside.

It landed on the ground only inches from Hosea. But Hosea, unable to free his wrists, was powerless.

Again Stalking Horse struck with his knife, but Watson caught hold of his attacker's wrist with one hand, and with the other he punched him in the face.

It had been a long time since Stalking Horse had utilized the techniques he had been taught as a boy by the senior warriors of his nation. Now he smashed a knee into the pit of his foe's stomach, then raised a foot and brought his heel down with hammerlike force. It caught Watson on the kneecap. The pain was excruciating, and the bounty hunter fell back onto the ice, releasing his grip.

Now Stalking Horse was free to use his knife, but to the surprise of the still helpless Hosea, he didn't drive it into the white man's body. The little Ashanti thought he was must be dreaming as he watched a scene that no man could have predicted.

Stalking Horse had chosen to fight in the style of the whites rather than his own people. Hauling the bounty hunter to his feet, the Cherokee battered him with punches, smashing his face and body with a succession of blinding lefts and rights.

The bounty hunter made an attempt to protect himself and fight back, but he was bloodied and groggy. The few punches that Watson managed to land were feeble and meaningless.

At last the punishment he received was more than he could tolerate, and he sank to the ground, unable to move. Stalking Horse quickly picked up his knife and severed Hosea's bonds. Then he took the same rawhide thongs and used them to secure Watson's ankles and tie his hands behind his back. In a final gesture of contempt, he propped the man in the same sitting position against the saddlebag lying on the ground that he had used as a cushion for Hosea.

Hosea managed to drag himself to his feet, but the effects of the drug had not yet worn off, and he wobbled in a precarious circle as he tried to walk. It was obvious to Stalking Horse that the Ashanti could not return to

Fort Madison on foot. He was still too weak. Picking up his friend, the Cherokee put him in the saddle on the back of the bounty hunter's gelding.

Then he mounted his own pony and picked up the gelding's reins. As a final gesture, he took up the reins of the two pack horses, too.

Watson realized he was being abandoned to his fate in the wilderness. He was being left with no mount, no supplies. Even if he managed to loosen his bonds, he would be forced to make his way back to civilization alone and on foot through hard-packed snow. And there was always the strong possibility that he would be attacked and killed by braves of the Omaha nation that patrolled the area.

"You can't leave me here to die!" he said in desperation, his speech thick because his lips were swollen and split.

Stalking Horse raised a hand in salute, then started off in the direction of Fort Madison. He had lived his whole life in a world where mercy to a defeated foe was unknown, and he felt only contempt for the man who had kidnapped his friend.

Hosea was too dizzy to look back; he clung to the saddle as his Indian friend led him back to safety and a future as a free man.

Watson heard the sound of hoofbeats growing fainter. He was alone in the snow and ice, struggling feebly to break his bonds, his own future sealed.

VIII

Spring came early and unexpectedly to the Great Plains. Little by little the weather became warmer during the last few days in March, and a week later the snow had virtually disappeared. Soon a pale green mantle of young grass began to spread across the vast prairie.

One of the first to be affected was Cathy van Ayl. After supervising the preparation of breakfast one morning in early April, she climbed the stairs to an empty watchtower and stepped into the open. She didn't quite know what had impelled her to come here, but the sun was gentle, its warmth covering and soothing her, and she sighed aloud.

The sight of the new grass extending as far as she could see was a startling sight. A wave of homesickness swept over her.

In her native Connecticut the oaks and maples would be budding now, bushes that had been brown and inert would be coming to life, and the apple trees in the orchard behind the house would be showing the first signs of green on their new branches. On Long Island, the earth would have a sweet smell and the new owners of her farm would be planting beans, squash, lettuce, cucumbers, and sweet corn. Flounder would be starting to appear in Long Island Sound, and within a few months great schools of bluefish would provide food for everyone. Even now there would be clams, oysters, and crabs waiting to be plucked from the sea. How she missed that world she had left behind.

And yet, in spite of her regrets and her desire to look back, she found herself staring hardest toward the West, the land of her future. Oregon still lay half a continent away, but in her new mood she felt confident she could make the journey. Certainly after all these months at Fort Madison, the Great Plains were no longer alien and frightening to her. Their very size inspired awe, and now that the land was turning green, it reminded her of the ocean she loved.

Yes, she told herself, there is beauty here. Perhaps she had been clinging to her love of home because the future she faced was so uncertain. Now, with the sun smiling from a cloudless sky and with the earth itself coming to life, something within her stirred. Perhaps it was the spirit of spring, perhaps it was something more.

She thought for a time, enjoying the warmth of the sun's rays, and all at once she knew. The Great Plains, like the Connecticut and Long Island she had left behind, like Oregon that lay beyond the horizon, were part of America. All of it was her land, all of it was her home.

That knowledge strengthened her resolve.

"When are we leaving?" she asked Whip later that day.

"Spring is giving you itchy feet," he said, grinning broadly. "Me, too."

"I'm ready," Cathy said, and at that moment she left the last of her idealistic, romantic dreams behind her. She was a woman meeting the frontier on its own terms, realistically prepared for new hardships because the goal she and her companions sought was worth any struggle.

"If the weather stays like this," Whip told Colonel Jonathan, "we'll soon be on our way."

Preparations for the journey to the Pacific became more intense. Axles and wheel hubs were greased, the floors of wagons were checked carefully, and those planks that had rotted during the harsh winter were replaced. Women devoted themselves to repairing rips and holes in

186

the canvas covers of their wagons. Ted Woods received so many requests for new metal wheel rims that he was swamped, and Hosea pitched in to help him fill the orders.

The hunters and fishermen stepped up the pace of their activities, too, and there was considerable excitement when Mack Dougall reported that he had sighted a herd of buffalo grazing on the new prairie grass just beyond the forest. Whip was eager to add to the store of smoked and dried meat before the trek was resumed. The army garrison was in need of more food, too, so a hunting party was formed, the regiment's scouts joining the civilians.

Thirty hunters were in the group that left Fort Madison early the next morning. They skirted the western edge of the forest and after about two hours they reached the prairie. Whip moved up to the head of the column to join Mack, who was acting as the guide. The sun was pleasantly warm, in spite of a cool breeze from the Rockies, and there seemed to be an elasticity to the drying ground. The men were in high spirits.

Late in the morning Mack sighted the buffalo herd not far from the place where he had seen them the previous afternoon. The beasts were still grazing peacefully, and Whip estimated that there were three to four hundred head in the herd. The buffalo were hungry so they continued to eat, and there was no indication they might stampede. Whip motioned for the group to move still closer. With luck they could bring down a good food supply before the beasts were aware of their danger and raced away.

Suddenly Stalking Horse pointed to the north. "Omaha," he said.

The men stared and could make out a party of at least fifty mounted warriors also riding toward the buffalo. It appeared that they, too, needed to replenish their meat supplies.

The Omaha edged slightly closer to the white men but continued to ride in the direction of the herd without slackening their pace.

Many of the men grew tense. They had heard that the Omaha were belligerent, refusing to acknowledge the peace offers that Colonel Jonathan had sent them, and some of the troops had told hair-raising stories about encounters with them. No one knew whether the stories were true that the Omaha tortured a white captive for days, scalping him before allowing him to die, and no one wanted to find out.

Whip remained complacent, however, and Stalking Horse, Arnold, and Mack were equally unperturbed, as were the army scouts. Like the band of Omaha, they continued to ride toward the buffalo.

"We're outnumbered!" an anxious Claiborne Woodling declared. "We've got to protect ourselves."

No one replied, but one of the army scouts snickered.

The young man moved up to the head of the column. "Whip," he said, "you're going to attack first, aren't you?"

"I don't aim to attack anybody," Whip replied calmly. "I came out looking for buffalo. I found them, and that's good enough for me."

"My God!" Claiborne's temper began to flare. "You heard Stalking Horse say those braves are Omaha. Sure, we have rifles and they don't, but if they're just half as mean as I've heard, they can kill and wound a lot of us before we drive them off."

"Sonny," Arnold said gently, "leave be."

Claiborne's anger increased. "Maybe all of you are afraid of the Omaha and don't think you can drive them off, but I'm not built that way!" He raised his rifle and began to take aim at the moving line of warriors.

Whip reacted instantly. Grasping his own rifle by the barrel and wielding it like a club, he struck the younger man's rifle so hard with the butt that the weapon fell to the ground, forcing the column to halt.

"Never open fire until you're given the order," Whip said in a mild tone of voice that belied his anger and the violence of his act.

A red-faced Claiborne dismounted, retrieved his rifle, and returned to the saddle.

"Those of you who are worried can just sit back in your saddles," Whip declared, raising his voice so everyone in the party could hear him. "The Omaha aren't on the warpath any more than we are. At this time of the year, after game has been scarce through the winter, they're more interested in hides than in scalps. Just pretend you don't even see them, and we'll have no problems."

Claiborne still was not satisfied. "Then why do they keep moving closer to us?"

"We're about to do the same," Whip said, and nodded to Arnold.

Arnold immediately rode off toward the south. The army scouts, Stalking Horse, and Mack followed him, and soon they moved into a formation parallel to each other.

"We're forming a single line now," Whip explained. "The Omaha are doing likewise. Between the two groups, we'll make a semicircle to prevent the buffalo from heading back this way when the shooting starts. If we don't bag enough game before they panic, it will be easier to follow them than to meet their charge."

It was inconceivable to Claiborne that the wagon train hunters and the Omaha warriors could be working together without either group acknowledging the other's presence. But that was precisely what was happening. Whip took the innermost position at the right end of the line. As he moved into place, the senior Omaha warrior shifted into the position adjoining his, less than a stone's throw away. The two leaders studiously ignored each other and both concentrated on the buffalo.

The attack on the herd was coordinated in the same uncanny manner. "Get ready," Whip called. "We're going to open fire soon."

As he spoke, the senior warrior raised an arm in a signal to his own party. Both groups simultaneously slowed their pace. Then Whip raised his rifle, and the senior warrior aimed an arrow. "Fire!" Whip called, and as the rifles discharged a volley, the Omaha sent a stream of arrows into the herd.

Both groups continued to advance, shooting as rapidly as they could.

A large number of buffalo, most of them bulls but a few of them cows and calves, fell to the groud before the herd quite knew what was happening. Then a mature bull took command and raced westward. In almost no time, the surviving members of the herd fell into place behind him. The stampede was under way.

But the men from the wagon train continued to press forward for a few more minutes, as did the Omaha. Whip was the first to call a halt, and shortly thereafter the Omaha pulled to a stop, too. Dead buffalo littered the ground.

Then the task of removing the skins and butchering the carcasses began. The men of both parties dismounted. There was enough game available so the two groups remained on either side of an invisible but definite line. The inexperienced members of the wagon train had the feeling that if just one man of either group stepped over that line, a wild battle would begin.

But no man stepped over the line, and no battle was even contemplated. Mack rode back to Fort Madison to summon several drivers and their wagons, and the warriors did not even glance in his direction as he galloped off.

The unrepentant Claiborne, forced to do his share of the dirty and unpleasant work of butchering, was the only man who seemed even remotely conscious of the presence of enemies on the prairie. The rest of the wagon train party followed Whip's example and concentrated on the task at hand.

Even when Mack returned, leading two wagons to the site, the Omaha stolidly continued to mind their own business. More experienced than the Oregon-bound settlers, they were finished first. Lacking the convenience of wagons, they hung their game on either side of their heavily burdened ponies and rode away toward the east, skirting the forest as they headed back to their own villages. After they had gone, some of the wagon train men mentioned that they felt as though they had been dreaming. The meeting still seemed unreal.

"From now on, we're going to see plenty of Indians," Whip said, "so let this be a lesson to all of you. When a brave minds his own business, do the same thing. Always wait until he proves to be unfriendly before you go after him. And when you do shoot, make sure your aim is accurate!"

For several days everyone at Fort Madison ate fresh buffalo meat. Meanwhile every available man and boy went to work smoking some of the meat and packing the rest in barrels filled with a mixture of salt and vinegar. The regiment took its fair share, and Whip was pleased to discover that the wagon train's portion was large enough for him to give each family a barrel of pickled meat as well as a smoked shoulder or hind quarter. What with more game moving into the prairie, where the grass steadily grew higher, it was certain that no one would starve during the spring, summer, and autumn to come.

Canvas roofing was taken out of storage, spread on the wagons, and then made secure. The people began their final task of moving their personal belongings from the fort back into the wagons where they would once again have to live.

On their last day at the fort, Whip wrote a letter to President Van Buren and one to former President Andrew Jackson, whose idea it had been to send the wagon train to the Oregon country hoping to strengthen the United States's claim. Whip also wrote to Sam Brentwood and considerately told Cathy that if she wanted to write to her sister, he would see to it that the letter was included in the packet that an army courier would carry.

In his letter to Sam Brentwood, Whip wrote with candor to his old friend and one-time fellow mountain man who was responsible for his role in the wagon train adventure.

By now the tenderfeet are getting calluses on their hoofs. The wild stallions and a few stray mares who were trying to break out of the corral are broken to saddles. I'm not saying there won't be stampedes now and again, but I'm keeping the herd under control.

I couldn't operate without Stalking Horse. And Ernie is the best president the company could have elected.

We're in for some rough times when we come across some of the mean Plains tribes, but I'm not alarming anybody just yet. We'll take our troubles one at a time.

Give my regards to your wife and tell her that her sister is surely a fine lady. She does her work, she never complains, and she inspires many of the other women. There are times I don't believe she likes me much, but I can't blame her. I never had much to do with ladies, and I can see in her face that sometimes I offend her without meaning to. Don't bet either way on whether she'll be speaking to me by the time we reach Oregon.

His letter to Martin Van Buren was formal.

I beg to report, Mr. President, that all goes well with us. As you've already heard from me, we now number almost five hundred persons, all in reasonably good health. Most are eager to go on with our journey. Like it or not, there's no turning back.

I reckon the War Department has shown you Colonel Jonathan's full report on our brush with an Imperial Russian agent. No harm was done, but we're keeping our powder dry. So far we have had no more trouble with the British, but we're alert to the danger and can deal with it.

God willing, we should reach Oregon next year. I hope we'll hit our goal of arriving at the mouth of the Columbia River by the early autumn of 1839 or thereabouts, if not sooner.

So far there's no need for military reinforcement, but I'll pass along the word in a hurry if a bad crisis develops.

In his communication to former President Andrew Jackson, Whip expressed the sentiments closest to his heart.

Not a day passes, General, but I wish you were making this trip with us. Every time I shoot a buffalo or meet up with ornery Indians or have a tangle with renegades, I think of you. I know how much you would enjoy this great trek.

It isn't all adventure and excitement, of course. I never let myself forget that we've got to beat the English and get to the Oregon country first. For all I know, they're sending a wagon train across Canada to get there first. If they are, put your bets on me, even though I don't know anything about diplomacy. I keep remembering what you said one time, that the best diplomacy comes out of the muzzle of a rifle.

What surprises me is that leading a wagon train can be such a heavy responsibility. I try to live up to it.

When we first talked about it, I didn't give much thought to the people. Now they are in my mind all the time. Most of them have strong guts and high spirits. They don't let bad happenings discourage them. All the same, they're civilians, not soldiers, and I know that often they're terrified, so scared they don't know what to do.

I can feel, in a very small way, how you must have felt when you were President. I not only have to look out for these folks and set an example for them, but I have to be father and mother to them, too. They depend on me for everything. A few natural leaders have been developing, but they don't know the country (except for a couple of old scouts, men you'd like to know).

Some days, and I'm sure you'll know what I mean, I feel like riding off by myself and never coming back to the train. I can't do that, of course, and I won't. Some nights I feel fifty years older, and for a man who has always been proud of his stamina, I get an ache in my legs I've never had before.

But what we're doing is worth all the effort and danger and hardship. The names of the folks in this train may not be written in the history books of the future, but they're going to make your dream come true. Thanks to them, America will stretch from the Atlantic to the Pacific. I'm proud to be one of them.

Cathy van Ayl's letter to her sister was personal.

Claudia dear, your baby sister is growing up. I have no choice, really, and I'm finding that being an adult has its advantages.

I've stopped being homesick for Connecticut and mooning over the Long Island farm. For some reason I don't understand, this wilderness no longer frightens me the way it did. Don't think I'm all that brave, of course. I am afraid, sometimes. But I see how good-humored all the people are (well, most of them, not including a newcomer who I think you met, that horrid Eulalia Woodling). They put up with so much; this journey would try the soul of a saint, but they're cheerful, and even the smallest children show great courage.

Cindy has become my good friend. Tonie is wonderful, as she has always been. I miss you badly, but they help cushion my loss.

I know that you and Sam have been hoping that Whip Holt and I would get together, but don't set your hearts on it, dear. You were none too subtle in hinting, and at the time I was inclined to agree with you, but now I'm not so sure.

Not that I dislike Whip in the least. On the contrary, I find him fascinating. I wouldn't have thought that someone who appears so simple on the surface could be so complex. He really cares about the people on this train, although he tries not to show it. I guess he's embarrassed by the idea of showing even a little of what he feels. At least that's the way I interpret him.

He's the most infuriating man I've ever known. One day he's kind and considerate, actually sweet. The very next day he becomes so remote that he doesn't know I exist. He's so frustrating.

I've met no one else who really interests me. Most of the new people (they aren't all that new any more) who joined us at Independence are married already.

All I know is that, although I'd prefer to be married than stay single, I have no intention of making the kind of mistake I made when I married Otto. As Cindy says, and she's right, no man is better than the wrong man. I've learned that lesson, and I intend to abide by it.

Civilians and soldiers mingled that night at a final celebration supper. The women who worked in the kitchen baked dozens of cakes in honor of the occasion. Drinking was strictly forbidden on government property, but glasses of dandelion wine appeared rather mysteriously, and Colonel Jonathan took care not to notice them.

A final breakfast was eaten before dawn the next morning. Then pots and pans, dishes and knives were packed, and bedding was carried out to the wagons.

"I wish I had a troop or two of cavalry to send with you as escorts, at least as far as the Rockies," Colonel Jonathan told Whip as they shook hands in the clearing behind the main buildings of the fort. "This was a rough winter, so the Indians are going to be rambunctious, and you'll need all the help you can get."

"We'll get along on our own," Whip replied, feeling as confident as he sounded.

"I hope so."

"We'll have to, Colonel. There's little choice."

Tonie Mell, wearing her buckskins for the first time in weeks, rode up to Whip, smiling broadly. "Everybody is set and raring to go," she said.

He quietly mounted his stallion and rode to the open rear gate of Fort Madison. "We're Oregon bound," he said, but his voice was so soft that only Cathy, who sat with Hosea on the boards of her lead wagon, was able to hear him.

No band played as the wagon train moved out and resumed the long trek along the north bank of the swiftly flowing Platte River, but the train made its own music. Harnesses creaked, and the hoofs of workhorses and oxen provided a background rhythm. Wheels squealed until the grease worked its way in, and occasionally objects that had been insecurely packed inside wagons clattered as they fell to the floor.

Tonie brought up the rear, waiting until the wagons moved into the three-column formation that had become so familiar to everyone the previous autumn. As she turned in her saddle to wave a final farewell to the officers and soldiers gathered in the clearing, two seven-inch cannon boomed, their roar echoing across the Great Plains, bidding farewell to the pioneers.

Progress that first day was slow, as Whip had anticipated. The work horses and oxen had received too little exercise through the winter, and consequently were out of practice; they had also eaten well and were fat and lazy. People took too long to unhitch their teams and then hitch them up again after the midday break. The scouts returned early to report that all was well, as they had known it would be so close to Fort Madison. When a halt was called that day and the wood- and water-gathering details went to work, Whip estimated they had covered only seven miles. But he wasn't worried. He knew that the wagons would increase their speed little by little as members of the company got back in stride.

Everyone had been in good health for at least a week, and that first evening only Eulalia Woodling excused herself from work as a cook and went to Dr. Martin's wagon.

"I'm feeling poorly," she told him.

Bob Martin thought she looked radiantly healthy, but nevertheless took her into the wagon, which was used as a traveling infirmary, and asked her to lie down on the cot.

Eulalia stretched sensually as she lowered herself on the cot.

"What seems to be the matter?" the physician asked, placing a hand on her forehead and assuring himself that she was not running a fever.

"I'm not sure."

"What are your symptoms?" he asked patiently.

"Well, I keep thinking I may faint," Eulalia told him, managing to flirt with him as he studied her.

He had a hunch she was malingering. "Sit up, please." He held out a hand to help her rise to a sitting position, and Eulalia clung to his hand while he examined the pupils of her violet eyes.

At that moment Tonie came in through the open flap, intending to resume her practice of helping the physician after her own day's work was done. Bob stood with his back to her, but she saw Eulalia grasping his hand and looking soulfully at him. Quickly and silently, she retreated.

There was one sure way of finding out whether his diagnosis was right, the doctor thought. He went to a chest at the far end of the wagon, unlocked it, searched through drawers filled with powders, elixirs, and other medicines until he found what he wanted. Fashioning a cone out of a small sheet of paper, he poured something into it, then closed and locked the chest.

"Take this in a cup of hot water," he said. "Make certain the water is boiling when you pour it into the cup and let this substance soak for about five minutes. Then drink all of the brew."

"What is it, Doctor?" She managed to look attractive even when she was apprehensive.

"An herb tea that should cure your condition. If you need more, don't hesitate to come back." As he escorted her firmly to the rear flap, he was willing to wager that she would enjoy a remarkably rapid recovery. She would indeed be drinking an herb tea, as he had told her, but he had deliberately refrained from mentioning that the brew was bitter, difficult to swallow, and left a thoroughly unpleasant aftertaste. It was a prescription frequently used to effect rapid cures in people suffering from imaginary ailments.

Eulalia thanked him profusely before making her way back to her own wagon, her hips swaying just enough to insure that he continued to watch her.

The doctor was watching her, all right, but she wouldn't have been flattered by his thoughts. Smiling slightly and shaking his head, he reflected that he had never known a more badly spoiled, self-centered young lady. Perhaps the right man could tame her and bring her to her senses, but he had no intention of becoming that man.

Meantime, a furious Tonie had stormed off to the cooking fire, and there she found Cathy. "A few weeks ago you wanted to kill that woman," she said, "and I wish you had!"

Cathy had rarely seen her friend so angry. "Eulalia?"

"Who else? Don't blame Whip for letting her confuse him. No man on this expedition is immune!" Still spluttering, Tonie related what she had just seen.

"Perhaps it didn't mean as much as you think," Cathy said.

"I reckon it means as much—or as little—as her flirtation with Whip in the kitchen. I keep trying and trying to get Bob to look at me, but nothing happens. I guess I'll have to develop a Southern drawl and some bold manners!"

Cindy, who was working on the other side of Cathy, had been listening quietly. Now she dried her hands on her apron, took Tonie firmly by the arm, and led her away from the fire. "I want you to listen to me," she said.

Tonie was in no mood for a lecture from anyone. "Why should I?"

Cindy's smile was wry. "Because I've forgotten more about men than you know."

Tonie felt chastised. "Sorry," she muttered.

"What will you do when you see Dr. Martin?"

"Either slap him across the face or pretend he doesn't exist."

"You'll do neither," Cindy said. "You'll forget what you just saw. You'll be as sweet as ever toward him. When I've been sick, I've had to lie down on that cot, too, but that doesn't make me Dr. Martin's mistress!"

Tonie was so startled by the other girl's frankness that she didn't know what to say.

Aware that she had made an impression, Cindy went a step further. "Was he stretched out with her, making love to her?"

"Hardly!"

"Then you're playing a childish game. You're as bad as Eulalia Woodling, and you're doing just what she'd do if your positions were reversed."

"That's unfair," Tonie protested.

"Unfortunately, it isn't," Cindy said. "Most men are polite—and embarrassed—when a woman flirts with them. Instead of telling her to go away and leave them alone, they tolerate her. But that doesn't mean they like her or admire her or want to have anything to do with her."

Tonie was incredulous. "You're sure?"

"Dead sure," Cindy said. "Cathy made a mistake when she started to snub Whip, although your experience may open her eyes and cause her to change her tactics. But you're making the same mistake. Few men are so stupid they can't see through somebody like Eulalia. She's all front, with no substance behind it. We had a saying about girls like her in Louisville. She promises, but she never delivers. And men know it."

Tonie was in no position to argue with her. "I guess I'll have to take your word for it."

"Please do. I'm sure Dr. Martin has put her out of his mind, so you'll be smart to forget her, too."

All at once Tonie's manner changed. Her anger faded, and she shrugged and smiled. "You know," she said, "I sound as though I desperately crave a man, which I don't. Not all that much. If Bob were foolish enough to fall for Eulalia's tactics, he'd be a simpleton I couldn't respect, and I'd want nothing more to do with him."

"Precisely!" Cindy declared.

"We're in the same boat," Cathy said, "all three of us."

Her friends looked at her.

"We're young and—without throwing bouquets—reasonably intelligent and more than reasonably attractive. All of us have been brought up to believe that marriage is the final goal in life—"

"Not I, thank you," Cindy interrupted, her voice dry. "My mother was a whore, and I never knew any other life, except that I learned to read and write—and think for myself."

"All the same," Cathy insisted, "you've been influenced by the society around you, just as Tonie and I have. But now we're in a completely different situation."

"I see what Cathy means," Tonie said. "This wagon train has changed us from ordinary stay-at-home women into pioneers, whether we like it or not."

"I didn't like it at first," Cathy said, "but now I'm becoming accustomed to living on my own, and I have to admit—just between us—that in many ways I enjoy it. Even though I'm still frightened at times."

"I wouldn't say frightened," Tonie said. "Occasionally I'm uneasy." She paused, then shook her head vigorously. "I'm a liar, or I'm fooling myself. Of course I get scared."

"Would the plains be any less strange or terrifying if you had husbands?" Cindy demanded.

They thought about the question.

"I guess not," Cathy said.

"Definitely not," Tonie declared. "The hardships and the hazards are real, very real, and no man could cushion us from them."

"The right man just might make me feel happier—if not more secure—because we'd be sharing the risks," Cathy admitted. "But the risks would be just as great."

"I find it challenging, not frightening, to face the hazards of the trail by myself," Cindy said. "Even to looking forward to a life alone in Oregon."

"Do you actually want to be alone?" Cathy asked.

"Yes and no," Cindy replied. "This winter at Fort Madison has been good for me. I've learned for the first time that men aren't necessarily lusting after me and that they—some of them, anyway—respect me as a human being. So the only way I can answer your question, Cathy, is to say that if I found the right partner, I'd be happy to live out my days with him. If not, I won't feel any great loss."

"I don't think I'd want to do without a man forever," Tonie said, "any more than most men would want to do without women for the rest of their lives. But I do see what you mean, Cindy, about our situation being a challenge. I think I'm in love with Bob. I'm not sure, really, because I've never felt like this before. But I'd want to be married to him only in a partnership, he'd have to respect me as much as I respect him. You'd never find me trailing four feet behind him the way Muslim women trail after their husbands on the Barbary Coast of North Africa, or so Ernie says."

Cathy laughed. "There was a time in my life when I

did trail around behind Otto. But I'm a big girl now, and I'll never do it again. That shouldn't be necessary in a happy marriage, and the women who behave that way are responsible for all the grief they create for themselves. Not for me!"

"Are you two telling me that you've come around to my way of thinking?" Cindy demanded. "That you're willing to cope alone—"

"I will if I must," Tonie said firmly. "My pride in myself must come first."

"I'm afraid there's no choice," Cathy said. "No matter what troubles lie ahead for us on the trail and in Oregon, if the choice is between staying single and making a bad marriage, I'll stay single, thank you. I've had the bad marriage, and nothing is worth that kind of life."

Routines were reestablished by the third day out of Fort Madison. The men, women, and older children knew what was expected of them and, for the most part, performed their tasks cheerfully. By now they realized they had entered a new phase of life; they had put the last outpost of civilization behind them, and they would see no towns, no villages, and no forts hereafter. The Great Plains and two chains of mountains, where potential enemies and other dangers lurked, stood between them and their longed-for destination.

On the fourth morning Grace Drummond made a discovery that she shared at breakfast with anyone who would listen to her. "You know something?" she asked in her booming voice. "We're pioneers!"

Most of the audience laughed heartily, but her words stuck in their minds. What she said was true: they *were* pioneers. Even though they had recognized their role, within themselves, the statement brought with it a stronger realization of that role, and gave them greater pride and dignity, as well as an increased sense of purpose.

Many people were still eating pancakes and drinking coffee, among them Lena Malcolm, who sat on the ground chatting with several other women while Lenore toddled off through the grass in the direction of a pile of rocks. Terence, who was now in charge of the water detail, had just gone off with members of his group to the river, where they would fill their pails so the cooking fires could be extinguished.

By now the travelers had regained their sense of timing. Those who were assigned the task of washing dishes were busy, but the others knew they could linger over their mugs of coffee for another quarter of an hour before the teams had to be hitched.

Lena kept her little daughter under observation as she talked with her friends, and suddenly she broke off in horror. Lenore had reached the pile of rocks and was bending down to examine something emerging from the pile.

Even at a distance, the young mother recognized it was a copperhead snake. About three feet long, it shimmered in the early morning sunlight. Lena could only scream in terror and point.

Most of the others were too petrified to move, but Whip went into action instantly and raced across the wagon circle. Lenore was unaware of her danger. Talking to the snake, the eighteen-month-old child extended her hand, hoping to pat the shiny creature.

Again Lena screamed.

Whip swiftly unwound the long lash that encircled his middle. At that moment the snake drew back its head to strike. Only inches separated its fangs from Lenore's chubby hand.

If the wagonmaster missed his target, he ran the risk of doing serious harm to Lenore. But he did not hesitate. He let fly with the whip, which made a hissing, singing sound as it cut through the air. Just at that moment the copperhead struck, but the rawhide severed its head, which seemed to disintegrate as the body writhed on the rocks.

Lena's fear propelled her across the grass, and she snatched up her baby. Lenore was not in the least frightened by the experience. On the contrary, she was amused by the sight of the harmless wriggling of the snake's body.

Lena was so relieved she began to weep and found it difficult to thank Whip. Then several members of the company who had hurried after her surrounded her and the child, all of them talking simultaneously.

Hosea approached Whip, who was winding his lash,

and the Ashanti's expression was doleful. "Bad to kill snake," he said. "Hosea could use."

Before Whip could reply, he became aware of further movement in the rocks. "Folks," he called, "move away, please, and give this pile a wide berth. It looks like there's a whole nest of copperheads in here."

The women needed no urging.

The news galvanized Hosea, who stared at the rocks for an instant, then sped off to Dr. Martin's wagon. Soon he returned with a glass container, and while others watched in fear and fascination, he removed the glass stopper, then moved close to the rocks.

Suddenly his hand darted into a crevice, and when he removed it, he was calmly holding a copperhead directly behind its head. The snake thrashed in his grasp, but he knew precisely how to render it harmless, and its fangs could not touch him.

Whip was on the verge of telling him to stop flirting with almost certain death, but changed his mind. It was plain that Hosea needed no advice and was well able to look after himself.

Some of the women were so sickened by the spectacle that they left the scene, but other members of the company gathered, watching from a safe distance. Soon the Ashanti had a silent, tense audience of more than fifty people.

Hosea was concentrating so completely on his task, however, that for all practical purposes he might have been alone. He placed the glass container on a flat rock, held the copperhead's head a fraction of an inch above it, and, with his free hand, began to stroke its lower jaw. The snake's fangs shot out, touched the inner rim of the container, and soon drops of a pale, somewhat milky fluid began to trickle from them down to the bottom of the glass.

Throwing the now harmless copperhead onto the far side of the rock pile, Hosea coolly reached into the crevice again and withdrew a second, even larger snake, which he proceeded to milk in the same manner. Totally fearless, his manner was brisk and businesslike.

Whip marveled, as did Ernie von Thalman, who joined

him. "If I weren't seeing this with my own eyes, I wouldn't believe it," the latter murmured.

The morning departure of the train was delayed while Hosea milked a third, then a fourth snake. By now the container was almost full, and Hosea sighed regretfully as he threw the fourth snake onto the rocks. "Two more in nest," he said, "but no more room in bottle."

Placing the stopper carefully into the container and making certain it was airtight, he dropped it into the pocket of his buckskin shirt and casually began to round up Cathy's workhorses.

Cathy moved her wagon into her regular place at the head of the line, and Hosea climbed up beside her. As they waited for other wagons to move into place, he removed the glass container and proudly showed it to her.

She had to use all of her willpower to force herself to look at the deadly fluid, for the sight of it made her ill. But she didn't want to hurt Hosea's feelings, and for his sake she feigned an interest. "That's—uh—wonderful, Hosea," she said.

He grinned and nodded complacently. Then, soon after they began their morning's ride, he reached into another pocket for some small, seasoned oak twigs. Removing a small knife from a hip pocket, he began the task of making darts, whittling and slicing, cutting notches and fashioning sharp points.

Absorbed and cheerful, he looked up only after he had finished making a half-dozen darts, a task that took him no more than an hour. Resting before he made still more darts, he took the glass container from his pocket and held it up to the light, somewhat disappointed because the sun had vanished and banks of dark clouds were rolling in rapidly from the western mountains, and he could not clearly see the fluid. "Kill many bad men now," he announced.

Cathy was relieved that he expected no reply.

Gradually the clouds overhead became thicker, the wind increased and the feeling of spring vanished as the air became raw and damp. In mid-morning, to the surprise of

Cathy and others who rode in the front portion of the train, Arnold Mell returned from his scouting duties and, riding beside Whip, conferred with him at some length. Those who realized he had come back to the train assumed that a problem with Indians might be developing, or perhaps another large herd of buffalo had been sighted.

Mack Dougall was the next of the scouts to arrive. Shoving his wad of chewing tobacco to the side of his mouth, he joined Arnold and Whip. Ordinarily undemonstrative, Mack gestured frequently, sometimes jabbing a finger skyward as though emphasizing a point.

Then Stalking Horse also returned to the train. Now Cathy was certain that something was happening. Never before had all three scouts rejoined the caravan so early in the day.

Whip raised two fingers to his mouth, and a sharp whistle summoned Tonie to the head of the line. He spoke to her briefly, she passed the word to her assistants, and then the entire company was notified that a halt was being called for the rest of the day.

Nearby was a wooded area where oak, elm, juniper, and pine grew. Nat Drummond was sent with his wood-gathering detail to bring back as much firewood as possible.

"Comb the woods for dead trees," Whip said. "I want enough to keep a roaring blaze going for at least twenty-four hours. If you must, chop down a few trees and cut them up, too. They'll take longer to burn, of course, but eventually they'll catch."

Although it wasn't yet noon, the wagons were placed in their overnight formation, the horses and oxen were set free to graze inside the circle, and Whip called a brief meeting of the entire company.

"Folks," he said, "some of you may find this hard to believe, but we're in for a day or two of unusual weather. Make sure your canvas wagon tops are secure. Keep the sides fastened, and stuff extra blankets along all the openings. I see that many of you are no longer wearing your greatcoats and cloaks. Get them out of your clothing boxes, along with your wool caps and mittens. The best we can do for the horses and oxen is to build a roaring fire and keep it going."

A stunned silence greeted his remarks. Some people stared at the carpet of green that stretched across the prairie to the horizon and found it impossible to believe that the problem was as grave as he made it out to be. Granted the weather had turned chilly, but the idea of donning heavy winter clothes seemed almost foolish.

"The change isn't all that unusual," Whip continued. "Take my word for it that many of the peaks in the Rockies are covered with snow all year, even during the height of summer. More years than not, there are severe storms in April, and when the winds are strong enough, the Great Plains get their share. Depending on how long the storm lasts, the grass may or may not be killed by frost and have to start again. But I'm worried about people and animals, not grass. So do as I say, and when the nasty weather strikes, stay in your wagons. All of you have ample supplies of emergency rations. Use them. We'll do no cooking during the storm. Right now I'd like everybody to give the water detail a helping hand. Fill your buckets and tubs and any other containers. You may have to thaw them at the fire, but at least you'll have drinking water for yourselves and your animals."

The wood-gatherers were the first to leave. Ted Woods and a number of other brawny men who weren't ordinarily part of the group accompanied them to saw logs, and soon a mound of firewood was piled in the center of the circle. Meanwhile, men walked to the Platte to fill water containers while women made sure the side flaps of canvas were secure and began to unpack the heavy winter clothing they had stored away.

The fire was lighted, and more logs were piled a safe distance from the flames. But the storm, if there was one, held off, and many people worked in a growing holiday atmosphere. In the past, Whip's advice had been sound, and he had never misled the company, but there were many who believed he was being too cautious this time or perhaps had misread the signs. Those who came from upper New York, Pennsylvania, Ohio, Illinois, and Indiana were familiar with late, freakish storms, but those who had spent their lives in the South found it difficult to believe that the flow of the seasons could be reversed.

The snow started to fall gently, shortly after noon, drifting down in tiny, lazy flakes that melted as they hit the ground. Gradually the snowfall increased, however, and by late afternoon a full-scale blizzard was raging. The ground turned white, and by nightfall the snow was several inches deep. The wind from the mountains became a gale and howled across the Great Plains; drifts piled up; the temperature dropped steadily.

Nat Drummond, Ted Woods, and a small group of volunteers tended the fire, which continued to burn, even though at times it seemed on the verge of being extinguished. Huddling together, horses and oxen edged closer and yet closer to the flames. Arnold, Mack, and Ernie supervised their feeding and watering, and although some animals were suffering extreme discomfort, none seemed to be in immediate danger. Thanks to the fire, they appeared able to survive.

The snow continued for more than fourteen hours, finally stopping in the early hours of the morning. Then the clouds dissipated, the stars appeared and a brilliant moon shone down on an endless sea of pure, silvery white. However, most people, burrowing under their blankets and wearing their heaviest clothing, remained inside their wagons and did not see the almost eerie beauty of the night. Only Whip and Stalking Horse had remained in the open, rolled in blankets near the fire. Thanks to their long experience in outdoor living, neither was the worse for wear.

Daylight came, and the flames of the fire still leaped high. People stayed in their wagons, however, and ate emergency rations of dried or pickled meat and parched corn for breakfast.

Only when the sun began to rise did the weather grow warmer. Then the temperature rose rapidly, and the thick snow began to melt. The older boys were the first to discover that the grass had not been destroyed, the thick layer of snow having protected it from the bitter cold.

Most of the animals were frisky, and only humans suffered real injury. A line formed outside Dr. Martin's wagon when many people found they were suffering from frostbite, and the physician, helped by the tireless, hard-working Tonie, treated more than fifty men, women, and children.

Members of the train congratulated themselves, believing they had escaped lightly, but their optimism proved premature. A woman's scream of anguish coming from one of the wagons indicated that one family, at least, had suffered.

People hurrying to the wagon found Ellie Fairbank, of Pennsylvania, hysterical. Her husband, Eb, was in agony, screaming deliriously that his left foot was on fire. In the other bed the two little Fairbank children, daughters of seven and five years, were dead, their tiny, pinched faces a pale blue color.

Women from neighboring wagons tried to comfort the distraught Ellie, while several men carried Eb to Dr. Martin's wagon. He fought them, cursing and shouting, flailing his arms and trying to escape from the "fire" that he screamed was consuming him.

Three men had to hold him down on the physician's operating table. A powerful man, he managed, nevertheless, to knock a glass of laudanum from Tonie's hand.

Without hesitation Dr. Martin amputated three of Eb Fairbank's toes. The task was grisly and difficult; Martin worked in grim silence, realizing the excruciating pain his patient was suffering. But he realized, too, that if he faltered or delayed, Fairbank well might lose his whole leg.

After the operation was completed, the doctor himself managed to pour a quantity of laudanum down the still-struggling patient's throat while the sweating volunteers continued to hold the man still. Gradually Fairbank calmed down, then fell into a deep sleep.

Ellie Fairbank no longer knew what was happening around her. Dr. Martin hurried to the Fairbank wagon and was able to persuade the hysterical woman to take a somewhat milder dose of the laudanum. Soon the sedative had the desired effect, and she, too, drifted off to sleep.

Meanwhile, another party of volunteers cleared away a patch of snow, and while Ted Woods and a carpenter from Kentucky hastily made two small coffins, another group of men quickly dug two graves in the soggy, drenched ground.

The two little Fairbank girls were buried there in a ceremony that was mercifully brief, and many of the women wept without shame, silently thanking God that their own children had been spared.

Ultimately the crippled Eb and his wife would have other children. But they would never recover completely from their tragic loss, and for the rest of their days, they would grieve for the daughters buried in shallow graves somewhere in the unmarked wilderness.

Everyone in the company realized anew that the price they were paying for their journey to Oregon was very high. Some even wondered as they stood by the two tiny graves whether the goal was worth it. But there was no turning back now.

There were some who were eager to leave the site without delay. But the snow was still too deep, and in many places the ground was too soggy for the journey to be resumed. Whip announced they would remain at their present campsite until further notice. Numerous volunteers accompanied the wood-gathering detail, and at Cathy's instigation, plans were made to prepare a hot meal at noon, the first since breakfast the previous day.

As the weather continued to improve, the owners of wagons came out into the open to feed and water their teams. Only then was it discovered that horses were missing. It seemed unlikely that the beasts could have wandered off during the blizzard, particularly as it would have been difficult for them to squeeze through the openings between the wagons.

A complete count was taken, with every wagon owner making a careful check. Nine horses were missing. The atmosphere became increasingly tense, and no one saw Whip and Stalking Horse quietly slip out and make a slow, thorough examination of the melting snow that surrounded the circle.

When they returned, Whip made an announcement. "I'm sorry to be telling you this," he said, "but it's plain that we were invaded during the storm. A party of Indians

—I can't tell you their tribe offhand—stole nine of our horses."

"How could they get around during a blizzard when I couldn't see more than a foot or two in front of my face?" a farmer from Tennessee demanded.

Whip's smile was thin. "The braves are accustomed to such weather. I reckon Stalking Horse and I could have done it, if need be. We've traveled in worse. But we're not accepting the theft as final. We've just found some prints out yonder, so I'm asking the scouts to follow them before the sun melts what's left of the snow."

Arnold and Mack immediately went off to saddle their horses, and Stalking Horse fetched his pony.

Hosea approached Whip. "Hosea go, too," he said, making a flat statement rather than a request.

Ordinarily Whip would have said no, but Hosea had amply demonstrated his ability to keep up with horsemen for long hours at a time. Whip also knew that Hosea felt he had been humiliated by his kidnapping and obviously wanted to restore his image as a warrior and scout in the eyes of the wagon train members. So Whip agreed.

Hosea carried his miniature clubs, blowgun, and poisoned darts with him at all times, but now he raced off to fetch his rawhide shield. He was ready to depart even before the three scouts gathered.

The hoofprints left by the raiders' mounts and the horses they had stolen were plain to see, and once assembled, all four members of the group moved off together, following the trail. The riders quickly increased their pace to a rapid canter, and Hosea ran beside them. When he went on a mission of this kind, he discarded his moccasins and preferred to be barefooted. Not until much later did he reveal privately to Stalking Horse that he had smeared his feet and calves with a coating of thick grease to protect them from the snow.

In places the drifts were still two and three feet high, but the group neither floundered nor paused. In a few hours, the snow would be reduced to puddles of water, and then the trail of the fleeing Indians would become more difficult to follow. Also, everyone in the party knew

It was imperative to cut off the thieves before they reached a larger body of their own people. It was apparent from the prints that the raiding party had been fairly large. If reinforced by scores of other braves, it would be too strong to be attacked.

One factor favored the pursuers, as they well realized. Although their foes had a long head start, they could travel far more rapidly than men who were herding nine lumbering workhorses, incapable of attaining speeds faster than a riding horse's trot.

It seemed miraculous to Arnold and Mack that Hosea could keep up with them. Never faltering, never out of breath, the little man ran easily, his wiry frame relaxed, his heavy rawhide shield seemingly weightless as he held it several inches off the ground. He was extraordinary, and the day was not far distant when true stories told about him would become legends.

In late afternoon, when the pursuit had already lasted five hours, Stalking Horse finally raised a hand in warning. He was even more adept at reading signs than his companions, and now he saw something in the thin, remaining layer of snow that made him cautious.

"Indians and wagon train horses not far now," he said. "Maybe a mile. Maybe not that much."

Arnold peered hard at the signs and had to nod in agreement. The indentations in the snow and the soft earth beneath it were fresh. The old man immediately assumed command.

"I'll take the left flank, and Mack will take the right," he said. "Stalking Horse, you and Hosea keep moving forward right smack on the trail."

Mack spat a stream of tobacco juice at a diminishing snowbank. "Do we attack together after somebody gives a signal?"

Arnold shook his head. "That's not practical. You and I will be making detours, traveling greater distances, so Stalking Horse and Hosea will come upon the braves before we do. And once they're close enough for an assault, there's no way to hide. I recommend that they open fire as soon as they think it's practical. Then you and

I will pitch in as soon as we reach the scene. It shouldn't take either of us more than an extra minute or two to get there."

"Is good," Stalking Horse said, and Mack nodded in agreement.

Hosea made no comment. As always, he was indifferent to matters of strategy and tactics; it was enough for him that he would be engaged in a fight.

Arnold and Mack fanned out, one going to the left and the other swinging to the right. Stalking Horse continued to move forward at his same, steady pace, Hosea calmly running beside him.

Soon they caught a glimpse of four warriors bringing up the rear of the raiding party and keeping the stolen horses in line. At first it was difficult to determine their nationality, but then Stalking Horse managed to see one in profile. The man's face was smeared with streaks of bright blue paint that identified him as an Osage. Members of that tribe had a reputation as stubborn fighters, although not particularly imaginative ones.

Stalking Horse notched an arrow on the string of his bow and drew the arrow back. The braves did not yet realize that enemies were moving up behind them.

Hosea was at a distinct disadvantage. Neither his clubs nor darts could carry far enough,

Stalking Horse did not slow his pace as he sent an arrow flying in the direction of the rider on the left end of the irregular line. The shaft penetrated the left side of the brave's back, and a spreading patch of crimson stained his buckskin shirt. He slumped in his saddle, quietly pitching forward onto the neck of his pony. But the animal continued to move forward, carried by its own momentum, and the other members of the rear guard were still unaware of the assault.

Stalking Horse knew his good fortune could not last indefinitely, but he was determined to take full advantage of his opportunity while he could. He aimed at the back of the brave on the right side of the line.

This time he missed the center of his target by two or three inches, the arrow merely wounding the brave, who screamed in pain and anger. At the same moment the corpse of the man on the left tumbled to the ground.

The alarm was given. The other two members of the rear guard turned and saw the approaching pair, and their warning shouts alerted the entire raiding party. The Osage halted, ignoring the wounded brave. Most of the raiders wheeled and moved back to join their comrades at the rear, with only a few staying in place at the front and flanks to hold the riderless horses in line and prevent them from bolting.

Stalking Horse fired another arrow, and again he hit his target. But he realized that he and Hosea were now facing a group of at least twenty-five Osage; no matter how courageously they fought, the odds against them were overwhelming.

Hosea was enjoying himself. Sticking the sharpened center rod at the bottom of his rawhide shield into the ground to hold it in position, he was protected by his mobile, miniature fort. Now that the Osage were closer, he could use his darts, and he showed himself at the left side of his shield for an instant, then at the right, each time firing one of his poison-laden darts.

The Ashanti rather than Stalking Horse drew the bulk of the Osage return fire. A man on foot appeared more vulnerable, especially when he seemed to be armed with no weapons of consequence and depended on a curious leather shield for safety.

As Stalking Horse let yet another arrow fly, he noted that dusk had come, and he was relieved. Thanks to good fortune rather than planning, the timing of the attack was perfect. The Osage would find it difficult to count their enemies and discover how few there were in the attacking force.

An arrow grazed the Cherokee's shoulder, slicing through his shirt and breaking the skin, but he suffered no real harm. He could still fire his next arrow.

Spears were bouncing off the rawhide shield, and arrows were digging into the outer layer, but none could reach Hosea, who had killed several warriors.

Suddenly a rifle shot erupted on one side of the field,

and even as a brave dropped and sprawled on the ground, another rifle shot roared on the opposite flank. It, too, claimed a warrior.

By now at least six of the raiders were dead, and no fewer than three others wounded. The Indians seemed to be surrounded, and the firesticks of the white men filled them with terror. Convinced that they could not compete against such odds, they held their positions only until the senior warrior in command shouted at the top of his voice, urging every brave to save himself. That was the only signal the Osage needed. The healthy fled, leaving their dead and wounded—as well as the captured horses—behind them.

Pursuit would have been impossible, but there was no need for it—they had recovered the horses. The horses had become skittish and would have scattered, but Mack and Arnold gave them no chance. The experienced scouts herded them together, speaking to them soothingly until they became docile again.

Hosea appeared from behind his shield and, as the stars appeared and the moon rose, quietly retrieved his spent darts.

Meanwhile, Stalking Horse was performing a task of his own, systematically scalping the dead Osage. Each time he came across a brave who was still alive, he quickly plunged his knife into the warrior's body, then added another scalp to his booty.

Some of the Indians' ponies had bolted, following the retreating war party. But five were rounded up by Arnold and Mack. The battle was ended, and the victory was complete; not only had all nine of the stolen horses been recovered, but five enemy mounts had been captured, too.

"Take your pick, Hosea," Arnold said. "You can ride back to camp in style."

The Ashanti shook his head. "Hosea walk," he said.

The four men placed themselves at the points of an invisible square and started back in the direction of the wagon train, keeping the workhorses and Osage ponies inside the square. After they had traveled for more than an hour, they halted briefly to eat their only meal, dried buffalo meat and parched corn. Then they resumed their march.

Sentries had been posted around the circle of wagons, and their shouts of joy, mingled with disbelief, aroused most of the company. Only the youngest children and a few women slept through the commotion.

Whip seemed unruffled, having expected no less of the group he had dispatched on the difficult errand. The Osage ponies would be distributed the following day, he said, and as the better part of the night was already spent, the wagon train would stay at its present site for an additional twenty-four hours in order to give the scouts and Hosea the opportunity to rest.

As the members of the company headed back to their wagons, their joy over the outcome was tempered by a sobering thought. Nat Drummond expressed it best when he said, "I wouldn't have thought anybody could have been abroad during that blizzard. Well, the Indians not only did it, but they even sneaked into our camp without anybody knowing it. If they can perform that kind of magic, just imagine all the troubles we have waiting for us on the Great Plains."

IX

Real spring finally came to the Great Plains in the wake of the late blizzard. The ground dried in the balmy breezes so the thin metal rims of the wagon wheels no longer cut into the earth and became mired. People and animals seemed to have greater energy. Sometimes, as they rode, the pioneers sang songs about the good life that awaited them in Oregon, making up new words to the tunes of familiar favorites. The grass grew higher, and prairie flowers of scarlet and bright yellow, pink, white, and orange dotted the landscape.

Terry and Lena Malcolm held hands at every opportunity, Eulalia Woodling flirted with any man who would talk to her, and many of the unmarried people became restless. Tonie Mell confided to Cathy van Ayl that she dreamed of Bob Martin, and a red-faced Cathy told her in return that she found herself thinking of Whip Holt in unguarded moments.

For no apparent reason, Ted Woods began to keep an even closer watch on Cindy than he had in the past. He changed the position of his wagon so he now rode directly behind her in the center column; he kept her under observation when she worked at the cooking fire before breakfast and supper; and on evenings when he wasn't working, he loitered in her vicinity.

His surveillance was harmless, but it made Cindy nervous. Unlike the girls who had led far more sheltered, inhibited lives, she had long been accustomed to speaking her mind candidly to men. So she ignored the well-meant advice of Cathy and Tonie. One night after supper, when she felt Ted lurking in the shadows of the fire behind her, she turned suddenly and went straight to him.

"I'd like a word with you, Ted," she said.

The burly blacksmith became uncomfortable. "What about?"

"Let's go sit on the stoop of my wagon, shall we? There are too many people around here."

With great reluctance he accompanied her to the far side of the circle, where her wagon sat in the shadows.

Cindy sat on the top step, motioned Ted to a lower step, and instinctively fluffed her red hair. "Now, if you please," she said, "I want to know what all this is about."

"All what, Cindy?"

"I'm not angry with you, Ted, and I'm not upset. You've been grand to me, and I appreciate it. Particularly the night you saved me from that loathsome mountain man back at Fort Madison. But I can't help wondering why you're always following me."

Ted's shock was genuine. "I wouldn't do a thing like that!" he protested.

She had guessed that he wasn't actually aware of what he was doing. So she spoke even more gently as she said, "Every time I turn around, there you are, keeping an eye on me. Before and during breakfast, before and during supper—even during the nooning. You were doing it just now when I asked you to come with me."

For a long time Ted was silent, thinking. Then he nodded. "I mean you no harm," he said.

"Oh, I know you don't," Cindy assured him, impulsively touching his bare forearm for a moment. When she removed her fingers, he clapped his hand over the spot she had touched and unconsciously ran his fingers back and forth across it.

"I've got to be honest with you," she said, "and I hope you'll be the same way with me. All right?"

"I always tried to be honest." He spoke slowly and with dignity. "I ain't much for lyin'."

Subtlety was a waste of time in dealing with a man of his temperament. "I believe," Cindy said, "that you're sweet on me."

Ted was so surprised at Cindy's frankness that he lost his voice. His Adam's apple bobbed up and down, and when he opened his mouth, he could make no sound.

"I'm not asking you to confirm it," Cindy told him. "Both of us know what we know. I just think you're making a mistake, that's all, Ted."

He looked as though she had stabbed him with a knife. "If there's somebody else, somebody I don't know about, all you got to do is say the word, Cindy, and I'll leave you strictly alone."

"I give you my word there's nobody else," she said. "There's no man in my life."

He looked relieved.

"No man now," she repeated. "And no man in the future, as far ahead as I can see."

"Then it's all right," Ted said.

"No!" Cindy cried fiercely. "No man! That includes you!"

"You're tryin' to tell me you don't think very highly of me, is that it?" He looked crushed.

"What I think or don't think of you is beside the point, Ted. You seem to have forgotten something I can't allow myself to forget. I'm a whore."

Ted's eyes blazed. "Nobody can call you that, not even you. Maybe it's what you were, but you ain't one now."

"I'm not practicing the trade any more, if that's what you mean. And I'd rather die than go back to it. But that doesn't change what I am."

He refused to accept her logic. "All right. Here's somethin' I never told you. I killed my wife and my brother. I put a bullet into her and a knife in him when I caught them in bed together. That's why I spent ten years in prison. So I'm a murderer."

Cindy had already learned about his background, so his revelations neither surprised nor shocked her. "You paid for your mistakes in jail, so you wiped your slate clean. Nobody can call you a murderer any more, Ted."

"If you're a whore, then I'm a murderer. There's no two ways about it," he insisted.

"You don't understand. I just stopped what I was doing, but nobody sent me to jail for it. Society has not punished me."

"You're sayin' a body has to be punished before the slate is wiped clean, huh?"

She hadn't thought about it in those terms before. "Something like that."

"Then you're absolved the same as I am. Because you been punishin' yourself. It's my guess you been doin' it for a long, long time. Long before you ever left that whorehouse in Louisville, I'll bet."

"Maybe so." Cindy had no intention of discussing the inner agonies she had suffered. "But that isn't important. What matters is that I'm not for you, not for anyone."

"You aimin' to live your whole life alone? A lady as pretty and young as you?"

"I'm not all that young," she replied indignantly. "I'm almost twenty-two."

Ted chuckled, then sobered. "Cindy," he said, "I ain't forcin' myself on you. I respect the way you feel, even though I think you're wrong. All I'll say is I'll be around —providin' you're sure it really doesn't matter to you that I killed two people."

"I can understand your reasons, and I don't blame you."

"Then I'll be waitin'. I won't push, and I'll do my best not to make you uncomfortable by hangin' around you too much. But any time you need help—in anythin'—all you got to do is holler for me."

"You're very sweet, Ted," Cindy said. It was astonishing that someone who had such great strength could be so gentle.

"Don't talk like that," Ted said. "I'm tryin' to behave myself."

She held out her hand to him. "We can be real friends now. I like that."

He stared at her small hand for a moment, then, wiping his palm on his trousers, he enveloped her hand in his, treating it as though it were a live bird that might be crushed to death if he squeezed it. Abruptly, he released her hand, then stood.

She smiled up at him.

Unable to speak again, Ted suddenly bolted, hurrying to his own wagon, which stood directly behind Cindy's in the circle. He was too embarrassed to look around at her and quickly lowered the flap, even though Danny, who still shared the wagon with him, hadn't yet come to bed.

Cindy continued to sit on the top step of her own wagon. Perhaps she had been wrong to speak so frankly. It had been her intention to discourage Ted Woods, but instead she had caused him to show an even greater interest in her. Cindy sighed. It was infuriating that her past life as a prostitute in no way turned him against her. Well, she had tried, and she couldn't be responsible for him or his feelings. She didn't want to hurt him, but having warned him that she wanted no man, she couldn't do anything more.

On the other hand, she wondered what life would be like as Ted's wife. A man like Ted didn't give his love easily. Certainly she could persuade him to do anything she wanted. She also knew she would have to be careful not to make him lose his temper—she would not like his rage to be directed against her.

What rubbish she was thinking! She was sick of men, and no one, Ted included, interested her physically.

She supposed she was drawn to the blacksmith because of his desire to protect her. After all, every woman wanted to be cherished. But the mere thought of physical contact nauseated her.

Well, she couldn't marry Ted—or anyone else—while she felt that way. Too many of her Louisville customers had confided that they had come to her because they were married to women who didn't care for them physically. She had been good at pretending she cared. But when she joined the wagon train, she had sworn that she would never again allow herself to be placed in a position where pretense would be necessary. And that was one promise that she fully intended to keep.

So goodbye to Ted Woods and everyone else! In years to come she might change her mind, but she hadn't changed it yet—although she knew that to an extent, she was recovering from the injuries to her soul that she had suffered. She was able to see men like Whip, Ernie, and Dr. Martin in their true perspective now, and she had learned, however reluctantly, to admire them for being upright, gallant, and courageous. The mere fact that she did not hate them and could recognize their good qualities was an improvement. She recognized the change and was grateful for it.

She had her friends to thank, at least in part, for that improvement. Cathy van Ayl and Tonie Mell accepted her without reservation, even though they knew of her past. Cathy, at least, was a lady, and Tonie, although harder to define, nevertheless was someone who had great inner strength. The mere fact that they had extended their friendship to her, sharing with her their inner thoughts, was something of a miracle. Never before had Cindy enjoyed such relationships with anyone; at the Louisville bordello, the other girls had been selfish and suspicious, ready to fight for what they regarded as their rights.

She was prepared, in return, to do anything she could to help both Tonie and Cathy. They had won her total loyalty.

At the same time, however, Cindy had to admit to herself that she envied them. They were living straight-forward, honest lives, uncluttered by shadows. Oh, it was true that Cathy had endured an unhappy marriage with a difficult, crabby miser, but she had done nothing of which to be ashamed, nothing that haunted her and kept her awake at night.

How wonderful it would be to clear the slate and start a fresh life, unsullied by the past! In a sense, of course, that was what she was trying to do by joining the wagon train and going off to Oregon. Ultimately she would put her past behind her, forget it, and emerge as a new woman. She was well on her way and would keep trying. Nobody, including the girl she herself had been, was going to stand in her way.

At length, Cindy became weary of her own thoughts.

Still too restless to go to bed, she rose from her seat on the wagon, walked slowly down the stairs, and then wandered around the inner edge of the circle. She was in no mood to make small talk with anyone, so she wandered aimlessly, then paused between two wagons to look out across the dark prairie. On a night like this the quiet of the wilderness was soothing.

Suddenly a hand touched her shoulder, causing her to jump, and a man's voice interrupted her thoughts. "You look lonely tonight."

Cindy brushed aside the hand as she whirled around, then grimaced when she saw Claiborne Woodling facing her. She still disliked the young man. The mere fact that he sought her company was irritating.

"I'm not in the least lonely, thank you," she said, and her tone was glacial.

Claiborne refused to recognize the rebuff. "Well, I am, and you're just the person to cure that feeling for me."

"I'm sorry," she said firmly, "but whether you're happy or sad—you or anyone else—is none of my concern."

"It was, not so long ago," he replied, moistening his lips.

Other members of the company were careful never to mention Cindy's past to her. Only this thoroughly unpleasant young man went out of his way to remind her of what she had been—as if she needed any reminders.

"I choose not to debate the point with you. Let me pass, please," she added when she saw he was blocking the opening between the wagons.

Claiborne did not move. Instead he folded his arms across his chest and grinned at her.

Cindy realized she had allowed herself to be placed in an uncomfortable position. The wagons on either side of her were dark; their owners were obviously still enjoying conversation over coffee at the fire. If she raised her voice, people would come running, but she dreaded creating an embarrassing personal situation. This was something she preferred to handle herself, if she could.

She was uncertain whether she was sorry or pleased that Ted Woods had given up watching her for the night. The proximity of the brooding giant might have deterred

Woodling. On the other hand, had Woodling persisted, Ted might have lost his temper—with consequences that even at this moment caused her to shiver.

"You're cold," Claiborne said, "but I can take good care of that."

"I don't care for your hints. If you really want to know, I don't like you."

"You'll change your mind when you come to know me better." His grin broadened.

"I don't intend to. Just because we happen to be traveling in the same wagon train doesn't mean we've got to be friends, you know." Cindy spoke stiffly, wondering whether to take the risk of pushing him aside and trying to squeeze past him. If she could time her move in a way that caught him off guard, she would be able to quietly rejoin those still lingering at the fire.

"What I've had in mind," Claiborne said, pulling her to him, "isn't exactly what I'd call friendship."

No escape was possible, but Cindy still wasn't ready to call for help. Virtually everyone in the train knew she had been a harlot. Some of the women still didn't like her, and she felt certain that many of them would believe that she had led Claiborne on.

Struggling, she pushed against his chest, but she was unable to break free of his viselike grip.

Claiborne laughed, his hold tightening. "I like it when a woman shows a little spirit—before I tame her."

"You'll never tame me," she gasped, fighting still harder to break loose.

He bent his head down to kiss her forcibly, but suddenly he released her and slumped to the ground. The astonished Cindy, breathing hard, saw that Claiborne was unconscious.

She turned around. There was no one there. Her deliverance seemed to be a miracle. Then she saw something lying on the ground; only a few inches from young Woodling's head. She bent down for it, then held it up to the dim light of the fire. Not until she saw it was a little wooden club did she realize what had happened.

Hosea materialized out of the dark and stood beside her. "Ted sleep," he said, "So Hosea keep watch." Calmly taking the club from her, he returned it to the loop around his middle.

Cindy thanked him profusely, feeling that anything she said would inadequately express her gratitude. At the same time she was worried. Claiborne had not moved, and she became increasingly fearful. "Did you—kill him?"

For an instant a faint smile hovered at the corners of Hosea's mouth. "Not kill," he said solemnly. "Whip and Ernie no like if kill. Get mad." He nudged Woodling with a foot, the gesture almost clinically impersonal. "Hosea make man sleep. Wake up in morning. Then head hurt all day."

A slight, barely perceptible shrug of disdain indicated his total lack of interest in any discomfort the young man might suffer the next day. Only one thing was important to him; again nudging the motionless figure at his foot, he said, "Not be bad with lady again."

Cindy's tension evaporated suddenly, and she hugged Hosea. In the future she felt certain Claiborne Woodling would take care to avoid her.

She knew, too, that there was no need for her to ask Hosea not to mention the incident to anyone. She trusted his discretion, and she realized, too, that he was wise enough to say nothing to Ted, who might be all too inclined to lose his temper.

Cindy, her spirits remarkably improved, decided to return to the fire for a last cup of coffee before turning in. Hosea walked beside her. He had developed an insatiable craving for the hot chocolate that the children drank instead of coffee, and Cindy decided that from now on, she would prepare a cup for him at every meal. That was the least she could do.

When they reached the fire she heard a man speaking in an angry, clear voice. Nat Drummond stood, feet spread apart and thumbs hooked in his belt, glaring at his wife. No one had ever heard Nat defy the overbearing Grace.

"Woman," he thundered, "I'm tired of being ordered around. Do this, Nat. Do that, Nat. I do my share and more. I supervise the wood-gathering detail, and I do it well. I hitch up our team twice a day, and I drive our wagon. I feed and water our team. I raise and lower the flaps on our wagon, and I repack the insides whenever anything is loose. That's all I aim to do!"

Grace glowered at him. "What about me? I work with the other women cooking meals—"

"Sure!" he interrupted, shouting. "But that's all you do!"

Some of those still gathered around the fire were embarrassed and turned away, talking to each other in low tones and pretending not to hear the surprising argument. But Cindy was fascinated, and she saw that Cathy van Ayl was listening, too, making no attempt to hide her broad smile. Obviously Cathy felt as she did, that Nat had been dominated for too long by a wife who treated him more like an indentured servant than a husband.

But that era appeared to have come to an abrupt end. Nat had gained a measure of self-respect on the long trek that he had never before known, and he was asserting himself with remarkable force. "It's too damn much when you order me to collect our dishes and take them back to the wagon. My sweat back home earned those dishes and mugs. Yes, and the knives we use when we eat. It's your place to wash them and keep an eye on them and take care of them. So you'll blame well do it from now on. Just as you're going to do a heap of other things!"

His rebellion was so strong and unexpected that Grace could only gape at him in stunned silence.

"I never believed in beating a woman," Nat said, "but I'm mighty tempted. Do what I tell you, Grace, and do it quick!" He clapped his hands together sharply.

All at once Grace sprang into action. Cindy thought she intended to pick up her husband and shake him. Instead she meekly went over to the fire, where piles of washed dishes were drying, picked up her crockery and a large kettle, then silently trudged off to her wagon.

Nat watched her for a moment or two, without any emotion. Then he quietly joined a group of people who were talking with Arnold Mell.

Cindy caught a glimpse of Grace Drummond's face as she turned away. The girl was surprised to note that Nat's tall, rawboned wife did not appear in the least upset. On the contrary, she was smiling and seemed to be at peace with herself. Some women were inexplicably contrary, and Cindy suspected that Grace would enjoy the new role she was being forced to play. When a woman truly loved a man, she didn't want to maintain the upper hand all the time.

Cindy thought it unlikely that she could ever love any man that much. Yet she knew she had been wrong, a short time earlier, about her ability to handle Ted Woods. Why was she even concerned about her relationship with Ted? She had promised herself that she would remain independent. Her freedom was too precious to her, and she fully intended to allow no one to interfere with it.

Chet Harris and Danny had developed into the most accomplished fishermen in the company. Armed with hooks made for them by Hosea, lines fashioned from remnants of cloth that Cathy van Ayl gave them, and poles cut under Ernie's quiet supervision, the pair organized all of the older boys in the caravan. Each night they returned to the circle with strings of fish. Trout were plentiful in the Platte River, but the boys preferred lake and pond fishing because they came away with larger, meatier catches. They were delighted when the train halted each night at one or another of a chain of lakes and ponds in the Nebraska country. These ran parallel to the route of march for more than sixty miles, so Danny was indulging in no idle boast when he said, "We'll be eating fresh fish for breakfast every day for at least a whole week."

On the third night of the journey past the chain of unnamed lakes, the older boys hurried away, as soon as camp was made, to start fishing in a small pond.

Mack had sighted a small herd of buffalo only a few miles from the campsite as he returned from his scouting duties, so a party had gone out hunting. Whip stayed behind deliberately—he didn't want the company to become too dependent on his efforts. Even those who had been new to this type of hunting were experienced by now.

Whip wandered through the woods that stood between

the campsite and the small pond, noting with approval that the wood-gatherers were concentrating their efforts on fallen and dead trees. The boys were hauling in a catch of fish and were completely absorbed in the task, while some of the older girls and women were busily gathering berries and edible roots nearby. The Oregon-bound settlers didn't yet realize it, but they were becoming increasingly efficient and more self-reliant in wilderness living. By the time these people reached Oregon they would be able to survive on their own.

Pleased with the progress they were making, Whip strolled back to the circle, where women were beginning to prepare supper. He stiffened slightly when he saw a strange gelding and a pack horse. Then he spotted a tall, broad-shouldered man wearing a shirt and trousers of heavy wool and store-bought boots. His rifle slung over his shoulder, he was engaged in conversation with several of the women.

The man introduced himself as Alvin Munson, but offered no other information.

The code of the wilderness was strict, and although Whip didn't much care for the man's looks, he had to extend the company's hospitality. "You'll stay for supper and the night?"

"Thanks," Munson replied. "I'm sure the ladies can cook better meals than I can prepare for myself, so I'll be glad to eat with you. Later, though, I believe I'll be on my way." He spoke with a faint accent that was impossible for Whip to identify.

Whip was surprised by the man's refusal to remain overnight. Only someone in a great hurry traveled through the Great Plains after dark. "Where are you headed, Mr. Munson?"

"Either Independence or St. Joseph, I don't much care which."

"You've spent the winter in the Rockies, then?"

The man nodded.

Again Whip felt a twinge. Munson's clothes didn't look like those of a mountain man, and he carried no furs— the only reason for anybody to endure the hardships of a winter in the Rockies. But common courtesy forbade Whip to question him too closely. Perhaps he was a fugitive on the run, or fleeing from personal enemies. A man was entitled to his privacy out here.

The hunters returned in time for supper, bringing with them the carcasses of three buffalo. One was lightly smoked so it would keep only until the following night, when both sides would be barbecued, and the others were cut up to be preserved in vinegar and salt, then added to the supply of emergency rations.

"This time of year," Whip said to Alvin Munson in an effort to make polite conversation, "nobody starves on the plains."

"So it seems," the visitor replied.

Very odd. The man spoke as though he were strange to the area. But that seemed impossible. In order to reach the Rockies and return from them, every mountain man had to cross the vast prairie twice, and anyone who managed that feat—and lived—became something of an authority on the prairie.

Various members of the company, happy to see a new face, sought out the visitor. But Munson, Whip observed, was uncommunicative with all of them. Perhaps he was naturally silent, as were many who spent a considerable length of time in the Rockies. Long months of solitude seemed to rob a man of his ability to converse with others. But this man seemed actively sullen.

Maybe it was wrong to judge the man, Whip thought. Although his appearance, attitude, and seeming lack of familiarity with the area belied his claims about himself, he was minding his own business and was harming no one. All the same, perhaps it was just as well that he had refused the invitation to stay overnight.

Only one member of the company seemed to attract his attention. When he heard someone speak Tonie Mell's name, he raised his head and peered at her intently for a few moments. Then he lost interest in her, too, and devoted himself to his dinner.

Night came long before the meal was finished. Whip again extended an invitation to remain overnight, but

Munson refused, although this time he was less curt. He expressed his thanks for supper, then mounted his gelding and, leading his pack horse, rode off into the darkness. Glad to be rid of him although he couldn't say why, Whip forgot about him.

The following morning the company stirred at daybreak. The fire, which had been allowed to die down but had not been extinguished, was rebuilt. As the flames rose again, the breakfast preparations began. Also more vinegar and salt were added to the new barrels of buffalo meat before they were closed and sealed.

The water-gathering detail went off to the little pond, armed with buckets, tubs, and other containers. As sometimes happened, they were accompanied by others who felt thirsty, among them Ernie von Thalman. Behind him sauntered Arnold Mell, who had already eaten breakfast and wanted a drink of fresh water before going off on his scouting duties.

Ernie dipped his silver mug embossed with his family crest into the pond, stood, and was raising the mug to his lips when Arnold suddenly knocked it from his hand. The startled Baron didn't know whether to protest the rude gesture or reply with a swift punch.

Arnold gave him no opportunity. He pointed to the pond. Dead fish were rising to the surface and floating there.

"Don't drink that water!" Arnold shouted to those who were filling their buckets. "Don't touch it!"

"Look at the dead fish!" Ernie called. "This pond is contaminated!"

"It was fine last night," someone said.

"Well, it isn't now," Ernie replied irritably.

They were interrupted by a woman's scream. Two men who had taken drinks of the water were writhing on the ground in agony. One was an earnest, bankrupt young farmer from Indiana, passionately devoted to the future he would enjoy in Oregon. The other man, easygoing and amiable, often entertained the company with his jokes and was liked by everyone.

A young boy raced back to the circle for Dr. Martin, who arrived, running, followed by Tonie. Whip came, too, and promptly sent everyone not directly concerned back to camp.

The physician couldn't prescribe an antidote. The best he could do was administer emetics, and by this time both of the sufferers were so far gone that Tonie had to open their mouths and hold their heads while Bob poured the medication into them.

Neither responded to the treatment. Both were bathed in cold perspiration, their skin a sickly, greenish-yellow, and both were struggling feebly.

Dr. Martin searched through his satchel for something to give them. "I can't imagine what's causing this," he muttered, "so I'm damned if I know what medication to use."

The victims were fading rapidly, their breathing now shallow.

Only the doctor remained calm. "Open their mouths again, Tonie," he directed. "This one first. Now the other. That's it." He poured quantities of a white powder onto the tongues of the men, both of whom had lost consciousness.

The patient stretched on the ground beside Tonie stopped struggling and lay still. "I—I'm afraid we've lost him," she said.

Bob examined him quickly, then turned to the other victim, who had also stopped moving. "They're both gone," he said. "I don't know what they drank, and I've never heard of any substance that would cause death that rapidly after ingestion."

Still squatting, resting his weight on his heels, he pondered for a time. "Tonie, did you notice anything unusual? Did you detect any strange odors?"

She nodded unhappily. "Now that you mention it, Bob, there was an awful smell on their breaths. Like rotten eggs."

"Sulfur of some kind, I believe. Whip, can you fetch one of those dead fish floating on the top of the water? Just handle it with care, please."

The wagonmaster returned with a fish. Bob sniffed it, his face contorting with disgust, then asked Tonie to do the same.

"That's the smell!" she exclaimed.

Bob Martin stood. "Whip," he said, "everybody drank water from the pond last night, and no one was hurt. All of us ate fish for breakfast that the boys caught, and there have been no adverse reactions."

Whip stared at the physician. "Are you telling me that somebody put poison into this lake between fishing and water-gathering time last night and this morning?"

"So it would seem." The doctor spoke reluctantly but firmly. "A poison, I'd say, with a sulfur base, one sufficiently strong to kill a man within a few minutes. I can't prove it, of course—but I'm willing to stake my professional reputation on it."

"Would you say it was deliberate poisoning?" Whip asked, speaking slowly.

"That I can't say," the physician replied. "All I can tell you for certain is that twelve hours ago fish were thriving in this pond. And right now there are hundreds of them dead out there. It's possible that an underground sulfur spring was diverted, causing the waters to become contaminated. It's also possible that someone poisoned the pond, although I find that difficult to believe."

"I aim to find out," Whip said grimly, then beckoned to Arnold and Ernie, who were standing nearby and had heard everything that had been said. "Get Stalking Horse to find the tracks of that fellow who was here for supper last night. Then take a small party, go after him, and find him. If he'll talk to you and his story makes sense, all well and good. If you have any reason to doubt him, bring him back to me."

"You'll stay in the camp right here, I assume," Ernie said.

Whip nodded, his expression somber. "We'll have to bury these poor devils and console their families as best we can. The whole company is bound to be upset."

Arnold had already moved off to find Stalking Horse, who could locate tracks more rapidly than any of their white scouts.

Tonie hurried after him. "Take me with you, Uncle Arnold," she said. "I haven't gone out on the trail in a long time, and you know I can be useful." She did not explain that she didn't want to spend the entire day with an indifferent Bob Martin. Arnold nodded, his mind already on the mission ahead.

Whip was preoccupied, too, or he would have forbidden Tonie to accompany the group. Certainly the search for Alvin Munson was no pleasure trip. A girl, no matter how expert at shooting, had no legitimate place in the party. Whip was, however, thinking of what consolation he could offer to the widows of the men who had died so suddenly and unexpectedly.

Stalking Horse needed only a short time to find Munson's tracks. It was significant that, although he had said he was traveling to Independence or St. Joseph, which lay to the east, he had ridden off to the west. Obviously he had a great deal to explain.

The search party consisted of the three regular scouts, as well as Ernie, Tonie, and the shield-bearing Hosea, who refused to be left behind. Stalking Horse had no difficulty in following the clear trail Munson's riding horse and pack horse had left in the grass, which was now calf high, and he led the party at a canter. Hosea ran directly behind him, tireless as always.

If it was true that the poisoning had been deliberate, a possibility so shocking it was difficult even to contemplate, the previous night's guest deserved to die, Tonie reflected. Ordinarily not vindictive, she couldn't help wishing that Hosea would kill him. It would be just retribution if someone who used poison was himself killed by a poison dart.

Crossing the prairie rapidly, the party headed inland a short distance from the Platte River. Arnold realized they were approaching a small pond, fed by natural springs, which he had selected as the next night's stopping place for the wagon train. A thick patch of birch trees and bramble-laden bushes stood near the pond in the damp, sandy soil, and there the trail came to an abrupt end. The party dismounted, waiting while Stalking Horse studied the ground more closely. The Cherokee stood, shaking his head, then bent down to the ground again.

The sound of a rifle shot emanating from the grove of

birch trees shattered the silence. A bullet passed so close to Tonie's ear that it sounded like the buzzing of an angry hornet.

Reacting instinctively, she threw herself to the ground. The others did the same. Armed with their rifles, they moved on their hands and knees toward the stand of birch, concealing themselves as best they could in the high grass.

Again a shot was fired, and again Tonie was the target, the bullet passing above her by inches.

Why should she be the object of the man's wrath, rather than one of the men, who presumably would be more dangerous? All at once the pieces of the puzzle fitted into place, and she knew. The man who had called himself Alvin Munson was a Russian agent. He had been dispatched by André Sebastian—or by someone like him —to interfere with the wagon train's progress. And finding the woman who had defied St. Petersburg in the party that had pursued him, he was trying to win extra credit for himself by killing her. The sun overhead was warm, but an icy chill crept slowly up Tonie's spine. She wished she had displayed the common sense to have remained behind at the camp.

Only Hosea was moving boldly now, advancing a few yards, his shield held before him, then halting for a few moments before starting again.

"Don't move for a spell, any of you," Arnold called softly. "He seems to be alone, so we'll wait until he fires again. This next time, keep watch for the flash of his rifle. Then we'll rush him before he can reload again." His companions agreed.

Tonie pressed herself against the earth, hoping she was invisible in the grass that stood almost a foot high. Only by arching her neck could she see the birch trees, and she discovered she was afraid to raise her head, afraid to move.

The heavy silence was almost unbearable. An ant started to crawl up the side of Tonie's face, and she felt a strong desire to brush it aside but managed to restrain herself. Then the insect began to move down the back of her neck, inside her open buckskin collar. She could hold off no longer. Reaching up impatiently, she brushed the ant away.

The enemy fired a third shot, again barely missing Tonie.

Her companions took careful note of the spot where the shot had originated. As Arnold, Ernie, and Mack leaped to their feet and charged toward the copse, Stalking Horse sent a single arrow through the brambles.

By the time the onrushing trio reached the spot, the man who had called himself Alvin Munson was dead, the Cherokee's arrow protruding from his heart.

It would be impossible to question him now. Arnold and Ernie were disappointed, but both refrained from lecturing Stalking Horse. In his world, a warrior had to kill or be killed.

However, they prevented him from scalping the man, and, as the others watched, they searched him. But he carried no documents, no identification of any kind. A manufacturer's stamp inside his boots indicated that they had been made in New York. His rifle had been made in New England, and the blade of his knife bore an insignia that Arnold recognized as the mark of a Pittsburgh metalsmith. Nothing on his person indicated anything about him.

They searched through his saddle bags, and finally, at the bottom of one of them, they found a cloth bag nestled inside a dirty shirt. When they opened it, they found an inner bag, made of thick paper. Opening it gingerly, they saw a handful of crystals, each the size of an almond. These crystals looked harmless, but they exuded the same pungent, nauseating odor that they had smelled at the pond.

At Arnold's suggestion a deep hole was dug, and the bag of crystals was buried in it. While the men were engaged in their task, Tonie walked to the bank of the spring-fed pond, with Hosea quietly keeping watch over her. Her knees felt weak. Fighting the desire to wretch, she inhaled deeply. Suddenly she recognized a faint but thoroughly unpleasant scent. Heavy clubs seemed to be beating at her temples.

"Uncle Arnold!" she called.

Within seconds she was surrounded by the anxious members of the party.

Tonie pointed toward the pond. "Smell that water!" she told them. "The stink of rotten eggs is there. It isn't strong, but it's the same."

Ernie dropped to his hands and knees, sniffing the pond cautiously. "Tonie is right," he said as he stood. "This pond wasn't rancid when you first saw it, Arnold?"

"It was pure and fresh and clean," the old man said quietly. "That means he must have come here after poisoning the first pond and poisoned this one, too, figuring the train would make its next stop here."

"We'll never know why he was so intent on killing innocent people who have done no harm to anyone," Ernie said, sighing. "At least we're rid of him, and that's all to the good."

Stalking Horse carefully removed the dead man's boots, knife, and pistol, along with his ammunition and powder, before carrying the body away from the wagon train's path, where it would be allowed to rot.

"We will give the pack horse or the rifle to Tonie, whichever of the two she prefers," Ernie said gallantly as they started toward the wagon train camp.

"Thank you," she replied, "but I want neither."

Ernie assumed, as did Mack, that the girl was depressed because the man had been killed.

She did not disillusion them, but signaled discreetly to her uncle, who fell back to the rear of the line and rode beside her.

"I wonder if you noticed," Tonie said, "that all three of the man's shots were fired at me. As far as he knew, I was the least likely to hit him, the least dangerous to him, yet he concentrated his fire only on me."

"I know," he replied, speaking in Russian. "The secret police is like a snake with many heads. Remove one, and hundreds of others grow. That is an old proverb, Antoinette. From now on, we take no unnecessary risks with your safety."

Tonie shuddered, then felt ashamed of herself. "I was

scared when he was shooting at me, Uncle Arnold. I'm not a coward, I swear I'm not, but I was afraid."

"Of course you were," he told her. "You're not lacking in courage. But anyone who isn't afraid of a powerful, unseen enemy is a fool."

When they reached the wagon train, they found that funeral services had already been held for the two men who had died after drinking from the pond that morning.

Ernie made a brief announcement. "As we suspected, the man who poisoned the pond was the same man we entertained at supper last night. He has also poisoned the pond at which we would have stopped tomorrow. But he'll cause no more harm to anyone. Stalking Horse saw to that."

At Tonie's suggestion, the dead man's riding horse was given to one of the widows and the pack horse was presented to the other. Then her uncle took her arm and led her to Ernie's elegant wagon. There the Baron and Whip were sipping tiny glasses of colorless Austrian schnapps, and another glass was filled for Arnold.

"Not until we came back here did I realize you were personally involved, Tonie. I should have realized when Munson made you his only target that he was working for the Russians."

The girl nodded.

"The question now," Whip said, "is whether to tell everybody that the Russian secret police want to kill you because you defied them."

"Do what you please," Tonie said in a dull voice. "It doesn't matter."

A tap sounded at the door, and Dr. Martin entered. "May I intrude?" he asked, and assuming the reply would be positive, seated himself on the top of a mahogany chest of drawers. "Mack Dougall was just telling me the details of your encounter with Munson," he said. "I knew at once why he was firing at Tonie, and I figured that's what you'd be discussing."

Ernie nodded and poured him a glass of schnapps.

The physician handed the drink to the girl. "She needs this. I don't."

237

Tonie shook her head, but Bob gave her no chance to speak. "Drink it," he said. "Doctor's orders."

She managed to down the drink, and shuddered.

"We've just raised the question of whether to tell the whole company why the Russians want to kill Tonie," Whip said. "Myself, I'm torn. I can see arguments in favor of both sides. I think you have to make the choice yourself, Tonie."

"I just told you," she said. "It doesn't matter." The schnapps seemed to be burning a hole inside of her, but she had to admit that she no longer felt lethargic. Perhaps Bob's presence rather than the liquor was responsible.

"I want to be fair to everybody," Ernie said.

"My only concern is being fair to Tonie," her uncle declared.

"I see no useful cause being served by making this information public," Bob Martin said, his manner unexpectedly vehement. "We'd only be drawing attention to her, unnecessary attention. In this instance I say that what people don't know won't hurt them."

Tonie was surprised that he was taking such a strong interest in her personal situation.

"Arnold," Bob continued, "you understand the Russian mentality, and we don't. Are they likely to attempt another attack on Tonie?"

"Perhaps," the old man replied, frowning as he tried to solve the puzzle for himself. "I would say they are determined to damage the wagon train because it is in the czar's interest that we fail to reach Oregon. Certainly the Russians are vindictive, and they patently hate Tonie because she refused to obey their orders. So I would guess they well might make another attempt on her life."

"In that case we must change her routines," Bob Martin said briskly. "I see no reason she can't continue to serve as chief monitor. She spends her days riding between the center column and one of the wing columns, so it would be very difficult to isolate her there. But I think it would be wrong for her to go off again as she did with today's search party. And I believe it would be too dangerous to allow her to go out hunting again."

"That makes sense," Whip said.

"It does," Ernie replied.

Even Arnold slowly nodded.

Tonie didn't know whether to laugh or weep. They were restricting her future activities, and no one was even bothering to consult her. Life would be far more boring if she couldn't go hunting any more, but she could console herself with the thought that Bob wasn't as unconcerned about her as he appeared. Certainly his interest in her welfare was personal, his involvement greater than that of Whip and Ernie. Or was it? She had no way of knowing.

X

The long trek continued, the wagon train creeping slowly through the heartlands of the Great Plains. They still followed the Platte River, and some members of the expedition were surprised when the broad stream rose higher and flowed more swiftly.

"It always does that," Whip explained, "but this year there must have been more snow than usual in the Rockies. The thaws come later on the heights than thcy do down below, of course, so the melted snow is just now beginning to reach us from the North Platte, the South Platte, and some of the smaller streams that flow into the big river."

During one nooning, when the sun overhead was actually hot, Danny and Chet, along with some of the older boys, decided to get undressed and go for a swim, but the water was so unexpectedly icy they soon changed their minds. They were dressing, threatening to push the last one who finished into the chilly water, when their horseplay was interrupted by Whip, who ran toward them from the circle.

"I ought to skin you lads alive," he said. "I ought to hang you up by the heels, like we do with dead polecats. But even that would be too good for you."

Rarely did the wagonmaster become so angry, at least

In public, and the boys were shocked. Danny, who had frozen in the midst of pulling on a stocking, was the only one of the group who had the courage to raise his voice. "What—what did we do wrong, Whip?"

"What did you do? You still don't know?" Whip's fury increased. "You think of yourselves as men, or close to it. But it looks to me like you're babies. About the same age as the little Malcolm youngster."

They were still at a loss to understand what they had done to inspire his wrath.

"Finish dressing!" Whip commanded, glaring at them. The boys wasted no time.

"Chet Harris!" Whip barked. "See that stick in the grass? Pick it up."

Chet quickly picked up a portion of a broken tree branch. It was two feet long, about three inches in diameter, and it was surprisingly heavy.

"Pass it around!" Whip ordered.

The broken branch moved from hand to hand, and none of the boys knew what to do with it. Some weighed it, others turned it over and over in their hands, while a few got rid of it very quickly, as though afraid it would contaminate them. At last it was passed back to Chet.

"Bring it with you," Whip commanded, "and all of you come with me." He led them to the bank of the river, forcing them to stand with him on the wet, soggy ground. "Look at the river and tell me what you see."

Again Danny was the only one to speak. "One mighty lot of water," he muttered.

Several of the boys started to snicker.

"You, Chet! Throw that stick into the river. Heave it as far as you can toward midstream," Whip instructed.

Using all of his strength, Chet hurled the broken branch toward the center of the rapidly flowing river.

"Now keep your eyes on it," Whip said, "and tell me when it disappears."

The boys crowded close to the bank. They saw the branch bobbing up and down as it was carried eastward at a rapid speed.

"It's gone!" one of them shouted.

"No it isn't," Chet said, correcting him. "I can still see it. Well, maybe not. I reckon you're right. It's gone."

Whip remained firm. "Now," he said, "I want somebody to tell me what you've just learned."

There was a long, tense silence. Then Danny said, "That stick got carried away awful fast. The river looks pretty strong, but the current is even faster than we think it is—and stronger, too. So we might have been in trouble if we'd gone swimming."

"*Might* have been in trouble?" Whip raised an eyebrow. "Some of you—especially you, Chet—think you're pretty good swimmers. Well, I guarantee you that every last one of you would have been washed downstream and drowned in almost no time."

The chastened boys stared down at the river bank.

"After this," Whip said, "you check with Ernie or with me before you start doing things on your own. You're in the wilderness, not on somebody's farm property, and God help those of you who forget it! Remember—your life and everyone else's depends on your alertness. So keep your eyes open every minute of the day." He turned and walked back to the circle.

The boys straggled after him, their lesson learned. Anyone who toyed with the forces of nature in the vast expanses of the Great Plains was running a dangerous risk.

As the spring advanced, rain fell more frequently, and usually at night. The Platte continued to rise, sometimes overflowing its banks for a distance of ten or fifteen yards on both sides. Whip kept the river under close observation and took the precaution of establishing the campsite some distance from the flowing waters.

There seemed to be less need to exercise such extreme care during the nooning period, however. It was far easier and simpler to form the circle fairly close to the river so that the animals could be led to the bank for watering. At nooning the wagons moved into the circle, experience enabling the drivers to perform the task quickly. Teams were unhitched and taken to the river for watering, then allowed to graze inside the circle. Hungry children were given smoked buffalo meat or, in some families, leftovers from breakfast, and any adults who were hungry did likewise. However, most of them had gone on a schedule of eating only two meals a day and preferred to wait until evening.

No one ever knew who first became aware of the approach of catastrophe that day. All at once men began to shout, women screamed, and somebody called, "My God! The river!"

The fear in their voices was so intense that virtually everyone jumped up, and those who had been taking naps awakened. What met their eyes was so unbelievable that it paralyzed them.

As they looked upstream, they saw a towering wall of water bearing down on them. No longer just a swiftly moving river, the Platte had been transformed into a wildly raging torrent. The boiling, churning water, carrying entire trees and other debris, bore down on the wagon train in a mighty tidal wave.

The initial reaction of fright gave way to frenzied panic as people struggled for survival in the midst of the nightmare. Those whose wagons stood nearest to the river were in the greatest danger. They began to run across the circle to the far side, some carrying small children.

Only Whip's and Hosea's instant response prevented the damage from being even worse. Reacting independently, they began to drive the bewildered horses and oxen toward the far edge of the circle, away from the raging flood. Whip fired his pistols, then his rifle, while Hosea roared in a deep baritone, clapping his hands together repeatedly, trying to get the animals moving away from the danger.

The animals began to stampede, and even those that had remained calm joined in the race. In almost no time, most were pushing against the wagons at the outer side of the circle. The horses and oxen had no idea of what was happening, but their instinctive panic led them away from the flood.

The wave approached at blinding speed, the gray waters

spelling doom for everything in their path. The wagons that stood nearest the bank bore the brunt of the attack. Wood splintered, loose objects were picked up and swept away, and the roar of the water was so loud that the screams of the women and children could not be heard.

Then, as suddenly as it had come, the wave was gone, still churning furiously as it raced eastward. Gradually the waters subsided, and although the Platte had spread beyond its banks, it once again became relatively harmless.

A woman screamed. Her husband and small daughter, who had been napping in their wagon, had been swept away by the wave, and her teenaged son, who had been whittling as he had sat on the rear stoop of the wagon had also disappeared. Some of the men found his battered, lifeless body about half a mile downstream later in the day.

Only a head count ultimately revealed that another family, who had joined the caravan in Indiana, had been swallowed up by the great wave. The husband, the wife, and all three of their small children had simply vanished as though they had never existed.

A young bachelor, a former bookkeeper from Cincinnatti who yearned for a life on his own farm, had suffered a broken leg when heavy debris had smashed into him. "I—I'm lucky I'm still here, I guess," he muttered through his pain as Dr. Martin set his leg.

Emily Harris required stitches in her thigh, where she had been gashed by a tree uprooted by the raging river. Terence Malcolm had suffered a sprained ankle, but had no idea how it had happened.

Grace Drummond was also injured. The wave had picked her up, then slammed her against a wagon, knocking her unconscious. As nearly as Dr. Martin could diagnose, she was suffering from a brain concussion. For hours Nat Drummond stayed at his wife's side, applying cold compresses to her forehead. Late in the afternoon, she stirred and opened her eyes. Sitting upright, she began to berate her husband for his idleness.

The grinning Nat knew she had returned to normal. Walking away from her bed, he left her to her own devices. Not until Grace finally realized what had happened to her did her anger subside.

Three workhorses were missing, as were a pair of oxen. One of the riding horses had broken a leg when it had been rammed by floating debris, and it had to be shot.

Aside from the tragedy of the man and his daughter, one entire wagon and its contents had been picked up and carried away by the wave. No portion of the wagon itself, nor its contents, remained. The owners, a young couple who had come all the way from the mountains of Pennsylvania, were forced to move into another wagon with the girl's parents.

There was debris everywhere, scattered as if by a giant hand. Two uprooted trees, one of them a forty-foot oak, complete with a portion of its roots, lay in the muddy ooze near the bank of the now-normal river. Branches of all sizes, torn from trees along the river, were everywhere. Even rocks and boulders had been strewn about by the raging wave.

What shocked the pioneers most was the waterlogged corpse of a cow buffalo washed up by the torrent. They could scarcely believe their eyes. The beast was huge and must have weighed at least fifteen hundred pounds.

Smaller animals had fallen victim, too. Rabbits and gophers, chipmunks, a raccoon and an antelope doe had been smashed almost beyond recognition by the furious river.

Several of the wagons, at least a half-dozen by preliminary count, were severely damaged, while a large number of others had been badly battered. Canvas tops and sides had been ripped away, then carried downstream by the wave. Struts that had supported the canvas roofs were either gone or reduced to kindling. Axles had been twisted and bent and were now useless, and one wagon teetered precariously because its wheels on the water side had been torn off.

It would be a long time before the owners of the stricken wagons would be able to judge accurately how much of their property had been lost. All they knew was that the remaining contents of their wagons were a muddy, soggy mess. Emergency food supplies were ruined. Pots, pans, and broken crockery littered the area, as did odd items of clothing, including a child's shoe and a torn woman's shift, which was draped around a bush.

Those who ventured near the river bank sank almost to their knees, and several had to be hauled out of the gripping, sucking mud. Hours would pass before the ground there had drained and dried off sufficiently to support the weight of a person.

Everyone pitched in to help. The circle of wagons was moved even further away from the bank of the Platte, although it was unlikely that the extraordinary phenomenon would be repeated. Then the remaining contents of the stricken wagons were spread out to dry, and the women went to work scrubbing down the muddy interiors.

Men with experience as carpenters made new struts from supplies carried in the special wagon, which also provided new canvas and axles to replace those that had been damaged beyond repair. Whip promised the dazed owners of the wagons that the hunters and fishermen would give them enough meat and fish to replace what they had lost. Other wagon owners contributed jars of preserves and sacks of beans, coffee, flour, and sugar.

The lost clothing was yet another problem, but Arnold and Mack promised to provide enough buffalo and deer hides so that people could replace their wardrobes.

The task of repairing the damage cost the company two days on the trail. No one objected to the extra labor involved, to be sure, and the hunters kept their word, shooting enough game in the next forty-eight hours to provide the stricken with at least the beginnings of new emergency food supplies and new wardrobes.

Everyone was appalled by the shocking and unexpected experience, and the entire company suddenly realized that the forces of nature were capable of inflicting cruel punishment on the unwary. The very word "wilderness" was enough to inspire respect.

Fortunately game was marvelously plentiful in the late spring. Whip wanted to replace the losses as rapidly as possible, so he asked for volunteers to join the regular hunting parties. Tonie was the first to offer her services, but Whip politely declined.

She was furious, telling herself that Bob Martin was to blame for wrapping her in a thick, protective mantle. Although she continued to help him in the infirmary, she made it clear to him that she was annoyed.

Another volunteer, much to everyone's surprise, was Nat Drummond. The hunters were working in pairs now, and Arnold said he would make Nat his partner. The combination seemed incongruous, but Arnold withheld judgment. "I want to see how he makes out before I'll listen to any criticism," he said.

The new team went out late one afternoon, returning a scant two hours later with a buck. But the initial flurry of excitement subsided when it was learned that Arnold, not Nat, had shot the deer.

The next day Arnold returned to the campsite early, his scouting duties completed, and he and Nat went out again. They headed toward a wooded area that the scout had seen, earlier in the day, off to the northwest.

Nat looked clumsy in the saddle, but he had no difficulty in maintaining the pace set by his companion, and he appeared to be enjoying the outing thoroughly. In a talkative mood, he began to chat as they cantered. "Can I tell you somethin' private, Arnold? It's taken a lifetime for me to do what I've always wanted to do."

Arnold nodded encouragingly.

"I grew up near the Kentucky border, you see, and when I was a boy, I heard all kinds of stories about Dan'l Boone and the others who tamed the wilderness."

"Most of those stories are exaggerated, I'm sure," Arnold said. "I've heard some of them just as I heard many others about this part of the wilderness when I lived in Independence. Hunters and trappers and guides have done some wonderful things, but a lot of them are also good liars. When a couple of them would get together with my wife and me in our kitchen, they'd start bragging, and before long they'd be trying to tell bigger and bigger stories so they could outdo each other."

"I reckon you're right," Nat said. "But you still don't know what this means to me, ridin' across the wilderness in search of game. When I grew up, I had a lot of hopes and dreams, but then I got married. And you know Grace.

I had to buckle down and make a living on the farm, or she gave me no peace. But this is a grand life. I couldn't ask for anythin' better."

They rode on in companionable silence, and ultimately the woods came into view on the horizon. As the pair drew nearer, six Indians rapidly rode out of the woods toward them.

"Oh-oh," Arnold said softly. "Now we'll see how your daydreams have prepared you for a real crisis. They're warriors—I'm not sure of their tribe at this distance—and they're bent on making mischief. I wouldn't be surprised if they were heading for the wagon train when they spotted us. They'll pause long enough to knock us out of commission, if they can."

Nat displayed remarkable calm. "First they got to do it," he said, eyeing the onrushing braves. "Just tell me what to do, Arnold. You're the boss."

Shading his eyes as they continued to canter, Arnold grunted. "We're in for real trouble. They're Paiute. I'd rather walk barefoot into a nest of rattlesnakes. Paiute can't be bluffed. Either we kill them or they kill us. There's no halfway measures, no evasions. If we run, they'll chase us and catch us. If we stop and wait for them, we'll be sitting targets, and we'll never get off a shot."

"Are you tellin' me we keep ridin'?"

"Right! No matter what happens, don't slow your pace. You understand?"

"Sure."

"All right," Arnold said. "Get your rifle ready. After you fire, reload as fast as you can, then fire again. Keep doing it."

"All right." Nat still seemed calm.

"They'll spread out as they come closer. We may move through their formation—provided they don't hit us first. Then we'll turn and come at them again from the rear." Arnold turned for an instant to look at his companion, afraid that Drummond would begin to show signs of panic when he realized how badly the odds were against them.

But the stubby farmer grinned, showing two rows of crooked, yellowed teeth. "It seems t' me we got one big advantage, Arnold. These rifles have a much longer range than their arrows."

Arnold chuckled. Nat was going to weather the crisis in good shape.

"If we can reload quick enough, maybe we can get off two rounds before they start sendin' their arrows at us."

"Not maybe, Nat. Two rounds are a minimum. And we've got to make those bullets count. At close range they'll overwhelm us. They're deadly shots with their arrows, and they can handle spears expertly, too."

Nat checked his rifle, hunching forward in his saddle. "I'm ready any time you give the word."

Together as they rode, they kept a sharp watch on the oncoming Paiute. The braves held their bows and were reaching for their first arrows.

Arnold Mell calculated the distance coolly. He felt reasonably sure that at least one of his bullets would find its mark, and he could only hope that Drummond would hold up. If the Indians realized they were dealing with a novice, they would redouble their efforts.

The two groups drew nearer.

"Now!" Arnold called, raising his own rifle and firing.

A brave seemed to rise high in the air from the back of his pony, then toppled to the ground.

Nat took deliberate aim and squeezed the trigger. A second brave flung his hands over his head, tried to steady himself in vain and fell to the grass, where he lay motionless, face down.

Arnold was quietly elated. He hadn't expected his partner to be this effective. "Keep up the good work," he called.

Nat reloaded with the speed of a marksman.

Arnold had his rifle up to his shoulder, and again he fired, then cursed as he saw he had missed by inches.

Nat's every move was as deliberate as though he were firing at a stationary target. He squeezed the trigger again, and a third brave clutched his chest, then dropped to the turf.

By this time the remaining Paiute were close enough to

enter the fray actively, and they sent their arrows in the direction of the pair cantering toward them. But the warriors were rattled because of the losses they had already suffered, and their shots went wild.

Seeing their consternation, Arnold knew he and his companion had victory almost in hand. "Again!" he shouted.

Nat doggedly reloaded, but by this time the Paiute had had enough of combat for one day. Swinging their ponies in an arc, they fled toward the north, quickly increasing their speed to a full gallop.

Two of the riderless ponies followed, their panic so great that they eventually caught up with the retreating band. The remaining pony was bewildered, however, and stood uncertainly, near his fallen master.

Arnold slowed his own mount to a sedate walk. "No point in chasing them, Nat. They won't want any more fighting today. You did a great job."

Nat slowed, too, and chuckled. "We didn't do too bad," he admitted as he followed his partner's example and turned back.

"This takes care of our hunting for the day," Arnold said, "but we'll bring a few souvenirs back with us so our friends won't think we're making up frontier tales."

The chunky little farmer stared at him apprehensively. "You ain't plannin' to take scalps, Arnold?"

The old man laughed aloud. "That's one habit I've never bothered to take up." He dismounted, then walked quietly toward the riderless pony, moving slowly and gently so he wouldn't alarm the animal. Removing a lariat from a hook at his belt, he twirled it, then threw the loop over the pony's head.

The animal balked, but as it pulled back, the noose tightened around its neck, and it had the good sense not to fight the inevitable. It stood still again.

Arnold pointed toward the crumpled body of one of the braves. "Help yourself to his weapons," he called.

Only now did Nat Drummond become diffident. He paused for a long time before he summoned the courage to bend down for the dead warrior's bow and quiver of arrows.

Arnold had no such inhibitions. Working swiftly as he led the docile pony, he removed knives from the belts of the other two corpses, picked up a spear, and then bent low to take a necklace of elk's teeth from the body of one warrior. "You may want to give this to your wife," he said, handing Nat the necklace. "Here. And take the pony, too, along with the spear and this knife."

Nat was overwhelmed. "You caught the pony, I didn't. And you're keepin' nothin'."

"Not so. I'll keep this one knife. It so happens that I've got all sorts of souvenirs from fights in the past. Besides, you deserve the lion's share. After all, you took care of two warriors to my one."

Flushing with embarrassment, pride, and gratitude, the heavily laden Nat mounted his own horse and, leading the captured Paiute pony, rode beside the older man as they started back toward the wagon train campsite.

"For a fellow who spent his early years daydreaming, you're a mighty fine partner to have around in an emergency," Arnold said. "From now on, I'm going hunting with no one but you."

Supper was almost ready when they reached camp, and a ripple of excitement passed through the company when they saw the enemy weapons and the pony. Arnold was lavish in his praise of his companion and described his exploits at length while Nat looked down at the ground and shuffled his feet.

The older boys were awed as they examined the captured weapons, and people clamored for the privilege of offering Nat their congratulations. Whip and Mack pumped his hand, Ernie clapped him on the back, and Stalking Horse caught hold of his wrist in a gesture of brotherly affection. Ted Woods and Hosea made no comment, but their expressions indicated that they shared the general opinion that Nat was a hero.

The excitement began to ebb when Cathy beat the side of a kettle with a heavy spoon to indicate that supper was now prepared. People formed a line to help themselves to a stew of buffalo meat and root vegetables, including wild beets. Nat deposited his booty in his wagon, then joined his wife in the line.

Grace gave him no chance to speak. "You think highly of yourself, Mr. Drummond," she said.

"Now that you mention it, Mrs. Drummond, maybe I do." He took the bone-handled Paiute knife from his belt, turned it over in his hand as he studied it, and decided that from now on he would always carry it with him. "Behave yourself like a wife should, and maybe I'll teach you how to ride that pony. He's a quiet creature, which is what you ought to be, so by-and-by the two of you ought to get along just fine."

Grace drew in a breath, steadying herself for a retort. Those who stood near them in the line waited for the inevitable, loud outburst.

Nat gave her no opportunity to explode. "Before I forget it," he said, "I brought you a little present." He reached into the breast pocket of his linsey-woolsey shirt, then handed her the necklace of elk's teeth.

Grace looked at the highly polished teeth, and all at once tears came into her eyes. "How—how do I wear it?"

"See them rawhide thongs? They tie at the back of your neck."

"Will you tie it for me, Nat?"

He was startled by the unexpected humility in her usually strident voice. "Sure," he said, putting the necklace around her neck and tying it.

"How does it look, Nat?"

He glanced at the necklace but was even more conscious of the tears that were trickling silently down her weather-hardened cheeks. "Right pretty, Grace. That necklace suits you just fine."

Not caring who might be watching, Grace Drummond hugged her husband, squeezing him until he was breathless. "It was your pa and your brothers who used to tease you for wantin' to be like Dan'l Boone, wasn't it?"

Nat nodded. "Now and again they'd have their fun with me," he admitted.

"Well, I just wish they could see you now!" she exclaimed, speaking in her normal, booming voice. "Because you have the last laugh. Gracious, but I'm proud o' you, Nat Drummond!"

Arthur Elwood was fed up. The discomforts and hardships of wagon train living were almost unbearable, he found the food intolerable and the company dull beyond endurance. He was a city dweller, and he missed the luxuries of the East that he had known only in small quantities. He was dismayed by the prospect of settling in the Oregon country, and when others spoke of that supposed paradise as a land of milk and honey, he refused to listen.

He had joined the train only because he had hoped he could buy the land claims of the future settlers for a dollar or two per acre. He had expected to be able to purchase several thousand acres and then reap an enormous profit by selling them to speculators in the East for as much as ten dollars per acre. But not one member of the expedition had been willing to sell to him. These stubborn farmers had destroyed his chance to become wealthy.

He should have turned back at Fort Madison. Now each day's journey carried him farther from the civilization he craved. To hell with these crude people and their dreams of the future. He wanted his creature comforts now, while he was still young enough to enjoy them. A man in his forties had to think in immediate terms.

So, little by little, Arthur Elwood came to the conclusion that he should make a break and go back alone. He had never spent a single day in the wilderness by himself, but that didn't matter, he thought. All he had to do was follow the Platte until he came to the Missouri, and he didn't care whether his journey took him to Independence, St. Joseph, or Council Bluffs. Once he reached a real town, he had enough money in his belt to arrange for transportation to Chicago or Cincinnati.

How he would live once he returned to the East was a problem he would solve later. His immediate task was that of getting away. He could just take off on his own, he supposed, but it wasn't that easy. Stupidly, no doubt, he hadn't bothered to collect any emergency supplies, and he needed them badly. If he could sneak into the special wagon, he could fill his saddlebags with quantities of smoked buffalo meat or venison, along with parched corn, none of which he would ever touch again when he reached

254

a world where people ate real food. He would be wise to take a spare rifle, too, along with plenty of lead, a bullet mold, and extra gunpowder.

In a sense, he told himself, he had earned whatever he chose to take with him. After all, he had worked as a member of the water-gathering detail, engaging in physical labor that he abhorred.

His greatest mistake, he knew, was that of having joined the wagon train in the first place. He had always had a desk job, working for various land speculation companies. He disliked the outdoors and loathed physical exertion.

Other men on the train had become hunters, fishermen and woodcutters. He was ashamed by the knowledge that he had been assigned to gather water because he had proved unfit for any other kind of service. Well, when he returned to the East, he would sit at a desk again and wouldn't ever leave it.

He simply had to get away from these people. The life they were leading and the future that beckoned to them kept them cheerful, even in the face of the same adversity and hardships that haunted him. He had no real friends in the company and had almost nothing in common with anyone. Claudia Brentwood had been kind to him, but she had remained in Independence. He had been attracted to Cindy, but she had rebuffed him. No one else interested him, and he spent the social hours alone each day, even eating by himself because there was so little he could discuss with the other travelers. He hated the wagon train and all it represented.

Elwood's desire to escape made him desperate. One warm evening in early summer, he found it impossible to sleep. After hesitating for a long time, he screwed up his courage and, sneaking out of his wagon, made his way to the special wagon. Just before reaching it, he stumbled, landing on the ground with a hard, noisy thud, but he ignored the pain and held his breath, hoping no one had heard him. There was no sound, and he was relieved.

It was easy enough to untie the back flaps and let himself into the wagon. First he dropped the flap behind him, but quickly realized his mistake. It was so dark inside that he could see nothing. So he raised the flap again and left it open.

After fumbling for a time, staring at boxes, crates, and barrels, he pried open a barrel with his knife. The strong odor of smoked buffalo meat almost gagged him, but he couldn't afford to take enough time to search for the milder-tasting venison. He crammed meat into his saddlebag, then carefully replaced the barrel cover. It took longer to locate a sack of parched corn, but now he acted quickly, making a small slit in one end with his knife and pouring enough of the contents into the saddlebag to fill it.

It took almost an hour to locate the spare arms and munitions. The rifle he selected was larger and heavier than his own weapon, but he was in no position to be particular, so he took it, along with a bar of lead and a horn filled with powder. Realizing it would be impossible to locate a bullet press in this gloom, he knew he had to alter his plans. He would hide his loot in his wagon. Then, when people were at breakfast, he would steal a press from a neighboring wagon that stood behind him. That meant he would have to wait until tomorrow night before he could leave. But no matter—he had attended to most of his needs, and after all these months, it wouldn't hurt him to wait an extra day.

The lead bar was heavy, but Elwood managed to squeeze it into his hip pocket before he climbed out of the wagon and lowered the flap behind him, carefully retying it. Then he hoisted the cumbersome saddlebag onto his shoulder, noting in surprise that day was breaking. He had finished his task none too soon. Staggering slightly under the weight of the bag and the lead, he turned away.

At that moment someone stepped out from between two wagons. Elwood saw Hosea, his blowgun in his hand, a dart already fitted into it.

Elwood panicked. "For God's sake, don't shoot that contraption at me! Look here, I—I have plenty of money, and I'll pay you well if you'll just forget that you've seen —"

"Whip decide what to do," Hosea said, gesturing in

the direction of the fire, which had burned low. "You come."

Fully aware that the blowgun could kill instantly, Arthur Elwood had no choice. His stomach, like his feet, felt leaden as he walked ahead of the grim Ashanti.

Whip was already awake, and he listened without comment to Hosea's explanation. Then he reached for the stolen rifle, examined the contents of the saddlebag, and asked, "What else did you take?"

It was useless to lie, so Elwood handed him the lead bar and powder horn.

"Don't say anything now," Whip told him. "I know what I'd do to you if it was up to me. But it isn't my place to decide." He led the way to Ernie von Thalman's wagon.

The Baron, who was just dressing, listened in stone-faced silence. "Hosea," he said, "keep Mr. Elwood under guard. Right here."

Soon the whole company was awake and stirring. Wood was gathered and the fire built up, water was carried from the Platte, and the women in charge of the cooking went to work.

Ernie waited until most members of the expedition had assembled, then made a short speech in which he explained what had happened. "I'm glad to say this is the first time we've faced such a situation, but now we've got to do something about it. As your president, I'm asking you—right now—to elect ten people as a jury. We don't want to delay our day's march too long, so I'll ask those who are elected to join me over yonder, in front of my wagon. Immediately."

Nat Drummond was the first to be elected. Whip declined the honor, as did the scouts, who departed on their regular missions as soon as they ate their usual early breakfast.

Before the meeting of the entire company broke up, Whip announced that he wanted to say a few words. "Folks," he began, "some of you may wonder why we're making so much of what's happened this morning."

"That's right," Cathy called out boldly, always willing to

champion an underdog. "It doesn't seem to me that Mr. Elwood committed any great crime. The food in the special wagon belongs to all of us. Every man here carries a rifle and ammunition, so I don't see what harm Mr. Elwood has done. Real harm, I mean. What he's taken is actually minor, so all this fuss strikes me as silly."

Whip had to respect her attitude. At the same time, he was glad she had spoken up because it would be easier now for him to emphasize the point he was trying to make.

"Mrs. van Ayl has a valid point," he said. "I think you folks know me well enough to realize I'm not vindictive, and I sure as shooting am not proposing that we boil Arthur Elwood in oil. But I'm afraid a lot of you may not realize the importance of the special wagon and what it means to all of us."

He paused, looked around at the people gathered in the circle, then spoke again very slowly. "That wagon is the key to our survival. It can mean the difference between life and death to every last one of us."

His words created a stir, and people muttered to each other.

"I mean what I say. Literally," Whip told them. "After the wave hit us, we'd have been in a pretty fix if we hadn't carried spare axles and canvas and wheels and such with us. We may have troubles with Indians before this trip ends, serious troubles, and I can see where one rifle and one lead bar that can be molded into bullets could make the difference between life and death."

The members of the company were beginning to understand, and Whip was rewarded by nods and other signs of recognition.

"On the day you joined the train, every last one of you was told that *nobody* is allowed to go into the special wagon, ever, without my own personal permission. I told you that included everybody—Ernie von Thalman, the scouts—I don't care who it is. Well, Mr. Elwood chose to disobey that order. I'll grant you that he didn't take much. But if fifty or a hundred others get the same idea and start taking things, what then? A rifle here, a barrel of pickled meat there, some gunpowder, an extra blanket or two. Pretty soon the special wagon will be plucked clean, and then—may God have mercy on all of us."

Cathy was forced to agree with him, her emphatic nod making the change in her attitude plain to everyone around her.

"There are no stores between here and Oregon. No stores once I get you there, either. The closest place you can buy a nail, a hammer, or a frying pan is way back in Independence. For at least two more years, until freight wagons start crossing the continent, you'll have to make do with what you already own or can make for yourselves. All that stands between you and sure disaster is that special wagon and the supplies it carries." He took a deep breath. "That's about all I have to say for now. I hope you'll remember it. For your own sakes, not mine, because I can get along on my own in the mountains." He stalked off, and the meeting broke up.

One by one the jurors gathered. Some of the older boys, who lingered, curious, in the vicinity, were sent on their way by a curt and unexpectedly stern Ernie. At last ten jurors stood in front of the wagon, and Ernie opened the wagon door. "You can come out now," he called.

A miserable Arthur Elwood appeared, closely followed by Hosea. Ernie thanked the Ashanti and dismissed him, sending him off for breakfast. Then he pointed to the saddlebag, rifle, lead bar, and powder horn. "These are the items Mr. Elwood stole from the special wagon. Do you admit it, Mr. Elwood?"

There was a moment's hesitation. "Not exactly. The saddlebag is my own."

Ernie was surprisingly patient. "Very well. But you took its contents. Meat and corn."

Elwood could only nod.

"Will you tell us your reasons?"

Suddenly the dam burst, and Arthur Elwood became eloquent, explaining in detail that he had long hated every aspect of wagon train living. "I took these things," he concluded passionately, "because I need them to get back to real civilization. I'm sick of this kind of living, and I just can't stand it any more. I'm not sorry I stole, and to hell with Oregon!"

His listeners were startled. It was unusual enough to hear someone refuse to express remorse for committing a crime. But people whose hearts and souls were devoted to the settlement of the Oregon country found it inconceivable that one of their number had lost the desire to make a new life in a land that was unique. What they failed to realize, of course, was that Elwood had had different desires from the very moment he had joined the company.

Ernie broke the heavy silence. "Let me see if I understand you correctly, Mr. Elwood. You want to detach your wagon from the expedition and go back East. Is that correct?"

"No!" Elwood had no idea that his voice was becoming strident. "I was planning to use one of my team as a pack horse and simply swap my other workhorse for a riding horse."

"Leaving your wagon behind?"

"I have no use for the damned thing." The man was bitter. "I couldn't tolerate the idea of creeping back across these infernal flatlands in it."

Ernie nodded, then turned to the jurors. "Gentlemen," he said, "I want to offer you a thought you can either accept or reject. The property Mr. Elwood stole from us has a strictly limited value. It's the theft itself, including that of the rifle, that's important. It seems to me that we can't compel a person to endure our company. All of us are voluntary members of this group, bound together by an unwritten compact and observing an unwritten code of conduct for the sake of our mutual good. Mr. Elwood chooses to break the contract, and in my opinion that's his privilege."

"We want no more to do with him than he wants with us," Nat said in a disgusted tone. "It ain't worth the fuss to turn his wagon into a jail and keep him in it. Let him go, that's what I say, and good riddance to him."

"You mean we ought to throw him out?" one of the other jurors asked.

Ernie shook his head. "We can't quite do that. These plains are inhospitable enough to men like Whip, who know the area well. I believe Mr. Elwood himself suggested the solution. We can trade one of the spare horses we've acquired for one of his workhorses. Let him take what he can carry of his belongings—food, clothes, cooking utensils and the like. Weapons, too, of course. Let him keep the food he's stolen, along with the rifle and ammunition. We'll take his wagon in return, along with any other belongings he chooses to leave behind. You needn't accept this idea, gentlemen. All I ask is that you consider it."

The jurors moved off down the line of wagons to confer privately. Some of the women brought them breakfast, then Ernie was given a plate, and Cathy insisted that Elwood be fed, too.

The jurors talked earnestly as they ate and needed no urging to reach a prompt decision, for they shared Whip's desire not to delay the start of the day's journey any longer than necessary.

Ernie ate in silence, refraining from conversing with Arthur Elwood.

Sipping their mugs of coffee, the jurors returned to the outside of the Baron's wagon. "Seein' it wouldn't be right to hang the bastard," Nat said, "we've decided your thinkin' is pretty good, Ernie. We'll make the trade, just like you said—on one condition. He's got to leave this mornin', right now. We don't want him hangin' around. And if you can spare the extra time, maybe you'll keep an eye on him while he packs to make sure he don't cheat us."

"You've heard the sentence pronounced by the jury, Mr. Elwood," Ernie said. "Do you have any comment?"

"It suits me just fine," Elwood replied angrily. "I'm happy to leave as fast as I can get myself organized."

The decision was communicated to Whip, and while the train made ready to leave on the day's march, Elwood returned to his wagon to pack another saddlebag and take his blankets, spare boots, and a frying pan. Ernie fetched one of the extra horses to give the man in exchange for his workhorse and brought it to his wagon, where Elwood was finishing his hurried task. Just then, a concerned Whip also appeared at the wagon. "I hope you know what you're doing, Mr. Elwood," he said. "Even men who have been hunters and trappers for years don't like traveling alone in these parts."

Arthur Elwood shrugged.

Whip looked at the saddlebags filled with food and made some mental calculations. "You're not carrying enough provisions to see you all the way to Council Bluffs or Independence. You'll need to shoot some game on the way."

"I see no problem, Mr. Holt. I'm not totally unfamiliar with the handling of firearms."

Whip had intended to enumerate the dangers of solitary travel in the Great Plains, but the man was being so hostile that he refrained. All the same, his conscience forced him to make one last remark. "In my opinion you're taking one hell of a big risk. I can't say I like or trust you after the way you broke into the special wagon, but we can't throw you out and let you flounder on your own."

"I'll make out fine," the tight-lipped Elwood replied.

Whip shook his head. "I know more about the Great Plains than you do, and I think you're wrong to leave our group at this time. I don't want to scare you, and I don't want to upset you, but I *am* suggesting you come all the way to Oregon with us. Other trains will be following us, and it won't be too long before there's a reasonable amount of traffic going back and forth between the Atlantic and the Pacific. Be patient, and eventually you can make the journey safely in a regular wagon train with an escort."

Elwood's laugh was unpleasant. "How long will it be before you reach the Oregon country, Mr. Holt?"

"I hope we'll get there a year from this October or thereabouts. If our luck holds, we'll be spending the coming winter in the mountains, and then it will take us another traveling season to reach our goal."

"And I suppose it will be another few years before trains will be moving back and forth regularly."

"Most likely." Whip spoke calmly.

"In other words, I might have to wait for as long as

three years before I could go back East with a convoy, Mr. Holt!"

Whip nodded. "It's better than starving on the prairie or being murdered or having a lot of disagreeable things happen, things I'd rather not even mention."

"You're very kind." Elwood was sarcastic. "I guess you mean well, but there's no way on earth that I could spend another three years with these people and retain my sanity!"

Whip made a final effort. "Don't give us your answer right away. I realize there's a lot of hard feeling against you right this minute, but if you keep your mouth shut, folks will forget what happened in a few weeks. Think, Mr. Elwood—and think hard—before you decide to work your way back to civilization alone. It's a long, tough, dangerous road."

"In another month, you'll be two to three hundred miles deeper into the wilderness, and it would be that much more difficult for me to go home. No, Mr. Holt, I'm leaving right now, as soon as I'm through organizing my belongings."

Whip looked at him sharply, recognizing a note of hysteria in his voice, and saw that his eyes were feverish. Until this moment he had thought that Arthur Elwood was rational, but now he knew better. Other men had reacted to prolonged stays in the wilderness in a similar way.

There had been a hunter who contracted what mountain men called "cabin fever" after being cooped up for too long in a remote hut in the far reaches of the Rockies one winter. His frozen body was found weeks later, after he had hanged himself.

Then there was the trapper who had run amok, murdering and scalping his partner.

Certainly Elwood had lost his balance, too, and although Whip knew it was a waste of breath to talk sense to him, at least he might be able to persuade the man to delay his departure until he recovered somewhat.

"Mr. Elwood," he said, "for your own good and well-being, I recommend that you stay with us for just a few more days."

"Ha! You're just trying to trick me, Holt. A few more

days in this wagon train, and I'll take leave of my wits!"

"I'm not asking you to take my word that you're doomed if you pull out. I only want you to give yourself a chance to reconsider, to weigh the odds more carefully than you've done."

"I'm going!" the man shouted, apparently unaware he was screaming. "And nobody in the world can stop me. You hear me, Holt? Nobody!"

"Well, sir," Whip said, speaking slowly, "we can use the wagon you'll be leaving behind. And we won't miss the rifle or the supplies you'll be taking with you. I wish you good luck."

"Thanks," Elwood said curtly, and swiftly turned to his blankets and frying pan so he wouldn't be required to shake hands.

Whip exchanged a long glance with Ernie, who had remained silent during the long exchange. Whip shrugged. He had done his best to dissuade the man from his venture and felt he could no longer be responsible for the consequences. He went off without another word to prepare for the day's journey.

"I'm compelled to agree with Whip," Ernie said. "You're being foolish. Just because you made one mistake doesn't mean you've got to compound it."

"I made no mistake," Elwood said. Leaving some of his belongings behind, he tied the saddlebags, slung them over the back of the pack horse, and then piled on the remaining property he was taking.

"Good luck," Ernie said, echoing Whip's farewell. Rarely at a loss for words, this was one occasion when he could think of nothing to say.

Elwood mounted his horse, picked up the reins of the pack horse and moved out of the circle, saying goodbye to no one. He ignored those who stared after him and did not bother to return the waves and calls of those who tried to bid him farewell. He set out toward the East along the Platte, riding at a trot.

Long before noon, Elwood had covered far more ground than the caravan had traveled in the opposite direction the previous day. When he finally stopped to water his horses and allow them to graze for a time as he ate a little of the despised buffalo meat and corn, he figured that he had already gone as far toward home as the train had achieved in two days. At this rate he would reach civilization easily by midsummer. The prospect made him lightheaded.

That afternoon Elwood again rode at a rapid clip, pleased because he was not pushing beyond his own endurance or that of his horses. Whip Holt, he decided, had deliberately exaggerated the hazards to be found in the wilderness in order to discourage him from leaving. The wagonmaster's reasons were not hard to guess. He would be discredited when it became known back home that the discomforts of wagon train existence were far greater than the proponents of the Oregon expedition had ever admitted.

Late in the afternoon Elwood came to a small patch of woods, and there he stopped. First gathering and cutting some dead birch and maple, he built a fire. Then, while his horses grazed peacefully, he fished in the Platte. Again he seemed to be enjoying the best of good fortune—within a remarkably short time he landed a fish considerably larger than a trout, big enough to provide him with supper as well as breakfast in the morning.

That night he cooked the fish, and for the first time since he had joined the train the previous year, he thoroughly enjoyed his meal. The day had been warm, but the night breeze carried with it a chill from the Rockies, so he built up his fire and, wrapping himself in a blanket, dropped into a deep sleep.

Arthur Elwood awakened at daybreak, but it wasn't the light that aroused him. Almost immediately he sensed an alien presence. When he opened his eyes, he saw three wiry Indian warriors, their faces hideously streaked with paint, staring down at him.

He tried to struggle to his feet, but a blow across the side of his head from the butt of one of his own rifles sent him sprawling. Too dazed to move, he lay crumpled helplessly on the ground while the braves tied his ankles and wrists with rawhide thongs that bit cruelly into his flesh.

As he regained his powers of speech, he protested, but the Indians paid no attention to him. It dawned on him that they spoke no English.

In any event, they were absorbed in searching through his belongings. Obviously they regarded his horses as valuable acquisitions. They admired his two rifles, passing them back and forth and commenting to each other in what sounded like grunts. The gunpowder meant nothing to them; one tasted it, made a wry face, and then shoved several pinches into the captive's mouth. They had no idea, either, that the lead bar was intended for the use of bullets. All they knew was that it was heavy metal, and one casually struck Elwood across the side of the face with it before dropping it onto the ground.

Elwood felt certain that his cheekbone had been broken, and his pain was so great that he whimpered. Now he realized what Whip Holt had meant about the hazards of wilderness traveling, but understanding did not help him. There was nothing he could do. He could only hope that the warriors would leave after taking what they wanted. Then he would find some way to cut his hands loose and proceed with his journey.

While Elwood watched in terror, two of the warriors produced knives, then slashed away his clothes and boots, unmindful of the fact that their blades sometimes cut into his skin. Meanwhile the third brave busied himself gathering long pine needles. The fire was built higher, then all three lighted needle after needle and applied them to their victim's body, first to the soles of his feet and gradually moving higher.

Elwood's screams echoed across the prairie as his flesh blistered and burned. Never had he known it was possible for any human being to suffer such torment, and his mind could no longer function clearly.

Arthur Elwood did not know that the warriors weren't being deliberately malicious. This was their customary way, their normal routine in dealing with a prisoner. He had no idea that they subjected their own young braves to similar torture before admitting them to full manhood and its rights.

The screams and sobs of the captive impelled the warriors to continue tormenting him. They applied burning needle after burning needle, until no part of his body was left untouched.

By now Arthur Elwood was delirious. No man could be subjected to such intense, constant torture and remain sane. He could no longer even hear the hoarse sound of his own voice as he brokenly begged his captors for mercy.

Then he felt a new pain, so intense and searing that he mercifully lost consciousness. One of the braves had scalped him while he still lived, and torrents of blood cascaded down his sagging, hideously distorted face.

There was no more the warriors could do. Taking the white man's horses and rifles, blankets and food, they mounted their ponies and rode away. Just as Elwood had not looked back when he had left the wagon train, the braves paid no further attention to the remains of the white man who would soon die.

The wilderness was quiet again, and there was no sound but the crackling of the fire. Elwood's agony was still so great that, even though unconscious, he sometimes groaned and stirred feebly.

After a time, several pairs of gleaming eyes peered out of the woods. Coyote, attracted by the smell of blood, stood, motionless. Patient as only wild beasts could be, they waited until the fire died down, waited until the wounded creature died before they devoured his body.

XI

Henry St. Clair had good cause to be pleased with himself and his accomplishments. His long winter with the Cheyenne had been completely satisfying. In return for several jugs of cheap liquor and a handful of rifles, along with instruction in their use, he had spent the worst season of the year in the tribe's main town, living in a hide tent that stood near a roaring fire that never burned low. He had eaten heartily of venison, fish, buffalo, and corn. He had been supplied with a squaw, too, and although he wouldn't have glanced twice at the girl under other circumstances, she had proved lively enough to satisfy him.

Most important of all, he had whetted the appetite of the Cheyenne for booty, and he knew for certain they would make small, repeated raids on the Oregon-bound wagon train. The promise of horses and rifles was sufficient to insure that such raids would be frequent.

It was unfortunate that he had been unable to persuade the leaders of the Cheyenne to conduct a major attack on the train with the hundreds of warriors at their disposal. Like so many of the Indian nations that lived north of the Platte, they were apprehensive about the intentions of their even more powerful and vigorous neighbors, the

Blackfoot, who badly outnumbered them. If the Cheyenne suffered appreciable losses in an assault on the wagon train, their weakened condition would almost certainly invite an invasion by the Blackfoot.

Henry St. Clair was content to leave well enough alone. The Cheyenne would create innumerable problems for the train, and that would be enough. Meanwhile, to lessen the chances of the wagon train ever getting to Oregon, he would go on to the land of the Blackfoot and try to persuade their sachem to wage all-out war on the large company of whites who, in the months ahead, would dare to pass through their sacred territory.

St. Clair was glad, too, that he had delayed well into the spring in the land of the Cheyenne. Their scouts had reported the approach of two white men, one coming from the southeast and the other from the northwest, both of them known to the tribe. In need of civilized reinforcements to help him deal with the Blackfoot, whom it would be dangerous for him to visit alone, St. Clair waited for the arrival of these unknowns, hoping they would be suitable aides and trusting in his own powers of persuasion if that proved to be the case.

The first to appear was André Sebastian, whom the elders of the Cheyenne greeted as an old and trusted friend. Somewhat surprised to see a member of his own race, Sebastian made no comment and instead presented the sachem, the principal medicine man, and the members of the council of elders with gold-handled knives. As nearly as St. Clair could determine, the gold looked real, at least from a distance of several feet, but for the moment, he said nothing. It was obvious to him that any man who gave the Cheyenne presents of such value was no ordinary visitor.

That night the two guests sat side by side at the cooking fire of the sachem. St. Clair was quick to note that Sebastian cut his meat with a knife similar to that which he had given to the Cheyenne. The pair were served by the young squaw who had been living with the Englishman. Both men sparred cautiously.

"Where are you from?" St. Clair asked in his best American accent.

"St. Louis. How about you?" Sebastian could not hide the trace of a foreign accent.

"Oh, I hail from Pittsburgh."

"I see. Going to the mountains to make your fortune in furs?"

"Something like that." St. Clair's judgment of men told him the other man was lying, but he bided his time.

An opportunity presented itself when the squaw handed him a gourd filled with the herb-flavored water that the Cheyenne customarily drank with their meals. Pretending it had slipped from the girl's hand, St. Clair contrived to overturn it in the direction of the other visitor. Sebastian half-squirmed, half-jumped out of the water's path to avoid a drenching, and, precisely as St. Clair had anticipated, he dropped his gold-handled knife.

St. Clair snatched it from the ground. Turning it over in his hand as he tried to read the inscription on the blade by the light of the fire, he simulated rage at the girl to give himself more time. "You clumsy woman!" he roared in her own tongue. "I shall beat you for this!"

The girl shrank from him, mumbling apologies.

His mission accomplished, St. Clair handed the other man the knife and offered his apologies. Sebastian graciously accepted them, and the incident was forgotten.

After the meal, however, St. Clair leaned toward him. "It so happens that I'm carrying some genuine French brandywine in my wagon. Could I persuade you to share a glass with me?"

"I don't need much persuasion," the darker man said.

Henry waited until the Cheyenne went about their own business. Then, fetching two generous gourds of the potent brandywine, he returned with them to the fire.

In spite of the warming drink, Sebastian remained taciturn. St. Clair was quiet, also. Extremely aware of the value of perfect timing, St. Clair waited until they had consumed about half the contents of the gourds, and then he spoke quietly. "I see your knife was made in St. Petersburg. I assume the knives you gave the Cheyenne came from there, too."

Sebastian's black eyes narrowed. "Sometimes it doesn't pay to be too observant. Indeed, it can be dangerous."

That was all Henry St. Clair needed to know, and he smiled lazily. "It's a long way from St. Petersburg to this Godforsaken part of the world. Even farther than it is from London."

André Sebastian stared hard at him. "London?"

"Your servant, sir." Henry allowed his own English accent to emerge.

The other man continued to stare at him, then chuckled.

"The only member of the secret police I know is Vladimir Raskovitch. We worked together in Constantinople some years ago when the Sultan and his Grand Vizier were thinking of expelling all foreigners from the Ottoman Empire. Together we managed to—ah—persuade them to change their minds."

"Vladimir sits at a desk now in St. Petersburg."

"Give him my fond regards when next you go there." It was Henry's turn to chuckle. "I was told before I left London that I might run across colleagues from another great power engaged in a mission similar to mine. I assume we have the same goal."

"I dare say we do." Sebastian sipped his brandywine with greater relish. "How odd it is that we should meet here, at the campfire of savages who have never heard of your great nation or mine. I assume you played a trick in order to read the printing on my knife blade."

Just because they were working on the same mission didn't mean St. Clair trusted his colleague, and his shrug was noncommittal. "I divined your identity," he said.

Sebastian let the question drop. The English were arrogant and opinionated. He had never liked them. But he, too, was prepared, for the sake of expediency, to work with someone who sought the same goal. "You are alone?"

"Always," Henry St. Clair replied proudly. "Most helpers are incompetent bunglers."

"How well I know it," Sebastian replied. "I gave my assistant the simple task of poisoning some of the wagon train's water holes, but he was so clumsy he allowed himself to be killed."

Reasonably assured the man was working without the assistance of subordinates, Henry felt more confident. He could handle the Russian, utilizing his services, telling him only what was necessary, and then dropping him when his presence became embarrassing. The interests of Great Britain and Imperial Russia coincided to an extent, but only to an extent. No English secret agent could allow himself to forget that Russia had once claimed the Oregon country. "Perhaps we could join forces," he said.

Sebastian had known the offer would be made and was ready for it. He would gladly give the Englishman his limited cooperation but would not go so far as to trust him. "Perhaps it would be to our best mutual advantage," he said, and the uneasy partnership was formed.

Martin Van Buren, the eighth President of the United States, had elected on the day of his inauguration to use the massive desk of his predecessor, Andrew Jackson. Old Hickory had been tall and slender, and the desk looked as though it had been made for him. "Little Van," as he had been nicknamed, was almost a foot shorter, so he gave visitors the impression of barely being able to peer over the rim of the desk. Consequently, many people came away from the President's office in the executive mansion with the unfortunate feeling that he was incompetent.

Nothing could have been farther from the truth. Martin Van Buren was a clear-thinking activist, and if he wasn't an innovator, he was nevertheless determined to carry out the policies established by Jackson.

No one knew his real nature better than the two men now seated in his orderly private office, John Jacob Astor and Major General Frederick Stovall.

Astor was often called the wealthiest man in the United States, and he, more than any other individual, had been responsible for striking the spark that was sending the wagon train to the Oregon country. His private funds had paid a substantial portion of the expense. He and Van Buren had worked together when the latter had been Secretary of State, and he had a high regard for the President's abilities.

Major General Stovall, Deputy Chief of Staff of the

United States Army and the nation's second highest rank-
ing military officer, shared Astor's opinion of the President. It had been his privilege to act as Van Buren's
aide-de-camp before being promoted to his present post,
so he knew him well and was one of his strongest ad-
mirers and supporters.

Therefore, the atmosphere was friendly, but there was
tension in the air. "Gentlemen," Van Buren said, "what
passes between us this afternoon must remain within these
walls. If any of the information should leak out or if the
remedies we may devise to solve the problem should become known, the United States may be at war with
Great Britain, Imperial Russia or both. Frankly, the eco-
nomic health of the nation is insufficiently strong at the
present time to permit us to become embroiled in a war
with a major world power. Such a war would be disastrous."

His listeners nodded, neither of them surprised by his
words.

Van Buren picked up a thin, leather-bound folder. "As
General Stovall already knows and as you may have
heard, Mr. Astor, American intelligence services have
done inadequate work since the bulk of our information-
gathering apparatus was dismantled by President Madison
after the War of 1812. President Jackson intended to
strengthen those services, but circumstances prevented it.
I've shared his aim, but we've lacked the funds." He ran
a hand across the top of his bald head. "Consequently, the
information that has just come to my attention arrives
here rather late in the day." He coughed behind his hand.

General Stovall knew that something of great significance had happened. Van Buren always paused before
making an important statement.

"Our intelligence people," the President said, tapping
the folder for emphasis, "have obtained incontrovertible
proof that both Great Britain and Imperial Russia are
taking active steps to prevent our wagon train from reaching Oregon."

"I'm not in the least surprised," John Jacob Astor said.
"The stakes in Oregon are high."

"If the British and Russians succeed," Van Buren said, "the United States stands to lose hundreds of thousands of square miles west of the Rocky Mountains. We'll lose a lucrative fur trade, about which Mr. Astor knows more than I do. We'll lose salmon fisheries, lumber, and minerals. We'll lose the opportunity to expand our borders all the way across the continent from the Atlantic to the Pacific."

"The wagon train can't be allowed to fail, sir," General Stovall said.

"Obviously," Astor murmured.

"So far several attacks have been made on the train," the President declared. "According to information obtained from Sam Brentwood, who has taken charge of our new depot in Independence, the attack was launched by army deserters—which was repulsed—was British inspired. Several vicious but relatively minor assaults of one kind or another have also failed completely or have been averted. But the people in the wagon train are in trouble over their heads. Most of them are simple farmers. Even the few relatively sophisticated members find it difficult to deal with the problems that London and St. Petersburg can create. The man in charge at the present time— Mike Holt—is a competent guide and hunter, but he's never dealt with such matters, either."

General Stovall frowned and drummed on the desk, and John Jacob Astor tugged at the gold-link watch chain that stretched across his expansive waistcoat.

"Something must be done, gentlemen," Van Buren said. "The wagon train needs help that only the United States government can provide. I await your suggestions."

The General's reply was prompt. "Mr. President," he said, "we already have a regiment stationed at Fort Madison in the Nebraska country, and we can form another from smaller units in garrisons at other frontier posts. Let the army send two fully equipped cavalry regiments to help. They can escort the wagon train all the way to the Oregon territory, and may the Lord help anyone who gets in their way, tries any tricks, or interferes!"

Astor was dismayed. "With all due respect to General Stovall, Mr. President, there's nothing this country might do that could harm us more."

The General's temper flared, overcoming his sense of discretion. "I must disagree. If Mr. Astor is thinking in terms of making diplomatic protests—"

"I'm not. The British and Russians would turn us aside by insisting they're doing nothing to harm us. I've seen the game played too often."

President Van Buren listened but made no comment.

"All the same, Mr. Astor," General Stovall said, "I believe in the principle of fighting fire by building a bigger and stronger fire."

"And I believe in using a rapier instead of a bludgeon, sir," John Jacob Astor replied. "Mr. President, I don't pretend to know how London and St. Petersburg would react if we sent two regiments of cavalry to escort the wagon train. I assume they'd be annoyed, and I assume they'd let us know it. The one thing I can tell you flatly is that such a move would be catastrophic for the fur business—one of the few industries in the country that remains profitable in these hard times."

General Stovall was still belligerent. "Perhaps you'd explain why the fur industry would suffer if we provide the wagon train with the protection the people need and deserve!"

"Of course." Astor spoke with the self-confidence of a man who knew precisely what he was doing and why. "Dozens of hunters and trappers in Oregon are working for fur companies, which also buy pelts from the independents. The British do the same thing. On the surface they—and we—are friendly. There is no reason not to be —there are enough furs for everyone, at least for the present. But the British, as well as the United States companies, are looking toward the day when the supplies will begin to diminish. Still, at present the two countries cooperate. Keep in mind that the one military post in the area is Fort Vancouver, which flies the Union Jack, not the Stars and Stripes. The British garrison gives protection to American hunters and trappers, just as it does those from Canada. If they should withdraw their support from us—and become openly hostile—we'll have a great many new problems that will be almost impossible to solve."

"I see your point," Van Buren said.

"That's not all," the magnate continued vigorously. "Most fur company employees in Oregon are Russians, subjects of the czar, who stayed behind when their government gave up its official claim to the territory. They're highly temperamental people, and I know that almost all of them dream about the future when the czar will reassert his claims. If we send the wagon train with two cavalry regiments, we're serving notice that the United States is prepared to fight for its rights in Oregon. Every last Russian will walk out on us, and the American fur business in the Northwest—a business that brings this country more revenues than any other—will collapse overnight. That will make the present precarious financial situation even worse."

"I understand your reasoning, Mr. Astor," Stovall said. "But we simply can't leave almost five hundred American citizens unprotected when British and Russian agents are conniving against them."

"I wouldn't dream of leaving them to their own fate, General," Astor replied. "That would be stupid and shortsighted."

"Then what do you suggest?"

"The British and Russians are being subtle. Surely this government isn't so primitive that it can't find equally subtle means to counter the threat!"

President Van Buren stared out of the window of the executive mansion at the new gate, where military sentries were now posted for the first time. "American citizens have the right to expect their country to help them when they're threatened by foreign foes. I quite agree that a subtle weapon is preferable to an obvious one, but I insist on giving our people the protection they need."

General Stovall, deep in thought, absently fingered the hilt of his dress sword. All at once he laughed aloud and slapped his knee.

Astor looked at him in surprise.

"You've thought of something, Fred?" Van Buren asked.

"Lee Blake!"

The President smiled. "Perfect! This situation is made to order for him."

"Mr. Astor," the General said, "there's an officer currently on duty right here in Washington who is capable of dealing with the foreign agents who threaten the wagon train. Leland Blake is a lieutenant colonel, the youngest in the army. He fought Indians in Alabama, Florida, and Tennessee with Andrew Jackson. This job suits him especially well, since he spent three years as our military attaché in St. Petersburg and four more in London. At present he's the director of the counterintelligence section at army headquarters, which means he's in charge of ferreting out foreign spies. He's been so restless that he regularly requests transfer from a desk job to the field. So he'll welcome an opportunity such as this."

John Jacob Astor looked pleased. "Your Colonel Blake sounds almost too good to be true."

"He's very good," the President said. "He worked directly for me when I served as our Minister to Great Britain, and he performed admirably. Fred, offer him the assignment at once!"

"Yes, Mr. President."

"Give him the authority he needs, but tell him to handle relations with wagon train members carefully."

"I know what you mean, sir. I'll see to it!"

The President invited Astor to stay for supper, and General Stovall quickly walked the two blocks down Pennsylvania Avenue to the three-story frame building that served as headquarters for the United States Army and Navy.

A few minutes later, Lieutenant Colonel Leland Blake came into his office and saluted. Tall, slender, and dark haired, with a deceptively gentle manner, he was in his mid-thirties, so handsome that Washington hostesses pursued him relentlessly for their dinner parties. Their efforts were in vain, however. The social life of the nation's capital bored him. Duty was always paramount in his eyes, and his only shortcoming, in the eyes of his superiors, was his refusal to relax.

"Sit down, Lee," Stovall said, returning the younger officer's salute. "Read this."

Colonel Blake needed only a few minutes to peruse the report of the attacks made on the wagon train by British and Imperial Russian agents. "None of this is surprising, sir," he said. "You may recall I had a meeting with Sam Brentwood, at President Jackson's instigation, shortly before the wagon train was scheduled to set out from New York. At that time I warned him that these troubles were likely to develop."

"I do remember, Lee. And they've become so serious that President Van Buren wants a counterintelligence operative to join the train and travel with it, at least until the threats can be ended. If necessary, of course, he can see them all the way to the end of their journey."

"You'll want a competent officer, I imagine, sir. He'll need to wear civilian clothes so he'll be inconspicuous."

"Right."

"It seems to me," Lee Blake said, his mind working with its usual rapidity, "that no one other than the wagonmaster and the president of the train should know his real identity."

"A good safeguard," Stovall agreed, concealing a smile as he asked, "Whom do you recommend?"

"Let me go through my list of available officers, sir. It won't be an easy assignment to fill."

"I'm aware of it, so I already have an exceptionally competent officer in mind."

Blake hated top-level interference, but was in no position to protest, so he waited politely.

"The President," General Stovall said, "agrees with me that Lieutenant Colonel Leland Blake has all the necessary qualifications."

A broad grin spread slowly across the younger officer's face. "I can think of no one better."

"How soon can you leave?"

"Immediately, sir! I'll stop off in Independence, and perhaps I can persuade Sam Brentwood to guide me out to the train, since I'm not familiar with the Great Plains. What authority will I have to mobilize the members of the train?"

"As much as you may want and need. The present wagonmaster, a hunter and guide named Holt, is competent and had President Jackson's confidence. But you may find yourself in a ticklish situation if he resents your presence."

"That would create unfortunate complications, and I'll do my best to avoid them."

"I'm sure you will. Handle the problems of dealing with the British and Russians as you see fit, Lee. I have no idea what you might encounter out there in the wilderness, so it would be foolish to give you any specific instructions. Do as you see fit. Just make certain the wagon train reaches Oregon intact!"

"You can depend on me, General," Lee Blake said quietly. "And so can President Van Buren."

Horses and oxen were browsing indolently during the nooning, the sun was shining from a cloudless sky, and a pleasant breeze from the west dissipated the heat that soon would become a problem. Members of the wagon train rested; the children ate cold leftovers from breakfast. The day was like scores of others, and the mood of the travelers was relaxed and serene.

Suddenly the quiet was interrupted by a sentry's shout. "A party of three is approaching from the east on horseback!" he called. "A white man and two Indians."

The train's leaders gathered to greet the new arrivals, and soon a large crowd surrounded the strange trio. The two Indians, warriors in their early twenties, were tall and slender, their skins a darker copper than those of other tribes. Christian crosses were embroidered in beads on their buckskin shirts, which were dyed in brilliant reds and greens. They spoke no English, and both Whip and Stalking Horse were unable to converse with them in any of the Indian languages they knew.

The white man was dressed even more unusually. His moccasins and fringed buckskin trousers were those of a frontier dweller, but he wore the formal black shirt and white clerical collar of a missionary. A Bible protruded from the top of his saddlebag, but he carried a brace of pistols and a double-edged hunting knife in his belt. He introduced himself as the Reverend Jason Lee, and Cathy van Ayl instantly recognized his nasal drawl as that of her native New England.

"I've just come from Oregon, where I've established a little mission," he said, "and I'm on my way to Washington. I hope to persuade President Van Buren and Congress to recognize the area as a formal territory and to set up a provisional government there."

At the mention of Oregon, a surprised and pleased murmur spread through the throng.

"We're headed for the Oregon country ourselves," Whip told the man.

The clergyman was only mildly surprised. "I had a letter from one of my friends at the New England Methodist Seminary a few months ago telling me a wagon train was coming out our way," he said. "You'll be welcome, very welcome. I'm hoping to return to Oregon by ship and bring some more settlers with me. We'll sail around South America."

Soon Reverend Lee, who was a husky man, was besieged with questions from the eager pioneers. Here was someone with firsthand knowledge of the region to which they were traveling, the future home for which they were enduring so many hardships.

The clergyman first told them about his two young companions. They were members of the peace-loving Chinook nation, and he had converted them to Christianity. Now they lived in the tiny settlement he had established on the Willamette River, less than a day's journey from Fort Vancouver.

"What's the attitude of the English there toward American settlers?" Ernie asked.

Jason Lee's face clouded. "Dr. John McLoughlin, the chief factor of the Hudson's Bay Company, is a fine Christian gentleman," he said. "He doesn't much care whether the territory is under British or American jurisdiction, and he's told me himself that he's prepared to do business with us, no matter what flag flies over us. I'm sorry to say, though, that the officers of the British military command at Fort Vancouver are less generous. They make no bones about their aim. They're determined that people who move there will live under the Union Jack—just as I'm determined that the Stars and Stripes will fly there. That's the chief reason I'm going East. When the President and Congress realize the situation is critical, I'm quite certain they'll give us their full support."

"I reckon the arrival of this train will tip the scale in favor of American jurisdiction," Whip said.

"Oh, it will," Lee replied enthusiastically. "You say there are about five hundred of you. How wonderful that my prayers are already being answered by the Lord. It will be very difficult for the British to force a group this large to swear allegiance to Queen Victoria."

"There's no chance of that," Cathy van Ayl said firmly, then blushed because she had spoken out of turn.

But the emphatic nods and vocal support of dozens of future Oregon settlers made her feel less embarrassed. It was plain that the wagon train was united in its intention to make Oregon an American territory.

Further travel for the day was out of the question. An overnight camp was made, and scores of people spent the afternoon and evening bombarding the Reverend Lee with requests for specific information. His replies fascinated them.

"Oregon truly is God's country," he said. "The climate is superb, particularly in the valleys. The higher you go in the mountains, of course, the greater the probability you'll run into snow. But there's none in the valleys and on the Pacific coast."

He was partial, obviously, to the Willamette Valley.

Whip said, "That's good country, all right, but I'm aiming to take these folks farther north by about fifty or sixty miles."

"You prefer the vicinity of the lower Columbia River, I take it," Reverend Lee said.

"I do. It's strictly a personal feeling," Whip said. "The salmon are more accessible, and so is the Pacific for fishing."

"Well," the clergyman replied, smiling, "it is all the same country, and there's ample space for hundreds of settlements, even thousands. You good people have never seen so much fine land!"

Just about everything that man needed for survival could be grown in the territory, Reverend Lee said enthusiastically. At his own small mission he already had apples, pears, peaches, plums, and a variety of berries. "Wheat takes naturally to our soil. So do oats and barley, corn, rye, and buckwheat. You won't believe the way crops such as beans and peas grow, not to mention cucumbers and squash."

The farmers listened intently, their eyes bright.

"Oregon is perfect for grazing, too. So far the only cows in the area are to be found at Fort Vancouver, but I predict the day will come when the cattle being raised there will outnumber people by at least ten to one. And I certainly expect that hundreds of thousands of immigrants will come to Oregon!"

The mineral deposits of the area were unknown, he said, because no one had ever explored for them.

"What kind of trees are there?" someone asked.

The clergyman laughed. "No matter where you may be from, I promise you've never seen so many kinds of trees. Our forests are endless. Let me see. There are firs everywhere, and pines, both yellow and white. There are spruce, hemlock, larch, and cedar. Some of our Indians use the inner bark of cedar for food. Cook it the way they do, and you'll find it delicious."

Someone inquired about the availability of fish other than salmon.

Reverend Lee grinned. "Well, sir—offhand, I can think of sturgeon, halibut, cod, herring, carp, and smelt. There are oysters and crabs, and strange lobsters that have only one claw instead of two. There are so many fish in our rivers and in the Pacific that they could feed the entire United States, with ample left over. Oh, yes—there's something I neglected to mention earlier when we were talking about grazing. Our hills are perfect for sheep. I myself started with a tiny flock, and right now I have several hundred."

Far into the evening, the members of the train listened in wonder and delight. Here was a man who had no need to exaggerate, who by profession undoubtedly was truthful. The beacon light of Oregon burned brightly.

The heat of early summer was so intense that many members of the wagon train suffered from stomach disorders, and the medicines Dr. Martin had brought with him failed to cure them. Stalking Horse gave the physician a small quantity of a prairie herb that, he said, the Plains tribes used for the purpose. Bob Martin tried it, giving the herb to two patients, both of whom recovered overnight.

The next day was Sunday, when the company rested, so the doctor went out alone, on foot, to gather as many of the herbs as he could. He began to find the plants about a mile from the campsite, and he pulled them carefully, stuffing them into a burlap sack. To his surprise and pleasure, he also found another herb, broad leafed and bearing seed balls that would turn into flowers later in the summer. This herb, whose Latin name he had forgotten, was identical to one he had studied when he had attended medical school in Edinburgh, but he hadn't actually ever seen it or used it in practice.

As he remembered the information in his textbooks, these seeds, when removed from their pods, had strong antiseptic qualities and could be utilized to pack wounds in order to prevent infection. He seemed to recall a lecturer at the university saying that this herb grew only in one known place, the vast plains or *pampas* of the Argentine. It was exciting to find it on the prairies of the American West, and Bob Martin gathered as many as he could locate.

He would experiment with the seeds, naturally, and devoutly hoped they were indeed the same as those found in the Argentine. If that should be the case, he had made a discovery of importance to the American medical profession. Ultimately, when mail service was established between the Oregon country and the Eastern Seaboard, he would write to a classmate who was now serving on the staff of Harvard Medical School and would enclose some samples in his letter.

Then, hearing horses approaching, he looked up and was startled when he saw three Indians smeared with paint riding rapidly toward him. A glance over his shoulder told him he had wandered so far from the wagon train that it was no longer in sight, and he realized he was in serious trouble.

His rifle lay on the ground beside the half-filled burlap sack, but it was too late now to use it. One of the braves had a spear poised in his hand, ready to throw it, and the others had their bows and arrows ready.

All he could do was raise his right arm, palm upraised, in the Indian sign of peace. At least he was glad he had persuaded Stalking Horse to teach him enough of the language of the Kiowa to make himself understood.

The peace gesture startled the braves, and they hesitated before firing their weapons.

"I am a man of medicine," Bob called, using the only Kiowan phrase that identified his profession with any degree of accuracy.

The warriors remained suspicious, but it was contrary to custom to kill any medicine man in cold blood. Besides, this white stranger was speaking a familiar tongue.

One of the braves dismounted and, after picking up Bob's rifle, looked in the burlap sack. There he saw some of the herbs used for stomach disorders, which he recognized instantly. Snatching one of the plants, he showed it to his companions.

To Bob's infinite relief, the herb seemed to provide corroborating evidence for his claim.

"The medicine man," the eldest of the trio said, "will come to the town of the Wichita."

The physician had no choice and was forced to mount the oldest brave's horse, riding double in front of the Indian, while the warrior carried the rifle and the burlap sack. They rode off in the direction from which they had come.

Cursing silently, Bob realized that his own careless preoccupation was responsible for his grim predicament. The savages of the plains, Whip had stressed in their many talks on the subject, were friendly only with whites they knew and had reason to trust. Strangers who intruded on the hunting grounds, which they regarded as inviolate and sacred, were either killed by torture and scalped, or were compelled to live as slaves. Neither prospect was heartening.

A Whip Holt or an Arnold Mell might find some clever way to either overpower the warriors or fool them long enough to escape and return to the wagon train. Although certainly not lacking in courage, he was a doctor and a scientist, devoted to the art of healing rather than the performance of daring deeds. He was incapable of breaking away from his captors.

So far, at least, they hadn't mistreated him or bound his arms and legs. He couldn't help smiling wryly. Obviously a middle-aged man with a slight paunch and graying temples posed no physical threat to a trio of healthy, strapping warriors in the physical prime of life.

The braves rode in silence for about an hour, and then Bob heard the soft throbbing of a drum, a sound that was very faint at first but that grew louder and more intense. What he found odd was that the beat of the drum was slow, solemn, and unvarying.

At last the braves and their captive came to a group of buffalo-hide tents, erected on center poles. In spite of his dangerous situation, Bob noted that the tent walls were double skins, with the outer portion heavily greased to ward off the elements. He even caught a glimpse of buffalo skins on the ground inside some of the tents.

About two hundred men and women dressed in the skins of young buffalo were sitting solemnly in a circle, while a number of naked children and many dogs played on the fringes. A fire was burning in the center of the circle, and a naked boy of eight or nine was lying unconscious on a robe of buffalo hide near the flames. On the far side of the fire, the drum beater pounded methodically on an animal skin stretched tightly over a kettlelike container. Dancing frenziedly around the fire and pausing occasionally to hover over the boy was a masked man, naked except for a breechcloth of buffalo hide. Streaks of paint covered his body and limbs, and he carried a bone rattle so large he needed both hands to shake it, which he did incessantly as he pranced and leaped.

Bob's escort dismounted and led him to the circle. The squaws and younger girls were weeping openly, while the braves stared straight ahead, their faces expressionless and their arms folded across their broad, bare chests. The faces, arms, and shoulders of all were smeared with a heavy coating of what looked like ashes.

Behind the boy, sitting cross-legged, was a warrior wearing an elaborate headdress of eagle feathers that descended down his back to his waist. Apparently he was the chief of this Wichita community, and Bob guessed he well might be the child's father. Directly behind the man was a squaw, her hands covering her face, who rocked back and forth in silent hysteria.

But it was the boy himself who most interested the physician. His left leg and thigh were bloated, swollen to several times their normal size, and neither his knee nor his ankle bones were visible. In spite of his own danger, the doctor paused to look at the child, who appeared to be suffering from an infection.

A member of the escort addressed the chief at length in a language that Bob did not understand.

The leader was impatient. "The stranger is a medicine man?" he demanded, speaking in Kiowan.

"It is so," Bob acknowledged.

"The son of Golden Bear suffers a great sickness. The Wichita have prayed to the gods of the sun, the moon, and the wind, but the boy is still sick. Will the magic of the strange medicine man cure him?"

"I must examine the boy before I can answer the question of the sachem," Bob replied.

The man gave a curt nod.

Some of the women stopped weeping, and a number of braves stared at the outsider as he approached the stricken child and dropped to one knee beside him. The tribe's medicine man halted his gyrations. Only the steady, mournful beat of the drum continued unabated.

The physician placed a hand on the boy's forehead. As he had assumed, the youngster was suffering from a high fever. A swift but thorough examination of his swollen thigh and leg revealed that the focal point of the infection was located in the calf. This spot was so tender that the unconscious child stirred when probing fingers barely touched the spot.

Bob stood and faced the chief. He realized that his own

situation was hazardous, but it was obvious to him that he had to make an attempt to save the boy. If his efforts failed, he thought it likely that he would be tortured until he died. But a combination of instinct and the little he had gleaned about the ways of Indians told him to magnify the task that awaited him, to wrap it in an air of mystery.

"I will cure the son of Golden Bear," he declared solemnly.

The warriors continued to glare at him, and the tribe's medicine man pulled off his mask and stared jealously at the white intruder.

Bob pointed a finger at the hysterical woman. "Let the mother of the boy place water in a pot. Let her put the pot over the fire and keep it there until it makes many bubbles. Let no one else touch the pot or help her."

The sachem's squaw hauled herself to her feet and moved off through the crowd, returning shortly with a huge iron pot that had been obtained in a trade with a representative of one of the fur companies. At the least, Bob thought, the simple function she had been asked to perform would occupy her attention sufficiently to let her tears dry.

"Let Golden Bear give me the knife he is wearing," the physician said.

Reluctantly the chief took a knife from his belt and handed it to the stranger.

Bob was disappointed because the blade was dull and badly nicked. "There is no magic in this knife," he said. "Bring the hunting knife of Golden Bear!"

A young brave hurried off to the largest of the tents, returning with a long bone-handled knife that he handed to the chief.

After another long moment's hesitation, Golden Bear gave it to the white man.

"Evil spirits fill the son of Golden Bear," the doctor declared solemnly, after assuring himself that this blade was what he needed. Obviously it, too, had been obtained in a trade with whites: it was fashioned of tempered steel, and was razor-sharp. "All the people of the Wichita will see the evil spirits leave the body of the son of Golden

288

Bear." And if my diagnosis is wrong, or if I'm too late and the boy dies, he reflected, I'll pay with my own life.

"Now," he continued, "let two women bring another pot filled with cold water."

This, too, was done.

The physician needed cloth, but none was available as the Wichita's clothing was made of leather. Removing his own shirt, he took the sharp knife and cut the shirt into strips several inches wide.

By this time the water in the first pot was boiling. Bob gestured, and the drummer fell silent. There was no sound now, and everyone could hear the labored breathing of the patient.

Bob dropped a strip of cloth into the boiling pot, allowed it to remain there for a few moments, and then fished it out with the knife. After waiting for it to cool just enough so that it wouldn't burn the boy, he placed it, still steaming, on the calf of his patient's leg, where he doubled it, then doubled it again. While the heat drew out the infection, he held the knife blade in the boiling water to sterilize it.

"Let the sack of the medicine man be brought to him," he ordered.

The burlap bag that had been taken from him was placed at his side, and he could only pray that he had properly identified the herb that had antiseptic qualities.

Many of the seated braves and squaws could not see him. Overcome by curiosity, they rose to their feet. The Wichita medicine man hovered nearby, and all at once it occurred to Bob to involve him directly in the proceedings.

"Let the brother of the white medicine man put two more pieces of cloth in the water that bubbles," he said. "Let him be ready to remove them with a stick when they are needed."

Slightly mollified but still jealous, the Wichita medicine man obeyed.

Bob removed the steaming cloth from the patient's leg, dropping it back into the boiling water. Then, taking the knife from the pot, he lowered himself to one knee. The focal point of the infection had risen to a bump, so he made an incision almost a half-inch deep and an inch long. Then, still moving swiftly, he cut through the center crosswise.

Large quantities of pus spurted out of the patient's leg. "The evil leaves the body of the son of Golden Bear," he announced loudly.

Then while the wound continued to drain, he cleaned the knife by plunging it into the boiling water. Motioning the Wichita medicine man, he watched closely as the savage, imitating what he himself had done previously, placed a steaming, folded section of cloth over the wound, which continued to draw and drain. As soon as the cloth stopped steaming, Bob ordered the process repeated. By now the swelling was somewhat reduced, although the child's leg was still puffed. When serum rather than pus began to drain from the cuts, Bob opened an herb pod. Using the sharp point of the knife, he pressed the seeds, one by one, into the wound. Then he took yet another strip of cloth from the boiling pot and allowing it to cool slightly, he made it into a bandage, placing it around the patient's calf and tying it securely, but not too tightly.

The boy opened his eyes, looking bewildered when he saw the stranger bending over him. Bob gestured to the chief and his squaw, who moved within their son's range of vision. The boy smiled and said something in the language of the Wichita. The chief replied, and his squaw dropped to both knees, then bent down to kiss her son on the forehead.

Bob's relief was so great he felt weak. The operation had been a success, so he had probably saved his own life. But his task was not yet done.

"Let no one lift the son of Golden Bear until the medicine man gives the word," he said. Later in the evening he would remove and replace the antiseptic seeds, and by morning the boy should be able to hobble around, with the help of a walking stick. The fever was already lower, and the thigh was less bloated.

The squaw sat on the ground and placed her son's head in her lap.

"Let the son of Golden Bear drink water," Bob said. Someone handed him a gourd, and he dipped it into the pot of cold water, then handed it to the squaw. Certainly the crisis was over, and he felt confident that the child's recovery would be complete.

Rising to his feet, he took the precaution of extending his thanks to the Wichita medicine man for the role he had played. The man's dignity had been restored, and he was so pleased that he exhibited no signs of jealousy. Another crisis had been averted.

Golden Bear enveloped the white man in a hug, then began to call orders to his people. A squaw appeared with a shirt of buffalo skin, which had been chipped so expertly that it was almost as thin as cloth. Two squaws pulled it over his head.

Then Golden Bear produced a square of buffalo bone about an inch and a half in diameter, on which a picture of the sun had been carved. It was attached to a loop of rawhide, and chanting an incantation, the sachem placed it around the doctor's neck. Not until it was in place did Bob Martin realize that Golden Bear himself wore an identical talisman.

"The new brother of Golden Bear is the greatest of medicine men," the sachem said in Kiowan. "Let all of the Wichita bend their knees to him and praise him!"

The entire assemblage began to chant, the drummer beat a lively rhythm, and, much to Bob's embarrassment, the people approached him one by one, prostrating themselves on the ground before him. Never, he thought, had any physician received such homage.

Eventually the men of the tribe feasted on antelope steak, the first that Bob had ever tasted, and with it they ate boiled ears of fresh corn, smeared with melted buffalo fat. The taste was unusual but surprisingly good.

After the meal, the physician removed the herb seeds from his patient's leg, and although the operation was painful, the child did not wince, a sure sign that he was improving rapidly. This time a poultice filled with seeds was placed on the outside of the wound, and at the doctor's orders, the child was moved into a tent.

"Now the son of Golden Bear will sleep," Bob said. "When the sun returns, he will be well again."

A special tent, complete with several rich buffalo robes

on the ground, was placed at the exhausted doctor's disposal. Before he dropped off to sleep, the squaw of the sachem came to him and offered herself to him, showing bewilderment when he declined the opportunity to spend the night with her. His willingness to abide by the customs of his hosts was limited.

Just before he fell asleep, he found himself thinking of Tonie Mell, and he wondered how she would react if he offered her his new shirt or buffalo bone talisman.

The entire wagon train was in an uproar when, at supper time, it was discovered that Dr. Martin had not yet returned. The night was cloudy, but the scouts and Hosea immediately went out beyond the circle of wagons to begin a search. It was the Ashanti who followed a trail of uprooted plants and who eventually found the place where the physician had been abducted.

Tonie Mell went wild when Hosea brought the word back to the camp. "We've got to organize a rescue expedition right now!" she said.

Whip disagreed. "On a night like this, it will be very difficult to follow signs across the prairie," he told her. "We'll do much better if we wait until morning."

"By then Bob could be dead!"

"Indians are never in that much of a hurry to kill their prisoners," he said.

"Then they could be torturing him," she insisted.

"Not at night," Whip replied. "They won't do him any serious harm before tomorrow."

Tonie refused to listen to him. "If you won't go tonight," she said, "I'll do it myself."

Only her uncle's persuasion and authority over her prevented her from dashing alone across the plains.

She was unable to sleep, and when a small rescue party was organized before dawn, she made such a fuss about accompanying the group that Whip decided to permit her to come along. Only he and the scouts would conduct the search, he said, refusing her request for a large party of armed men.

"If there are too many of us," he explained, "they'll kill Bob before we can get near him. You'll have to trust my judgment and let me handle this in my own way."

He refrained from telling her that he was taking the cured skin of the pure white buffalo calf with him. If necessary, he would offer it to Dr. Martin's captors in exchange for the physician's release, and he felt confident that no Indian would be able to resist such a bargain.

"We want to avoid open warfare with any nation," Whip said before they departed, and although his remarks presumably were intended for all his companions, he looked only at Tonie. "We can accomplish a great deal more through peaceful negotiations. I'll do the talking, and I want no one to fire a single shot without my express permission. Our aim is to save Bob, not punish a tribe for abducting him."

Giving the girl no chance to reply, he led his stallion out of the circle.

Arnold brought up the rear, Tonie riding directly in front of him, and Stalking Horse took the lead. It was a simple matter for the Cherokee to read and follow the tracks made the previous day by the band of warriors, and by the time the sun rose, the group had traveled a considerable distance from the campsite.

An hour later, as they still pushed forward, Stalking Horse suddenly raised a hand in warning. "Indians come," he called.

The group moved into a horizontal line, leaving ample space between their mounts. Rifles were checked, and Whip spoke casually to Tonie, who sat on his left. "Remember," he said, "keep your trigger finger quiet."

She nodded, but made no comment. If Bob Martin was in great danger, she reserved the right to act in any manner she saw fit, and to hell with the wagonmaster.

Stalking Horse recognized the distinctive warpaint worn by the approaching braves. "Wichita warriors come," he announced.

There were about twenty braves in the approaching party, so even Whip, Arnold, and Mack became tense, and Stalking Horse moved his quiver a few inches toward one side of his shoulder, where he could draw arrow after arrow quickly, should the need arise.

Tonie noticed that these Indians were riding horses as

large as those used by members of the expedition. "They're not mounted on ponies," she said.

"That's because we're in the real West now," Whip said. "These horses are the descendants of the herds originally brought to Mexico by the Spaniards. Wild herds were formed by runaway horses, and the Plains Indians who know about them go off into the mountain canyons, catch them, then tame them."

"The Wichita are good fighters," Mack said, "and they don't like strangers." He took a firmer grip on his rifle.

Whip waited until the approaching horsemen drew closer, then raised his arm in the sign of peace.

Two of the warriors responded with the same sign, much to the relief of the outnumbered little band.

Then one brave, wearing a beaded shirt and a headdress studded with eagle feathers, detached himself from the Wichita party and rode forward alone.

Even Whip was confused for a moment because he wore a white man's trousers and boots. The astonished Tonie was the first to recognize a broadly smiling Bob Martin.

"Put down your rifles," Bob called. "My brothers, the Wichita, are your friends forever."

Arnold chuckled quietly. "I might have guessed he'd do something like this!"

The two groups merged and dismounted. Golden Bear made a long, impassioned speech in which he praised his new brother, the great medicine man. Then, at his signal, his braves mounted their horses again, while Whip and his comrades followed their example.

Before turning back toward his village, Golden Bear looked at Tonie, then muttered something that caused every man present to laugh. The parties separated, and the wagon train group headed back toward their campsite.

Only Tonie was totally silent, and Bob fell into line beside her. "Thank you for coming after me," he said. "You had no idea what might be awaiting you, and I'm grateful you risked your life for me."

"Not really," she replied, shrugging. "I knew Whip and Uncle Arnold wouldn't let any harm come to me." Again she was silent for a time, but something continued to bother her, and at last she could not hold it in. "What made him think I'm your squaw?"

He shrugged, her belligerence making him defensive. "I don't know. The mere fact that you came after me with Whip and the scouts, I suppose."

"I'm no man's squaw," Tonie said firmly.

Bob had thought of offering her the buffalo bone amulet that was still hanging around his neck, but he decided it was best to take no chances when she was in an angry mood.

XII

Prince Nicholas Orlev, the personal representative of
the czar and the most distinguished of his subjects ever
to visit Washington, was weary after spending a day hag-
gling with State Department officials in their current trade
negotiations. But now, relaxing in the spacious Russian
Legation office of the *chargé d'affairs* he brightened as he
raised his glass of cooled Ukrainian wine. "To the czar,"
he said.

"The czar," Baron Alexis Tarnoff, the *chargé,* replied
automatically.

"These Americans," Prince Orlev said, after swallowing
half of his drink without stopping, "have the souls of
merchants. All of them, including the President and Secretary of State. What boors they are."

"Greedy boors," Baron Tarnoff replied. "They are always hungry for trade advantages, for cash, for land—for
anything and everything they can take."

"Ah, yes." The guest drained his glass and immediately
refilled it, then belched. "That brings up a matter I find
painful. These trade negotiations are not my only reason
—or even my principal reason—for coming to America.
Surely, my dear Tarnoff, you realize from the dispatches
sent to you by the Ministry of External Affairs that the
czar himself is deeply worried about the status of New

Russia—the land the Americans and the British call the Oregon country."

"It is always in my mind," the *chargé* said. "I become distressed when I read that the English are strengthening their garrison at Fort Vancouver. I become even more upset when I read that hundreds of Americans have joined the wagon train to Oregon and that other, similar expeditions are being planned. At the moment our own claims are distinctly small. We take third place."

The Prince struck the table before him with the flat of his hand, causing the glasses to jump. Then, rather clumsily, he rescued the wine bottle before it toppled. "If you know all this, my dear Baron, why do you procrastinate? Why hasn't the wagon train been destroyed? You had a perfect pawn in the young woman whose parents are still being held in St. Petersburg as hostages."

The Baron's face twisted. "You refer to the person who calls herself Tonie Mell. I interviewed her myself, you know, and offered to send her father and mother to America if she successfully sabotaged the train. But she has done nothing. No, that is not accurate. She has actually dared to defy Imperial Russia by remaining loyal to this upstart country."

"Then you are growing soft, my dear Baron." Orlev took a small knife from his pocket and began to dig at the grime that had accumulated beneath his overly long fingernails. "The woman should be killed as a lesson to all who defect. And others should be found who will attend to the sabotage of the train."

The *chargé* became bitter and spat in the general direction of a china bowl that sat on the floor beside him. "Do you suppose for one moment, my good Prince, that I am insensitive to the wishes of His Imperial Majesty? I have served him for almost thirty years, and I know what needs to be done!"

Orlev's smile was thin. "Why hasn't it been done, then?"

"Would you have me send a regiment of Cossacks chasing across the American wilderness? You forget, Prince Orlev, that the situation in which Imperial Russia finds herself is complicated by the bad advice given by your Ministry of External Affairs to His Majesty."

The Prince bristled. "That was done by my predecessors, not by me. They were stupid and shortsighted to abandon their claims to New Russia. But, now that the czar has changed his mind, we are required to do his bidding. First, the American wagon train must be crippled so badly it will either halt or turn back. Then we will notify the world that His Majesty is restoring his claim to Oregon. We will demand it for ourselves, and we are prepared to send a fleet from our colony of Alaska to take full possession of it!"

"Surely you have agents whose services you can command."

"Naturally. I have already called upon one such man. I'm sure you'll recall Daunevsky, who did such splendid work for us in the Balkans and who came to America under the name of André Sebastian. I sent him to force the Mell girl to commit sabotage, to kill her if she refused to halt the train herself."

"But of course. There is no agent in the entire network superior to Sebastian. His talents are unlimited."

"Indeed they are, and for that reason I sent him after the wagon train. I thought surely that between him and his assistant Munson the Americans would be stopped. Alas, I have heard nothing from either agent."

"It is impossible that Sebastian is dead. Munson—well, who knows? But Sebastian is indestructible!"

"That is my reasoning also," Baron Tarnoff declared. "I remain confident that Sebastian, at least, will do what is required of him."

"I hope so, but you cannot and must not place your sole reliance on one man. This Tonie Mell person represents a threat to the Imperial Crown, don't you understand? She was offered a generous bargain, and she rejected it. It is maddening to think that the demands of the czar himself are being frustrated by a stubborn, ignorant peasant girl."

"She deserves slow torture," the *chargé* said. "I would like nothing better, myself, than to spend a few hours with her alone—with a fire, a pair of tongs, a knife, and a hearth poker. Her screams would be music more joyous than the singing of the Imperial choir at the Church of St. Michael!"

"Then see to it!" the Prince rasped. "Send still more agents to catch up with the train, capture the woman, and bring her back to the legation. I don't care how you dispose of her, but in the name of the czar, I demand that the wagon train be halted or destroyed!"

A party of Cheyenne warriors rode out into the prairie wilderness at a gallop, and an hour later they returned in triumph, escorting a red-haired, heavily tanned white man in faded buckskins. The new arrival was a giant who stood at least six feet, six inches tall; he was lean and sinewy, which gave him the illusion of being even taller. He embraced the sachem, clasped forearms with the senior warriors, and even hugged a number of the squaws, a gesture in which no outsider would dare to indulge.

Pierre le Rouge was a native of the village of Montreal in French-speaking Canada. He had spent virtually all of his adult life in the Rocky Mountains, and his three pack horses, laden with bundles of furs, were proof of his skills. He hadn't seen another white man in almost three years, he told Henry St. Clair and André Sebastian, so he had interrupted his season's hunting, intending to take his furs to Independence and then return to the Rockies for the autumn season, when even more beaver and lynx would be available.

The Cheyenne declared a holiday in their visitor's honor. A bear, two deer, and an antelope were killed, with the best parts of the meat barbecued for the feast. Pierre seemed to know everyone in the Indian town by name and was on intimate terms with all of the Cheyenne, teasing them, joking with them, and playfully chiding them.

Henry St. Clair rejoiced quietly and bided his time. As he told Sebastian in confidence, the addition of such an experienced mountain man to their company would further guarantee their success. Late that night, after the Indians had retired, Henry offered the delighted Pierre a cup of his precious brandywine. "How do you happen to know these savages so well?" he asked.

"Pierre has made it his business to know all of the Indians—the Blackfoot and the Cheyenne in the plains, the Arapaho in the mountains—even the Comanche, who hate all foreigners and would rather take a white man's scalp than break bread with him. Most mountain men have partners, but Pierre works alone. He needs no partners." His words were boastful, but he spoke quietly, relating what he regarded as simple facts.

"You make a living that way, I presume?"

"Pierre is not rich, but he cannot complain."

"You're a subject of Queen Victoria, as I am," Henry St. Clair said.

"That is true." Pierre le Rouge inhaled the fragrance of the brandywine.

"How would you like to earn more in a few weeks than you could make in several years of hunting and trapping?"

Pierre's booming laugh echoed across the silent Cheyenne town. "Pierre always listens when men speak of money," he said.

Henry was encouraged. "You'd also be performing a service for the Queen," he said. "I'm sure you'd be awarded a medal."

"Pierre likes gold better than medals."

Henry offered him a simplified explanation of the situation. An American wagon train was traveling to the Oregon country, and it was in the best interests of Great Britain that it be halted and forced to turn back.

"There are farmers in this train?"

Henry admitted that most were farmers.

"They bring their families with them, their wives and children?"

"Yes, of course."

"Then they must not be harmed."

Henry was relieved that he had not admitted too much. "We don't want to harm them," he replied. "It will be enough if they become discouraged and return to their homes in other parts of the United States."

Pierre le Rouge stared at him for a long time, sizing him

up and making no comment. Then he spoke abruptly. "Pierre will think about this," he said. "In a day, maybe two days, he will give you his answer." He drained his cup, rose effortlessly to his feet, and went off to his own dwelling.

Henry felt uneasy. The stupid mountain man hadn't reacted as he had wished, but it would be unwise to press him for a positive reply, so there was nothing to be done except wait. Pouring himself more brandywine, he took it off to his own quarters.

Still restless, Henry remained half-awake until dawn. Only when day broke did he drop off into a deep sleep. It was almost noon when he awakened, and after he emerged into the open, he discovered that many of the braves had gone hunting, while most of the women and the older children were at work in the fields where they grew corn, beans, and sunflowers, whose seeds they prized as a delicacy. André Sebastian sat with the chief outside the latter's hut, lazing in the sun, but there was no sign of Pierre le Rouge anywhere. Neither his stallion nor his pack horses were grazing in the fenced compound beyond the dwellings.

"Where is Pierre?" Henry asked, interrupting the conversation.

The sachem displayed a double row of filed teeth when he grinned. "Pierre was gone before the sun came," he said. "That is his way."

Henry felt stricken.

Sebastian saw his expression and asked in English, "What's wrong?"

"I tried to recruit him last night. He was evasive and said he'd give me an answer in a day or two." Henry made no attempt to hide his anxiety. "If he locates the wagon train, he could warn them. I don't like this!"

"Neither do I!" Sebastian replied.

The sachem looked first at one, then at the other, puzzled by their use of the foreign language.

Henry quickly addressed him in Kiowan. "If the warriors of the Cheyenne will find Pierre le Rouge and bring him to me, they will be rewarded with two barrels of whiskey and many firesticks."

302

The sachem sat upright. This seemed serious. "What has Pierre done?"

"He has broken the trust of his brothers," Henry said.

Virtually no Indian would blame a man for stealing the property of another, which they regarded as a legitimate activity, but the breaking of a brother's trust cast any warrior beyond the pale. The sachem was shocked.

"The Cheyenne have been told that much booty awaits them when they attack the wagon train that comes soon into their country," Henry said. "Pierre has gone to warn the white men that they will be attacked!"

The sachem was stunned by the revelation.

As a gesture of good will, Henry handed him a knife with a tempered steel blade. "We will leave this very day for the land of the Blackfoot so they will be ready when the wagon train enters their land," he said. "Thanks to the treachery of Pierre, we cannot stay here any longer. Send me the scalp of Pierre, and the warriors of the Cheyenne will be rewarded."

That, he reflected, was the best he could manage in a difficult situation. The Cheyenne were already primed to attack the train, and if they could apprehend Pierre le Rouge, he would pay them a bonus. He was relieved that he hadn't told the mountain man too much about his plans, but just the fact that the wagon train would be alerted would make attempts to sabotage it more difficult.

He had to rely on the Cheyenne now, and if his mood weren't so vindictive, he could almost feel sorry for the simple-minded Pierre.

Only a short time had passed since Claudia Brentwood had learned for certain that she was pregnant, but she couldn't yet afford the luxury of daydreaming about the day when she and Sam would be parents, for they were too busy establishing the depot. Day after day freight caravans arrived from the East, bringing supplies and provisions, wagon axles, wheels, and rifles for the depot. Sam had hired a number of men to help him load the various supplies in the outbuildings beyond the ranch house, so it was Claudia's place to prepare the meals for these hired hands, some of whom slept in the barns. Sam frequently needed her help and as frequently consulted with her, so there was little time she could call her own.

Today was Sunday, so there were only two extra mouths to feed. Most of the hired hands had gone into Independence to spend their week's pay on liquor and women, but the pair who remained behind would work until noon.

Jacob Levine sat at the breakfast table in the kitchen, silently devouring his fried fish and scrambled eggs. He was short and so slender that he looked as though a strong wind would break him in half; but Sam said that no hired hand worked harder. A former fur cutter from New York whose one ambition in life was to go to Oregon and settle there, Levine was hard-bitten and surprisingly resilient.

So, in his own way, was the Reverend Oscar Cavendish, who was tall, almost as slender as Levine, and very talkative. Freely admitting he had been discharged by his congregation and defrocked for deeds he refused to discuss, he shared Levine's appetite for work and food and had been infected with his partner's enthusiasm for life in the Oregon country.

As Claudia brought a second platter of eggs and fried fish to the plain wooden table, then joined the men for coffee, Cavendish launched into a discussion of his favorite subject.

"As we learn in Ezekiel," he said, "the flock of my pasture are men. Sam has said there are hundreds of souls in the wagon train that is traveling across the Great Plains at this very moment. Other people are beginning to gather in town for the next train, and still others will follow. It stands to reason there will soon be several thousand settlers in Oregon—men, women, and children who will need the counsel of a man of the cloth. They'll need someone to baptize them, to marry them, and to bury them. I feel I'm called by the Lord to help them."

Sam coughed behind his hand to hide his amusement. "I thought you were thrown out of your church, Reverend."

Cavendish was unabashed. "The Lord has forgiven the congregation's transgression, so I have done the same. A new pastorate awaits me."

"All I know," Levine said as he helped himself to more fish, "is that I won't be happy until I get to Oregon. This afternoon I'm going to spend a few hours at target practice on the range in back of the stables. You ought to come with me, Reverend. The Indians out yonder ain't going to leave you alone just because you put your collar on backwards."

Cavendish shook his head. "Beasts shall be at peace with me, just as the Lord promised Job they would be at peace with him. If I am unjustly attacked, I'll know what to do, but I cannot prepare for war."

Levine smiled faintly. "If you were pushed around the way I was, you'd have a good-sized chip on your shoulder, too."

"Just exactly how do you both intend to get out to Oregon?" Sam Brentwood asked them. "It's a long, long journey from here."

"The Lord will find a way," Cavendish replied.

"Maybe so, maybe not," Levine said. "Me, I'm saving my money. I've already bought a good horse and a rifle, and before I'm done, I'll have a team of mules and a snug wagon, so I'll be ready to join the next train. But sitting here ain't earning money. Thank you for breakfast, Mrs. Brentwood. Come along, Reverend. We got lots of work to do this morning."

The pair made their way to the barns, where sacks of gunpowder and piles of harness leather had to be unpacked and stored.

Sam lingered for another cup of coffee with his wife. "I'm sorry you have all this extra work to do, Claudia," he said. "It's something I didn't count on when we set up the depot."

"I don't mind, darling," she replied, brushing a lock of blonde hair away from her face. "If there's still so much cooking to be done after the baby comes—well, maybe we'll have to hire a woman to help. By that time I dare say we'll be able to afford it. But I refuse to worry about what will happen six months from now."

Before Sam could reply, there was a knock at the door.

Lieutenant Colonel Leland Blake stood in the frame,

his uniform and boots covered with dust. He shook hands with Sam, introduced himself to Claudia, and then added, "I've taken the liberty of feeding and watering my horse and turning him loose in your back pasture, Mr. Brentwood. We've been on the move all night, so he's as tired as I am."

Claudia offered the new arrival breakfast, which he gladly accepted, and Sam waited until he returned from the pump, where he went to wash away his grime, before questioning him.

"You're in a hurry to get some place, Colonel?" he asked.

"This is my first stop," Lee Blake said, handing him a sealed letter.

The wax imprint on the communication was that of the President of the United States, and Martin Van Buren's message was brief. "This letter will serve to inform you that Lieutenant Colonel Leland Blake, U.S.A., has my full confidence. I will appreciate your cooperation with him. Colonel Blake will discuss his mission with you, as the situation warrants."

As Claudia began preparing breakfast for the weary officer, Lee Blake seated himself at the kitchen table and glanced at his hostess, then his host. "Would you prefer that I wait until later to talk about business, Mr. Brentwood?"

Sam shook his head. "You can say anything in front of my wife that you can say to me."

"As a start, then, perhaps you can give me some information. I'd like to know everything you can tell me about the attempts made by British and Russian agents to sabotage the wagon train that's headed for the Oregon territory."

Sam spoke steadily and at length. Claudia chimed in too, having known Henry St. Clair fairly well after he had joined the train as a supposed Oregon-bound immigrant.

"He sounds like one of London's upper-echelon agents," Lee said thoughtfully. "All of them are dangerous, so I'm sure I have my work cut out for me." He went on to explain that he was being sent to join the wagon train in order to bring a halt to the incidents that were plaguing them.

"I can see why you've been riding hard, Colonel," Sam said.

"I can't afford to waste time, Mr. Brentwood. I'm hoping you will be able to provide me with a guide who can lead me to the expedition. Or, at the very least, perhaps you can give me a detailed map that will allow me to locate the train myself."

"I don't know of any reliable guides in Independence," Sam said. "Anybody who claims to be a mountain man and is hanging around these parts in summer can't be worth his salt."

Claudia, sensing what was coming, braced herself.

"Have you ever crossed the Great Plains, Colonel?"

"Never, Mr. Brentwood. I spent a long time in the Everglades, and I was part of a group that prevented the British from moving down into Minnesota from Canada, but the plains are new to me."

"Then I strongly urge you not to make the journey alone. Game is plentiful at this time of year, and so are berries and other edible plants, so food will be no problem. But many of the Indians between here and the mountains resent outsiders—especially the Blackfoot and the Cheyenne, along with any number of smaller tribes."

"Certainly no two Indian nations are alike," Lee replied, "and any man who values his scalp tries to minimize the risks he's required to take. But I don't see where I have much choice. I've been ordered to join that wagon train, and if there are no competent guides available, I'll have to travel alone."

"If my wife will give me her permission," Sam said, "I'll take you across the prairies myself."

Claudia swallowed hard, resisting the temptation to close her eyes for a moment. Her hunch had been right. She was certainly competent to take charge of the growing depot and supervise the laborers who were putting away the supplies. And even though she was afraid for Sam's safety, she could not and would not use her pregnancy as an excuse to keep him at her side.

"I won't pretend that I'll enjoy spending weeks—or

months—by myself," she said. "And of course I'll worry. But I have good friends on the wagon train, and my sister is a member of the company. So I can't be selfish and refuse you the right to do what you think is best, Sam. I couldn't live here, all safe and snug, knowing that the train is in constant danger."

Sam reached for her hand. He had known she would make the sacrifice without hesitation, and he was proud of her. "That's settled, then," he said. "Get all the rest you can today, Colonel, and we'll leave early tomorrow. How strong is your horse?"

"He's a big, tough stallion. I couldn't ask for better."

"Then I won't offer you one of mine. But I think we'll need to take a couple of spare mounts with us. We can make much better time if we alternate horses."

After Lee finished his breakfast, he was shown to one of the guest rooms in the ranch house, and Sam went out to the stables to check on the work being done by Jacob Levine and the Reverend Cavendish.

Both reacted instantly when he revealed that he was leaving the following day to guide a visitor, whom he carefully refrained from identifying as an army officer, to the wagon train.

"Take me with you," Levine said. "I already have one horse, and I have enough cash to buy another. I don't really need or want a wagon of my own."

"I want to go, too," the clergyman declared. "The Lord guided Moses through the desert of Sinai, and you shall be our guide, Sam. I believe I can scrape together enough cash to pay you for a couple of good horses."

Sam was impressed by their zeal, even though he remained dubious about their ability to make the journey. "I aim to set a fast pace," he warned them. "I'm not making this trip for pleasure or convenience. So, if you can't keep up, you'll be left behind, which could mean the end of you."

Jacob Levine's jaw jutted forward. "Nobody will leave me behind," he said. "I've spent my whole life waiting for the day when I can claim land of my own and farm it. Nobody's going to deprive me of that chance. Don't worry about me keeping up with you!"

Reverend Cavendish hesitated for a moment. "I've never fired a gun or used any other weapon. The Bible is my only protection, and the Almighty will give me the strength to maintain any pace that you choose to set. I refuse to be left behind!"

Sam shrugged. He had warned them, and he fully intended to keep his word. The safety and future of the wagon train members was of far greater importance than the fate of two adventurous strays.

When he returned to the house, he found Claudia preparing Sunday dinner, a rib roast of beef. She was concentrating on peeling potatoes and carrots, but Sam noticed that her eyes were red. Going to her, he put his arm around her shoulders.

"I wouldn't leave you alone if I thought you were unable to manage, honey," he said. "But you can handle a rifle as well as any man. You know what needs to be done here. In fact, you're better at it than I am."

"I have no worries about myself, only about you." She smiled up at him, unwilling to let him see the depth of her concern.

"Have you ever known me not to be able to look after myself?" he demanded.

She shook her head. It was true that his self-reliance was awesome. She put her arms around him, and she knew he would survive.

Pierre le Rouge knew he was being followed by a band of Cheyenne warriors, but the maneuver didn't surprise him, and he easily managed to outdistance his pursuers, simply by traveling each night for several hours after dark. Most Plains Indians halted their journeys at sundown.

So he reached the wagon train without further incident, arriving late one afternoon, after camp had been made and the hunters had gone out for fresh meat. He was in high spirits, pleased with himself after his efforts, and his mood improved still more when the first person he saw was Eulalia Woodling. She had become a member of the water-gathering detail and was filling two buckets in a small lake behind the circle of wagons.

The mountain man halted, removed his hat with a flourish, and bowed from the saddle. "Pierre le Rouge knows he has died and ascended to heaven," he declared, his English strongly accented. "Never on earth did I see such a lovely angel!"

Eulalia stared up at the bearded, red-haired giant. In spite of his rough attire, this stranger had the manners of a gentleman, and his gleaming eyes indicated that his compliment was sincere. All the same, she had spent enough time in the wilderness by now to recognize the dangers of engaging in conversation with strangers.

Smiling slightly to temper the severity of her attitude, she said, "Our wagonmaster has gone hunting, but you'll find people in the train who will look after you until he returns."

"Ah, but you will allow Pierre to carry those pails for you. Beautiful ladies should not be expected to perform such hard work."

"I do what I must," Eulalia replied, and insisted on carrying the pails herself. She tried to hide her reactions but was flattered by this man's attention. It had been a long time since she had been treated with the courtliness she felt she deserved.

Pierre bowed again, then rode on, turning once in his saddle and grinning broadly to indicate that she had not seen the last of him.

Ernie von Thalman was in camp and greeted the newcomer courteously but was unable to elicit much information from him. It was obvious to Pierre that Ernie was new to the plains, and he would tell his story only to the wagonmaster, who would be better able to make his own judgments.

Then Eulalia returned with her buckets of water, and Pierre instantly devoted his full attention to her. He hadn't known any ladies for more years than he could recall, having attended to his needs by visiting brothels in Independence and other towns on his infrequent journeys to civilized communities. This dignified young woman had the air of the great ladies he had seen from a distance coming in and out of the Citadel, the governor's palace-fort in Quebec, and perhaps for that reason she fascinated him.

Whatever the cause, Eulalia was delighted and flirted with him subtly. At the very least, she was showing other women in the company that, regardless of their opinion of her, men were still drawn to her.

A short time later the hunters returned. They had killed a bull buffalo, which they had already butchered. Whip dismounted and, seeing the new arrival from the rear, went to him. "What can we do for you?" he asked as the man continued to chat with Eulalia.

Pierre le Rouge turned, recognized him instantly, and pounded him on the back. "Whip Holt!"

"Pierre!" Whip was equally overjoyed.

"Not since we fought the Comanche together near the South Pass have I seen you! Are you the wagonmaster of this train?"

"Of course. What are you doing here?"

"Pierre must have words with you in private," the French-Canadian mountain man declared, his tone ominous.

They adjourned to Ernie's wagon, where the president of the company joined them, and there Pierre told them of the offer made to him by the British agent. "Never has Pierre le Rouge done harm to ladies and children," he concluded. "So I went away quickly. I was followed by a band of Cheyenne, but they couldn't catch me. Or, if they could, they had the good sense not to attack me."

"Tell us more about this British agent," Whip said, plainly concerned.

"His name, I believe, is St. Clair—"

"Say no more. That no-good bastard again. I was hoping we had seen the last of him, but we're in for more trouble. Real trouble."

Ernie nodded in sober agreement.

"You will need help?" Pierre wanted to know.

"We could sure use your rifle, if that's what you mean," Whip said. "But if you go along with us, you'll be heading in the wrong direction, if you aim to sell those furs your pack horses are carrying."

Pierre's roar of laughter shook the walls of the hard-roofed wagon. "Pierre was a little crazy for the company of people, that's all," he said. "The money I would earn from the furs I would spend in Independence on women and whiskey. The whiskey I do not need, and in this wagon train there are beautiful ladies. So I will be happy to travel with you."

"Just remember they're ladies," Ernie cautioned him, "not the kind you'd find in a town."

"Pierre knows when he must behave like a gentleman," was the indignant reply. Turning to Whip, he added, "How long Pierre will stay with you I do not know. Long enough to make certain that St. Clair is beaten."

At supper that evening, Whip announced to the company that his old friend was joining the train, at least for the time being, and would act as assistant wagonmaster. Now that they were entering the land of the Cheyenne—and the territory of the even more dreaded Blackfoot lay ahead—Pierre would be a valuable addition to the company.

As soon as the meal was finished, Pierre sought out Eulalia. Now that she had learned his identity, she was even more cordial to him, rightly suspecting that her presence was at least partly responsible for his decision to accompany the caravan for a time.

"There is a favor Pierre wishes to ask of you," he said.

"Tell me what it is," she replied coyly, "and then I'll decide whether to grant it."

He pointed to the bales of beaver and lynx skins that he had removed from the backs of his pack horses. "Do you have the space in your wagon to store my furs? I would like my pack animals to enjoy the rest they deserve."

"I'll make room for them," Eulalia replied quickly. It shouldn't be difficult to persuade this man, who so obviously liked her, to make her a gift of enough furs to fashion a lynx coat for the coming winter. Confident of her powers, she reflected that a few smiles and an occasional encouraging word should be enough to win her a prize that other women would envy.

Lieutenant Colonel Leland Blake looked like any other civilian frontier dweller in the old buckskin shirt and trousers he had borrowed from Sam Brentwood. Only his boots would have revealed to a sharp-eyed observer that he might be an army officer. Not even Jacob Levine and the Reverend Oscar Cavendish were told his true identity or the reason for his presence on the journey.

Sam took the lead, with Lee riding beside him, each of them leading a spare horse. Levine and Cavendish rode a short distance behind the pair, and they, too, had spare horses. After a few days in the wilderness, Sam's doubts about these volunteers began to disappear. Levine never complained, gathered firewood and water, and cheerfully accepted the chore of cooking breakfast and supper.

Cavendish proved to be even more surprising. In the saddle, he resembled a loose-jointed scarecrow. It seemed miraculous that he could keep his seat. Yet he managed to maintain the blistering pace that Sam set. He claimed to know nothing about the outdoors, but he caught several fish every evening, and he proved adept at lighting fires in the Indian manner, by rubbing sticks together. It was difficult to actually enjoy the company of a man who seemed incapable of speaking a complete sentence without referring to the Scriptures, but he was resilient and tireless.

By riding one horse mornings and another afternoons, it became possible to travel even more swiftly than Sam had dared to hope. They covered forty to fifty miles each day. If they could maintain the pace, they expected to catch up with the wagon train in two weeks or less.

No unexpected incidents occurred during the first days of their journey. On the fourth morning, however, the placid routine was broken when Sam suddenly pointed to some dark objects in the distance.

"There's a small herd of buffalo yonder," he said. "We'll shoot one—just one—to give us meat for the days ahead."

"I need the practice," Jacob Levine said. "I hope nobody will mind if I bring him down."

"All right," Sam told him, "but make a semicircle north-

313

ward away from the Platte so you'll approach the herd downwind. And don't get too close before you shoot. Buffalo tend to avoid riders, but can be dangerous to men when they stampede."

Levine handed the reins of his spare horse to the clergyman, checked his rifle, and directed his mount on a wide swing so he wouldn't alert the herd. The others continued to follow the river, slowing their pace, and for a time Sam nodded approvingly. Then his attitude changed, and he spoke softly. "He's close enough now for a clean strike. He ought to stop and shoot."

Levine continued to move closer to the grazing buffalo. Lee Blake saw nothing wrong with what the former fur cutter was doing, but his knowledge of buffalo was limited. "What's wrong?"

"He isn't a good enough horseman to get out of the way in a hurry if the herd stampedes. It's an unnerving experience to have tons and tons of wild animals galloping toward you. I've known men to become so rattled they've been thrown and then trampled to death."

"Isn't there some way we can warn him?"

"Not without firing ourselves and maybe scaring off the whole herd." Sam increased his own pace, quietly checking his rifle to make certain he could fire it instantly.

"Ah," the relieved Lee said. "He's slowing down now."

"But not quite enough."

Reverend Cavendish started to pray softly, but they ignored him.

At last Levine halted, raised his rifle and, after what seemed like a very long time, squeezed the trigger. His shot struck a bull, which weighed at least two thousand pounds, but it only wounded the animal. Crazed by the pain, the beast lowered his head until it almost touched the ground, then charged his attacker, his hoofs pounding as he advanced.

"Get out of the way, Jacob!" Reverend Cavendish shouted. "Move, man!"

Levine was so startled by the unexpected assault that he continued to sit motionless. Finally, instead of urging his mount out of the path of the crazed bull, he began to reload his rifle, too confused by now to realize that he would have no opportunity to fire again before he and his horse were gored.

The others were two hundred yards away, but Sam Brentwood knew there was only one way to save the man's life. His rifle had a range of no more than two hundred yards, but he had no choice. He spurred his stallion, and as the great horse broke into a gallop, he raised his rifle, took careful aim, and fired.

His bullet entered the brain of the bull buffalo, who died instantly, plunging forward and collapsing almost at the feet of Levine's badly frightened gelding.

The other buffalo in the herd, unaware of the first shot, were at last alert to the danger. A wise, elderly bull was the first to bolt, and then the entire herd of about fifteen buffalo followed him as he raced off to the northwest, away from the scene.

Levine was still trembling when Sam led the others to him. "You don't have to lecture me," he said. "I know all the things I did wrong. Next time I won't make the same mistakes, and I thank God there will be a next time!"

He was the first to leap to the ground and begin butchering the bull, his experience as a fur cutter making him exceptionally adept at the task. Sam and Lee Blake exchanged glances. They both had to admire Levine's courage. Many men who had escaped death so narrowly would have been useless for the rest of the day. For the first time, it occurred to Sam that Levine might prove to be a welcome addition to the wagon train.

Pierre le Rouge quickly became accustomed to the routines of wagon train living. Sometimes he relieved Whip at the head of the column, he had to be dissuaded from going out with the scouts, and he was as skilled as Whip and Arnold at shooting game. Pierre and Hosea frequently went hunting together, each fascinated by the other's techniques. When they were joined by Stalking Horse, they made a formidable trio, and never failed to return with game.

Pierre delighted in teaching the older boys bawdy songs, which they sang at the top of their voices. As they sang in French, only Ernie von Thalman and Cathy van Ayl could understand the words; the former kept his own counsel so the fun wouldn't be spoiled, and Cathy resolutely ignored the lyrics.

The only objection anyone could find to Pierre was that he continued to devote too much attention to Eulalia Woodling. No one minded his open interest in the girl, but there were many—particularly the women—who resented the way Eulalia used him. She flirted with him when it pleased her and calmly accepted his help when he offered to do her chores for her.

On the night the wagon train reached the junction of the North and South Platte rivers, Whip announced to the company that they had reached a significant place in the Great Plains. Pioneers who chose to follow the South Platte would travel across Colorado, then head toward the southwest onto what was known as the Old Santa Fe Trail, eventually reaching Spanish California. Their wagon train, Whip said, would follow the North Platte to its headwaters in the mountains and would travel by way of the Wyoming country and the land of the Ute Indians, to the Great Divide, then cross yet another range of mountains that would bring them to Oregon.

They still had a vast distance to travel, but they had made good progress, and there was at least a chance they would be able to reach a sheltered, wooded canyon in the Rockies before they would have to establish a permanent winter camp.

"You've come a long way from Long Island," Whip told Cathy. "You have a right to be proud of yourself."

"I haven't done much of anything, except follow where you've led us," she replied honestly.

A scant twelve hours after starting to follow the North Platte as it meandered westward, its waters deeper and less sandy than those of the Platte itself, Stalking Horse returned early from his scouting duties. He reported without delay to Whip; then Pierre was summoned. The three

conversed at length, speaking in an Indian tongue so no
one would know what they were saying. As Whip pointed
out, there was nothing to be gained by alarming the company prematurely.

At the insistence of Stalking Horse, they sent for Hosea,
too, and Whip explained the situation to him succinctly.
"We've come to the land of the Cheyenne now," he
said. "Next to the Blackfoot and the Comanche, maybe,
they're the meanest tribe there is. They hate foreigners
as much as they hate other Indians, even more. They've
had a quarrel with Pierre, who was their friend, because
an enemy turned against him. Now Stalking Horse be-
lieves they've sent a large party of scouts to keep watch
on us, and that means trouble. What we need to know,
right off, is how many men there are in the Cheyenne
scouting party. That will tell us something about their
intentions. You understand me so far?"

The Ashanti, listening carefully, nodded but made no
reply.

"Stalking Horse and Pierre are going out," Whip said.
"They'll ride in the direction that Stalking Horse spotted
the Cheyenne."

"The Cheyenne will recognize Pierre," the French Ca-
nadian mountain man interrupted. "That much will be
good."

"They'll also see Stalking Horse," Whip went on. "Both
of them will keep their distance. That should attract the
attention of the Cheyenne—and, we hope, should keep
that attention. Meantime, Hosea, maybe you could steal
close enough to count their number and find out how heavily they're armed. That's information we badly need."

"Hosea do," the little man said, his manner confident
and calm.

He immediately moved out into the prairie and began
to pluck clumps of the knee-high grass. While members of
the company watched, he covered his shield with grass,
then hastily made and donned a plaited-grass shirt and cap.
The members of the company were astonished at his in-
genuity, and the results were almost magical. The camouflage was so effective that, at a distance of a scant one

hundred and fifty yards, Hosea blended completely into the landscape of the prairie. One moment he could be seen, and the next he vanished.

Stalking Horse and Pierre left at once, riding at a canter through the tall grass toward the northwest. Hosea ran beside them, tireless as always. Even Whip could follow his progress only because the grass parted and waved slightly wherever he moved.

Voices carried across the open country, so there was no talk. After the trio had gone about three or four miles, Stalking Horse grunted quietly, and the two horsemen slowed their pace, moving apart until they were separated by several hundred feet.

Hosea moved off on his own, staying parallel with them but making his own way. Stalking Horse paid no attention to his friend, confident of his ability to take care of himself.

Although Pierre had gone hunting with the Ashanti every day for a week, he was seeing a new facet of Hosea's talents and was amazed.

All at once Stalking Horse raised a hand, pointed, and said in a clear voice, "Cheyenne!"

A cluster of horsemen could be seen in the distance, but it was impossible to make out their number. The two riders moved into single file, Stalking Horse in the lead, and rode parallel to the Indians, neither closing in nor allowing themselves to drift farther away.

The braves obviously were not intimidated by men who had no intention of challenging them. They respected Pierre, whom they were able to identify at a distance because of his height and beard. But the strange Indian who rode with him did not impress them, and they remained confidently on their own course.

Stalking Horse had learned patience in the long trials he had been forced to endure as a child and as an adolescent before he had been admitted to the councils of the Cherokee as a full-fledged warrior. He was able to play this seemingly simple game indefinitely, and he felt no stirring of impatience.

When Pierre le Rouge went hunting or was about to confront an enemy in combat, he, too, could be patient, but this situation annoyed him. He peered continually across the sea of grass that separated him from the Cheyenne scouts, but he could make out no sign of Hosea, even though he looked for a telltale parting and waving of grass. Perhaps, he thought, the little man had outsmarted himself. Certainly there seemed to be no way he could be moving through that grass.

The better part of an hour passed, and Pierre stared hard at Stalking Horse until the Cherokee looked at him. Then he shrugged to indicate his bewilderment. Stalking Horse merely grinned at him in return. Suddenly a voice was raised only a few feet from Pierre's mount, causing him to start violently.

"We go back to train now," Hosea said calmly, still hidden from view in the grass. "Hosea find out what Whip want to know."

Stalking Horse immediately turned back in the direction of the North Platte River, and Pierre moved up beside him. There was no sign of Hosea, however, until they left the Cheyenne patrol far behind. Then the Ashanti moved his shield slightly and could be seen running only a short distance from the two riders.

He was so eager to report his findings that he actually raced ahead of them and was the first to reach the spot where the wagon train had halted for the night. When the others arrived shortly thereafter, Pierre found it difficult to believe that the Ashanti was breathing normally, as though he had not exerted himself at all.

Whip was waiting.

"Count eighteen warriors in party," Hosea told him. "All carry bows and arrows. All carry big spears."

Whip sucked in his breath. "That's exactly what I needed to know," he said. Eighteen braves in a scouting party meant reconnaissance in force. The warriors obviously were ready for a serious engagement if they carried spears as well as bows and arrows.

That very night a new routine was established. Sentry posts were set up, and the men of the wagon train, particularly those who were able to make out potential enemy moves after dark, were on constant duty until daybreak.

XIII

Lee Blake kept up the pace that Sam Brentwood set, but he had to admit to himself that at no time in his army career had he traveled at such a steady speed. Jacob Levine pushed hard, his determination making it possible for him to follow, and Reverend Cavendish, to the surprise of his companions, seemed untroubled. His resources were endless.

The quartet shot enough game to provide themselves with fresh meat each day, and the clergyman's fishing provided them with a measure of variety in their diet. On two different evenings, Levine found wild berries, which he presented to his companions. They slept in the open, rolled in their blankets, and at dawn each day, before they began their ride, they bathed in the always-cold waters of the Platte River.

Sam and Lee struck up a firm friendship on the trail and, after the manner of men who liked each other, began to exchange confidences.

"I'm more worried about my wife than I was willing to admit to her," Sam said. "But she's the most resourceful, courageous woman I know. If any man at the ranch steps out of line—well, I feel sorry for him. Only a mission like this would have taken me away from home when she's expecting a baby, though. All the same, I'll be back in Independence long before our son shows up."

"You know," Lee said, "I can't help envying the members of the wagon train. Oh, I'll grant you life can't be easy for them, crawling across the entire continent in all kinds of weather, facing hostile Indians and other hazards. But there's something solid waiting for them when they finally reach Oregon."

"You never married, Lee?"

"An officer in my kind of work never settles in any one place long enough to have a wife and a family. Every few years I've been moved to a new assignment, and I can't ask any woman to share that kind of a life."

"The right woman wouldn't mind."

"If there is such a woman, Sam, I haven't had time to find out. Between you and me, I had a private meeting with President Van Buren before I left Washington City. He told me there's a possibility, if I have to travel all the way to Oregon, that we'll establish an army post there to protect our citizens. I could have the command of that post if I wanted it, I'm sure. It's a temptation, but I'd be out of the mainstream, and it would take a very special girl to persuade me to spend the rest of my life on the Pacific."

Sam refrained from commenting that he had been a confirmed bachelor, too, until Claudia had come into his life.

Summer was the lush season on the Great Plains, so most of the nomadic Indian tribes stayed in one place, raising the crops they would store until the harsh winter arrived. Autumn was the season when they were on the move, hunting the vast herds of buffalo that had grown fat and sleek on the rich grass of the prairies.

Even in summer, however, Indian patrols were on the prowl, constantly watchful and alert, so their nations would not be subjected to surprise attacks launched by traditional enemies. On several occasions Sam and the members of his party saw mounted braves in the distance, but the warriors showed no interest in a group of only four white men.

One day, however, eight Kansa warriors emerged unexpectedly from a grove of trees.

"Hold your rifles ready, but don't shoot," Sam warned. "We may get out of this without any trouble, but the whole blamed tribe will be after us if we kill any of them."

Lee nodded and remained calm. Levine clutched his rifle, waiting for an order to fire. Reverend Cavendish raised his voice in a recitation from the Book of Psalms, but his companions paid no attention to him.

The Kansa came closer, and one of their number approached and raised a hand in greeting. Sam returned the salute. The Kansa addressed him in Kiowan, Sam responded in the same tongue, and then the braves rode off without further ado.

"What was that all about?" Lee wanted to know.

Sam was embarrassed. "Indians may steal," he said, "but they almost always speak the truth. They were planning to attack us, but they recognized me and changed their minds. I guess it occurred to them that they'd have a real battle on their hands if they insisted on a fight."

The army officer laughed appreciatively. "Now I can understand why you wanted to be my guide," he said. "I had no idea that even Indians were afraid of you."

"Not of me," Sam replied modestly. "Only of my rifle. They'd be leery of you, Lee, if they felt the sting of some of your bullets."

In the following days, they encountered more Indians on the prairies, including Wichita and Osage. A band of the latter appeared to be hostile, so Sam put a single bullet in the head of the leader's pony. The discouraged braves quickly disappeared.

At last the day came when the quartet caught up with the wagon train. They reached their destination during the nooning hour, and within moments, most of the company surrounded Sam, eager to shake his hand and inquire about Claudia. He spent a few moments alone with Cathy, managing to tell her that Claudia was expecting a baby, and he promised to spend the evening with her.

Then, while Levine and Reverend Cavendish began to acquaint themselves with the men and women they had joined, Sam and Lee Blake went off to confer privately with Whip. The wagonmaster read a letter that President Van Buren had sent him and seemed perturbed.

"It appears to me that you're replacing me, Colonel," he said.

"Not at all," Lee replied quickly. "I don't know the terrain—either here or what lies ahead. I'm totally unfamiliar with the operation of a wagon train, and I've never dealt with any of the Indian nations of the plains or Rocky Mountains. Even if I wanted to replace you—which I don't—I'm not qualified. I'm here because the War Department regards me as something of an expert in countering the work done by foreign agents. I'll step in only when I think it necessary, and I'll ask you for specific help only when I believe there's an opportunity to put British or Imperial Russian spies and saboteurs out of business."

"Fair enough," Whip said, but he still had reservations.

"Lee has become my friend," Sam Brentwood said. "He's our kind of man."

His friend's approval reassured Whip somewhat, and he brought the army officer up to date, telling him about the visit of André Sebastian to Fort Madison, the subsequent poisoning of the lake water, the death of the Russian agent and, finally, the current flurry being caused by the Cheyenne.

"I'm blame near positive the British are behind the Cheyenne," he said. "Pierre le Rouge saw St. Clair and another white man in a Cheyenne town to the northwest of us, and St. Clair tried to enlist his services. I reckon you'll want to talk with Pierre yourself."

"So I shall," Lee said. "But I don't want my real identity revealed to him or to anyone else. Let everyone think I'm just a new recruit, like Jake Levine and Reverend Cavendish. I don't want to restrict myself by starting to sleep in anybody's wagon, and I prefer not to join any of your hunting parties. I'll help out with various chores, but I don't want to be tied down to a regular job. From time to time, I may ask you and your assistants for specific help, but mainly I'll be working by myself."

"I reckon we're going to get along," Whip said, and

extended a hand. Lee's grip was equally firm, and Sam was relieved. A clash between these two could have had catastrophic results.

"After I've had a long chat with Pierre le Rouge," Lee said, "I plan to become acquainted with every adult in the wagon train. A good many of them won't require much of a check, but I want to make as certain as I can that there are no British or Russian agents currently in your company."

Whip was startled. "I think that's unlikely."

"I hope so, but it's my job to find out," Lee replied firmly. "Henry St. Clair once posed as an Oregon-bound immigrant, and from what Sam here reported to Washington, he almost wrecked the train. What one agent has done, another could do all too easily, so I intend to make good and sure that the inside of the house is clean before we start looking outside."

They separated, and that afternoon, while Sam rode in his familiar place at the head of the column beside Whip, Lee dropped back a few paces and fell into conversation with Pierre. Prodding gently, he managed to elicit the entire story of what had taken place in the town of the Cheyenne, but he did it so subtly that Pierre had no idea he was being interrogated.

When the caravan made camp for the night, Lee had a few additional words with Whip, in Sam's presence. "You probably realize this already," he said, "but I can almost guarantee that the Cheyenne will launch a serious attack on the train soon. An agent of St. Clair's caliber wouldn't rest until he managed to provide them with strong inducements. Apparently he was planning on pushing ahead into new territory, so his work with the Cheyenne seems to be finished. The only reason he'd move on would be that he's convinced the Cheyenne will follow through with his plan."

"My hunch," Sam said, "is that his next stop is the Blackfoot, and then the trouble will be even worse."

"I've been worried about the Blackfoot—and the Comanche in the mountains—ever since Andy Jackson asked me to join you in this whole enterprise, Sam," Whip said. "They're both strong and mean, and they hate everybody outside their own tribes. The best thing that could happen would be a war between them. If they bled each other enough, there would be peace in the wilderness for a few years. In the meantime, the Cheyenne are nasty enough."

"I think," Sam said, "that I'll spend a few days with you before I head back to Independence. My horses need resting, and I'd be perturbed if I left too soon to help you out."

"We sure can use you," Whip said.

"What precautions have you taken?" Lee wanted to know.

"I've posted sentries at night, and all our scouts are on the alert," Whip replied. "I'll double the sentry detail, just to make sure we aren't surprised in the middle of the night. And I'll tell our hunters not to roam too far from camp. I've already reminded the men to carry their firearms with them at all times, so there isn't much more that I'm able to do."

"How many men can the Cheyenne muster in an attack?" Lee asked.

Whip thought for a time. "They've never been a nation that uses mass assaults as a tactic, maybe because their towns and villages are so scattered. Myself, I've never heard of them sending more than a couple of hundred braves into battle at any one time."

"That's pretty much true," Sam added. "Of course, two hundred determined warriors can cause one hell of a lot of damage."

"And how many effectives can you use for defense purposes?"

"A dozen to eighteen marksmen, and another one hundred and fifty who range from fair shots to poor."

Lee Blake smiled and patted his own rifle. "It will be good exercise," he said. "After spending years sitting at one desk or another, all the way from St. Petersburg and London to Washington City, it will be interesting to do what any officer worth his salt enjoys most."

Supper was almost ready by the time they joined the rest of the company. Lee saw that Cathy was alone and decided to join her. For all practical purposes, he had already ruled her out as a possible enemy spy, but he told himself he had done enough work for one day. She was the most attractive girl in the wagon train, and he saw no reason he shouldn't indulge himself for a time.

"You and your sister don't look in the least alike, Mrs. Van Ayl," he said as he joined her.

"Oh, you've met Claudia?"

"I stayed with the Brentwoods for a day and a night before Sam brought me out here," he replied.

Cathy kept her suspicions to herself, but it was evident to her that Lee Blake was no ordinary immigrant. Joseph Levine and the Reverend Oscar Cavendish had tagged along on the journey, but she realized that Sam wouldn't have left Independence unless it had been important. She was in no hurry, however, to find out who this man was. It was enough for her that he was personable, handsome enough to arouse the attention of any romantically inclined woman, and well-mannered.

"Then you found Claudia well and happy?"

"Yes, and busy."

"That's an old family tradition," she said.

"I've noticed you preparing this meal. It can't be easy to direct the cooking for so many people."

"I do what I must."

Lee's curiosity about her was aroused. "Forgive me if I seem to be prying, but Mrs. Brentwood told me that she and Sam offered you the opportunity to stay with them in Independence. I find it surprising that an exceptionally pretty young lady should be going out to the Oregon country by herself."

"I don't like being beholden to anyone," Cathy told him. "That's an old family tradition, too."

"You intend to build your own house and farm your own property once you reach Oregon?" He was impressed by the task she was willing to undertake.

"Well, I lived on a farm with my late husband on Long Island, so farming isn't going to be a new experience for me," she said. "I realize I might be intending to try doing more than I can handle, but I won't really know until I make the effort, will I?"

"I salute you," Lee said, realizing it was the type of

spirit Cathy van Ayl exhibited that would establish a solid, viable American colony in the rich farm country in Oregon.

Their talk was interrupted by Whip, who was carrying his plate. "Cathy is spoiling fellows like me for wilderness living," he said. "I'm not sure I'll ever be satisfied to eat with my fingers again, even though it was the only way I took my meals for more than ten years."

Lee laughed.

Cathy smiled, too, hiding her surprise. This was the first time in days that Whip had actively sought her company, and for a few moments she didn't know what to make of his unexpected initiative. Lee was standing on her left, and when Whip deliberately moved to her other side and began to discuss ways to use leftover buffalo meat for breakfast, she realized he was deliberately trying to freeze the other man out of the conversation.

Then it dawned on her that Whip was jealous of the attention that Lee Blake was paying her. It was almost too good to be true. Whip Holt was actually jealous! So he wasn't indifferent to her, and he certainly wasn't taking her for granted.

Although Cathy showed no sign of the way she felt, she was elated. She had been so young when she had married that she had never had to deal with more than one suitor, but her instinct came to her aid. She managed to talk to both men, sometimes separately and sometimes together, taking care not to show a preference for either one.

She was very much aware that Whip bristled every time she addressed a remark to Lee Blake or smiled at him. Perhaps it was unfair to use this handsome stranger this way, but she told herself she was doing him no harm. Certainly the effect on Whip was almost magical.

Cindy, who saw the two men jockeying for position, looked at Cathy from a distance, then winked solemnly. It was all Cathy could do to keep from laughing aloud in triumph. At last she had proved to herself that Whip Holt was really interested in her.

Ultimately Sam appeared, put an arm around her shoulders, and started toward the stoop of her wagon with her.

"Sorry to break in," he said cheerfully, "but we're going to have us a little family chat."

As they made themselves comfortable on the wagon steps, he gave her a letter that her sister had written her, then answered her eager questions about Claudia.

"I think it's wonderful that you and Claudia are so right for each other," she said at last. "I find it hard to envision her being so domestic and so happy doing the things she always said she despised. What will the baby be named?"

"We've agreed to call him Andrew Jackson Brentwood. After all, it was Old Hickory who brought us together."

"What if Claudia has a girl?"

"She won't," he said firmly.

Cathy giggled.

Sam backtracked. "Well, Claudia says she'd name a daughter Martha, after your mother, and that's fine with me. But it won't happen."

She tried in vain to keep a straight face. "Of course not."

Sam was uncomfortable, and changed the subject. "You're not having any serious problems, I take it. You look just grand."

"To tell you the truth," Cathy replied, "I've never felt better in my life. Wagon train living agrees with me. I don't know how I'll act when we finally get to Oregon. It seems as though we've been traveling forever."

Sam leaned closer to her and lowered his voice, even though no one was within earshot. "Claudia and I have had many talks about you, Cathy. I wouldn't repeat this outside the family, but she's convinced you're in love with Whip."

Cathy hesitated for a long time before she spoke again. "One day I'm convinced I am, and the next—when he ignores me—I change my mind. You saw the way he was hanging around at supper tonight. That's because the new man, Lee Blake, was paying attention to me, and Whip was jealous. So that's a good sign, Sam."

"Maybe so." He drew his knife from his belt and absently slashed the tall blades of grass at his feet with it. "This isn't easy for me, so bear with me, Cathy. I've got to speak out because I promised Claudia I would. You know how firm she is when she makes up her mind to something." He paused, then took a deep breath. "Claudia and I hope you don't have your heart set on marrying Whip."

She wanted facts, not hints. "Why not?" she asked bluntly.

"Hellfire, girl, he's a mountain man. He's spent year after year by himself in the wilderness, never knowing a permanent home, cooking most of his own meals, going wherever he wants any time he's felt like going. Most of all, he's never been responsible for anybody but himself."

"But you were a mountain man, Sam. You spent longer in the Rockies than Whip has. Now you're happily married, settled in a permanent home, and about to become a father. So it does happen, even to the best of mountain men."

"For one thing," he replied, cutting the blades of grass more rapidly, "Claudia kind of crept into my bloodstream before I even realized what was happening. Every now and again a mountain man *does* find the right woman, and then they get married. But most fellows who have been hunters and trappers for any length of time just can't stand being tied down. When they see a woman—which doesn't happen very often—she's the wrong kind—not a lady, if you follow me. Look at Pierre le Rouge, who is almost my age and has been living in the Rockies ever since he was a youngster. A man like that will never marry."

Cathy thought of Pierre's obvious interest in the spoiled Eulalia Woodling. "Don't place any wagers on that."

He slid his knife back into his belt. "Claudia and I just don't want you to get hurt, that's all. I've known Whip ever since he first came out to the Rockies, when he was little more than a boy. He was a wild one, especially when he was younger, and he's always been the most independent cuss I've known. He doesn't get close to anyone, and he never lets on what he really thinks and feels."

"I'm convinced that's a front. People who are lonely often behave that way."

"Maybe so," Sam replied, sighing. "You'll do as you

please, of course, seeing you're a grown woman. And if you weren't headstrong, you wouldn't be Claudia's sister. Just remember that I warned you, Cathy."

The day began like any other. The sentries reported that nothing suspicious had happened during the last hours of the night. The campfire, which had burned low, was rebuilt. Small children emerged from their wagons to play, their shouts and laughter awakening many of the adults who otherwise would have slept later.

Members of the cooking contingent gathered at the fire, and under the direction of Cathy and Cindy began to prepare breakfast. Ted Woods, aided by Hosea, made emergency repairs on an axle that was sagging suspiciously. Some of the older boys would have gone fishing in the North Platte River but were stopped by Pierre, who told them to postpone their sport until that night's halt, when there would be more time for it.

Instead the boys were put to work cutting grass to be set aside as fodder for the horses and oxen. That noon they would be stopping in a sandy area where nothing grew, so the fodder had to be prepared in advance. Members of the water-gathering detail walked off through a patch of thick elm and pine to a clear, swift-flowing stream that flowed into the North Platte farther upstream.

Soon, Whip had announced the previous night, they would come to rolling countryside where they would catch their first glimpse of buttes—steep hills, each of which stood alone. Their appearance would mark the beginning of the Rocky Mountain foothills. Everyone was excited by the prospect and was filled with a sense of accomplishment.

As usual, Eulalia Woodling was the last member of the water-gathering detail to appear. The others had already returned to the camp after performing the chore, and she looked around for Pierre, hoping he would offer to take her buckets off to the stream and fill them for her. Unfortunately, he was supervising the grass-cutting efforts of Danny, Chet, and the other boys.

So Eulalia sighed petulantly and went off alone. All

through the long spring and summer, she had hated being obliged to perform such menial duties as cooking, washing dishes, and hauling buckets of water, but she had discovered that there was no escape from the chores. Whip and Ernie von Thalman showed her no sympathy, and even her father merely shrugged when she complained to him. Only Pierre showed her any kindness, but when he was otherwise engaged, she had to do the work herself.

Eulalia pouted as she left the circle. Instead of walking around the woods, as members of the detail had been instructed the previous evening, she elected to take a shorter route by going through them to the little river. Sometimes, she thought, Whip and Ernie deliberately made up rules for the perverse pleasure of forcing people to work harder.

Nothing stirred in the woods, and there was no sound. Eulalia dawdled, deliberately postponing her chore.

Then a brawny, brown-skinned arm caught her from behind, encircled her neck, and pulled her backward, knocking her off her feet. At the same instant, a soft gag of leather was shoved into her mouth, muffling her scream.

Eulalia looked up in terror as she fell, catching a glimpse of a husky Indian brave bending over her, his face and bare torso streaked with paint. In his scalp lock he wore several eagle feathers, and the stench of bear grease that was smeared over his whole body made her sick to her stomach.

She struggled, thrashing her arms and legs, but the man easily subdued her, binding her wrists behind her back with a strip of rawhide that he tied so tightly the leather cut into her flesh. He used another strip of rawhide to bind her ankles, then threw her over his shoulder, carrying her as though she were a sack of grain.

Eulalia realized he was taking her to a waiting horse, and again she tried to scream, but the gag muffled her voice. All at once she noticed that the woods and the open area to the north were alive with scores of other Indians, all mounted on large horses and armed with bows and arrows, spears, and long poles padded with dried grass.

The brave who had made her his prisoner threw her

over the folded buffalo robe that he used as a saddle, then mounted his horse and began to ride through the ranks of his comrades. The other warriors, intent on the grim business that awaited them, paid scant attention to the terror-stricken girl. Obviously her capture had been an unexpected bonus and had no bearing on what they were doing.

The brave continued to ride his horse slowly northward across the prairie. Not until he had gone several hundred yards did he strike the mount smartly on the flank. Then the horse bounded forward swiftly, and Eulalia was carried off.

Unaware that anything was wrong, Cathy beat on the bottom of an empty kettle with a large metal spoon to indicate that breakfast was ready. People began to line up for slices of buffalo fat cut from the center strip across the back of the huge beasts—a dish that, when fried, closely resembled bacon. With it the company was being served biscuits and a jam that some of the women had made from wild raspberries; pots of coffee were beginning to boil.

Suddenly one of the workhorses screamed and collapsed onto the ground, an arrow protruding from its head. Terence Malcolm staggered backward and sat down hard on the ground, staring foolishly at an arrow that was sticking out of his shoulder. And an indignant Grace Drummond plucked an arrow from her apron and brandished it over her head.

The mountain men were the first to react.

"Cheyenne!" Pierre le Rouge shouted as he recognized the short, thick arrows used by the warriors of the most dreaded Plains tribe.

"Cheyenne attack!" Sam Brentwood called in the same breath.

Whip instantly began to organize the defense of the circle. The entire company was caught by surprise, as Indian attacks almost always took place either at dawn or sundown. This assault, however, obviously had been planned for a time when it was least anticipated.

Most of the men moved to the openings between the

wagons, and the older boys, knowing from past experience what was expected of them, raced to the special wagon for spare ammunition, powder, and the extra rifles they would load while others were being fired.

The women, children, and animals were moved toward the river side of the circle, which was farthest from the area of active combat. Grace Drummond took charge of this maneuver, her booming voice rising above the shouts and the sound of rifle fire that was already starting to erupt. "Take your time!" she called. "Don't stampede like cattle or you'll trample your own little ones. Every mother is responsible for her own young. And look after your animals. Keep them away from the arrows as best you can. Don't let them stampede, either."

Whip was everywhere, organizing the resistance. Sam immediately slipped back into the role he had played for so long, mustering a number of the best marksmen into a special group. These included the scouts, Lee Blake, Pierre, and Ernie von Thalman, and they were joined voluntarily by Hosea and Claiborne Woodling, neither of whose talents Sam knew. Then Tonie Mell came to them, too, crawling close to the ground just inside the shelter of the wagons, and Sam didn't have the heart to turn her away.

Wiser and shrewder by far than other tribes, whose tactics usually consisted of a bold frontal attack, the Cheyenne remained in the woods, where they could see the defenders but could not be seen. From that shelter, they sent showers of arrows into the circle.

Cathy realized the cooking fire made an easily seen target. She began to extinguish it, indifferent to the arrows that fell around her. Cindy came to help her, and although terrified, the two girls tried to perform the task alone. Then Ted Woods saw them, and, his prowess with a rifle being limited, he came to join them. Wielding a heavy shovel, he piled dirt onto the flames, and as soon as they were extinguished, he shepherded the girls to relative safety on the river side of the circle, then devoted himself to calming the horses and oxen.

Meanwhile, the members of the elite unit huddled behind the special wagon, and there Whip conferred with them.

"There's no telling yet how many warriors are out yonder," he said. "We won't know until they show themselves."

"It looks to me like most of our shots are going wild," Sam said. "That's because too many of the men have never fought in a battle."

"I don't believe that matters," Lee Blake said.

Whip, aware of his high military rank, paid particular attention to this remark. "Why not?"

"Any kind of rifle fire is enough to hold savages at bay until we establish some kind of order here. And that's a job you seem to have done already. I'm not at all familiar with the Cheyenne, but if they're in any way like the tribes I know, they'll keep firing arrows until they think they've weakened us, and then they'll charge us on horseback and try to overwhelm us."

"I'm sure you're right," Whip said. "We've just got to be extra careful some of them don't sneak around to the river side."

"Some of us will see to that," Arnold Mell said. He worked his way around to the left, accompanied by Tonie, while Mack Dougall and Pierre le Rouge moved to the right. Any Cheyenne who tried to sneak down to the river side of the circle would be greeted by the accurate fire of sharpshooters who took pride in rarely missing their targets.

"Somebody is showing good sense," Lee said. "Instead of trying to pick targets in the woods, which is impossible, he's just sending a stream of fire into the trees to disrupt the enemy."

Whip grinned. "That's the new man, Levine," he said.

He beckoned to Chet and Danny, who were waiting nearby, hoping they would be chosen to reload the rifles of the marksmen. "Lads," he said, "make your way to every wagon opening that's being used for firing. Tell our men not to bother with individual targets. Tell them to just make certain their shots go into the woods. Easy now, boys. Take your time, don't expose yourselves in the open, and come back here as soon as you're done passing the message."

Soon all of the wagon train men understood what was

expected of them and concentrated on firing into the woods.

"There are fewer arrows coming this way now," Lee observed.

"A lot of the braves must be moving to the back side of the woods, where it's healthier for them," Whip said.

"But we mustn't be fooled by that maneuver." Sam was grave. "The Cheyenne don't scare easy. They won't give up—not with all the booty and scalps they could pick up here, not to mention firearms and horses."

Suddenly Arnold and Tonie opened fire, reloading and firing again as rapidly as they discharged their rifles.

"Ah," Lee said, "the enemy is growing impatient. Does that couple want any help?"

"Arnold will let us know if they do," Whip said.

The rapid fire continued. The army officer was impressed by Tonie's speed and dexterity as she reloaded again and again. Never had he dreamed any woman could handle firearms so well.

At last the firing stopped.

"We brought down three of them and got two of their horses as well," Arnold called. "I don't think they'll try sneaking around this flank again."

All at once the canvas of a wagon burst into flames. There was no way of extinguishing the fire, and not only was the canvas top eaten away but much of the contents were destroyed.

Now many more flaming spears soared over the roofs of wagons and landed inside the circle, making the animals restless and terrifying the women.

Whip made a quick decision. "Hosea," he said, "Get Ted Woods to help you and use as many of the men as you need. Smother those torches before they cause any more damage."

Hosea streaked away, organizing the task with astonishing rapidity. Apparently the Cheyenne were using something to launch the flaming spears, which continued to clear the tops of the wagons before they came to earth. But Hosea and Ted were equal to the task. A dozen men were helping them, but the pair managed to put out more of the fires than all of the others.

"If the savages had more sense," Lee Blake said, "they'd set fire to every last wagon we have. Then we'd be in real trouble."

"The Cheyenne are too greedy for that," Whip replied, smiling grimly. "They're already counting on all the food and blankets and other loot they're going to take home with them, and they don't want to destroy it."

Whip, Lee, and Sam continued to watch the woods for any sign of a decisive move on the part of the enemy. They were concentrating so hard that none of them saw Cathy van Ayl come up behind them. There was dirt on her hands, face, and clothes, and her hair was flying. She started to speak, panting from the exertion of running across the center of the circle.

Whip turned at the sound of her voice. "What the hell are you doing, going out in the open?" he demanded, his fear for her safety making him angry.

Cathy ignored his tone. "Dr. Martin needs help," she said, fighting to regain her breath. "Some of our people have been wounded by arrows—I can't tell you how many —and a little girl broke her leg getting away from one of the workhorses that almost crushed her."

"Well," Whip said, "Tonie can't be spared. We need her right where she is, doing what she's doing."

"Bob Martin knows that, and he isn't asking for her. Cindy and I would be glad to do what we can for him, but he needs somebody who knows what to do about the wounded without having to be told every step."

"Find that new man, Reverend Cavendish," Whip said. "A clergyman should be able to help a doctor in a situation like this. No, Cathy! Not you!" Whip shouted, as Cathy turned to go and look for Reverend Cavendish. "Go back to the other side, but work your way around, and stop taking needless risks with your life!"

Then he shouted, "Danny! You find Reverend Cavendish and take him to Dr. Martin's wagon. And let me know if he doesn't work out all right."

Whip turned back to observing the woods. Obviously he intended that his orders be obeyed, so Cathy meekly returned by a circuitous route to the far side of the circle. She knew that his anger had been sparked by his concern for her welfare, and that knowledge comforted her.

The shower of flaming spears continued, and Hosea and Ted gradually developed a new technique for disposing of these dangerous weapons. The blacksmith snatched them, sometimes catching them before they landed, his calloused hands not bothered by their heat. And Hosea calmly stamped out the flames with the hardened feet that had already carried him across so much of the continent.

The pair's courage and skill were remarkable, but they could not perform miracles. The roof and some of the contents of another wagon were destroyed. A farmer from Pennsylvania was struck by a burning spear; the man rolled on the ground to extinguish the flames, but he was burned seriously and had to be carried to the doctor's wagon.

The Reverend Cavendish, as calm as ever, understood exactly what was required of him. He worked in tandem with the frantically busy physician. None of the wounded laughed at the uninterrupted stream of Biblical quotations the clergyman uttered, and later many would express their gratitude for the comfort he had given them.

Then tragedy struck blindly. A flaming spear launched with greater force than those that preceded it reached the far side of the circle, where the women and children were gathered with the animals, and the point lodged in the ground, only inches from where Tommy Harris, the youngest of Emily Harris's surviving sons, was standing.

The nine-year-old boy, disappointed because he could take no active part in the battle, had been admiring the efforts of Hosea and Ted Woods. Now he had his chance to imitate them, and before anyone could stop him, he seized the flaming spear with both hands. His scream of agonizing pain and fright echoed across the circle.

Ernie von Thalman had been prowling the entire perimeter, doing his best to maintain order until such time as he was needed by the members of the group who were shooting into the woods. When he saw Tommy enveloped in flames, he dashed across the open to the child, ignoring his own safety.

The stunned Emily seemed paralyzed, unable to act, unable to move. Ernie threw the child to the ground, then fell on top of him, smothering the flames with his own body. After what seemed like an eternity, he put out the fire. Leaping to his feet and ignoring his own relatively minor burns, he picked up Tommy's limp body and raced with the boy to Dr. Martin's wagon. Cindy picked up his rifle, knowing he would soon need it, and followed behind, as did Cathy, who supported the staggering, weeping Emily.

Ernie knew even before he reached the physician's wagon that it was too late. Tommy was no longer breathing, and his sightless eyes stared vacantly from his small, scorched face. Gently he laid the body of the boy on a cot in Dr. Martin's wagon. Then, refusing treatment for himself, Ernie hurried to the command post behind the special wagon and related what had happened.

Whip was the first to break the long, tense silence. "We owe Tommy Harris a victory," he said. "Men who make war on little children deserve no quarter."

The Cheyenne gave the defenders no opportunity to alter their tactics or reverse the tide of battle. The attackers continued to remain hidden in the woods, and the flow of flaming spears into the compound seemed endless. Hosea and Ted worked doggedly, as did the men who were assisting them.

Sam Brentwood made a shrewd assessment of the situation. "I'm not making light of our casualties or property losses, which hurt," he said. "But we're not in too bad a shape. The women and youngsters are less panicky now, and the oxen and horses are quiet, except when a flaming torch lands near them. If we can just sit tight long enough, the Indians will have to try a more direct approach."

"When they attack another tribe's town," Whip declared, "their burning lances usually drive the defenders into the open. Then the Cheyenne divide and scatter them, which makes it easy for the major part of their force to capture the town, take the women and youngsters as prisoners, and go off with as much booty as they can carry. Right about now they must be getting a mite upset because we aren't reacting like their other enemies."

Pierre was aware of yet another significant development. "Their lances become fewer," he said. "They must be running out by now. Soon there will be a change."

"It seems to me," Whip said, "they've got to convince themselves we've been badly weakened. They can't move around our flanks, so they've just about exhausted their choices. Before long they'll have to make a big frontal attack, mustering their full strength and riding at us hard in the hope they can smash through the wagons and overwhelm us."

Such an assault sounded suicidal to Lee Blake, and he shook his head. "I think they'd be deterred by realizing they'd suffer one whale of a lot of casualties that way."

"The Plains nations aren't like others," Whip explained. "They believe that when a warrior is killed in battle, his spirit lives on forever in the land of their gods. That's what makes them fearless."

Gradually the stream of flaming lances thinned to a slow trickle.

"I reckon we'd best get ready for the main attack," Whip said. "I want our sharpshooters spread out—two to each wagon opening between us and the Mells on the left. Pierre, go back to your place with Mack, and we'll fill in the openings to the right, too."

The men began to move off.

"Danny, I want you to stay right here with Sam and me," Whip said. "Reload the spare rifles as fast as you can and keep feeding them to us. Chet, you do the same for Lee Blake and Ernie at the other end of the special wagon. We'll be the focal point of the attack, and we've got to hold them off here in the center."

The two boys obeyed eagerly.

"Where's Stalking Horse?" Whip demanded.

"Here," the Cherokee replied, materializing beside him.

"Get hold of Hosea. There's no need to tell either of you what to do. Station yourselves wherever you think you're most needed, and move around from one point to another any way you see fit to strengthen a position. And while you're at it, tell Ted and the men working with him to take complete charge of the animals as soon as the torches stop coming over. The riding horses are used to the noise and shouldn't be bothered by it, but the wagon horses and oxen will become excited when they hear sustained rifle fire. If they panic and start to stampede, they're likely to smash out of the circle and leave an opening big enough for the Cheyenne to pour through. We can't allow that to happen, no matter what, so tell Ted we're depending on him to keep the animals quiet!"

Stalking Horse glided away, returning a few minutes later, accompanied by Hosea. Whip and Sam had already stationed themselves on either side of the small opening between the special wagon and the smaller vehicle that stood adjacent to it, so there was little room there for Stalking Horse and the Ashanti.

Hosea solved that problem by stretching out in the tall grass in the open area between the two wagons, his shield on the ground in front of him, and Stalking Horse dropped on one knee beside him.

"We start here," the Cherokee said. "Move if get bad other places."

Whip and Sam agreed. The firepower massed at this one defense station would be so great that the attackers would quickly learn to avoid it. Both mountain men were relying on the knowledge they had acquired over the years about Indian behavior in battle. They knew that Pierre, Arnold, and Mack were equally well aware of the basic situation. No fighting men anywhere were more courageous and persistent than a body of Indian warriors, provided they were advancing. They would take risks that far more cautious white soldiers, even seasoned veterans, would not. However, once an Indian drive was blunted and the braves were thrown onto the defensive, they quickly collapsed, their bravado vanishing. When an attack failed, they were inclined to lose their zest for combat and frequently withdrew from the field.

"Here they come!" Ernie von Thalman shouted.

A long line of Cheyenne horsemen emerged from the woods and began to gallop toward the wagons, firing arrows as they rode. Behind them came a second wave, then a third, and a fourth. It appeared that, as usual, they were holding none of their band in reserve; any warriors who failed to take part in the initial assault would feel they had been slighted and would lose face.

Lieutenant Colonel Lee Blake, more experienced than his colleagues in judging the size of an enemy force, estimated there were approximately fifty warriors in each of the four lines, or about two hundred in all. Certainly the attackers outnumbered the defenders in what would long be remembered as the first major engagement fought by members of the wagon train.

Claiborne Woodling won the distinction of being the first to dispose of a foe. His rifle spoke a fraction of a second before any of the others, and he caught an oncoming brave between the eyes. The man was killed instantly.

Then Sam and Whip calmly opened fire. By unspoken agreement, they concentrated on the Cheyenne leaders, the warriors who wore the largest number of eagle feathers in their headdresses. Both knew that the braves were more likely to lose heart if they were deprived of their leadership.

Stalking Horse was taking his time, making each of his arrows count. Unflustered by the fury of the enemy drive, he fitted an arrow into his bowstring, let fly, and then reached for another.

Hosea was less fortunate. A number of Cheyenne arrows had already cut into his shield, but he himself was unharmed. The darts from his blowgun were effective only at short range, however, so he had to wait until the braves in the front row drew still closer before he could launch his own counterattack. He waited patiently, his dark eyes narrowed and gleaming with suppressed excitement. He knew that the battle presented him with an opportunity to repay the loyalty and trust the members of the wagon train had shown him, and his hand was steady.

After a wait of only a few seconds, which to him felt like a very long time, he had his chance. One of his darts

342

caught an onrushing warrior in the throat, and a moment later the man slumped, then slid to the ground.

Lee and Ernie were methodically sending round after round of bullets at the foe, with deadly effect. Pierre and Mack more than held their own, and Tonie, keeping up the pace set by her uncle, brought down her share of attackers.

Arrows were sticking out of the ground, some were lodged in the canvas of wagon tops, and a number found their targets. Whip suffered a minor wound in his left arm but ignored it. Claiborne Woodling, who was proving his mettle as a man, discovered that an arrow had dug into his thigh. He pulled it out, paying no attention to the pain, and continued to fire, reload and fire again, despite the spreading bloodstain on his throbbing thigh.

Some of the less able defenders didn't fare as well. One member of the expedition who appeared in an opening between wagons was killed instantly by an arrow, and two others were wounded. Then Major Woodling, accustomed to the more formal type of battle fought by civilized armies, became careless. He allowed himself to be seen in the open for a brief moment. Those few seconds were enough to seal his doom. An arrow penetrated his body, killing him even as he fired his old-fashioned musket.

His body sagged, but remained upright, leaning against the wagon beside him. Frozen on his lips was the faint smile of pleasure that had mirrored his feelings when he had peered down the barrel of his musket and seen a brave.

The thrust of the first wave was broken, and a number of riderless horses milled around the area just beyond the wagons. Confused and frightened by the sound of gunfire, they panicked and took off across the prairie.

The second wave of Indians replaced the first, and the warriors in the front rank either turned aside in bewilderment or tried to join their comrades, who were now suffering the same fate that they themselves had endured.

"I need more gunpowder!" Tonie Mell called. "Gunpowder!"

She repeated the cry several times, but none of the

older boys who were helping the marksmen heard her above the roar of gunfire and the hoarse cries of the warriors who were trying to encourage each other. But Cindy, who was pressed against a wagon a short distance farther down the line, made out the voice of her friend, listened carefully, and knew something had to be done. She picked up a powder horn lying on the ground beside one of the farmers, and, not taking the time to find an appropriate messenger, she began to work her way toward Tonie, crouching low each time she came to an opening between wagons.

Terrified by the Indians' arrows, Cindy paid little heed to the ground underfoot. A harness was coiled there, and she caught her toe in a leather loop. Losing her balance, she pitched forward onto the ground. The powder horn she was carrying flew out of her grasp and landed on the ground just beyond her reach.

Although she didn't realize it, she was directly in the path of a Cheyenne warrior who had been thrown from his horse just beyond the outside of the circle. In the confusion, none of the defenders had realized that the brave was still alive and uninjured, determined to work his way inside the perimeter and kill enough of the riflemen to permit his comrades to make a breakthrough.

His presence unseen and unsuspected, the warrior was moving slowly on his stomach under a wagon, gradually making his way inside the circle. He had lost his quiver of arrows and broken his bow when he had been thrown, but he still had his knife. Carrying it in his hand, he had no concern for his own safety, but was intent on killing as many wielders of firesticks as he could.

All at once, as the breathless Cindy struggled to rise from the ground, she saw the face and painted body of this husky brave a scant yard from her. The warrior saw her at the same instant, and Cindy screamed in terror.

Claiborne Woodling stood at the next wagon opening, reloading his rifle after firing at another oncoming horseman. He heard the girl's cry above the din of battle, then took in the situation swiftly. The warrior, as startled as Cindy, took a firm grip on his knife and poised himself, raising the blade above his head in order to plunge it into the body of this squaw who was raising an alarm.

There was no time for Claiborne to reload and fire at the man. So he took the only course open to him. He raced down the length of the wagon. Grasping his rifle by its hot barrel, and wielding it like a club, he brought the oak butt down with all his might on the back of the warrior's head, just as the Indian was about to strike Cindy. The man died at once, his blood and brains oozing onto the ground.

Cindy felt ill, but she still had a duty to perform. The din of battle made it impossible for her to thank Claiborne, who seemed to want no thanks and had raced back to his post, resuming his fire. Cindy scooped up the warrior's knife, along with the powder horn she had dropped, then delivered the horn to the hard-pressed Tonie.

The battle raged furiously, both sides realizing that the climax had been reached. The defenders' burden fell on the marksmen. They were equal to their task, holding their places and firing again and again, until their arms grew weary.

The Cheyenne were growing increasingly frustrated by their inability to penetrate their foes' line. Some of the braves threw their spears in desperation, rather than waiting until they could fight at closer quarters, but the lances caused no substantial harm. Arrows were proving useless, too, and the attackers' casualties were mounting so rapidly that the surviving senior warriors finally realized they would be wise to withdraw while they could.

No formal order was given. One moment the braves were sending arrows at their enemies, trying their best to keep pushing forward in the face of murderous rifle fire, and the next moment their ranks broke, and they were in flight, some skirting the woods as they retreated, others plunging into the cover immediately.

Stalking Horse and Hosea wanted to pursue the warriors, but Whip objected. "Let them go," he said. "We've hit them so hard they won't come back."

The expedition's casualties were the worst the Oregon-bound settlers had ever suffered. Six members of the company were dead, including little Tommy Harris and Major Woodling, while a score of others, including three children, had suffered injuries. Dr. Martin was still at work, looking after the wounded. As soon as the warriors had vanished from sight, Tonie went to help him and Reverend Cavendish.

Fire had destroyed the contents of several wagons, but most of the losses could be replaced. There was spare canvas in the special wagon, and ample food supplies were on hand, thanks to the successes of the hunters and fishermen. Clothing of skins could be made to take the place of wool and cotton that had gone up in flames. At least the wagons themselves were intact, and miraculously, the horses and oxen had all survived.

Whip decided it was best, for the sake of the company's morale, not to delay the funeral services. Graves were prepared, and a number of the men helped Ted cut down trees and fashion coffins.

The hunger of the smaller children reminded their elders that no one had eaten anything that day. But the adults had little appetite, so no hot meals were prepared. People made do with strips of dried buffalo meat, parched corn, and preserved berries.

Cindy looked for Claiborne Woodling and found him near the bank of the North Platte, staring down at the clear, swift-running water. She found it strange to be in the debt of this brash young man who had caused her trouble in the past, but she forced herself to face him without flinching.

"I want to thank you," she said. "I was so scared I didn't know what to do when I saw that Indian. You saved my life."

"Anybody would have done what I did," he replied, showing none of the aggressiveness that had made him so unpopular in the past.

"Not anybody," the girl replied, correcting him. "Besides, you did it. I never saw anybody move so fast, and I'm grateful to you."

"I'm glad I could be of help," he muttered, and turned away to look down into the water again.

Cindy couldn't help feeling sorry for him and touched

his arm lightly. "I—I'm sorry about your father," she said.

Claiborne looked at her, his expression reflecting something unfathomable in addition to sadness. "It may be just as well," he said. "Papa joined the wagon train only because he could see no other future for himself or his children. But he never felt at home in the train, and I know he'd have hated setting up a homestead for himself in Oregon. He lived a different kind of life, and in a sense he died when we lost our plantation."

The girl took a deep breath. "I suppose—you'll be—going back East with Sam Brentwood when he leaves for Independence."

"Not I," Claiborne said, shaking his head. "There's nothing for me in South Carolina. I'm going all the way to Oregon with you people, and I'll make a life for myself there." He straightened his shoulders, but sounded forlorn as he said, "That's the least I can do in Papa's memory. If I don't justify the faith he showed in me when we joined this wagon train, I'll never be able to look at my face in a mirror again."

It occurred to Cindy, as she made her way back to the circle, that Claiborne had grown to manhood more in a few hours than he had in all his preceding years.

Not until the funeral procession to the open graves was about to start did anyone notice that Eulalia Woodling was missing. Her brother noticed her absence when he returned to the vicinity. A hasty search was conducted for her, and when she couldn't be located the search was temporarily called off. For the sake of the grieving members of other families, Whip didn't want to delay the funeral any longer. When Sam and Ernie agreed with him, the procession started slowly upstream, then turned northward away from the river, beyond the place where it might overflow in the autumn and spring. As they made their way to the waiting graves, they began to sing.

This was not a time for a hymn, even though they were mourning those who had been taken from them. Their hope for the future had to sustain them, no matter how much they missed the departed, and those who first raised their voices expressed the faith of the entire company in what lay ahead by singing "America." By the time they came to the last stanza, even the members of the families of those who had died joined in, tears streaming down their faces:

> Our fathers' God, to thee,
> Author of liberty,
> To thee we sing;
> Long may our land be bright
> With freedom's holy light;
> Protect us by thy might,
> Great God, our King.

Reverend Cavendish conducted one service for all who had died, and there was no sound but the gentle whisper of the breeze through the tall grass of the Great Plains as he began to recite the familiar words: "I am the resurrection and the life, saith the Lord: he that believeth in me, though he were dead, yet shall he live: and whosoever liveth and believeth in me, shall never die. . . ."

Emily Harris stood with her surviving children, the younger in front of her and Chet on one side of her. Ernie von Thalman flanked her other side, as he had done on a similar, sad occasion in the past. He placed a comforting arm around her shoulders to sustain her and hold her upright.

Claiborne Woodling stood alone, his hands clasped behind his back, his feet apart, as though he were bracing himself in a strong wind. His eyes were fixed on his father's coffin. Although his expression was stiff, betraying no emotion, the arrogance that had been so much a part of his nature had been drained from him.

Cindy looked at him and had to restrain the impulse to move to a place beside him and take his hand. She knew he was suffering from loneliness, and she who had been alone so much of her life felt a deep pity for him. But she was afraid that others, including Claiborne himself, might misunderstand her gesture; besides, she was uncertain how Ted Woods might react. So she made no move and she, too, stared straight ahead, listening to Reverend Cavendish.

Before the service ended, many of the adults were thinking the same thought: the unknown perils that lay ahead were many, and before they reached Oregon, other graves would mark the long trail. But that knowledge could not deter them from reaching their goal. The promised land awaited the strong and the brave. They felt compelled to go on, so those who had lost their lives on the endless trek would not have died in vain.

At the end of the service, a group of volunteers filled in the graves with dirt and erected markers. Then a common grave was dug near the woods, and the bodies of the Cheyenne braves who had died were placed in it. Forty warriors had been killed in the abortive attack—a surprisingly large number. No one knew how many had been hurt because they had taken their wounded with them when they had withdrawn.

Claiborne Woodling stood alone outside the wagon he had shared with his father and sister, seeking solace from no one in his time of grief. Cindy found him there. Not speaking, she handed him the knife of the warrior he had killed when he had saved her life. For an instant her eyes met his, then she moved quickly away.

Whip quietly asked Stalking Horse and Hosea to search the entire area for any sign of the missing Eulalia. No warriors had entered the compound, except for the one brave Claiborne had killed, so it appeared impossible that the Cheyenne had captured the girl.

Late in the afternoon Hosea returned to the circle, caught Whip's eye, and beckoned. "Whip come," he said.

Together they went out into the woods. At the far side, near the bank of the little stream that flowed into the North Platte farther to the west, lay two of the expedition's wooden buckets. One of them had been crushed almost beyond recognition beneath the hoofs of a retreating warrior's horse.

Whip returned to the circle for a private talk with Sam, and then they went together to Claiborne, taking him with them into the woods.

"Look yonder," Whip said, pointing to the buckets. "I'm only guessing, but I think it's a pretty good guess, and so does Sam. We believe your sister was abducted by the Cheyenne while she was gathering water this morning. Before the attack even started."

The young man nodded. "I imagine you're right. What do we do now to get her back?"

"This isn't easy to say," Whip told him. "But—for the immediate future—we can do nothing."

Claiborne looked as though he had been struck; he started to protest. Sam raised a hand to silence him. "Hear us out," he said. "The Cheyenne's hunting grounds are extensive. It's impossible to know how many towns and villages they have in the area. At least twenty, I'd say, and maybe twice that number."

"In order to find Eulalia," Whip said, "we'd have to send out a search party—not just a few men, but a really strong party, in force—at least thirty well-armed men who know how to handle rifles. We've just beaten the tar out of the Cheyenne, and they won't forget that defeat in a hurry. It wouldn't surprise me any if Pierre le Rouge would like to hunt for your sister, and I'm sure you'd want to join him—"

"Of course!" Claiborne said.

Whip shook his head. "As Pierre would be the first to tell you, once he cooled down, such a mission would be suicidal. We can't afford to halt the entire train for weeks or even months while a big party of armed men travels from one Cheyenne town to the next. We can't afford to let our people run the risk of spending another winter on the prairie, this time in the open, without adequate shelter or firewood."

"Then you propose to abandon Eulalia?" Claiborne asked in a choked voice.

"Not at all," Whip said. "There's only one way to handle a situation like this. We keep on with our own journey, and that gives the dust time to settle. We haven't seen the last of the Cheyenne. They won't dare attack us again in force, but they'll undoubtedly send small groups of braves to make nuisance raids on us."

"That's their way," Sam added.

"When that happens," Whip said, "we'll find some way to detain one or two of them. They sure can't be holding any other white girl as a prisoner, and we'll be able to find out for sure where they're holding Eulalia. Then we'll go after her. Until then, we'll have to be patient."

"What's to stop them from killing her?" Claiborne asked, still visibly upset.

"Nothing," Whip said. "But it isn't their style to murder women." He refrained from mentioning how the Cheyenne *did* treat any unfortunate females held captive.

XIV

The buttes appeared suddenly in the midst of the flat prairie, their presence dramatic because it was so abrupt. The first buttes were small, standing only ten or fifteen feet high. Their sides were steep, sometimes almost perpendicular to the ground. Some were solid rock, like so many in the Dakota country that lay to the north, but many had soil on them and were covered with grass and weeds. Vegetation was not as lush as it was in the flatlands, however, and each butte stood alone in isolated splendor, rising by itself in the midst of the Great Plains.

André Sebastian was familiar with the area, but Henry St. Clair was seeing the region for the first time. Although he took pride in his ability never to show surprise, he realized this terrain was unique.

They rode side by side, leading the horses that pulled the Englishman's wagon, and Sebastian gestured toward the buttes. "We're in the land of the Blackfoot now, God help us."

"We'll get along with them." Henry showed his customary confidence.

"Don't try to trick them, that's all. Even the Cheyenne are afraid of them, you know. And only the Comanche of the mountains have an agreement of sorts with them, with neither invading the land of the other. It's the only way they both avoid total annihilation. Listen!"

Henry raised his head, strained, and heard the faint sound of drums in the distance.

"They know we've arrived on Blackfoot soil," Sebastian said. "Obviously we've been seen by their sentry outposts—who have made certain we haven't seen them. So we've got to watch our step now."

"In what way?"

"We do no hunting. It doesn't matter if a deer stops right in front of us. We ignore him. If we see a herd of buffalo, we ride around them. And if we should run across an elk or a bear, and there are both in the foothills, we close our eyes to them. Nobody hunts in Blackfoot country without the permission of their chiefs. If we brought down even small game, we'd be signing our own death warrants."

Henry was pleased rather than dismayed. "I believe I'm going to enjoy my visit with the Blackfoot. If they are as reliable as they are rugged, they're the very Indians I've been looking for, ever since I began my mission."

"Oh, they're reliable. They always keep their word— provided you do the same with them." Sebastian shaded his eyes with a hand and glanced up at the sun, which stood somewhat lower at this time of afternoon, now that autumn was at hand. "We'll arrive at one of their larger towns before dusk."

"Good."

"Most of their warriors will be off hunting buffalo, of course," Sebastian said. "This is the time of year when the animals weigh the most and have the best coats, so all the Plains tribes hunt them in force. But the Blackfoot are different. The sachems stay at home, and they keep enough warriors behind to protect their women and children. They're like Peter the Great, you know, always staying ahead of those who might become their enemies."

"They sound more like our Henry the Fifth." Henry allowed himself a slight smile.

Sebastian had no interest in a verbal duel with him. "Even their method of buffalo hunting is different. Closer to the mountains, where the hills become steeper, they send out parties of warriors who light firebrands, form a semicircle, and approach a herd of buffalo. The animals are afraid of the fire, so they take off in the opposite direction, and the Blackfoot drive them off the edge of a cliff. That kills the buffalo rather neatly, and the warriors simply go to the base of the cliff and collect the carcasses."

Henry stared at the Russian agent to see if he was joking but saw he was serious. Certainly he had made his point. Any Indians who managed to force buffalo to commit suicide by the hundreds while putting themselves in virtually no danger, deserved to be treated with both respect and great caution.

"The sachem we're going to see today is Gray Antelope. He claims he's fought more than a hundred battles and won them all. By the way, he'll expect us to prostrate ourselves on the ground when we first approach him."

"I must draw the line there. As a representative of Queen Victoria, I'm obliged to remember Her Majesty's dignity as well as my own."

"You won't look very dignified with your head stuck on the end of a spear," Sebastian said.

"On second thought," Henry declared, speaking emphatically, "I won't in the least mind abasing myself. In fact, I'll do anything the Blackfoot want if they'll cooperate with us and put an end, once and for all, to those people in the wagon train who have been leading such charmed lives!"

Eulalia Woodling labored on her hands and knees under a hot autumn sun, breathing in dust as she pulled weeds from the field of corn, soon to be harvested, in the land of the Cheyenne. She was barefooted and clad only in a skimpy breastband and short skirt of buffalo skin. Her hair was braided in two tight pigtails.

As she worked, she ignored the bugs and worms, paid no attention when she broke a fingernail, and barely paused to stifle a sneeze with one grubby hand. Certainly she didn't dare run the risk of looking up to see if the squaw who was in charge of the slaves was anywhere in the immediate vicinity. The woman, armed with a short, ugly whip made of several strands of rawhide, liked nothing better than to apply the whip to the back of any slave she caught malingering.

There were days when Eulalia no longer cared what became of her. Certainly she had abandoned hope that the wagon train leaders would send an expedition to rescue her from her miserable fate. The days ran together, and only the cold that settled over the Cheyenne town each night told her the season was changing and that autumn had arrived.

Nevertheless, today was different, perhaps because there had been enough buffalo stew left in the cooking pots at breakfast for the slaves to eat their fill after the Cheyenne had finished their meal. They had been able to eat before the slave mistress appeared with her whip and drove them like cattle into the fields, to work until sunset. A full stomach could make a great difference, even when the only food on hand was a greasy, somewhat rancid stew of tough buffalo meat.

There was another reason today was different, Eulalia realized. A large herd of buffalo had been seen only a few miles from the town, and almost all of the Cheyenne had gone off to hunt. That meant none of the older girls were on hand to torment the slaves when they had nothing better to do. The little boys had gone, too, so they couldn't prod the slaves with sharp sticks and then laugh when they squealed. And even the damned dogs that nipped at the heels of the slave women had departed. Her relief was infinite.

Tomorrow, to be sure, Eulalia knew that she and the others who shared her bleak existence would pay for the relative peace they were currently enjoying. Experience had taught her they would be sent to the scene of the hunt and required to perform the most loathesome of tasks—disemboweling the dead buffalo. But at least, if the hunt was successful, there would be enough to eat before the remains of the buffalo meat spoiled. She had learned to be grateful for the smallest favors.

Without warning the whip descended, wielded with such cunning that, although it caused welts, it did not break the skin. Startled, Eulalia straightened involuntarily, then wearily pulled herself to her feet, and fell into line behind the slave mistress. The work in the fields had come to an end.

One by one, other captives joined her. All were Indians, who concealed their feelings as only Indians could. Two were Wichita, Eulalia knew, another was an Omaha, and several came from small tribes whose names were new to her. One squaw was a Sioux whose nation lived in the Dakota country to the north. She was treated somewhat more leniently, perhaps because the Cheyenne and Sioux regularly exchanged prisoners.

There was one member of the shabby group whom Eulalia pitied more than herself. A Cheyenne, this miserable creature was actually a man who had shown cowardice in battle. He was condemned to spend the rest of his days as a slave—dressed as a woman. His hair was braided in long pigtails, and he was accorded the same treatment meted out to the others.

The captives were marched through the town and taken to a lake just beyond it. There they were required to strip and bathe in the chilly waters, itself an ordeal, but only a taste of what lay ahead. As they shivered, their bodies drying in the air, they were required to smear each other with pungent bear grease, which the Cheyenne regarded as attractive. Eulalia was convinced that, no matter how long she lived, the stench of that grease would remain in her nostrils.

Then the slaves were required to daub their lips and nipples with a red berry stain and smear the oil of a black plant root on their eyelids. The women were marched off to a row of small tents, set apart from the rest of the town. Each occupied her own tent, which had a buffalo rug on the floor.

Now the real ordeal began. Each slave was required to attend to the sexual desires of the Cheyenne warriors. A slave had no choice, accepting any brave who elected to appear at the entrance to her tent. The system was both simple and cunning. The unfortunate prisoners were given no food at night and were forced to rely on their clients for their evening meals. When a warrior was satisfied, he presented the woman with a portion of a buffalo tongue, regarded as the greatest of delicacies, part of an elk liver, or a chunk of grilled antelope heart.

Eulalia had been horrified and heartsick at first but had been driven by hunger to do what was expected of her. Some of the braves were stingy and she soon learned, through necessity, to dispose of them as quickly as possible. Others, who were more generous, she learned to treat to simulated pleasure.

The intimacies in which she was forced to participate no longer had any meaning to her. As best she could, she separated what was left of her spirit from her body and allowed the savages to use it as they pleased, all the while hating them and loathing herself.

To her astonishment, she was becoming expert in the tricks of the alien trade. She soon discovered that she and the former male warrior were the most popular of the prostitutes because they were different. When she was given more than she could eat, she shared the excess with the women the braves had ignored.

Her instinct for survival, she learned, was strong. Gradually, as she began to understand more and more of the language of the Cheyenne, she found out there was only one escape from her hard and degrading existence. A warrior, if he wished, could make a prostitute one of his squaws and take her off to his own quarters. There she would be subjected only to his authority and that of his senior wife. Such a position would mean no more beatings, a far less rigorous work schedule, and the need to take only one man to bed.

So Eulalia found herself exerting all of her charm on the senior warriors, the medicine man, and the son of the local sachem, who ultimately would succeed his father as the leader of the community. If she had to be an Indian whore, she told herself repeatedly, she would be a successful one.

Her endurance and attitudes were limited, however, and Eulalia found she could not allow herself to think of the life she had once led as a South Carolina belle. Even her wagon train existence, which she had despised, now seemed to her to have been such a paradise that she closed her memory to those months.

Sometimes she felt like giving in to hysteria, but the Indians had no patience with tears and tantrums. The slave mistress would punish her by administering a whipping that would leave her raw and bleeding, and she would still have to work the fields by day and service the braves at night.

She knew there was no way she could make her way back to civilization, no way she could rejoin the wagon train. If she was condemned to stay in the land of the Cheyenne until she died, she wanted greater comforts and a less exacting, grueling day-by-day existence. She had to earn them, so that was what she was doing. There was no way she could influence the harsh slave mistress who supervised her work in the fields and made her daylight hours such a hell on earth. But her smiles and pretended ecstacy well might persuade one of the more powerful men to ease her lot.

Fighting her way through the weariness that enveloped her, Eulalia willed herself to become more energetic. She ignored the vile stench of the bear grease that covered her and paid no attention to the sting of the berry stain or the smarting of her eyes as the plant root oil ran into them. She walked steadily to the entrance flap of her tent and forced herself to stand there naked, her pose provocative, a sultry smile on her lips, as she waited for the first of her evening's clients to appear. She was so ravenous that even the prospect of eating a piece of buffalo tongue appealed to her.

Everyone in the wagon train had heard by now that Eulalia Woodling probably had been captured by Indians, but nothing was being done to rescue the girl. The arrival of cooler weather, particularly at night, caused Cathy van Ayl to worry about Eulalia, and Cathy's own dislike for Eulalia increased her sense of guilt.

Ernie refused to discuss the problem with her, as did Arnold Mell. Claiborne, who had become friendlier with Cindy, kept his opinions to himself. She hesitated about going to Whip, not wanting to jeopardize the greater warmth he had been showing since Lee Blake had joined the train and had started paying attention to her.

The caravan came at last to the buttes. Soon, Cathy knew, the company would begin to search for an appropriate site, perhaps even in the mountains, to spend the coming winter. The realization that the Great Plains soon would be left behind had a sobering effect on Cathy, who was increasingly haunted by the fear that Eulalia would be forgotten. Sam, to whom she would have gone for advice, had returned to Independence some weeks before. So, one day during the nooning rest, she decided to confide in Lee.

He listened with the sympathetic understanding he consistently displayed toward her, then shook his head. "I've been concerned, too," he said, "but I'm sure Whip knows what he's doing. He's waiting until we can learn for certain whether the girl is being held by Cheyenne and, if she is, in which of their towns."

He did not tell her that he had a deep interest of his own in the developments. The Cheyenne also would know whether Henry St. Clair, having created a nasty problem for the wagon train during his visit with them, had moved on to the land of the Blackfoot or that of the Comanche in an effort to stir up even more serious trouble.

"Eulalia is no friend of mine," Cathy told him, "but the Cheyenne are vicious savages and might be torturing her or—worse. That's a horrible thought."

Lee had no voice in the matter and had to admit it. Unable to hold off any longer, Cathy went to Whip and told him her fears.

"I won't pretend to you that I think Eulalia Woodling is having an easy time of it as a captive," he said. "But I'm reasonably sure she's alive. It might take us months to search the whole Cheyenne country for her, so we've got to wait."

"Wait for what?" she demanded.

In recent days Whip had been developing a scheme of his own whereby it might be possible to obtain information, not only about the missing girl but about Henry St. Clair's intentions. But he wasn't ready yet to discuss his plan. Lacking the tact of more sophisticated men, he spoke abruptly, "You'll have to trust me to do what I'm able in my own way."

Cathy became angry. "If anything happens to her, that girl's blood will be on your hands."

"Have I ever shirked my responsibilities?" he demanded.

Although neither realized it, their near-romance had created its own tensions, which had been intensified by Whip's reluctance to tell Cathy of his growing interest in her. It seemed to her that his years on the frontier had made him insensitive to the feelings and sufferings of others, and her temper rose higher. "You wouldn't be so calm if you were the prisoner of the Indians!"

"I'd be dead," he said bluntly. "They wouldn't keep me alive very long."

"Well, I think—"

"Look here, Cathy. I don't tell you how to cook meals—"

"Now I'm not good for anything except cooking!" She knew she was being unreasonable and that the argument was no longer sensible, but she couldn't stop herself. "If you ask me, Michael Holt, you've lived around savages so long that you've become one yourself." Cathy turned and stormed off toward her wagon, but in spite of her rage she was ready to stop short and then forgive him if he offered her an apology.

Whip was in no mood to apologize, however. He couldn't remember when anyone had spoken to him so rudely, and he wanted to shake this headstrong girl until her teeth rattled—or kiss her until she melted in his arms. Or both.

His confusion was so great that, although he was almost always in command of his emotions, he now stood indecisively, clenching and opening his fists. The argument was absurd, and he tried to dismiss it from his mind.

What bothered him most was the suspicion that he was actually in love with Cathy van Ayl. That possibility horrified him. She had just now indicated that she thought of him as a rough mountain man, unmannered and crude. She was not only lovely, but a lady—and an heiress as well, having inherited two thousand dollars in gold from

361

her late husband. Whip saw no chance that she would consider the suit of a man so far beneath her, a man who had nothing of substance to offer her.

Damnation! He *was* in love with her! But she had made it clear what she thought of him, and she would laugh if he declared himself to her. If he had any brains greater than those of a buffalo, he would keep his feelings to himself.

A young woman's scream of terror brought Whip back to the present. Turning in the direction of the sound, he saw that Tonie Mell, who had been climbing a butte, had fallen forward on the steep hillside. For some reason she was unable to move. He noticed she had dropped her rifle, which lay beyond her reach.

As he started toward the hill, he saw why she had screamed, and he broke into a run. A rattlesnake, the longest and thickest he had ever seen, was coiled on the side of the butte less than a yard from Tonie's face, its head moving back and forth as it prepared to strike. The girl might have escaped if she had rolled down the hill, although it was probably already too late. She seemed mesmerized, however, and remained motionless as she stared at the reptile.

Others were hurrying toward the hill, too, and Stalking Horse was already preparing to shoot.

"No!" Whip shouted at him, unwilling to let him take the chance of killing Tonie if his arrow missed.

By the time the wagonmaster arrived at the base of the hill, he had uncoiled his whip. He made a lightning calculation, hoped the whip was long enough to reach his target, and then lashed out with all of his skill and strength. The leather sang through the air, decapitating the snake before it could sink its fangs into its victim.

Still Tonie lay where she had fallen. Whip raced up the butte, shouting, "Get up, Tonie! Where there's one rattler, there's often another."

"I know," the girl replied through clenched teeth. "But I—I can't move. Something happened to my leg."

As Whip came closer, he saw that she had stepped into a gopher hole, which had caused her to lose her balance.

The lower part of her left leg stuck out at an angle; it was obvious her leg was broken.

"Here," he said, kneeling and gently rolling her over. "Put your arms around my neck, and I'll see if I can get both of us back down to the prairie without taking a tumble that will break our necks."

Obviously in pain, Tonie did as she was told. As Whip carried Tonie down the butte, Dr. Martin arrived. Hosea, who had witnessed the scene, had run to get him.

"Bring her to my wagon," Dr. Martin ordered. A white line showed around his compressed lips, but he made no comment until Whip had departed. Then, as he measured and cut straight oak branches that he kept on hand to use as splints, he addressed Tonie for the first time.

"May I ask what in the devil you were doing climbing that hill?"

"I wanted to see the real foothills of the Rockies up ahead of us." Tonie gritted her teeth, swallowed a gasp of pain, and continued. "Danny and Chet told me they saw the big hills, so I wanted to see them, too."

"You're somewhat older than Danny and Chet—or are you?" he demanded acidly as he tore a portion of an old sheet into narrow strips. "You not only broke your leg, but you almost got yourself bitten and killed by a snake. It's too bad you weren't born wealthy, Antoinette. You need a governess."

She knew he called her by her full Christian name only when he was exasperated with her. "Don't scold me, Bob. Please. I was so eager to see the hills—"

"Since you're not wealthy, what you need is a keeper," he declared. He fell silent as he removed her boot, then cut away her buckskin trousers and stockings above her knee.

The girl's pain made it difficult for her to speak. "You're ruining my buckskins," she said. "And I don't have all that many spare stockings."

"You have only one leg left," he said curtly. "Hold on to the sides of the table and save your breath. This won't be pleasant." Before she could reply, he began to scrub her leg with a cloth soaked in brandywine.

Her leg felt as though it were on fire. Ordinarily Tonie would have moaned, but under the circumstances her pride would not allow her to do so.

"Here," he said, handing her a block of hard wood about an inch deep, two inches wide and six inches long. "Bite down on this. It will help when you start to scream."

She had helped him so often that she knew what would happen next. "I won't chew wood," she said, "and I promise you that I won't scream."

"Woman, I wonder if you ever do what you're told. Even a keeper isn't enough for you. What you need is a jailer!" Bob studied her leg intently. "All right. I warned you. Now, whatever happens, don't twitch and don't thrash around. For once in your life listen—and follow orders!"

His hands firm, his touch deft, he set her leg swiftly and expertly. Tonie's agony was so great she thought she would faint, but through sheer willpower she managed to cling to consciousness. And, having given her word, she not only refrained from screaming but made no sound.

Bob put the splints in place, then bound them. Not until the operation was completed did he move to the head of the table.

Tears were streaming down Tonie's face, but she was still silent. Bob reached out behind him, his eyes filled with admiration for the rare, stubborn courage she had displayed, and then handed her a glass of milky liquid. "There will be no more pain, Tonie. Drink this."

"I don't want any laudanum," she declared. "I won't be put to sleep."

"Tonie," he told her, raising her head. "You're going to drink this, every drop of it, if I have to pry your mouth open and pour it down your throat!"

Tonie drank the laudanum.

Bob's manner changed abruptly, and his voice became tender. "I was wrong," he said. "You don't need a governess, a keeper, or a jailer. What you need is a husband. You're so obstinate and ornery that I can think of only one man stupid enough to marry you."

He bent down, then kissed her. As his lips met hers, Tonie reached up, her arms encircling him, and clung to him. Surely the laudanum had already taken effect and she was dreaming.

The flatlands of the Great Plains gradually gave way to more rugged terrain. By early October the wagon train was following the North Platte through the western reaches of the Nebraska country, where hills were high. The sense of elation that members of the company felt after crossing the prairie was tempered by the knowledge that another winter was on its way and the Rocky Mountains lay directly ahead.

The days were cool now, and frost was beginning to threaten at night. At least firewood was plentiful, the tall grass of the prairie being replaced in many areas by thick stands of pine and hickory, ash and juniper.

The buffalo hunting season was at its height, the cumbersome beasts having grown sleek and fat after feasting on grass for months. At Whip's instigation, large quantities of meat were smoked, and the basic Indian system of preservation was used, too. Meat was cut into long, thin strips, which were dried in the open air on crude frames, some of which were tied to the sides and tops of wagons. It was essential to put aside provisions for the winter that loomed ahead, and no one needed to be told the importance of hoarding. The travelers were veterans now, acclimated to the tribulations of the trail, and they were already making preparations for the hardships that awaited them.

The women put away their dresses of cotton and dimity, changing into wool, and the men rolled down their shirtsleeves. Those of both sexes who owned clothes of buffalo or deerskin changed into them and were so comfortable that others demanded similar garments. Cindy and several of the other women began to learn the difficult Indian art of chipping away layers from tough buffalo hide to make it thin enough for wear. These skins were rubbed with mixtures of salt and the brains of the animals to cure them, then lightly smoked to keep them flexible. By the time winter came, virtually every member of the company would own at least one leather outfit.

Frequently the hunters saw Indians in the distance, ob-

serving the size of buffalo herds and the direction in which
they were moving. At Pierre's request, he was added temporarily to the roster of scouts, and Whip issued the group
new instructions.

"One of these days soon," he said, "you're going to
run across a party of Cheyenne keeping watch on a buffalo herd. Whenever that happens, don't wait until the
end of the day to notify me. Let me know right off. It's
high time we bear down and try to locate Eulalia Woodling."

Although the need to find a site for satisfactory winter
quarters was on everyone's mind, a halt was called for
twenty-four hours to celebrate the marriage of Tonie Mell
and Dr. Robert Martin. Two antelope and a buck were
shot for the feast, and Tonie herself was one of the hunters
who brought down geese. The splints had been removed
from her leg, and she walked with only a slight limp that,
her future husband said, would soon disappear. Precious
flour was used to make a wedding cake. Virtually every
family contributed a jar of preserved fruit for the gala
meal.

Tonie owned no white dress, so Cathy loaned her one,
made of silk, and Cindy provided a delicate hat with a
wide brim and a bunch of artificial flowers near the
crown. The bridegroom wore his best suit, a high-col-
lared white shirt, and a black stock, and Arnold Mell, who
would give his niece away, was attired in linsey-woolsey—
the first time on the journey that he had worn anything
other than buckskins. Cathy was the matron of honor,
and Bob asked Whip to serve as his best man.

The circle of wagons had been formed on a bluff overlooking the North Platte, and as safety precautions took
precedence over the wedding, the horses and oxen grazed
nearby as the company assembled for the ceremony.

A radiant Tonie emerged from the wagon she had
shared with her uncle. She couldn't stop smiling as she
took Arnold's arm and made her way slowly across the
clearing to the spot where Bob and Whip stood, in front
of Reverend Cavendish. Cindy was already weeping, and
tears came to Grace Drummond's eyes, too.

Then a hush fell as the minister intoned the words of

the wedding ceremony. During the vows, even the nervous bridegroom couldn't help smiling broadly when Tonie promised to obey as well as love and honor her husband. Certainly he knew, as did everyone else, that marriage would not change Tonie's fierce sense of independence.

At the end of the ceremony the bride and groom kissed with tender enthusiasm, and some of the teenaged boys and girls began to cheer. In a moment or two everyone joined in.

As people formed a line to kiss Tonie and offer Bob their congratulations, several younger couples conferred with each other in whispers, then started to laugh. The usually sedate Terence Malcolm cupped his hands and called, "Now the best man has to kiss the matron of honor!" A dozen others took up the cry.

Whip's face became red, and he pretended not to hear. Cathy, unable to look at him, felt her own face turning scarlet. But there was no escape for them. Their obvious discomfort encouraged their tormentors, and it soon became evident that the chant would continue until they complied.

Whip took a deep breath, mumbled something unintelligible, and grasped Cathy by the shoulders. She began to tremble at his touch and hoped he wouldn't notice. Then he kissed her, lightly but firmly, and everything else faded from her consciousness. She didn't even hear the cheers of the company. When he released her, she refrained from looking at him. Flustered, she turned and hurried to the cooking fire to supervise the last phase of the preparations of the wedding feast.

An even more serious business occupied Whip. Mack, Pierre, and Stalking Horse had not been present for the ceremony, having gone out to scout the neighboring area, and now the Cherokee returned, his usually expressionless face grim.

Whip hastily left the wedding party, and, feigning unconcern so he would not put a damper on the festivities, he sauntered off with Stalking Horse toward the far side of the compound.

Stalking Horse spoke in his own tongue so possible eavesdroppers wouldn't understand. "About three miles from the camp, there are many buffalo. There the son of Roaring Thunder saw Cheyenne."

"How many?"

Stalking Horse held up five fingers, then added, "One was a senior warrior, maybe a sachem. There were seven feathers of the eagle in his bonnet."

"He must be captured and brought back here. Alive," Whip said emphatically.

The Cherokee nodded. "It will be done," he replied, a light of anticipatory pleasure appearing in his eyes. "Hosea will come with me, and we will return with the Cheyenne."

Whip frowned. "It will be best to send a strong war party to make him prisoner."

Stalking Horse shook his head. "No. Then many fire-sticks will be used to kill Cheyenne. Their sachems will thirst for vengeance, and a new battle will be fought. Hosea and the son of Roaring Thunder will need no help from their brothers."

Whip trusted him and was satisfied. "Do what you will," he said.

They returned to the company, and Stalking Horse next drew Hosea aside. No one noticed the Cherokee and Ashanti leave the circle together, on foot.

As soon as they left the wagon train behind, they began to jog, slowing to a walk only when they sighted the buffalo herd in the distance. They moved forward cautiously, and at last Stalking Horse grunted. "Cheyenne," he said.

Hosea smiled when he saw five horsemen, all of them loitering near the herd, facing in the opposite direction. He and his friend were about to engage in a game of wits, and he was already enjoying himself.

Stalking Horse dropped to his hands and knees in the tall grass, disappearing from sight. Hosea advanced very slowly now, seemingly alone. His companion, accompanying him, could no longer be seen.

At last, as the pair had hoped, the Cheyenne braves became aware of Hosea, who appeared unarmed except for his cumbersome shield. The warriors turned, their horses spreading out, and began to move toward him.

Ordinarily they would have killed a man alone, but they were unaccustomed to the sight of a man with black skin, and their curiosity brought them still closer.

Showing no fear, Hosea continued to advance. When he was no more than a hundred yards from the mounted braves, he halted, planted his shield in the ground, and waited.

One of the warriors began to circle toward the right as he continued to edge toward Hosea. Hosea made no move until the man came within his range. Then he removed one of his little clubs from a loop at his waist and threw it. The weapon caught the brave on the forehead, instantly knocking him unconscious, and he slumped on the back of his mount. The other Cheyenne were alarmed and immediately reached for their arrows.

Hosea had eyes only for the man who wore seven feathers in his headdress—he would leave the other three Indians to his friend. Stalking Horse was still unseen, his presence in the high grass unsuspected. Then he let loose an arrow and brought down a warrior, who fell from his horse without making a sound.

Several arrows landed almost simultaneously in Hosea's shield, penetrating the outer layer of leather. But the Ashanti remained unharmed behind the "wall" of his unique fort.

Again Stalking Horse fired an arrow, and again his aim was true. Now only two of the Cheyenne remained. One was the brave with the headdress. Hosea took careful aim with a club, then sent it spinning through the air with all of the strength he could command. It landed against the warrior's temple, and he tumbled backward onto the ground.

The remaining Cheyenne, having had enough of foes seen and unseen, galloped away, presumably to bring the unhappy news back to his town. Some of the horses followed.

Hosea and Stalking Horse raced forward together. They were elated when they saw that the Cheyenne with the fancy headdress had been knocked unconscious. They used strips of rawhide to bind him to the back of his bewildered horse, which had not left the scene, and were so anxious to take him back to the wagon train that Stalking Horse regretfully collected no scalps. Not only had their mission been successful, but neither the survivor who had fled nor the other, still unconscious, would be able to identify their foes as members of the wagon train.

Leading the Indian's horse, Stalking Horse and Hosea returned as quickly as they could to the campsite. Their captive was still unconscious when they arrived, so they took him to Ernie von Thalman's wagon, then quietly summoned Whip.

The wagonmaster tried to arouse the captive, but failed, although the brave's deep, regular breathing convinced him that the man was not seriously disabled.

The wedding feast had not yet been served, so Whip drew the bridegroom aside. "I hate to ask you to work today of all days, Bob," he said, explaining the situation. "But, as you can see yourself, it can't be helped."

The physician slipped away from the wedding party, went to his wagon to get his medical bag, then went to Ernie's wagon. Only Whip accompanied him. The doctor held a small vial of smelling crystals under the warrior's nose, and he stirred, groaned, and opened his eyes.

"Who are you?" Whip asked him, speaking the language of the Cheyenne.

When the brave saw that his interrogator was white, his eyes became sullen, even though he was still groggy. He made no reply.

"Do you want me for anything more?" Bob Martin asked as he packed away the vial in his black leather bag.

Before Whip could reply, the warrior caught sight of the Wichita buffalo-bone amulet hanging from the physician's neck. "You are a sachem," he said. "I am the son of a sachem!" With great pride he displayed the amulet that he was wearing.

Bob didn't understand a word, but Whip was quick to seize the opportunity. "Stay for a couple of minutes," he said, and translated the warrior's remarks.

Bob's smile was reassuring as he looked down at his patient on the cot.

"The son of the Cheyenne sachem will suffer no harm," Whip told the warrior. "We found you sleeping in the fields, and we will return you this day to your own town."

The confused Indian hauled himself to a sitting position, one hand clutching his aching temple. Uncertain as to whether or not he was being tricked, he waited warily.

"The Cheyenne will be our friends." Whip continued to speak soothingly. "We will prove our friendship by taking you to your own people. You can also prove you are our friend."

"How so?" the brave asked cautiously.

"Tell me if a young, white squaw is a prisoner in the land of the Cheyenne."

"It is so," the warrior replied at once, relieved because the request was so simple.

"Can you take us to her?"

The man nodded. "She is in the town of Rising Moon, next to the town of my father."

"Then we will take you to the town of Rising Moon, and you will be free to join your people there."

"It is agreed," the warrior said, and although he was not yet fully recovered, he folded his arms across his chest to indicate that a bargain had been struck.

Bob Martin returned to the wedding festivities, and Whip asked him to send Mack and Pierre, who had just returned from their scouting duties, to the wagon.

"You'll have to eat your wedding dinner later," the wagonmaster told them. "Our Cheyenne here—who doesn't realize we kidnapped him—has told me where we can find Eulalia Woodling and will lead us to her."

Mack looked incredulous. "Three of us will invade a Cheyenne town?"

Pierre was equally disturbed. "That is suicide! We will be scalped alive and tortured to death!"

"I don't aim to lose the top of my head," Whip said. "Just trust me."

Pierre and Mack were still dubious, but Whip gave them no choice. They got their horses, then rejoined him as he slung a saddlebag over his stallion's back. He even had the presence of mind to saddle a mare for Eulalia. The Cheyenne warrior was still weak, but his dignity compelled him to mount his own horse unassisted. The group sneaked away from the festivities, with no one but the bridegroom knowing they had gone. This was Tonie's great day, and Whip wanted to do nothing that would detract from it.

The four men rode at a rapid clip. It was evening by the time they reached their destination, a Cheyenne town rich in fields planted with corn and beans. A sentry halted them just outside the community, then admitted them when he recognized the warrior.

In almost no time the sachem of the town appeared, surrounded by fifty warriors armed with knives and spears, bows and arrows. Mack and Pierre exchanged glances as they clutched their rifles. If they were attacked, it would be difficult to save themselves, but they were prepared to make the savages pay dearly.

The warrior who had escorted the strangers explained that these men had saved his life after he had been attacked by a large, fierce band of Indians he had been unable to identify.

So far so good, Whip thought, and gave the gathered Cheyenne no time to think about possible flaws in the story. Addressing himself to the sachem alone, he said boldly, "We have come to bargain with Rising Moon. Give me the white squaw who is your captive, and I will give you a priceless gift in return."

Before the chief could reply, he dismounted, opened his saddlebag and, as the warriors crowded around him, removed the skin of the white buffalo calf. The braves fell back, muttering to each other in awe.

Mack and Pierre understood now what Whip was trying to do, but their apprehension grew. There was nothing to prevent the sachem from ordering the visitors murdered and calmly taking possession of the precious white hide.

But Whip promptly demonstrated that he knew even more about the ways of Indians than did these experienced mountain men. "There is magic in this skin," he said.

The Cheyenne nodded in assent, and Rising Moon's eyes gleamed with avarice.

"The skin keeps its magic when its owner presents it freely to a friend. It will bring good luck in the hunt to its new owner and his people if they keep faith with their friends."

"It is so," Rising Moon replied gravely.

At that moment Mack and Pierre knew that they were safe.

The sachem sent two senior warriors for the white captive. After what seemed an interminable time, they returned, leading Eulalia by a rawhide leash looped over her neck. She was barefooted, clad in the leather breastband and short skirt that were her only attire. She had already prepared for her evening activities, so her skin was greased, her eyelids were smudged, and her lips were stained with berry juice.

"Don't say a word," Whip cautioned the startled girl as he took the loose end of the leash from the warrior, handed it to Pierre, and then helped Eulalia onto the back of the mare. "Mack, Pierre—get started back to the wagon train. I'll make a farewell speech to our new friends and catch up with you."

The trio promptly rode off, and it appeared to the Indians that the white squaw was being treated like a slave by her new owners.

Whip made a long, rambling speech—the kind the Indians enjoyed and expected—stressing his friendship and that of his people for the Cheyenne. The words did not come easily, but he persisted until he felt certain that Eulalia and her escorts had gone at least a mile.

At last he left the Cheyenne, letting his stallion gallop at full speed. Soon he caught up with the little party. Whip's first act was symbolic. He slashed the leash with his knife. "I know you've had a rough time," he said, "but you're safe now."

Eulalia nodded, but made no reply. Even though her unexpected rescue was a miracle that gave her infinite relief, she knew that her appearance told these men, experienced in the ways of Indians, that the Cheyenne had used her as a prostitute. She was so ashamed that she could look at none of them.

She tried to stammer her thanks for her deliverance. Then, after she fell silent, tears streamed down her face.

Pierre tried to comfort her by reaching out to pat her on the arm, but she shrank from his touch.

Guessing how she felt, Whip decided it would be wise to ease her gently back into the mainstream of wagon train life. So he waited until they were approaching the campsite before he said, "We'll take you straight to your wagon, and then we'll tell your brother you've come back." It would be best if Claiborne told her their father had been killed.

"Tonie Mell and Dr. Martin got married today, so I don't want to take away from the attention they're getting. You can get a decent night's sleep and change into your own clothes, and tomorrow morning will be time enough for folks to know you've returned."

Again Eulalia tried to express her thanks, but again words wouldn't come.

They approached the Woodling wagon from the outside of the circle. Not until Whip had seen the girl safely inside her wagon did he go in search of her brother. He found Claiborne eating wedding cake with Cindy, both of them chatting while a glowering Ted Woods stood nearby.

Whip quietly explained the situation.

"I'm coming with you," Cindy told Claiborne, and they walked together to the Woodling wagon.

They found Eulalia sitting cross-legged on the floor, still in her Indian attire. She looked dazed, and Cindy took charge. "Let me talk to her alone," she told Claiborne. "Wait until I come for you."

Claiborne had learned to trust Cindy's judgment and moved a short distance away. Cindy moved around the wagon, lighting lamps and, as she did, noting every detail of the other girl's appearance, including the welts on her back.

"I'll bring you some water so you can wash that grease away before you change into your own clothes," she said, then started to rummage in a leather clothing box. "Ah, here we are. A brush that will help you unsnarl those Indian braids."

Eulalia took the brush, then let it fall to the floor. "I wish I was dead," she said listlessly.

"I often felt like that in my day." Cindy remained calm.

"They shouldn't have brought me back here. It would have been better to leave me where I was."

Cindy went to the flap, beckoned to Claiborne, and sent him for two buckets of warm water.

"I'm useless here. Nobody will want anything to do with me," Eulalia said.

Cindy sat behind her on the clothing box, then began to unbraid and brush her hair. "Maybe it isn't as bad as you think."

"You don't understand. The Cheyenne made me be a whore. Man after man, night after night."

"Oh, that. I figured as much the second I saw you."

"It isn't just that they forced me to do it," Eulalia said. "I—I cooperated with them. I flirted with them. I pretended I loved every minute of it. Because they gave me food, and without it I would have starved."

"I would have starved, too, if I hadn't pretended to love entertaining my customers," Cindy said quietly. "You're no worse than the rest of us."

"Except that I had to sleep with savages."

Cindy was still unruffled. "Most men are savages in bed, especially with the women they pay." She went to the flap, took the buckets from Claiborne, and motioned him away again. "Here. Start to wash yourself. And scrub your face hard. You'll feel much better."

The lethargic Eulalia made no move.

"Here's one of your washcloths and a little jar of soft soap. Go to work, or I'll have to bathe you myself."

Eulalia heard the determination in her voice and, stripping herself, began to bathe.

"I'll grant you've had a nasty experience," Cindy said. "But those marks on your back will go away. And so will the marks inside you—if you let them."

"Everybody will know what happened to me."

"I very much doubt that they will—unless you tell them. But suppose they *do* find out. Just about everybody on this train knows I was a whore. But I have plenty of good friends, and I really wouldn't much want to know the others." She handed the other girl a towel, then took undergarments, stockings, a dress, and shoes from the clothing box.

Mechanically, Eulalia began to dress. "Civilized clothes. You can't imagine!"

"Yes, I can. You should have seen the flashy dresses I had to throw away." Cindy laughed, then sobered. "I'll tell you a secret. You can become twice the person you would have been without this experience."

"You're just trying to make me feel better. People will laugh at me—and shun me."

"A few will, I suppose," Cindy said candidly. "Let them. You don't need that kind. Start feeling proud of yourself. You had a hard time, but you lived through it, and you learned something. You'll be surprised, from now on, how easily you'll be able to distinguish between the men who just want your body and the men who like you for yourself."

Eulalia finished dressing, and a faint flicker of her old pride returned. Staring hard at the other girl in the flickering light of the oil lamps, she asked, "Why are you being so kind to me?"

"Because you'd do the same for me if our positions were reversed," Cindy replied promptly. "The person you used to be wouldn't have done it, but you're not that person any more. I can see the change reflected in your eyes, and I know a little something about what you've had to go through. Men are men, and it doesn't matter if they're Cheyenne warriors or the leading citizens of Louisville."

Eulalia took a deep, unsteady breath. "I think—I'd rather—let people know tonight that—I've come back. Instead of—waiting until tomorrow. If you'll come with me."

"Of course!" Cindy opened the flap, and for a moment they stood together on the top step. Then with one accord, they linked arms and started to walk toward the festive crowd.

Gray Antelope was the most powerful Indian leader in the West, perhaps in all of North America, and he knew it. All of the lower-ranking chiefs of the Blackfoot paid homage to him. For more than a decade he had ruled his nation as sachem of sachems. Although his face was becoming wrinkled, his hair was still a deep black, his build was still muscular, and, above all, he exuded an air of authority.

He sat cross-legged on the buffalo-hide rug in his tent of double skins, facing the fire outside, puffing slowly on his long pipe and studying the two white-skinned visitors who sat opposite him. After two long days of intensive discussions, it was plain to him that this pair were' trying to use him. Fair enough—and he would use them. So he concealed the instinctive dislike he felt for any men who were not Blackfoot. Adjusting his cape of buffalo skin adorned with feathers, he spoke slowly so the darker of the pair could translate his words.

"Twice the sun has risen, and twice the sun has gone again while we have talked. Now Gray Antelope has made up his mind."

Henry St. Clair started to speak, thought better of it, and waited.

"You have told Gray Antelope of the riches in horses and slaves, firesticks and cooking pots, blankets and other good things that await the Blackfoot when they attack the carts of the white men and squaws who will soon come to this land. So be it. The Blackfoot can make good use of all those things. But you offer too little in return. You say you will give us one hundred firesticks. Not enough!"

"Your senior warriors have counted them in my cart. I offer you all I own." Henry sat back and waited for André Sebastian to translate.

Gray Antelope shook his head, and the many feathers in his ornate bonnet danced. "The Blackfoot can send more than one thousand warriors against their foes. The white men of the moving carts have more than one hundred firesticks. So the Blackfoot will need five hundred more before they will strike a bargain with you!"

Henry exchanged a quick glance with Sebastian. He had been afraid of this development, knowing of the greed for which Gray Antelope was noted. Fortunately he was prepared for it. "There are many soldiers of my country at Fort Vancouver, which stands beside the waters of the Great Sea," he said. "I will write to them. Let a swift messenger of the Blackfoot ride to them. They

377

will send five hundred firesticks across the mountains at once!"

Gray Antelope felt a surge of elation, which he did not allow to show on his face. Armed with six hundred firesticks, his warriors could not only subdue the people of the moving carts, who were only a minor consideration, but they could use those firesticks to conquer the Arapaho, the Ute, and, above all, the hated Comanche. Those firesticks would make them the masters of all the flatlands and the mountains—of the entire world that was within reach.

"So be it," he said. "And while the messenger goes and the firesticks are sent, the visitors to the land of the Blackfoot will stay here. You will teach the warriors of the Blackfoot to use the one hundred firesticks you have already given us. You will teach my braves to shoot as well as you shoot."

The old man drove a hard bargain, Henry thought, but the price was worth paying. He felt certain the rifles would be sent from Fort Vancouver, along with ammunition and powder, no matter how much the brigadier in command disliked the idea of arming Indians with modern weapons. Even his own position as a semi-hostage while he acted as an instructor in marksmanship would be tolerable.

Now there would be no escape for the American wagon train. Attacked by one thousand Blackfoot, six hundred of them armed with rifles, they would perish. His own mission would be achieved without the government or people of the United States ever knowing that Great Britain had been involved.

"So be it," he replied solemnly.

The autumn wind that blew down from the nearby Rocky Mountains was chilly, and the sky overhead was leaden, as it had been for several days. But Cathy van Ayl was unconcerned about the approach of a new winter.

The wedding of Tonie and Bob Martin had made a marked change in her own life. When Whip had been teased into kissing her after the ceremony, the wall that had stood between them had crumbled and vanished. He was no longer as shy in her presence and sought her company whenever he wasn't busy. For the first time he spoke freely—not only about his past, but about his future.

The day before, he had told her in confidence that he was seriously thinking of settling in Oregon after he led the wagon train there. She had felt as though a bolt of lightning had struck her. She hadn't dared to hope that he might be willing to exchange his hard, nomadic existence for a settled future. Above all, the mere fact that he had taken her into his confidence was significant. Her instinct told her that he was thinking of establishing a homestead of his own because he wanted to share it with her.

So, at long last, she could admit to herself that she was seriously interested in him. Her sister had found happiness with one former mountain man, so it wasn't too much to hope that she could be equally successful as Mrs. Michael Holt.

Now, during the nooning halt, he came over to her again to talk. "This morning while we were riding," he said, "I got to thinking about a little valley I know in the Oregon country. There's no place in the whole world like it. The Pacific is on the western end, and on the other three sides it's surrounded by mountains. The forest is thick, so there's wood aplenty for building snug homes and for firewood. There are so many salmon in the river that flows along one side that nobody would ever go hungry. And the soil is as black and fertile as the soil you saw in Illinois."

"Is there enough room there for everybody in the wagon train?" Cathy asked.

"Enough and more," he assured her. "Even with the head of every family claiming six hundred acres, there's enough space for a couple of more wagon trains filled with people."

She was enjoying herself. "Surely there must be something wrong with it. I suppose we'll have to fight the Indians who live there."

Whip shook his head vehemently. "That's the beauty of my valley. Nobody lives there. There are Indians to the north and others directly to the east. But my valley isn't occupied. I've had a half-dozen sites in mind, but seeing as I may want to settle out yonder myself, my valley is going to be our goal."

Before Cathy could reply, someone shouted for Whip. He excused himself, and Cathy watched him as he hurried off to greet some unusual visitors—three mounted Indians, each of whom led a pack horse.

The trio dismounted, and it was plain that Whip knew them well. The two warriors exchanged greetings with him by raising their hands in the peace sign, and then, to Cathy's surprise, he embraced them each in turn.

But it was the third of the new arrivals, a young woman, who most attracted Cathy's attention. The girl appeared to be in her early twenties. Her chiseled features were flawless, making her a beauty by any standards. Her doeskin shirt and skirt fitted her closely, revealing a tall, perfectly proportioned body, and her hair, unlike the thick braids of the Plains squaw, cascaded down her back in a blue-black wave to her waist.

As Cathy stared at her, the girl prostrated herself on the ground before Whip. He quickly drew her to her feet, then embraced her, and a sense of jealousy surged up within Cathy as she saw the girl cling to him. At that moment, Stalking Horse came forward with great dignity and embraced the girl, who, Cathy later learned was his half-sister. He and his mother had traveled West many years before, where his mother had married her second husband, an Arapaho. Then the trio engaged in a spirited discussion with Whip.

Lee Blake was summoned, as was Ernie, and they joined in the talk, with Whip translating. The conversation went on for so long that, contrary to custom, the nooning was extended for a considerable period of time. The talk seemed endless.

At last Whip gave the order to resume the march. The three newcomers mounted their horses. Apparently they were attaching themselves to the wagon train. Lee Blake came to Cathy's assistance, helping her round up her horses and harness them. She knew better than to ask questions out of turn, but her memory of Whip's embrace with the lovely Indian girl still bothered her. "Who are these people?"

"Old friends and allies of Whip Holt's," Lee said.

He refrained from telling her the significance of their arrival, which she would learn soon enough. Mountain dwellers with whom Whip had spent several winters, they had brought word that the dreaded Blackfoot were being armed with rifles and were receiving instructions in their use from two white men. That portion of the news concerned Lee alone. It was his duty not only to learn more about the men but to counter their influence.

It was being rumored in the mountain tribes that the wagon train was coming into the Rockies and that the Blackfoot intended to annihilate the entire company. Lee realized he had his hands full, that he faced an unparalleled challenge. He would think in depth about the problem after he mounted his horse. Right now he was conscious of Cathy's steady gaze and knew he had to say something more to her. "They're members of the Arapaho tribe," he said.

Their nationality meant nothing to her. "The girl, too?"

"I believe so," Lee said. "She—ah—appears to be Whip's woman."

Cathy stiffened involuntarily.

Lee hoped that he hadn't said too much. He wondered if Cathy had more of a personal interest in Whip then he knew. Well, that couldn't be helped; by tonight the entire company would know of Whip's relationship with the young woman.

Mounting the board of her wagon, where Hosea was already sitting, Cathy saw the Indian girl look at Whip. The intimacy in her dark eyes required no further explanation. Too late Cathy realized she should have heeded Sam Brentwood's warning when he had told her not to become too involved with Whip. While she had indulged in foolish daydreams about a future in Oregon, Whip's common-law Indian wife had been traveling to him, and now she had joined him.

What had happened in the past didn't concern Cathy. In fact, she would have been surprised if Whip had remained celibate through the years. So the fact that he had chosen to live with a beautiful Arapaho girl was strictly his own business.

But that girl had joined him and was riding beside him at this very moment. Tonight they would sleep together. The realization was so crushing, so humiliating, that Cathy felt an almost overpowering urge to weep hysterically. How stupid she had been to pin her hopes for the future on such a man! Only the presence of Hosea on the seat beside her fueled her pride and kept her face immobile.

Cathy felt sure that, deep within, something precious and irreplaceable had been stolen from her.

Out of the corner of her eye, she caught a glimpse of Lee coming toward her again, his expression solicitous. Perhaps her preoccupation with Whip had blinded her to anyone else. How foolish she had been. Perhaps. Certainly Lee was good-looking and intelligent, sensitive and a man of integrity. And obviously, now that she thought about it, he was developing a deep and sincere interest in her.

But she couldn't think about him now, any more than she could allow herself to dwell on her disappointment in Whip. There was something far more important at stake.

Oregon still beckoned. The promise of the land that lay ahead was more vital than any personal relationship. She was more determined than ever to remain a member of the wagon train until it reached its goal.

Book III in the Wagons West Series

WYOMING!
DANA FULLER ROSS

In this unforgettable book, the dauntless band of pioneering men and women—members of America's first wagon train featured in INDEPENDENCE and NEBRASKA—continue their hazardous trek west through the Rockies.

Savage attacks by Indians, treacherous acts by English and Russian agents are only a few of the dangers they face. Yet Whip Holt, Cathy van Ayle, La-ena and others show amazing courage and remain steadfast in their determination to reach their ultimate goal—Oregon.

Read WYOMING!

★ WAGONS WEST ★

A series of unforgettable books that trace the lives of a dauntless band of pioneering men, women, and children as they brave the hazards of an untamed land in their trek across America. This legendary caravan of people forge a new link in the wilderness. They are Americans from the North and the South, alongside immigrants, Blacks, and Indians, who wage fierce daily battles for survival on this uncompromising journey—each to their private destinies as they fulfill their greatest dreams.

☐	22808	**INDEPENDENCE!**	$3.50
☐	22784	**NEBRASKA!**	$3.50
☐	23177	**WYOMING!**	$3.50
☐	22568	**OREGON!**	$3.50
☐	23168	**TEXAS!**	$3.50
☐	23381	**CALIFORNIA!**	$3.95
☐	23405	**COLORADO!**	$3.50
☐	20174	**NEVADA!**	$3.50
☐	20919	**WASHINGTON!**	$3.50

Buy them at your local bookstore or use this handy coupon:

RELAX!
SIT DOWN
and Catch Up On Your Reading!